Mother looked up at Father in awe. "My elbow still hurts, where it struck the floor," she said. "It still hurts very much."

A hurt that lasted! Who had heard of such a thing! And when she lifted her arm, there was a raw and bleeding scrape on it.

"Have I killed you?" asked Father, wonderingly.

"No," said Mother. "I don't think so."

"Then why does it bleed?..."

ORSON SCOTT CARD
THE WORTHING CHRONICLE

ACE SCIENCE FICTION BOOKS
NEW YORK

Some portions of this book appeared
previously as parts of the author's books
Capitol and *Hot Sleep*.

THE WORTHING CHRONICLE

An Ace Science Fiction Book/published by arrangement with
the author

PRINTING HISTORY
Ace Original / July 1983

ISBN: 0-441-91810-7

Ace Science Fiction Books are published by Charter Communications, Inc.
200 Madison Avenue, New York, New York 10016.
PRINTED IN THE UNITED STATES OF AMERICA

*For Laird and Sally,
because the right tales
are true to you.*

The Day of Pain

In many places in the Peopled Worlds, the pain came suddenly in the midst of the day's labor. It was as if an ancient and comfortable presence left them, one that they had never noticed until it was gone; and no one knew what to make of it at first, though all knew at once that something had changed deep at the heart of the world. No one saw the brief flare in the star named Argos; it would be years before astronomers would connect the Day of Pain with the End of Worthing. And by then the change was done, the worlds were broken, and the golden age was over.

In Lared's village, the change came while they slept. That night there were no shepherds for their dreams. Lared's little sister, Sala, awoke screaming in terror that Grandma was dead, Grandma is dead!

Lared sat up in his truckle bed, trying to dispel his own dreams, for in them he had seen his father carry Grandma to the grave—but that had been long ago, hadn't it? Father stumbled from the wooden bedstead where he and Mother slept. Not since Sala had been weaned had anyone cried out in the night. Was she hungry?

"Grandma died tonight, like a fly in the fire she died!"

Like a squirrel in the fox's teeth, thought Lared. Like a lizard in the cat's mouth, trembling.

"Of course she's dead," Father said, "but not tonight." He took her in his vast blacksmith's arms and held her. "Why do you weep now, when Grandma has been dead for such a long time?" But Sala wept on, as if the grief were great and new.

Then Lared looked at Grandma's old bed. "Father," he

whispered. Again, "Father." For there lay her corpse, still new, still stiffening, though Lared so clearly remembered her burial long ago.

Father lay Sala back in her truckle bed, where she burrowed down against the woven straw side, in order not to watch. Lared watched, though, as his father touched the straw tick beside his old mother's body. "Not cold yet," he murmured. Then he cried out in fear and agony, "Mother!" It woke all the sleepers, even the travelers in the room upstairs; they all came into the sleeping room.

"Do you see it!" cried Father. "Dead a year, at least, and here's her body not yet cold in her own bed!"

"Dead a year!" cried the old clerk, who had arrived late in the afternoon yesterday, on a donkey. "Nonsense! She served the soup last night. Don't you remember how she joked with me that if my bed was too cold, your wife would come up and warm it, and if it was too warm, *she* would sleep with me?"

Lared tried to sort out his memories. "I remember that, but I remember that she said that long, long ago, and yet I remember she said it to you, and I never saw you before last night."

"I buried you!" Father cried, and then he knelt at Grandma's bed and wept. "I buried you, and forgot you, and here you are to grieve me!"

Weeping. It was an unaccustomed sound in the village of Flat Harbor, and no one knew what to do about it. Only hungry infants made such cries, and so Mother said, "Elmo, will you eat something? Let me fetch you something to eat."

"No!" shouted Elmo. "Don't you see my mother's dead?" And he caught his wife by the arm and flung her roughly away. She fell over the stool and struck her head against the table.

This was worse than the corpse lying in the bed, stiff as a dried-out bird. Never in Lared's life had he seen one human being do harm to another. Father, too, was aghast at his own temper. "Thano, Thanalo, what have I done?" He scarcely knew how to comfort her as she lay weeping softly on the floor. No one had needed comfort in all their lives. To all the others, Father said, "I was so angry. I have never been so angry before, and yet what did she do? I've never felt such a rage, and yet she did me no harm!"

Who could answer him? Something was bitterly wrong with the world, they could see that; they had all felt anger in the past, but till now something had always come between the thought and the act, and calmed them. Now, tonight, that calm was gone. They could feel it in themselves, nothing soothing their fear, nothing telling them wordlessly, *All is well.*

Sala raised her head above the edge of her bed and said, "The angels are gone, Mama. No one watches us anymore."

Mother got up from the floor and stumbled over to her daughter. "Don't be foolish, child. There are no angels, except in dreams."

There is a lie in my mind, Lared said to himself. The traveler came last night, and Grandma spoke to him just as he said, and yet my memory is twisted, for I remember the traveler speaking yesterday, but Grandma answering long ago. Something has bent my memories, for I remember grieving at her graveside, and yet her grave has not been dug.

Mother looked up at Father in awe. "My elbow still hurts, where it struck the floor," she said. "It still hurts very much."

A hurt that lasted! Who had heard of such a thing! And when she lifted her arm, there was a raw and bleeding scrape on it.

"Have I killed you?" asked Father, wonderingly.

"No," said Mother. "I don't think so."

"Then why does it bleed?"

The old clerk trembled and nodded and his voice quivered as he spoke. "I have read the books of ancient times," he began, and all eyes turned to him. "I have read the books of ancient times, and in them the old ones spoke of wounds that bleed like slaughtered cattle, and great griefs when the living suddenly are dead, and anger that turns to blows among people. But that was long, long ago, when men were still animals, and God was young and inexperienced."

"What does this mean, then?" asked Father. He was not a bookish man, and so even more than Lared he thought that men who knew books had answers.

"I don't know," said the clerk. "But perhaps it means that God has gone away, or that he no longer cares for us."

Lared studied the corpse of Grandma, lying on her bed. "Or is he dead?" Lared asked.

"How can God die?" the old clerk asked with withering scorn. "He has all the power in the universe."

"Then doesn't he have the power to die if he wants to?"

"Why should I speak with children of things like this?" The clerk got up to go upstairs, and the other travelers took that as a signal to return to bed.

But Father did not go to bed: he knelt by his old mother's body until daybreak. And Lared also did not sleep, because he was trying to remember what he had felt inside himself yesterday that he did not feel now, for something was strange in the way his own eyes looked out upon the world, and yet he could not remember how it was before. Only Sala and Mother slept, and they slept together in Mother and Father's bed.

Before dawn, Lared got up and walked over to his mother, and saw that a scab had formed on her arm, and the bleeding had stopped. Comforted, he dressed himself and went out to milk the ewe, which was near the end of its milk. Every bit of the milk was needed for the cheese press and the butter churn—winter was coming, and this morning, as the cold breeze whipped at Lared's hair, this morning he looked to winter with dread. Until today he had always looked at the future like a cow looking at the pasture, never imagining drought or snow. Now it was possible for old women to be found dead in their beds. Now it was possible for Father to be angry and knock Mother to the floor. Now it was possible for Mother to bleed like an animal. And so winter seemed more than just a season of inactivity. It was the end of hope.

The ewe perked up at something, a sound perhaps that Lared was too human to hear. He stopped milking and looked up, and saw in the western sky a great light, which hovered in the air like a star that had lost its bearings and needed help to get back home. Then the light sank down below the level of the trees across the river, and it was gone. Lared did not know at first what it might be. Then he remembered the word *starship* from school and wondered. Starships did not come to Flat Harbor, nor to this continent, nor even, more than once a decade, to this world. There was nothing here to carry away to somewhere else, nothing lacking here that only other worlds could supply. Why, then, would a starship come here now? Don't be a fool, Lared, he told himself. It was a shooting star, but on this strange morning you made too much of it, because you are afraid.

At dawn, Flat Harbor came awake, and others gradually

discovered what had come to Lared's family in the night. They came, as they always did in cold weather, to Elmo's house, with its great table and indoor kitchen. They were not surprised to find that Elmo had not yet built up the fire in his forge.

"I scalded myself on the gruel this morning," said Dinno, Mother's closest friend. She held up the reddened skin of her fingers for admiration. "Hurts like it was still in the fire. Good God," she said.

Mother had her own wounds, but she chose not to tell that tale. "When that old clerk went to leave this morning, his donkey kicked him square in the belly, and now he's upstairs. Too much hurt to travel, he says. Threw up his breakfast."

There were a score of minor, careless injuries, and by noon most people were walking more carefully, carrying out their tasks more slowly. Not a one of them but had some hurt. Omber, one of the diggers of Grandma's grave, crushed his foot with a pick, and it bled for a long, long time; now, white and weak and barely alive, he lay drawing scant breath in one of Mother's guest beds. And Father, death on his mind, would not even take the hammer in his hand on the Day of Pain: "For fear I'll strike fire into my eye, or break my hand. God doesn't look out for us anymore."

They laid Grandma into the ground at noon, and all day Lared and Sala were busy helping Mother with the work that Grandma used to do. Her place at table was so empty. Many a sentence began, "Grandma." And Father always looked away as if searching for something hidden deep in the walls. Try as they might, no one could think of a time before this when grief had been anything but a dim and wistful memory; never had the loss of a loved one come so suddenly, with the gap in their lives so plain, with the soil on the grave so black and rich, fresh as the first-turned fold of earth in the spring plowing.

Late in the afternoon, Omber died, the last blood of his body seeping into the rough bandage. He lay beside the wide-eyed clerk, who still vomited everything he swallowed and cried out in pain when he tried to sit. Never in their lives had they seen a man die still in his strength and prime, and just from a careless blow of a pick.

They were still digging the new grave for Omber when Bran's daughter, Clany, fell into the fire and lay screaming for three hours before she died. No one could even speak when they laid her into the third grave of the day. For a village of a scant three hundred souls, the death of three on the same day would have been calamitous; the death of a strong man and a young child undid them all.

At nightfall there were no new travelers—they always became rarer when the cold weather came. That was the only good thing about the night, however, the fact that there were no new guests to care for. The world had changed, had become a harsh place, all in a single day. As Sala got into her bed, she asked, "Will I die tonight, like Grandma?"

"No," said Father, but Lared heard in his voice that he wasn't sure. "No, Sala, my Sarela, you will not die tonight." But he pulled her truckle bed farther from the fire, and put another blanket over her.

Lared did not need to be told, once he had seen. He also moved his truckle bed from his place near the fire. He had heard the sound of Clany's screams. The whole village had heard them—there was no shutting them out. He had never been terrified of flames before, but he was now. Let the cold come—better that than the pain. Better anything than this new and terrible pain.

Lared fell asleep nursing the bruise on his knee where he had carelessly bashed into the woodbox. He awoke three times in the night. Once because Father was weeping softly in his bed; when Elmo saw that Lared was awake, he got up and kissed him and held him and said, "Sleep, Lared, sleep, all's well, all's well." It was a lie, but Lared slept again.

The second time he awoke because Sala had another nightmare, again about Grandma's death. It was Mother who comforted her, singing a song whose sadness Lared had never understood before.

> Saw my love at river's side
> Across the stream.
> The stream was wide.
>
> Heard my love say come to him
> Across the stream.
> I could not swim.

> Got myself a little boat
> But the day was cold.
> I had no coat.
>
> Got a coat and put it on
> But it was night.
> Now wait till dawn.
>
> Sun came up and night was over
> I saw my love.
> I saw his lover.

Lared did not know what else Mother might have sung. He was lost in the dream that wakened him the third and last time that night.

He sat beside the Endwater in spring flood, with the rafts coming down, the lumbermen poling them a safe distance from each other. Then, suddenly, there was a fire in the sky, and it fell down toward the river. Lared knew that he must stop the fire, must shout for it to stop, but though he opened his mouth he could not speak, and so the fire came on. It fell into the river, and all the rafts were burned at once, and the men on the rafts screamed with Clany's voice, and burned, and fell into the river, and drowned, and all because Lared did not know what to say to stop the fire.

Lared woke trembling, filled with guilt at his failure to save anyone, wondering why it was his fault. He heard a moaning sound upstairs. His parents were asleep. Lared did not wake them, but climbed the stairs himself. The old clerk lay on the bed. There was blood on his face, blood on the sheet.

"I'm dying," he whispered, when he saw Lared by the moonlight through the window.

Lared nodded.

"Can you read, boy?"

Again he nodded. This village was not so backward that the children had no school in the winter, and Lared read as well as any adult in the village, even when he was ten years old. Now he was fourteen, and beginning to get a man's strength on him, and still he loved to read, and studied whatever letters he could find.

"Then take the Book of the Finding of the Stars. It is yours. It is all yours."

"Why me?" whispered Lared. Perhaps the old clerk had seen him eyeing his books last night. Perhaps he had heard him recite the Eyes of Endwater to Sala and her friends after supper. But the clerk was silent, though he was not yet dead. Whatever his reason, he meant Lared to have his book. *A book that is my own*. And a book about finding stars, on the day after the Day of Pain, the day after he had seen a star fall into the forest across Endwater. "Thank you, sir," he said, and he reached to touch the old clerk's hand.

Lared heard a noise behind him. It was Mother, and her eyes were wide.

"Why would he give his books to you?" she asked.

The clerk moved his lips, but made no sound.

"You're nothing but a boy," said Mother. "You're lazy, and you argue."

I know that I deserve nothing, said Lared silently.

"He must have family—we'll send his books to them, if he dies."

The clerk tortured himself by shaking his head violently. "No," he whispered. "Give the books to the boy!"

"Don't die in my house," cried Mother, in anguish. "Not another dead in my house!"

"I'm sorry for the inconvenience," said the old clerk. Then he died.

"Why did you come up here?" Mother whispered fiercely to Lared. "Now see what you've done."

"I only came because he was crying out in his—"

"Coming to get his books, and him on the edge of death."

Lared wanted to argue, to defend himself, but even his own dream had blamed him, hadn't it? Her eyes looked like a ewe's eyes, when the pain of birth was on her, and he dared not stay or quarrel. "I have to milk the ewe," he said, and ran down the stairs and out the door.

The night had turned bitterly cold, and the frost was thick on the grass. The ewe was ready for the milking, but Lared was not. His fingers quickly became too cold, despite the warmth of the animals.

No, it was not the cold that made his hands tremble clumsily. It was the books that waited for him in the old clerk's room. It was the three new graves heaped up in the moonlight, where soon a fourth would rise.

It was, above all, the man and woman who walked across the river, angling their steps to combat the current. The river was ten feet deep from bank to bank, but they walked as if the water were hard-packed dirt, whose only oddity was that it slid away underfoot as they walked. Lared thought of hiding, so they would not see him; but instead, without deciding, he stood from his stool by the ewe, set the milk bucket up high where it could not be kicked over, and walked out across the cemetery to meet them.

They were on the riverbank before he reached them, looking at the new graves. There was sorrow in their eyes. The man was white-haired, but his body was strong, and his face was kind and sure. The woman was much younger, younger than Mother, yet her face looked harsh and angry, even in repose. There was no sign that either of them had been in the water—even their footprints on the riverbank were dry. And when they turned and looked at him, he could see even in the moonlight that their eyes were blue. He had never seen eyes so blue that even without sunlight their color was bright and visible.

"Who are you?" he asked.

The man answered in a language that Lared didn't understand. The woman shook her head, said nothing. Yet Lared felt a sudden desire to tell them his name.

"Lared," he said.

"Lared," she answered. His name sounded strangely twisted on her tongue. He felt a sudden urgency not to tell anyone that he had seen them walk on Endwater.

"I'll never tell," he said.

The woman nodded. Then he knew, though he still did not know how he knew, that he should take them home.

But he was afraid of these strangers. "You won't hurt my family, will you?"

Tears came to the man's eyes, and the hard-faced woman did not look him in the face. The thought came into Lared's mind: "We have already hurt you more than we can bear."

And now he understood—or thought he understood—his dream, and the falling star on the Day of Pain, and the Day itself. "Have you come to take away the pain again?"

The man shook his head.

The hope had been brief, but the disappointment was no less deep because of that. "If you can't do that," he said, "then what good are you to us?" Still, he was an innkeeper's son, and so he led them carefully through the cemetery, past the sheepsheds, and into the house, where Mother already had the water boiling for the morning gruel.

2

The Making of
Parchment and Ink

Mother greeted them. "Do you want a meal? Have you been traveling all night?" Lared watched for her surprise when they spoke inside her mind, but there was no surprise; there was no answer at all, it seemed, for she repeated her question, and it was into Lared's thoughts the answer came.

"They're not hungry, Mother."

"Let the guests speak for themselves," she said sharply. "Will you eat?"

The man shook his head. Lared felt an urgent desire to get the Book of the Finding of the Stars. He started for the stairs.

"Where are you going, Lared?" Mother asked.

"To get the book. Of the Finding of the Stars."

"Now is not the time for playing. There's work to do."

"They want me to read it to them."

"Do you think I'm a fool? They haven't said a word, I don't even think they speak Werren."

Lared did not answer. Instead, Sala said, "It's true, Mama. They speak to Lared and me without words, but they don't want to talk to you and Papa."

Mother looked from Sala to Lared. "What is this? They only talk to you, and not to—" She turned to the strangers. "I don't need people coming into my house and telling me I'm not worth talking to. We don't need you."

The man put a single shining jewel on the table.

Mother looked at it with contempt. "What can I do with *that?* Will it draw grain out of the soil? Will it make my husband's forge burn hotter? Will it heal the scabs on my arm?" But she reached out and took it. "Is it real?" she asked them; and then, helpless in the face of their silence, she asked Sala, "Is it real?"

"It's perfect," said Sala. "It's worth the price of every farm in Flat Harbor, and every building, and all the earth that's

11

under it and all the air that's over it and all the water that runs through it." And she put her hand to her mouth to stop the torrent of words.

"Get the book they asked for," Mother said to Lared. Then she turned sullenly back to the gruel.

Lared ran upstairs, to the room where the body of the old clerk lay. The eyes were closed, with pebbles on them. The belly under the blanket was slack. Did it move, just a little, with a faint breath?

"Sir?" whispered Lared. But there was no answer. Lared went to the pack the old man had so heavily borne. Five books were within it, and a sheaf of parchment, perhaps twenty sheets, with a small horn of ink and several quills. Lared knew something of making parchment, and one of the first lessons of winter school was to sharpen and split a quill for writing. The ink was a mystery, though. Lared reluctantly set the inkhorn back in the pack; he had been given books, not the tools of making books. He quickly sorted out the titles from the decorations of the tooled leather covers; never did cattle and sheep so docilely lie together as in the sheepskin pages and the cowskin covers of a book. The Finding of the Stars.

He had barely set the other books aside when he heard footsteps on the stairs. It was Father, come with Han Carpenter to take away the corpse. Their boots were lightly crusted with soil—the grave was already dug.

"Come to rob the dead?" asked Han cheerfully.

"He gave the books to me—"

Father shook his head. "Han thinks there's jests to make in death rooms."

"Keep the ghosts at bay," said Han. "If they're laughing, they'll cause you no pain."

Lared looked suspiciously at the old clerk's body. Had he a ghost, perhaps? And did that ghost bear sharp pen-knives, ready to carve Lared like a quill, perhaps when he slept? Lared shuddered. To believe such things would be the end of sleep.

"Take the books, lad," Father said. "They're yours. But be careful with them. They're worth the price of the iron I'll use in my life."

Lared made a wide circle around the bed, where Father and Han were winding the old man in a faded horseblanket—it would make no sense to send good cloth into the ground with the dead. Lared left the room and fairly flew down the stairs. His mother's fingers caught him at the bottom, stopping him, nearly pulling him off his feet. "What, do you want another burial today? Be careful, there's no angels now to pick up your feet when you start to fall."

Lared pulled away, answered sharply: "I didn't stumble till you near pulled me down!"

She slapped his face harshly, hurting his neck and leaving his cheek stinging. They looked at each other in surprise.

"I'm sorry," Lared whispered.

Mother said nothing, only turned back to the table to set out the horn spoons for their guests. She did not know they had walked on water, but she did know the worth of the jewel they gave her, and that was miracle enough to warrant the best treatment.

Lared did not want to go to the strangers now, however, for they had seen him ashamed and in pain. In spite of himself there were tears in his eyes—no one had purposely hurt him in his life, and though the pain was fading, the fear of it was not. "She never," he began to explain in a whisper, but they spoke into his mind again, spoke calmly to him, and he handed the Finding of the Stars to them.

The man held the book, opened it and traced the words with his finger. Lared saw at once that he could not read, for his finger moved from left to right instead of from the top to the bottom of the page. You can do miracles, but you cannot read, Lared thought triumphantly.

Almost at once an image leapt into his mind, of pages of strange words in even stranger letters, letters that spread across the page loosely, as if the parchment were not hours of labor and the ink not worth its volume in hard-earned tin. Then he saw, as if in memory, the young woman bending over the page. "Sorry," he murmured.

The man pointed at the first word, drew his finger down the first sentence, and asked with his eyes. Read, said the silent voice in Lared's mind.

"After the worlds were slain by Abner Doon, ten thousand years of darkness passed before the fires again burned their threads between the stars."

The man's eyes grew wide. "Abner Doon," he said aloud. Lared pointed at the two words.

Only two letters to say this man's name? asked the silent voice.

"No—those are words, not letters." Lared got a kindling twig from the firebox and drew in the thin dust on the floor. "Here's *ab*, and here's *un*, and here's *er*, and they fit together like this. This tie tells you that the *un* is quick, and this one that the *ab* is longest, and the binding tells you that the words are names."

The man and woman looked at each other in surprise, and then laughed. At Lared? He thought not.

No, said the voice in his mind. Not at you. At ourselves. We thought to learn your language and your writing, but it's plain your letters are too hard for us.

"No, they're easy," said Lared. "There are only a hundred ninety-eight letters, and thirteen ties, and seven bindings at the ends."

They laughed again, and the man shook his head. Then he got an idea. "Jason," he said, pointing to himself. "Jason." And the voice in Lared's mind said, Write.

So he wrote: *J* and *es*, and *un*, and joined them to make it say *jesun*, and bound it to say, not name, but name of God. It was a dignity only offered to great rulers, but Lared did not hesitate to use it with this man. With Jason.

But apparently the man could understand somehow what the binding meant. He took the stick from Lared's hand and put the binding of God's name on the word of Abner, and put the common name binding on his own name.

An image came into Lared's mind, of a small man dressed in a strange and ugly costume, smiling with mocking amusement. Lared didn't like him. The voice in his mind said, Abner Doon.

"You knew him?" asked Lared. "The Unmaker of the Universe? The Breaker of Man? The Waker from the Sleep of Life?"

The man shook his head. Lared thought he meant that he did not know Abner Doon. How could he, after all, unless he was a devil, too? That thought crossed Lared's mind. Their powers were more than human; how did Lared know that they were good?

In answer came a soothing feeling, a warmth, a calm, and Lared shuddered. How could he doubt them? And yet, even deeper, he still asked himself, How can I not doubt them? They come too near to the Day of Pain.

Jason handed him the book again. Read, said the voice in his mind.

He understood only some of what he read. Making the sounds was easy, since he knew the alphabet. But many of the words were too hard for him. What did he know of starships and worlds and explorers and embassies? He thought that perhaps the two strangers would explain to him what the words meant.

We can't.

"Why not?" he asked.

Because the words mean nothing to us. What we understand is your understanding of them. What you don't know, we can't know.

"Then why don't you learn our language, if you're so wise?"

"Don't be fresh," said Mother from the kitchen, where she was grinding the dried pease for the pot.

Lared was angry. She understood nothing of the conversation, but still could tell when Lared was doing something wrong. Jason reached out and touched him on the knee. Be calm. It's all right. The words weren't put in his head, but he understood them all the same, from the gentle hand, from the calm smile.

Jason will learn your language, said the voice in his mind. But Justice will not.

"Justice?" said Lared, not realizing at first that this was the woman's name.

She touched herself and echoed his word. "Justice," she said. Her voice was uncertain and soft, as if little used. "Justice," she said again. Then laughed, and said an incomprehensible word in a language Lared had never heard before.

That is my name, said the voice in his mind. Justice. Jason's ame is mere sound, the same no matter what language you speak. But my name is the idea, and the sound of it changes from language to language.

It made no sense to Lared. "A name's a name. It means you, and so what if it means something else besides?"

They looked at each other.

Tell us, are there words about a place named—
And Justice said a word: "Worthing."

Lared tried out the name on his tongue. "Worthing," he said. Then he wrote down the name in the dirt, so he would be sure to know the sign for it, if he met it in the book.

He did not notice that at the saying of the name Mother's eyebrows rose, and she slipped out of the kitchen without so much as an I'll-be-back.

He found Worthing at the end of the book. "It was believed for thousands of years that two of Doon's arks had gone astray, or their colonies had failed. Indeed, if Rivethock's Ark resulted in a colony, it remains unfound to this day. The world called Worthing, however, from Worthing's Ark, was found at last, by a Discoverer IV-class ship in the Fifth Wave, whose geologer marked the planet as habitable—and then, to the shock of the crew, as inhabited."

This time, where the words were hard, brief explanations often came into Lared's mind, using ideas that he was familiar with. Doon's Arks were huge starships equipped with everything that 334 passengers would need to start a world. A colony was a village in newly cleared land on a world without human beings. A Discoverer IV of the Fifth Wave was a starship sent by the government to chart the inner reaches of the galaxy some five thousand years ago. A geologer was a machine, or a group of machines, that looked at a world from far away and saw where lay all forests and oil and iron and farmland and ice and ocean and life.

And if we read at this rate we'll get nowhere, said the voice in his mind. The impatience on Justice's face matched the words, and for the first time it occurred to Lared that it might be *only* Justice who spoke to him. For Jason only smiled at whatever she silently said to him, and when he answered her it was in words from their strange language, spoken aloud.

"Who are you?" demanded Father.

He stood at the door that led into the kitchen shed, his strong arms and massive shoulders filling the door, silhouetting him against the light from the kitchen fire.

"They're Jason and Justice," said Sala.

"Who are you?" asked Father again. "I'll not be answered by my children's voices."

The words came into Lared's mind, and he spoke them. "You'll not be answered any other way. Don't blame us, Father—they only speak to me because they don't know another way. Jason plans to learn our language as soon as he can."

"Who are you?" asked Father a third time. "You dared to cause my child to say the dark name, the hidden word, and him not yet sixteen."

"What hidden name?" asked Lared.

Father could not force himself to say it. Instead he walked to where Lared had written the sign of it upon the ground, and scraped the mark away with his foot.

Jason laughed, and Justice sighed, and Lared spoke without waiting for them to give him words. "Father, I found the name *Worthing* in the old cleric's book. It's just the name of a world."

Father slapped Lared brutally across the face. "There is a time and place for uttering the name, and that is not here."

Lared could not help but cry out from the pain—he had no strategies for coping with this unhabitual distress. It was too cruel, that with the coming of pain the greatest danger of it should be, not from fire or water or beast, but from Father. So even after the first impact of the pain wore off, Lared could not keep himself from whimpering like a bee-stung dog.

Suddenly Jason slapped the table and jumped to his feet. Justice tried to hold him back, but he stammered out a few words that they could understand. "Name of my," he said. "Name this mying be."

Father squinted, as if seeing better would help him understand the twisted words. Lared translated for him. "I think he means that *his* name is—is *the* name."

Jason nodded.

"I thought you said your name was Jason."

"Name of my is Jason Worthing."

"My name is Jason Worthing," prompted Lared.

The moment Lared uttered *Worthing,* Father's hand snaked out to slap him again. But Jason was quicker, and caught the blacksmith's hand in mid-act.

"There's no man in Flat Harbor," said Father, "who dares to match strength with me."

Jason only smiled.

Father tried to move his hand again, but Jason tightened his fingers almost imperceptibly, and Father cried out in pain.

Justice, too, cried out as if the pain had touched her. The two of them babbled in angry language as Father held his wrist, gasping. When Father could speak again, he ignored them, too. "I don't need them as guests, and I don't need you getting into forbidden things. They're going, and you won't have another thing to do with them until they're gone."

Jason and Justice left off their argument and heard the end of his speech. As if to stop the blacksmith, Justice took from her clothing a thin bar of pure gold; she bent it to show its softness.

Father reached for the gold and took it. Between two fingers he folded the bar flat, and with two hands folded it again, and tossed it against the front door. "This is my house, and this is my son, and we have no need of you."

Then Father led Lared from the room, unfed and unhappy, to the forge where the fire was already growing hot.

Lared worked there all morning, hungry and angry, but not daring to do anything but what his father asked. They both knew that Lared hated the work at the forge, that he had no desire at all to learn the secrets of smithing. He did what he had to, just the way he bore his share in the field—and no more. Usually that was enough for Father, but not today.

"There are things you'll learn from me," Father shouted above the roar of the flames. "There are things no half-witted strangers are going to teach you!"

They aren't half-witted, Lared said silently. Unlike Justice, however, when he held his tongue his words went unremarked. It was one of the things he did best, holding his tongue.

"You're no good at smithing, I know that, you've got weak arms like your mother's father, narrow shoulders. I haven't pushed you, have I?"

Lared shook his head.

"Pump harder."

Lared bore down on the bellows, pumped faster even though his back ached.

"And in the fields, you're a decent hand, and if you aren't big enough yet for a man's load, you're good at mushrooms and herbs and I won't even be ashamed of you if you end up a swineherd. God help me, I'd even bear having my son be the gooseboy."

"I'll be no gooseboy, Father." Father often made things out worse than they really were, for effect.

"Better gooseboy than a clerk! There's no work for a clerk in Flat Harbor, no need for one."

"I'm not a clerk. I'm not good enough at numbers, and I don't know but half the words in the book."

Father struck the iron so hard that it split, and he cast the piece that was in the tongs onto the stone floor, where it broke again. "Name of God, I don't want you not to be a clerk because you're not *good* enough! You're *good* enough to be a clerk! But I'd be ashamed to have a son of mine be no more useful than to scratch letters on leather all day long!"

Lared leaned on the bellows handle and studied his father. How has the coming of pain changed you? You're no more careful of your hands at the forge. You stand as close to the fire as ever, though all others who work near fire have taken to standing back far, and there's been a rash of calls for long strong sticks for spoons twice as long as anyone thought to want before. *You* haven't asked for longer tongs, though. So what has changed?

"If you become a clerk," Father said, "then there'll be nothing for you but to leave Flat Harbor. Live in Endwater Havens, or Cleaving, somewhere far."

Lared smiled bitterly. "It can't happen a day too soon for Mother."

Father shrugged impatiently. "Don't be a fool. You just look too much like her father, that's all. She means no harm."

"Sometimes," Lared said, "I think the only one who has a use for me is Sala." Until now. Until the strangers came.

"I have a use for you."

"Do I pull bellows for you until you die? And afterward pull for whoever takes your place? Here's the truth, Father. I don't want to leave Flat Harbor. I don't want to be a clerk. Except maybe to read for a guest or two, especially late in the year, like now, with nothing to do but leather work and spinning and weaving and slaughter. Other men make up songs. *You* make up songs."

Father picked up the wasted iron and put the pieces in the

scraps pile. Another bar was heating in the forge. "Pull the bellows, Lareled."

The affectionate name was Lared's answer. Father's anger was only temporary, and he'd not bar him from reading, when it didn't keep him from work. Lared sang as he pulled the bellows.

> "Squirrilel, squirrilel, where go the nuts?
> In holes in the ground or in poor farmer's huts?
> Steal from my barn and I'll string out your guts
> To make songs with my lyre
> Or sausaging wire
> Or tie off the bull so he no longer ruts."

Father laughed. He had made up the song himself when the whole village gathered in the inn during the worst of last winter. It was an honor, to have a song remembered, especially by your own son. Lared knew it would please his father, but there was no calculation in his singing. He *did* love his father, and wanted him to be glad, though he had no common ground with him, and was in no way like him.

Father sang another verse, one that Lared didn't like as well. But he laughed anyway, and this time he *was* calculating. For when the verse was over and the laughter done, Lared said, "Let them stay. Please."

Father's expression darkened, and he pulled the bar from the fire and again began to beat it into a sickle. "They talk with your voice, Lared."

"They speak in my mind," Lared said. "Like—" and he hesitated before saying the childhood word "—angels."

"If they are angels, why is the cemetery so full today?" Father asked.

"*Like* angels. There's no harm in it. They—"

"They what?"

They walk on water. "They mean no harm to us. They're willing to learn our language."

"The man knows ways to cause pain. Why would an angel know ways to cause pain?"

There was no good reason. Before yesterday no one had known what real pain was. Yet Jason could reach out his hand

and stop Elmo the Smith with a subtle agony. What sort of man would even want to know such things?

"They can put thoughts in your mind," Father said. "How do you know they haven't put trust in your mind as well? And hope and love and anything else that they might use to destroy you? And us as well? Times are perilous now. Word is that upriver there was killing. Not just death, but killing yesterday. From such anger that had never been let out before. And here is a man who knows pain like I know the insides of iron."

And the sickle was complete. Father plunged it back in the fire, to let the iron know its true shape, and rubbed it on the hearthstone so it knew the earth, and would not offend at harvest time. Then he dipped it smoothly into the cistern, and the iron sang.

"Still," said Lared. He handed the whetstone to his father, to work an edge onto the iron.

"Still what?"

"Still. If they want to stay, how can you stop them?"

Father turned sharply. "Do you think I'd let them stay from fear?"

"No," said Lared, abashed. "But there's the jewel. And the gold."

"It's a low sort of man who changes his mind for the hope of wealth. Who's to say what gold and jewels are worth, if things get worse upriver? Will gold bring Mama back from the grave? Will it make Clany's flesh hold to her bones? Will it give the old clerk sight? Or heal the iron-bitten foot?"

"They've caused no harm, Father, except that he reached out to protect me, when I sinned at his bidding."

Father drew back, thinking of the name Lared had offended by saying. "That's the name of God," said Father. "You're not supposed to learn it until you kiss the ice in your sixteenth winter."

Lared, too, grew solemn. "You would turn away one who comes teaching the name of God?"

"The wicked can use God's name as well as God."

"How can we ever know, then, unless we try them? Or should we cast away all men who use the name of God, for fear they're blasphemers? What name will God use, then?"

"Already you talk like a clerk," said Father. "Already you

want them here too much. I'm not afraid of pain, I'm not afraid of wealth, I'm not even afraid of a man who blasphemes and thinks he does no harm. I'm afraid of how you want whatever it is they promised you—"

"They promised me nothing!"

"I'm afraid of how you'll change."

Lared laughed bitterly. "You don't much like the way I am. What difference does a difference in me make?"

Father ran his finger along the sickle's edge. "Sharp," he said. "I barely touched her, and she cut me a bit." He showed the finger to Lared. There was a drop of blood on the finger. Father reached out and touched the bloody finger to Lared's right eyelid. Usually the rite was done with water, but it felt all the more powerful with blood. Lared shuddered—touch his left, and instead of a protection to Lared the rite would have been a fending, to drive Lared himself away. "I'll let them stay," Father whispered. "But all your winter work must come first."

"Thank you," Lared said softly. "I swear it'll do no harm, but end up serving God."

"All things end up serving God." Father set down the sickle on the bench. "There's another ready for a handlemaker. Blade's no good unless it fits somebody's hand." He turned and looked down on Lared—they were near the same height, but always he looked down to see his son. "Whose hand were *you* made to fit, Lared? Never mind, God knows."

But Lared's thoughts were all on Jason and Justice, and the work they had for him. He spared no thought, not now, for his father's pain. "You'll not let Mother invent more work than last year, just to keep me from them?"

Father laughed. "Nor will I." Then he touched Lared's shoulder and looked gravely in his eyes. "Their eyes are the sky," he said. "Beware of flying. It isn't the hunter's shot that kills the dove, but the fall to earth, they say."

So except for Mother's brittle silence and sharp remarks, Lared was unhindered that winter. From the first, even before the snowfall, he and Jason were every day together, every*where* together. Jason had a language to learn, he said, and he could earn more of Lared's time if he helped him in his work. So he came with Lared into the forest, searching for mushrooms before the first snow killed them all. And Jason had an eye for herbs, too, asking which was which yet knowing more of the answers than Lared, who had thought he knew them all.

"Are the herbs the same as here, where you come from?" Lared asked him one day.

Haltingly, Jason answered, "All worlds come are same ships from. Are come."

"From the same ships."

"Yes."

Lared had been puzzling out coincidences. "The world of Worthing, that the book of the Finding of the Stars talks about. Have you ever lived there?"

Jason smiled as if the question caused him secret pleasure and secret pain. "Seeing it. But *live* there, no."

"Does this world called Worthing have something to do with the name of God?"

Jason did not answer. Instead he pointed at a flower. "Did you eat this ever?"

"It's poisonous."

"Flower be—is poisonous." Jason broke the stem at the ground, and tossed the flower far away. Then he freed the soil around the root and brought it up. It was almost perfectly round and black. "For winter eating." He broke it open. It was speckled black inside. "Water hot," he said, struggling for the word.

"Boil it?"

"Yes. What is going up?"

"Steam?"

"Yes. Drinking steam from this, it makes children." Jason grinned as he said it, to show he didn't believe *that* particular cure.

They walked on. Lared found a patch of safe mushrooms, and they filled their bag. Lared kept up a constant chatter, Jason answering as he could. They came to the boggy ground near the edge of the swamp, and Lared showed Jason how to use his quarterstaff to vault the fingers and arms of water. By the end of the morning, Jason and Lared were running madly at the water, plunging in the staves, and overleaping the stream without getting wet. Except once, when Jason set the staff too deeply, and it didn't come away when he reached the other bank. Jason seemed at a loss for words, as he sat there covered with mud. Lared taught him some of the more colorful words of the language, and Jason laughed.

"Some things is the same between languages," he said.

Lared insisted, then, that Jason teach him the words *he* used. By the time they got home, they were both thoroughly bilingual in cursing.

The cry of "Boat upriver!" came late in the day, at the time when travelers would often put to shore and spend the night in a friendly village. So Father and Mother and Lared and Sala all ran to the dock to watch the coming boat. To their surprise it was a raft, though the logging season wasn't till the break-up of ice in the spring. And what seemed a large cook-fire was much greater—one end of the raft itself was afire, right down to the waterline.

"There's a man aboard!" shouted someone, and the villagers at once put out in their rowboats. Lared was in a boat with Father, whose strong arms brought them to the raft before any of the others. The man was lying atop a pile of wood, surrounded by flame. Lared pulled himself across the short distance between boat and raft, thinking to pull the man from the boat before the fire reached him. But, standing aboard the raft, Lared saw that the fire had already reached him, that it was burning his legs; Lared smelled the flesh, the smell he knew from Clany's death. Lared staggered back to the edge of the raft, reached out and pulled the boat near enough to get in.

"He's dead," Lared said. Then the stench and the fear of having been aboard the flaming raft and the memory of flames rising from the man's naked flesh had Lared leaning over the edge of the boat, casting up his guts. Father said nothing. He's ashamed of me, Lared thought. He looked up from the water. Father had taken his hands from the oars and turned to signal the others to go back. Lared saw his face, how grim he looked. Is he ashamed of me, for being so afraid? Or does he think of me at all? Then Lared looked at the raft, clearly in view behind Father, though already growing distant as the midriver current drew it on. As Lared watched, the arm of the burning man rose into the air, black and flaming; the arm stayed erect in the air and the fingers uncrumpled like paper in a fire.

"He's still alive!" Lared cried.

Father turned to look. The hand stayed up a moment more, then collapsed back into the pyre. It took a long time before Father again took the oars in hand and pulled for shore. In the bow, Lared could not see his father's face. He did not want to.

They had been so long without rowing in the current that they came to shore well downstream from the dock. Ordinarily Father would have worked the boat upstream in the calm water near the bank, but this time he sprang from the boat and pulled it onto Harvings' gravel beach. He was silent, and Lared did not dare to speak to him. What could be said, after what they had seen? The people upriver had put a living man on a burning raft. And though the man had been silent, no sound of agony, the memory of Clany's death was too near; she had screamed into their minds enough to sear them again and again.

"Maybe," said Father, "maybe the heat made his arm rise, and him long dead."

That was it, thought Lared. They had seen the sign of life, but it was no sign of life.

"Father," shouted Sala.

They were not alone, after all. On a rise of ground above Harvings' landing stood tall Jason, holding Sala in his arms. Only when Lared was halfway up the embankment did he realize that Justice was there, too, curled around Jason's legs like a game animal freshly killed. But she was not dead; her body shook.

Jason saw the question in Lared's mind, and answered it. "She looked into the mind of the man on the boat."

"He was alive then?" asked Lared.

"Yes."

"And you, too, looked into his mind?"

Jason shook his head. "I've been with men when they died before."

Lared looked at Justice, wondering why *she* had wanted to look at death so closely. Jason looked away. Justice raised herself partway from the ground, and looked at him as the words came into his mind: I am not afraid to know anything. But that was not all, was it? Lared was not sure, but he felt an overtone of meaning, as if she had really said, I am not afraid to know anything *that I have done*.

"You're so wise," said Father behind them. "What was that raft? What did it mean?"

The words of answer came to Lared, and he spoke them. "Upriver they have made pain into a god, and they burn the man alive so pain will be satisfied and go away."

Father's face went ugly with disgust. "What fool would believe such things?"

Again Lared spoke the words they gave him. "The man on the boat believed it."

"He was already dead!" shouted Father.

Lared shook his head.

"I say he was already dead!" Father stalked away, disappearing quickly in the scant moonlight.

When his footsteps died away, Lared heard an unaccustomed sound. Quick, heavy, uncontrolled breathing—it took a minute to realize that it was Justice, cold and immovable Justice; she was weeping.

Jason said something in their language. She answered sharply, and lifted herself away from him, sat up and bent her back so her head was clasped between her knees.

"She will stop crying," Jason said.

Sala wriggled in Jason's arms, and he let her down. She went to Justice and patted her trembling shoulders. "I forgive you," Sala said. "I don't mind."

Lared almost rebuked his sister for saying such silly, meaningless things to an adult—Sala was always saying inappropriate things until Mother's hand was nearly raw from swatting her. But before he could speak, Jason laid a firm hand on his shoulder and shook his head. "Let's go home," Jason said softly, and drew Lared from the hill. Lared looked back only once, and saw in the moonlight how Justice sat with Sala on her lap, rocking back and forth, for all the world as if it were Sala who wept, and Justice who comforted her.

"Your sister," said Jason. "She is good."

Lared had never thought of it before, but it was true. Slow to argue, quick to forgive: Sala was good.

For all their friendship in the field and forest, Lared still felt shy of Jason, and terrified of cold Justice, who did not want to learn the village speech. Jason and Justice had been there three weeks before Lared worked up the courage to ask even such a simple question as, "Why don't *you* ever speak in my mind, as Justice does?"

Jason deftly peeled the last shaving from the spade edge, and this time the iron blade-tip fit smoothly. He held it up. "Good work?"

"Perfect," Lared said. He took the spade and began to nail down the iron sheathing. "Why," he asked between blows, "don't you want to answer me?"

Jason looked around the shed. "Any other wood work?"

"Not unless you count smoking the winter's meat with the scrap wood. Why don't you ever speak in my mind?"

Jason sighed. "Justice does it all. I do little."

"You hear what I think even when I don't speak, the same as her. You walked on the—walked where she did, just the same, the day I first saw you."

"I hear what I hear—but what you saw me do, *she* did."

Lared didn't like that, for the woman to be stronger than the man. It wasn't the way of Flat Harbor, anyway. What would it be like, if Mother had Father's strength? Who would protect him from her then? And would Mother work the forge?

Where I come from, Justice said silently in Lared's mind, Where I come from men and women care nothing for strength, only for what you do with it.

She had been listening in from the house, of course. Since she wasn't interested in learning the language, she often avoided their company, preferring to work at spinning and weaving with Mother and Sala, where songs were always being sung, and Sala would say whatever words Justice needed to say. Still, Justice was no less with them, just because her body wasn't there. And it annoyed Lared that he and Jason were never really alone together, no matter how far away they went, no matter how quietly they spoke. Justice even knew that it annoyed him, no doubt, and did it anyway.

As to what Justice claimed about her people, Lared was not surprised that they made no difference between the sexes. Where Justice and Jason came from people walked on water and learned to cause pain and talked to each other without opening their mouths. Why shouldn't they do everything else oddly, too? It was something else that interested Lared. "Where *are* you from?"

Jason smiled at the question. "She won't tell you," he said.
"Why not?"

"Because where she's from is gone."

"Aren't you from the same place?"

Jason's smile faded. "Where she's from, came from *me*.
Where *I'm* from is also gone."

"I don't understand your puzzles or your secrets. Where are
you from?" Lared remembered the falling star.

Of course Jason knew what was in his thoughts. "We're
from where you think we're from."

They had voyaged between the stars. "Then why are you
here? Of all the places in the universe, why Flat Harbor?"

Jason shrugged. "Ask Justice."

"To ask Justice, I only have to think. Sometimes even *before*
I think, she knows. I wake up in the night and I'm never alone.
Always there's someone listening in on my dreams."

We are here, said Justice silently, for you.

"For a blacksmith's son? Or a mushroom hunter? What do
you want from me?"

"What you want from us," said Jason.

"And what is that?"

Our story, answered Justice. Where we're from, what we've
done, why we left. And why pain has returned to the world.

"You have something to do with that?"

You've known all along that we did.

"And what do you need from me?"

Your words. Your language. Written down, simply, truthfully.

"I'm not a cleric."

That's your virtue.

"Who would read what I write?"

It will be true. Those who know truth when they see it will
read it, and believe it.

"And what does it matter if they do?"

It was Jason who answered. "Our story won't bring burning
rafts down the river."

Lared remembered the burning man who gave his pain as
a sacrifice to some imagined god. Lared wasn't sure yet whether
Jason and Justice were good or evil—his very liking of Jason
made him more suspicious sometimes than his dislike of Justice. But good or evil, they were better than torture in the name

of God. Still, he couldn't figure out what need they had of him. "I've never written anything longer than a page, no one's read anything longer than my name, a million billion people in the universe, you still haven't told me why me!"

Because our story has to be written simply, so simple people can read it. It has to be written in Flat Harbor.

"There are a million places like Flat Harbor."

But I knew Flat Harbor. I knew you. And when all else that I knew was gone, where else could I go home?

"How could you know this place? When have you ever been here before?"

"Enough," said Jason. "She's told you more than she meant to."

"How can I know what to do? Can I write it? *Should* I write your story?"

Jason would not decide for him. "If you want to."

"Will the story tell me what it means? Why Clany died the way she did?"

The answer to that, said Justice, and to questions that you haven't yet thought to ask.

Lared's work began as dreams. He awoke in the night four, five, six times, ever more surprised to see still the split-log walls, the packed-earth floor, the half-ladder stairway that ran upward into the tiny guest rooms. Fire, barely contained within the chimney. A cat stretching before the fire. The sheepskins half-ready to be parchment, drying on their frames. The looms in the corner—of course the village loom was kept here. All this had been in Lared's eyes since infancy, and yet after the dreams it was strange. Strange at first, anyway, and then unpleasant, for compared to the world that Justice showed him in his sleep, Father's inn was filthy, disgusting, poor, shameful.

They are not from *my* memory, Justice told him. I give you dreams from Jason's past. Unless you live in his world, how can you write his tale?

So Lared spent his nights wandering the clean white corridors of Capitol, where not even dust dared to settle. Here and there the passageways opened into bright caverns, teeming with people—Lared had never seen so many people in his life, had not thought so many might exist. And yet in the dream he knew they were but a tiny fraction of the people of this world. For

the corridors were miles from top to bottom, and covered the
world from pole to pole, except a few patches of ocean, the
only place where life renewed itself. There was some attempt
to remember living worlds. Here and there among the corridors
were little gardens, carefully tamed plants artfully arranged, a
mockery of forest. A man could hunt mushrooms here forever,
and find no life but what was planted and tended.

There were trains that flew through tubes connecting place
to place; and in his dream his palm contained a disc, and he
laid his hand on glowing plates to do everything—to travel,
to pass through doors, to use the booths where people who
weren't there talked to you and told you things. Lared had
heard of such things, but they were always far away, and never
touched the life of Flat Harbor. Now, however, the memories
were so real that he found himself walking through the forest
with the stride of a corridor dweller, and the tracks of wild
swine took him by surprise, for there were no impressions of
the passage of living things on the floors of Capitol.

As the setting grew more familiar, his dreams began to be
stories. He saw life-loop players whose whole lives were re-
corded for others to see, even what ought to have been done
by dark of night or in the privy shed. He saw weapons that
made a man come afire inside, erupting through the eyes like
flames through spoilt cloth. The life of Capitol was always on
the edge of death, precarious as an autumn leaf resting on a
fence rail on a windy day.

Nowhere was the death of Capitol more clearly promised
than in the catacombs of sleepers. Again and again Justice
showed him the people lying down on sterile beds, having their
memories drained away into balls of foam, and then waiting
docilely as quiet servants injected death into their veins. Death
in the form of the drug somec, death that only delayed itself
while the frozen corpses waited in their tombs. Years later the
quiet servants awakened them, poured back their memories,
and the sleepers got up and walked around, as proud of themselves as if they had accomplished something.

"What are they afraid of?" Lared asked Jason as they stuffed
sausages together in the butchery shed.

"Dying first."

"But they still die, don't they? Sleeping like that gives them
not another day of life, does it?"

"Not an hour. We all end up like this." And he bound off another link of tightstuffed gut.

"Then why? It makes no sense."

"It worked this way. Important people slept longer and woke up less. So they died hundreds of years later."

"But then all their friends died first."

"That was the point."

"But why would you want to live, if all your friends were dead?"

Jason laughed. "Don't ask me. I always thought it was stupid."

"Why did they do it?"

Jason shrugged. "How can I tell you? I don't know."

Justice answered into Lared's thoughts: There is nothing so stupid or dangerous or painful that people won't eagerly do it, if by doing it they will make others believe they are better or stronger or more honorable. I have seen people poison themselves, destroy their children, abandon their mates, cut themselves off from the world, all so that others would think they were a better sort of person.

"But who would think such cripples were better?"

"There were people who felt like you," Jason said.

But they never took somec, said Justice. They never slept, and so they lived their century and died and those who lived for the honor and power of sleep, thinking it was eternal life, they only despised the ones who refused somec.

It made no sense to Lared, that people could be such fools. But Jason assured him that for thousands of years the universe was ruled by people who lived only for sleep, who died as often as possible in order to avoid the sleep that would never end. How could Lared doubt it, after all? His dreams of Capitol were too powerful, the memories too real.

"Where is Capitol?"

"Gone," said Jason, stirring the spiced meat before funneling another handful into the casing.

"The whole world?"

"Bare rock. All the metal stripped away long ago. No soil left, no life in the sea."

Give it two billion years, said Justice, and maybe something will happen.

"Where did the people go?"

"That's part of the story you're going to write."

"Did you and Justice destroy it?"

"No. Abner Doon destroyed it."

"Then Abner Doon was real?"

"I knew him," Jason said.

"He was a man?"

"You will write the story of how I met Abner Doon. Justice will tell you the story in your dreams, and when you wake up, you'll write it down."

"Did Justice meet Abner Doon?"

"Justice was born twenty years ago. I met Abner Doon— fifteen, sixteen thousand years ago."

Lared thought that Jason, still uncertain of the language, had got the numbers wrong. Justice corrected him. The numbers are right, she said. Jason slept for ten thousand years at the bottom of the sea, and before that slept and slept and slept.

"You—used somec, too," said Lared.

"I was a starpilot," Jason said. "Our ships were slower then. We who piloted the ships, we were the only ones who had a need for somec."

"How old are you?"

"Before anyone lived here on your world, I was already old. Does it matter?"

Lared could not grasp it, and so he put it into the only terms he knew. "Are you God?" he asked.

Jason did not laugh at him. Instead he looked thoughtful, and considered the question. It was Justice who answered. All my life I called him God, she said, until I met him.

"But how can you be God, if Justice is more powerful than you?"

I am his daughter, five hundred generations from him. Shouldn't the children of God learn something in that time?

Lared took the finished chain of sausages from Jason's hands and looped it above the smoky fire. "No one ever taught me that God could make sausages."

"It's one of the little skills I picked up along the way."

It was afternoon already, and so they went back to the house, where Mother sullenly served them cheese and hot bread with the juice of the overripe apples. "Better than anything on Capitol," Jason said, and Lared, remembering clearly the taste of the tasteless food of Jason's childhood, agreed.

"Only one job left before your writing days begin," said Jason. "Ink."

"The old cleric left me some," Lared said.

"No better than mule piss," said Jason. "I'll teach you how to make ink that lasts."

Mother was not pleased. "There's work to do," she said. "You can't take Lared out on some foolish task like ink-making."

Jason smiled, but his eyes were hard. "Thano, I have worked in this village like your own son. The snow will be here soon, and you have never before been so well-prepared. And yet I have paid *you* for my lodging, when by rights you ought to have paid me. I warn you, don't begrudge me your son's time."

"You *warn* me? What will you do, murder me in my own house?" She dared him to hurt her.

But he only needed to strike her with words. "Don't stand in my way, Thano, or I will tell your husband that he isn't the only one in this house who keeps a little forge. I will tell your husband which travelers you have had pumping the bellows handle for you, to keep your little fire hot."

Mother's eyes went small, and she turned back to cutting turnips into the supper soup.

Her docility was confession. Lared looked on her with contempt and fear. He thought of his thin body, his narrow shoulders, and wondered what traveler had sired him. What have you stolen from the chain of life? he demanded silently.

You are your father's son, said Justice in his mind. And Sala is his, too. Those who protected you from pain prevented bastards as well.

It was scant comfort. Cold and fearsome as Mother had always been, still he had never thought she was false.

"I'm learning the language very well, don't you think?" said Jason cheerfully.

"Go make your ink." Mother was sullen. "I don't like having you indoors here."

I don't much like to be here, either, Mother.

Jason kissed Justice lightly on the cheek as he left. Justice only glared at him. Jason explained to Lared when they got outside. "Justice hates it when I make people obey me out of fear. She thinks it's ugly and not nice. She always used to make people obey her by changing what they wanted, so it didn't occur to them to disobey. I think that's degrading and turns people into animals."

Lared shrugged. Just so long as Mother let him learn how to make good ink, it didn't matter to Lared how Jason and Justice got it done.

Jason looked for a certain fungus growth on certain trees, and gathered it into one bag; he had Lared fill another bag with blackthorn stalks, though they cut his hands. Lared did not complain of the pain, because it gave him pleasure to bear it wordlessly. And as dark came on, and they were nearly home, Jason stopped and tapped a pine tree, which still had enough life in it to fill a little jar with gum.

The funguses they boiled and ground up and boiled again, then strained out the thin black fluid that was left. They crushed the blackthorn into it, and strained it again, and then boiled it for an hour with the pine gum. At last they squeezed it through fine linen, and ended up with two pints of smooth black ink.

"It will stay black for a thousand years, and readable for five thousand. The parchment will turn to dust before the ink is too faint to see," said Jason.

"How did you learn to make such ink?"

"How did you learn to make such parchment?" Jason answered, holding up a sheet of it that Lared had made. "I can see my hand through it."

"There's no secret to parchment," Lared answered. "The sheep wear the secret on their bodies till they die, and give it up when we butcher them."

That night Lared dreamed of how Jason met Abner Doon. How God met Satan. How life met death. How making met unmaking. The dream was given to him by Justice, as she remembered it from finding the memory complete in Jason's mind. Memories of memories of memories, that was what lay in Lared's mind the next morning, when with trembling quill he began to write.

3

A Book of Old Memories

Here is how Lared began his book:

"I am Lared of Flat Haven Inn. I am not a cleric, but I have read books and know my letters, ties, and bindings. So I write, with good new ink on parchment I made myself, a story that is not my own. It is my memory of my dreams of another man's childhood, dreams that were given me so I could tell his tale. Forgive me if I write badly, because I have had little practice at this. I have not the elegance of Semol of Grais, though my pen longs to write such language. All you will have from me is the plain tale.

"The name of the boy I tell you of was Jason Worthing, then called Jase, without respect, because no one knew what he was or what he would become. He lived on a world of steel and plastic called Capitol, which now is dead. It was a world so rich that the children had nothing to do but go to school or play. It was a world so poor that no food grew there, and they had to eat what other worlds sent them in great starships."

Lared read it over, and felt at once pleased and afraid. Pleased that he could write so many words at once. Pleased because it did sound like the beginning of a book. And afraid because he knew how uneducated he was, knew that to clerics it would sound childish. But I am a child, he thought.

"You're a man," said Jason. He sat on the floor, leaning against the wall, sewing the leather boots he had volunteered to make for Father. "And your book will be good enough, if you only tell the truth."

"How can I be sure I'll remember everything?"

"You don't have to remember everything."

"Some things in the dreams I don't even understand."

"You don't have to understand it, either."

"How do I even know it's true?"

Jason laughed, driving the long, heavy needle through the leather and drawing the thread tight. "It's your memory of your dreams of Justice's memory of my memory of things that happened to me in my childhood on a planet that died more than ten thousand years ago. How could it help but be true?"

"What should I start with?"

Jason shrugged. "We didn't choose a tool, we chose a person to write our story. Start with the first thing that matters."

What was the first thing that mattered? Lared thought through the things he remembered of Jason's life. What mattered? Fear and pain—that's what mattered to Lared now, after a childhood without either. And the earliest fear, the earliest pain that mattered, that was when Jason nearly lost his life because he did too well on a test.

It was in a class that studied the movements and powers of the stars, one that only a few hundred of the thirteen-year-olds of Capitol knew enough to take. Jase watched as the problems appeared in the air below the stars, and Jase entered his answers on a keyboard.

Jase knew all the answers easily, for he had learned well, and he grew more confident as it became clear the test was below his abilities. Until the last question. It was completely unrelated to the rest of the test. He was not prepared for it. They had not studied it in class. And yet as he looked at the problem, he thought he understood how the answer might be found. He began calculating. There was one figure that baffled him. He thought he knew what it meant, but did not know how to prove it, to be sure, to be exact. A year ago he would have called it a good guess and entered his answer. But this year had changed everything. He had a way of finding out what he needed to know.

He looked at the teacher, Hartman Torrock, who was gazing around the room. Then he shifted something in his mind, the way things shifted when his eyes suddenly focused on something far, when they had been seeing something near. It was as though he could suddenly see behind Hartman Torrock's eyes. Now Jase could hear his present thoughts as if he were thinking them himself—his mind was on the woman who had quarreled with him this morning, and whose body he wanted to cause pleasure to and cause pain to this night. It was an ugly sort of desire, to rule her and make her be like his own tongue, to speak only his thoughts, to disappear inside him when she was not in use. Jase never liked Hartman Torrock, but loathed him now. Torrock's thoughts were not pleasant scenery.

Jase quickly plunged deeper than Torrock's present thoughts, moved among his unthought-of memories as easily as if they were his own, finding Torrock's knowledge of stars and motions, seeking the meaning of the unfamiliar figure. And the exact figure was there, perfect to the fourteenth decimal place. Then he slipped gratefully from Torrock's mind and entered the result into the keyboard. No more problems appeared above his table. The test was over. He waited.

His score was perfect, when it came. And yet a red glow appeared, and hung in the air above Jase's table. The red glow meant a failing score. Or a computer malfunction, or cheating. Torrock, looking worried, got up and came to him. "What's wrong?" asked the teacher.

"I don't know," said Jase.

"What's your score?" He looked, and it was perfect. "Then what's wrong?"

"I don't know," said Jase again.

Torrock went back to his own table and began talking quietly with the air. Jase, as always, listened to Torrock's mind. The mistake had been Torrock's. The last question should not have been on his test. It dealt with secrets that children should not learn until years later. Torrock had written it last night, meaning to append it to an examination he would give to his advanced students tomorrow. Instead he had added it to his beginning class today. Jase should not have been given the question at all; above all, he should not have been able to get it right. It was a sign of cheating.

But how could he cheat? thought Hartman Torrock. Who in the room knew the answer, except me? And I never told him.

Somehow this boy stole secrets from me, thought Torrock. They will think that I told him, that I broke my trust, that I am not fit to know secrets. They will punish me. They will take away my somec privileges. What has this boy done to me? How did he do it?

Then Torrock remembered the darkest truth about Jase Worthing: his father. What do you expect from the son of a Swipe? thought Torrock. He knew my secret because he is his father's son.

Jase recoiled from the thought, for it was his darkest fear. He had grown up with the horror of who his father was: Homer Worthing, the monster, leader of the Swipe Revolt, the foulest murderer in all history. He had died in space years before Jase's mother had decided to conceive a child. The Swipe war was over then. But the universal loathing for the Swipes remained, tinged with the memory of the eight billion people Jase's father had burned to death.

It had been nearly bloodless until then. In the seemingly endless war between the Empire and the Rebels (or the Usurpers and the Patriots, depending on which side you were on), both sides had begun using telepathic starpilots. The results were devastating—non-Swipes were helpless, and it quickly became clear to both sides that the Swipes, who could silently communicate with each other, might easily unite against both Empire and Rebels, unseat all government, take control of somec and therefore of the entire bureaucracy. As long as normal people could not tell what the Swipes had in mind, the Swipes could not, must not be given starships.

In fact the Swipe starpilots had been conspiring to end the war and impose peace on both sides. They thought, when both sides tried to remove them from their commands, that they could still bring off such a victory. So they seized their ships and declared both governments dissolved. In response, Empire and Rebels united, briefly, to exterminate the Swipes. At first the Swipe starpilots allowed themselves to be harried from here to there. Though Swipes were always killed as soon as they were captured, yet they tried to avoid causing too much harm, hoping at first for victory, later for compromise, at last for mercy. But the universe had no place for them; the Swipes must die. Homer was at the end of his last hope of escape. But in that moment he had chosen to destroy eight billion people rather than to die alone.

And I am his son.

All this came in a moment's memory to Jason Worthing.

Hartman Torrock did not know what went on behind the mask of Jase's face.

"Blood test," Torrock said.

Jason protested, wanted to know why.

"Hold out your hand."

Jase held out his hand. He knew the test would show nothing. They were so smart, the ones who hated Swipes. They were sure they knew how the power to see behind the eyes was passed from mother to children, to lie dormant in daughters, to become active in sons. Jase's mother did not have the Swipe, and so Jase could not have it, *did* not have it. And yet he *was* a Swipe, *could* see behind the eyes. Someday, he knew, it would occur to someone that perhaps there was another way to be a Swipe, a way that might be passed from father to son, along with eyes as blue as a quepbird's breast. The gift to see behind the eyes had only come gradually to his mind, like the hair of manhood to his body. When he first realized what was going on, he feared that he was going crazy; later he knew that somehow the impossible had happened, and he had inherited his father's curse. That was terrifying enough—how much like his father, the mass murderer, was he? And yet the Swipe was not something he could refuse. He tried to be careful, tried to remember to pretend not to know the secrets he learned in other people's minds. The simplest way to do it, of course, would be not to look in their minds at all. But he felt like a cripple whose legs had just been healed—how could he not run, now that he had learned that it was possible? So in these months—or had it been a year?—he had grown more and more daring as he learned to better control and use his power. And today he had been careless. Today he had plainly known what he could not know by any other means.

And yet, he told himself, I did not *learn* it from Torrock's mind. I only *confirmed* it, clarified it. The shape of the answer came to me from my own thoughts.

Jase almost explained this aloud—I thought of the answer to the last question myself!—but he caught himself in time. Torrock had not yet told him aloud that he was worried about that last question. Don't be a fool, Jase told himself. Admit nothing, if you want to live.

The test result came in a moment, rows of figures scrolling up from the table and then slipping backward through the air until they faded out of sight, like sheep being led to the shearing shed. Negative. Negative. Negative. Jase had none of the signs of the Swipe.

Except one. He could not possibly know the answer to the question.

"All right, Jase. How did you do it?"

"Do what?" Jase asked. Am I a good liar? I'd better be— my life depends on it.

"The last question. We never studied it. I never so much as wrote down Crack's Theorem."

"What's Crack's Theorem?"

"Don't be an ass," Torrock said. He touched the keys and called up into the air the answer Jase had given to the last question. He made one set of numbers glow brighter than the others. "How did you learn the value of the curve of the straight line at the edge of light?"

Truthfully, Jase answered, "It was the only number that could fit there."

"To the fourteenth decimal? It took two hundred years even to know the problem existed, and years of work by the best mathematicians of the Empire to determine the value of the curve to *five* places. Crack only proved it to the fourteenth place some fifty years ago. And you expect me to believe you duplicated all this work here at your table in five minutes?"

The other students had been looking away from him, till now. Now, to learn that he knew the value of Crack's Theorem and how to use it in a problem—now they looked in awe at Jase. Whether he cheated to get the value of the curve or not, he had known how to *use* it, when they were only just getting the hang of Newton, Einstein, and Ahmed. They hated Jase with all their hearts, and hoped that he would die. He made them all look so stupid, they thought.

Torrock, too, noticed the other students watching them. He lowered his voice. "I don't know how you got the value of the curve, boy, but if they think I wrote it down or taught it to you, which by God I did not, then it's my job, it's my *somec*, and God knows I get little enough as it is, one year under for three years up, but it's a *start*, I'm a *sleeper*, and you're not going to take it away from me."

"I don't know what you're talking about," Jase said. "I

figured it out on my own. It's not *my* fault if you asked a question that made the value of the curve obvious."

"It was not obvious to fourteen places," Torrock whispered fiercely. "So get out of here, but come back tomorrow. There'll be questions to ask you, you and your mother and anyone else, because *I know what you are,* and test or no test I'll prove it and see you die before I let you ruin everything for me."

Jase and Torrock had never gotten along, but it still horrified Jase to have a grown man say in words that he wanted Jase's death. It frightened him, like a child that meets a rabid wolf in the forest would be frightened, able to watch nothing but the foaming jaws, the streaming teeth, able to hear nothing but the low growl in the throat.

Still, he must pretend not to know what Torrock meant. "I didn't cheat, Mr. Torrock. I've never cheated."

"There are only a few thousand of us on Capitol who know how to use the curve, Master Worthing. But there are millions of us who know how to notify Mother's Little Boys about a person who seems to show symptoms of the Swipe."

"Are you accusing me of—"

"You know what I'm accusing you of."

I know, said Jase silently, that you're frightened half to death of me, that you expect me to be like my father and kill you where you stand, small as I am, powerless as I am—

"Be prepared for questioning, Master Worthing. They'll know how you learned to use the curve, one way or another—there's no honest way you could have done it."

"Except figuring it out on my own!"

"Not to the fourteenth decimal."

No. Not to the fourteenth decimal.

Jase got up and left the classroom. The other students were careful not to look at him until his back was to them. Then they stared and stared. The explosion had come, after all, from nowhere, out of silence, out of the tension of a test that *they* had all been struggling with. What have I done to myself?

He put his palm on the reader at the worm, and the gate chimed to let him through. As long as he was going home from school, there was no charge. The worm was not crowded at this hour, which made it more dangerous—at the levels where Jase and his mother could afford to live, the wall rats were bold enough to come out into the worm and take what they could. For safety, Jase walked forward from segment to segment as the worm rushed smoothly through its tunnel, until he came to a place where several people were gathered. They looked at him suspiciously. He was no longer a little child, he realized. He no longer looked safe to strangers.

Mother was waiting for him. He never found her doing anything when he got home—just sitting there, waiting for him. If it weren't for the fact that she still had her job, still earned what pitiful money they had, he would think she sat down across from the door the moment he left for school, and sat there the whole time until he came back. Her face looked dead, like a slack puppet. Then, after he said hello, after he smiled at her, the corners of her mouth twitched; she smiled, she slowly stood up. "Hungry?" she asked.

"Not much."

"Something wrong?"

Jason shrugged.

"Here, I'll call up the menu." She punched in the one-bark meal menu. Not much choice today—or ever. "There's fish or fowl or red meat."

"It's all algae and beans and human feces," answered Jase.

"I hope you didn't learn to speak that way from me," said Mother.

"Sorry. Fish. Whatever you want."

She punched it in. Then she folded down the little table and leaned on it, looking across at Jase, where he sat on the floor in the corner. "What's wrong?"

He told her.

"But that's absurd," said Mother. "You can't have the Swipe. I was tested three times before they let me have Homer's— your father's child. I told you that when you were young."

"Somehow that doesn't reassure them."

And it didn't reassure Mother, either. Jase realized that she looked genuinely uneasy, frightened. "Don't worry, Mother. They can't prove anything."

Mother shrugged, bit on her palm. Jase hated when she did that, holding her hand palm up and gnawing on the fleshy part. He got up from the floor and went to the bedwall and folded down his bed. He swung up onto it and stared at the ceiling.

At the spot on the ceiling tiles that Jase had known was a face since he was a child. When he was very little he had dreamed about that face. Sometimes it was a monster, come to devour him. Sometimes it was his father, who had gone away but still watched over him. When he was six Mother had told him who his father was, and Jase had known that he was right both times—it *was* his father, and his father *was* a monster.

Why was Mother so afraid?

Jase longed to look behind *her* eyes, but he never had before. Oh, her conscious thoughts, now and then, but nothing deep. He was afraid of the way she gnawed her hand, and sat slack-faced in the chair when he wasn't home, and knew the answer to every question he asked her and yet never seemed interested in anything—he was afraid, instinctively, that whatever was in her memories, he did not want to know it.

For he experienced other people's memories as if they were his own, and remembered them as clearly, so that once having dwelt in their minds for a time he could easily become confused about which things that he remembered were actually things that he had done. Many hours late at night he had lain in his bed, letting his mind wander, searching the nearby rooms—he did not know how to range farther than that with his listening, prowling gift. No one suspected his intrusions. They thought their thoughts, held their memories, dreamed their dreams as always, unaware of this spectator. In his memory, Jase was no virgin—with the prurience of childhood he had been man and woman in acts he did not think his neighbors had imagination enough to perform. In memory, Jase had beaten his children, killed a man in a riot on a lower level, stolen from his employer, quietly sabotaged the electrical system—all the most memorable, painful, exhilarating acts of the people whose minds he entered. It was the hardest thing about the Swipe, remembering when he awoke in the morning which things he had really done, and which things not.

He did not want his mother's memories to have such force upon him.

And yet she was too afraid, still gnawing at her hand there at the table, waiting for the commissary to send them supper. Why are you so afraid because someone has accused me of having the Swipe?

So he looked, and, looking, learned. She had married Homer Worthing before the rebellion, so she had rights. She had gone to sleep with somec, as starpilots' wives do, to be wakened when he returned. And one day, when her flesh burned from waking, when her memories were still newly returned to her head, the kind people in their white sterile clothes told her that her husband was dead. Outside the sleep rooms, some less kind people told her how her husband died, and what he had done in dying. She remembered having seen him only a few minutes ago, just before they bubbled her memory. He had kissed her good-bye, and she fancied she could still feel the pressure of his lips, and now he was dead, had been dead a year before they thought it was safe to waken his widow; he was a murderer, a monster, and she hadn't had his child yet.

Why did you have a child, Mother? Jase looked for the answer, forgetting that his errand in her mind was to find out why she was so afraid. It didn't matter: his curiosity and her fear led to the same place. She wanted Homer's child, Homer's *son*, because Homer's father, old Ulysses Worthing, had told her that she must.

Ulysses Worthing had the same blue eyes that Jason saw each day in the mirror, those deep, pure, markless blue irises that looked like God had erased a spot of Jason and let the pure sky of a living world shine through. He looked at young Uyul, the girl his starpilot son had brought home to meet him, and she did not know what he saw in her that seemed to puzzle him so. "I don't know," said old Ulysses, "I don't know how strong you are. I don't know if there'll be much left of Uyul when she takes Homer into herself."

"Now, don't make her scared of me," said Homer.

I don't want to hear your voice, said Jason to his mother's memory of his father. I am no part of you, I have no father.

"I'm not afraid of you," Uyul said. But was she talking to Homer or Ulysses? "I might be stronger than you think." But what she thought was this: if I lose myself and become nothing but the woman half of Homer, that is fine with me.

Ulysses laughed at her. As if he could read her mind, he said, "Don't marry her, Homer. She's determined to be less than half a human being."

"I don't even know what this conversation means," Uyul said, laughing nervously.

Ulysses leaned closer to her. "I don't care who or what my son marries. He doesn't ask my consent, and he never will. But listen close, young lady. This is between you and me, not you and him. You will have his child, and it will be a son, and if it doesn't have blue eyes like mine, you have another until you have one that does. You won't leave me without inheritance, just because you're too weak to know your own name without Homer whispering it to you every night."

It made her furious. "It's none of your business how many children I have, or what sex they are, or what eyes their colors are. Colors their eyes are." She was furious that she had gotten her words twisted up. Ulysses only laughed at her.

"Never mind, Uyul," Homer said—hold your peace! cried the listening Jason—"he's only pretending to be an impossible son-of-a-bitch. He's just testing to see if you can stand him."

"I can't," Uyul said, trying to make the truth sound like a joke.

Ulysses shrugged. "What do *I* care? Just have Homer's sky-eyed son. And name it Jason, after my grandfather. We've been cycling those old names through the family for so long that—"

"Father, you're getting tedious," said Homer. So impatiently he said it. So urgently. Jason wished, for just a moment, that he could have been there, and listened to Homer's mind, instead of getting only Mother's memory of it.

"What Homer is," said Ulysses, "I am, and Homer's child will be."

Those were the words that Mother remembered. What Homer is, I am, and Homer's child will be. Have a son with sky-colored eyes. Name him Jason. What Homer is, I am, and Homer's child will be.

"I'm not a murderer," Jason whispered.

His mother shuddered.

"But I do see all that Father—"

She rose and rushed toward him, knocking down the chair, stumbling over it, rushing to put her hand across his mouth.

"Hold your tongue, boy, don't you know the walls are ears?"

"What Homer is," Jason said out loud, "I am, and Homer's child will be."

Mother looked at him in horror. He named her worst fear to her, that in posthumously obeying Ulysses' charge to her she had unleashed another Swipe upon the world. "You can't be," she whispered. "Mother to son, that's the only way—"

"There must be other gifts in the world," Jase said, "than those that reside in X chromosomes, only showing up when paired with a stunted Y."

Suddenly she doubled up her fist and brought it down like a hammer on his mouth. He cried out in pain; blood from his lips rushed into his mouth as he tried to shout at her, and he choked. Mother backed away from him whimpering, gnawing on the hand that had just struck him. "No no no," she said. "Mother to son, you're clean, you're clean, not his son but mine, not his but mine—"

But in his mother's mind Jason saw that she looked at him with the same eyes that had seen and loved her husband. After all, Jason had Homer Worthing's face, that well-known face, that face that frightened children in the textbooks in school. He was younger, thicker of lip, gentler in the eyes, but he still wore Homer's face, and his mother both loved and hated him for that.

She stood in the middle of the room, facing the door, and Jason saw that she was seeing Homer, as if he had come back to her, as if he smiled at her and said, "It was all a misunderstanding, and I've come back to make you whole again." Jase swallowed the blood in his mouth and got off his bed, walked around Mother and stood in front of her. She did not see him. Still in her mind she saw her husband, and he reached out to her, reached out and touched her cheek and said, "Uyula, I love you," and she took a step toward him, into his embrace.

"Mother," said Jason.

She shuddered; her vision cleared, and she saw that it was not her husband she held, but her son, and his mouth was bleeding. She dissolved into sobs, clung to him, pulled him to the floor and wept upon him, touching his bleeding lips, kissing him, saying over and over, "I'm sorry, I'm so sorry you were ever born, will you ever forgive me?"

"I forgive you," Jason whispered, "for letting me be born."

Mother is insane, said Jason silently. She is insane, and she knows I have the Swipe, and if they interrogate her we both are dead.

• • •

He had to go to school the next day. If he stayed away he would be confessing; he would be begging them to come to his home, where they would find Uyul, who was nobody except Homer Worthing's wife—Uyul the monster's wife, that was the name he found inside his mother's head. I wish I had never looked, he thought again and again all night. He lay awake for a long time, and awoke often, always trying to think of a solution that was not terrifyingly desperate. Go into hiding, become a wall rat? He did not know how the people with uncoded hands survived on Capitol, living in the ventilation shafts and stealing whatever they could. No, he would have to go to school, face it down. They had no proof. He *had* answered the question himself. Pretty much. As long as his genes didn't show it, Torrock had no proof that he was a Swipe.

So he left his mother in the morning, and dozed in the worm on the way to school. He went to his morning classes as usual, ate the free lunch that was usually his best meal of the day, and then the headmaster came and invited him to his office.

"What about history?" Jase asked, trying to act unconcerned.

"The rest of your classes today are cancelled."

Torrock was waiting in the headmaster's office. He looked pleased with himself. "We have prepared a test. It's no more difficult than the one you took yesterday. Except that I didn't write the questions. I don't know the answers. Someone will be with you all the time. If you could perform an act of genius yesterday, surely you can do it again today."

Jason looked at the headmaster. "Do I have to? I was lucky yesterday, I don't know why I have to go through this test."

The headmaster sighed, glanced at Torrock, and raised his hands in helplessness. "A serious accusation has been made. This test is—an allowable act."

"It won't prove anything."

"Your blood test is—ambiguous."

"My blood test was negative. It was from the time I was born. I can't help who my father was!"

Yes, the headmaster agreed silently, it's hardly fair, but— "There are other tests, and your genetic analysis shows—irregularities."

"Everybody's genes are different."

The headmaster sighed again. "Take the test, Master Worthing. And do well."

Torrock smiled. "There are three questions. Take as long as you like. Take all night if you like."

Shall I take your secrets out of your memory and tell them to the world? But Jase did not dare look behind Torrock's eyes. He had to take this test with no knowledge of anything he should not know. It might have been his life at stake. And yet even as he denied himself any illegitimate knowledge, he wondered if it might not be better to know as much as possible. To know what the real object of the test was. He felt helpless. Torrock could make him do anything, could make the test mean anything, and Jase had no recourse.

At the table, staring at a pattern of stars moving in the air, he despaired. Even the question made no sense to him. There were two symbols that he didn't understand, and the movement of the stars was eccentric, to say the least. Who were they, to play God with his life?

They had been playing God with his life from the beginning. He was only conceived because of old Ulysses' command; Jason was not brought to life because of love, but because a half-mad widow followed someone else's dead and ancient plan. Now, his life hinged on someone else's plan, and he couldn't even be sure that knowing what it was would help him to survive.

But despair led nowhere. He studied the stars and tried to understand the eccentricity; studied the figures and tried to eliminate possible causes.

"Do I have to answer the three questions in order?" Jase asked.

The headmaster looked up from his work. "Hmm?"

"Can I answer these out of order?"

The headmaster nodded and went back to writing letters.

Jason went from question to question, one-two-three, one-two-three. They were related problems, building from bad to worse. Even the curve theorem wouldn't help. What did they think he was, a genius?

Apparently they did. Either a genius or a Swipe. If he didn't prove himself one, he would prove himself the other. So he set to work.

All afternoon. Torrock came in at dismissal time, and took the headmaster's place in the room. The headmaster left, and came back an hour later with dinner for all three of them. Jase couldn't eat. He was getting a handle on the first problem, learning things from the data on the second question that helped explain what was going on in the first. Before Torrock had disposed of the tray, the first question was answered.

He fell asleep about eleven o'clock. The headmaster was already asleep. Jase awoke first, hours before school was supposed to start. The second question was still there, waiting for him. But Jason saw the answer at once, in a different direction from anything he had been pursuing. It meant a slight revision to the way he had understood the curve, but now it worked. He entered the second answer.

He tried for a while longer with the third question, but with what he had discovered on the first two, he realized that there were too many variables and he couldn't solve it with the present data. He could solve a few cycles in it, but that was all. So he entered what he could, called the rest unanswerable, and closed the test.

There was a red glow above the table. Failure.

He woke up the headmaster. "What time is it?" the old man asked.

"Time to get somebody else to take tests for you," Jase said.

The headmaster saw the red glow and raised an eyebrow.

"Good-bye," Jason said. He was out the door before the headmaster was awake enough to do anything more.

His school was nested inside the university, and he went straight to Gracie, the university library. His student status would give him better access to Capitol's information system than he could get from the public stations. However, he might not have much time. The red light at the end of his test might mean many things, and none of them were good. It might mean that he failed the test, and thereby "proved" to them that he could not have passed the first one without being a Swipe, and they would be looking for him to kill him. It might mean that he passed the test, but that they did not believe he could have done it without being a Swipe. The truth was that neither the first nor second test proved anything. But if they thought it proved something, he was just as dead.

Where could he turn for help? He could think of only one possibility. Mother believed that Jase's grandfather was also a Swipe. If what Jase had was indeed a version of the Swipe that could be passed from father to son, and it had been going on long enough for Ulysses Worthing to know that it was hereditary, then there should be other Worthings with the same gift. Of course, the fact that Mother's Little Boys didn't know about it meant that all the others had succeeded in keeping their gift secret.

Row on row, hundreds of dusty pink plastic carrels with the gray-blue letter *C* of the Communications Bureau in prominent display. He had been here often enough before to know where the older students went, and where they didn't. He went to where they didn't, the older section without individual printouts in each booth—and where there weren't enough externals to play the most popular games. Jason had sat for hours playing Evolution, in which constant environmental changes forced the player to adapt animals to fit. He got to the level where eight animals and four plants had to be adapted at once. Jase had a knack for it, but he wasn't here to play.

He carded the reader for charges, then palmed it for identification. The air over the desk went bright with directory entries. He flipped through it up, back, and to the left, until he got to the genealogical programs. He brought Genealogy: Relatives by Common Descent into the window and punched Enter. A much simpler menu appeared. He chose Male Relatives by Male Lines Only and entered his own name and code. Gracie identified him at once—his birth date and place appeared in the middle of the air, then settled slow as a dustflake toward the bottom. Above him, connected by a little line, was his father's name, and *his* father's name, and so on: Homer Worthing, Ulysses Worthing, Ajax Worthing, another Jason, another Homer. And spiraling around and out from the central column were all the cousins, hundreds of them, thousands of them. It was too much to handle.

Nearest five living cousins only, he entered.

All but five names disappeared. To his surprise, there were two near ones, and the next three were quite distant relatives, branching from his line more than fifteen generations back. Only the first two were close at all.

Full current address, he entered.

The nearest in blood was Talbot Worthing, a grandson of Ajax Worthing. But he lived on a planet forty-two light years away. The other cousin was nearer in space: Radamand Worthing, a great grandson of the first Homer. He was on Capitol, working as a government employee on the district manager level. Nice to know that a relative had done so well for himself. Jase asked for a print-out. He heard the choke of a printer a few carrels away, and immediately went to get it, without signing off. On his way back he only happened to glance at the carrel he had been using.

"Attention: You are required to remain where you are until a proctor comes to your carrel and gives you further instruction. Failure to comply will seriously endanger your academic standing."

Right now Jase figured it wasn't his academic standing at stake. It was his life. If the test results were enough to call for the proctors, there was little hope the results would be benign. Fortunately, it would be a while before they could get permission to call for Mother's Little Boys—that was a power far above what the university could normally command. The Swipe would bring that power, of course. But it would take time.

If the test had convinced them he was a Swipe. How could he be sure? Whose mind could tell him the truth? He didn't know how to search at a distance, how to look for strangers that he couldn't see.

Cousin Radamand was far enough away that he was well under the curve of the earth; Jase took a deep worm, and in an hour he stood in the anteroom of the office of Radamand Worthing, supervisor of district 10 of Napa Sector.

"Do you have an appointment, young man?" asked the receptionist.

"I don't need one," said Jase. He tried to search for someone behind the door of Radamand's office, but without knowing who was there, or where in the other room he was, he hardly knew how to begin. As always when he could not see the person he searched for, he saw only flashes of random thoughts, connected to no one person, telling no particular story.

"Everyone needs an appointment, little boy." There was

menace in her voice. Jase knew she was not to be trifled with. She looked decorative, but in fact she was trained to kill; Radamand kept a bodyguard in front of his door.

Jase studied her a moment, took a potent name out of her memory. "Would Hilvock need one? If he came wearing white?"

Her face went a deep red. "Never," she said. "How did you know?"

"Tell Radamand Worthing that his blue-eyed cousin Jason is here to see him."

"Do you think you're the first to pretend to be a relative of his?" But she stared at his pure blue eyes and he knew she did not doubt him.

"I'm the first to know how much money he makes from opening the foundation space to manufacturing. And from child labor, since Mother's Little Boys have no eyes down there."

He did not take this from her mind. He had finally found his cousin in the other room. And now he could not so much as notice the woman who watched him. He could see only the memories in Radamand's mind. Radamand had the Swipe, all right; it was hereditary, all right; the question was if Jason would live to escape this place.

Radamand was wise—he knew there was profit in knowing secrets. District supervisor, that was all he was—but he knew so much about so many, had such a quiet reputation, that his power extended far into the heart of Capitol. And power breeds power, for the more you are believed to have, the more you have as others fear to cross you—Radamand knew that, too. Who could take him by surprise? He seemed to anticipate every move to thwart him. There were corpses here and there in Capitol that he had arranged for—but murder was not a thing that pleased him much. He took far more pleasure out of watching people who thought they were fearless as they learned to fear him, tasting the panic when they realized what was known about them, things that no one could know.

Worst for Jase was this: that Radamand was stronger than he was, that the mere memory of Radamand's will was stronger than Jase's present self. Radamand's memories inhabited Jason's mind as if they were his own. Jase tasted Radamand's delight in making others obey him, and it was as sweet to him as it was to Radamand.

As sweet to him, and yet there was Jase's own self, revolted at what he had done, at the murders he remembered committing, the lives he remembered having destroyed, and he could not bear to have such memories inside his head. How could I have done it! cried Jase silently. How can I undo what I have done!

He cried out. The receptionist was startled. He *was* a child, but a dangerous one, and all the more dangerous because of his seeming madness, to seem suddenly to be in pain like this. She got up slowly, walked to the door that led to Radamand.

Jase finally reached the bottom, the worst acts, the only murders Radamand had committed with his own hands. For Radamand knew that a man who profited from knowing others' secrets could not afford to have a dangerous secret of his own— not one, at least, that anyone else might know. And who would know that Radamand was a Swipe? Why, his own dear kin. As the first murder occurred to him, all the others had to follow. He killed his older brother on impulse, in the family's swimming pool; but from his father and younger brothers he could not possibly hide his guilt. They could see his memory of the act as well as he could. So he ranged through his house, killing every male that was kin of his; and using Gracie he located as many as he could find, all who had the pure blue eyes of the Worthing gift, and killed them. Evading arrest was easy—he had information to sell to powerful men about other powerful men, and made himself too valuable to lose; and for those not interested in buying or selling, he held their reputations hostage, and they dared not harm him. Only two of his kin with the gift had he let live. Talbot, who was on a far-off colony, and Homer, the starpilot who had made it impossible to be known as a Swipe and live. Homer, who had died in a holocaust of his own making. Radamand was safe. His hands were foul with his brothers', with his father's blood, but he was safe.

It did not occur to him that some thirteen years ago or so Homer's widow would choose to inseminate herself and bear Homer's son. Radamand was not expecting Jason. But when he knew that Jason lived—and worse, that Jason knew—

"Cousin," whispered Radamand from the door.

Jase saw the death in Radamand's mind and threw himself to the floor before the pellet was fired.

Radamand did not move to try again, not at once. Radamand was looking now into Jason's memories. Jase watched his own memories unfolding in Radamand's mind, saw that Radamand searched for only one thing: who knew that Jason was a Swipe. And in spite of himself Jase thought of his mother. And as he thought of her, he saw his memory of her knowledge pass through Radamand's thoughts, but not neutrally, no—it was overlaid with the decision to kill her also. Mother and son, they would die, because if once it was discovered that another sort of Swipe could be passed from father to son, it would be only a matter of time before Radamand was found.

The world would end if Radamand died—it would end, at least, for Radamand, and he cared for nothing else.

It was too much for Jason, to have to hold within himself memories of his mother with intent to kill her. He screamed and threw himself at Radamand, who dodged easily and laughed at him.

"Come, child. Try to surprise me."

How can I think of something that he doesn't know I've thought of? His only hope was not surprise at all; with an enemy who was more skilled than he in seeing behind the eyes, it was not quickness that would count. It was chess, and what stopped the checkmate would be check: force him to move another piece.

"You have no pieces," Radamand said. He was searching in Jase's mind for Jase's address, so he wouldn't have any trouble finding Jase's mother.

"Radamand Worthing is a Swipe," Jason said aloud. "So am I. It's hereditary, father to son."

Did Radamand's receptionist believe him? Indeed she did.

Radamand had no choice. If he did not kill her, she would surely kill him—Swipes were the most loathsome creatures imaginable, and she could not possibly be trusted now. Jason was only a boy. He was no direct physical threat to Radamand. The woman was a killer, as he well knew. He dared not leave her behind him.

As Radamand fired a pellet at the receptionist, Jason fled. It would take time for Radamand to arrange things so that he wouldn't be charged with her murder. Was it time enough for Jason to escape?

From the office, yes. From Radamand's sector, yes. But

Radamand knew his address, and would find him wherever in the world he hid. Even among the wall rats, Radamand had friends and would hunt him down.

And what could Jason do in return? If he denounced Radamand it was surely his own death, too. His only hope was to do what Talbot Worthing had done—go light-years away from Radamand, where he could not possibly be a threat.

There were two routes off Capitol that a boy of Jase's age could take. He could join the military, or he could go to a colony on one of the newly opened worlds. That would be far enough away for Radamand, surely. And once enrolled in the Fleet or the Colonies, even Radamand could not touch him— the administration of Capitol had no power in imperial services like those.

But he could not go directly to the colonies. For if he did, Radamand would find Mother, and she would die. He must act to save her first. And the Fleet was not open to her, at her age. Only the Colonies for Mother.

He had no choice but to go home now, at once. Yet Radamand surely knew that Jason thought this way, and would be waiting somewhere along the path, ready to destroy him.

At the thought of Radamand and death, his newly acquired memories flooded back. He remembered his brother's face as he broke his arm at pool's edge and then held him helplessly under the water until he drowned. I have no brother, thought Jason. But he remembered the brother, and his brother's death. And pushing a knife into his sleeping father's eye. And loving it. And could not bear the memories. Could not bear to be himself, with such a past.

Not my past! he cried out to himself. It is not my past!

But the memories were too strong for him. He could not disregard what he so clearly remembered having done. He wept aloud in the worm as it hurtled through bedrock, skirting the molten furnace of the world. It caused no particular commotion, that he cried. They were used to weepers in the worm.

When Jase got home, Mother was angry. "What have you been doing? The butler went off in the middle of the day and said that you took a trip to the other side of the *world!* How will we live through the month now? Half the food budget, in one day—I should have restricted you, but you always—"

Then she realized his face was raw from crying, and she

looked at him in wonderment. "What's wrong?" she asked.

"You never should have given Homer Worthing a son," said Jase.

Mother looked distractedly toward the butler, which still showed a red alarm light. "It was naughty of you to run away from school. The proctors called. They sealed the doors for a while, till they were sure you weren't in here."

Jason immediately ran to the door and opened it, set a stool in front of it to keep it ajar. "Why did they say they wanted me?"

"Something about your answer to the third question."

The one that he missed.

"He said you knew things that you couldn't have known," said Mother. "You must be more careful, Homer. You must never know things that you couldn't possibly know. It makes people upset."

"I'm not Homer."

She raised her eyebrows. "He was a starpilot, you know."

"We have to leave, Mother."

"I don't like to leave. You go do whatever you must, and I'll wait here. That's what I like to do—wait here while you're gone. And then you'll come back to me. That's what I like. When you come back to me."

"If you don't come with me now, Mother, I'll never come back."

She turned away. "Don't threaten me, Jase. It isn't nice."

"If the proctors don't get me, Mother's Little Boys will! I have a man after me, trying to kill me, and he's very powerful, and he *will* succeed."

"Oh, don't be so serious, you're only a boy, Jase."

"He means to kill you, too."

"People don't go around just—killing people."

Jase exploded. "Everything they say about Swipes is true, Mother! Father killed billions of people, and Radamand Worthing is a killer, too! His own father and brothers and every cousin he could find—that's what Swipes are, is killers, and he knows I was coming here and he knows you know what I am and he means to kill us and he *will!* I'm a Swipe, too, Mother! That's what you did when you had me—brought one more Swipe into the world."

She clamped her hand over his mouth. "The door is open, and other people might not know you're joking."

"The only way to save our lives is—" But she was not listening. She was only waiting. That was all that was in her mind—waiting for Homer to come back. Then everything would be all right. This was all too much for her to handle, and so she had to wait till Homer came back.

"Mother, he won't come here. We have to go to him."

She looked at him wide-eyed. "Don't be silly. He forgot me years ago."

But he knew that she believed him, in her madness. He could control her, because she believed him. "It means a long voyage."

She followed him docilely out the door. "Does that mean somec? Does that mean sleep? I don't like sleeping. They keep changing things while you're asleep."

"This time they promise that they won't."

All the way through the corridor Jase expected to be stopped by a constable, or even one of Mother's Little Boys—Radamand wouldn't hold back anything, he'd use all his power to find Jason and stop him. So it was almost with surprise that Jase found himself at the local Colonies station, and led his mother inside.

The room was cool, with a breeze machine going somewhere. One end of the room was given to a scene near the brink of a cliff, surrounded by trees shedding their leaves in autumn. Far across a canyon was a slope thick with brightly-colored trees. "Earth Colony," whispered the room gently. "Return home again." Then the scene changed to a snowy hill, with skiers madly careening down the slopes. "Makor, the land of eternal winter."

"Where is he?" asked Mother.

"Catch stars on Makor, and bring them home as frozen light." The scene showed some of the fantastic crystals growing in the crevices of a cliff, with a climber making his way up to harvest them.

Jason left her looking at the crystal-hunter, and made his way to the man at the desk. "She's not herself today, but she wants to make a long voyage anyway."

The Colonies were not fussy. No one in his right mind would

travel fifty light years and wake up on a world where there was no hope of return, no hope even of somec, just work through the natural span of life to the end. "We have just the place for her."

"A place where you can walk around in the open," Jason said. None of those pressure suit colonies for his mother.

"We have just the place. Capricorn. It's a yellow sun planet, just like Capitol."

Jase looked behind the man's eyes. That was the assigned planet to push for the week—they needed more platinum and aluminum miners, and women to service them. Not what Jase had in mind. He searched the man's memories until he found a planet that would do. "How about Duncan?" asked Jason.

The man sighed. "Why didn't you tell me you had a tip from inside? Duncan it is." A place so good they hadn't even had to terraform it.

Mother stood at his side. "Where are we going?"

"Duncan," said Jason. "It's a good place."

"You just have to sign these papers." The man began entering information at a keyboard. It was one of the ancient screen-view kinds. You'd think the Colonies could afford something better than *that*.

Name? Occupation? Parents? Address? Birthdate? As he demanded more and more data from her, Mother began to retreat from her illusion. Marital status? "Widow," she said. She turned to Jason. "He's not waiting for me, Jase. He's dead."

Jason looked her in the eyes, trying to think of an answer. This was not a good time for Mother to be sane.

The man smiled cheerfully. "And of course you're taking your son with you."

"Yes," said Mother.

In that moment Jason realized that he never intended to go. Even to save his own life, even though it was likely he would be arrested or killed the moment he left this office, he would not go to a Colony. Would not go off to the end of the populated universe and disappear. The Colonies were the only place his mother might be safe, but he had another alternative. The Fleet. In the Fleet he would be safe enough, might even become a starpilot. Like his father.

"No," said Jase.

"You're the legal guardian, according to this," said the man. "If you say he comes, he comes."

"No," said Jase.

"You're leaving me!" she cried. "I won't have it!"

"It's the only way to save your life," said Jase.

"Did you ever ask me," she said, "if I wanted my life to be saved?"

Jase knew his mother, better than she knew herself. "They put you under somec," he said. "For as long as the voyage takes."

It stirred all the old memories. All the sleepings and wakings. Usually to find Homer there. The last time, though, she awoke alone.

"I don't think so," she said. "I don't think I want to do it."

"I'll be there," he lied.

"No you won't," she said. "You mean to leave me. You plan to leave me, just like your father did."

It was unnerving. How could she know him so well, without the Swipe herself? But no, she didn't *know*, it was only her own fears. The worst thing in the world, to wake up and have him not be there. I am doing the worst thing in the world to her, for the second time.

"Just sign here," said the man. "Your personal code." He pushed a keypad across the desk to them.

"I don't want to do it," said Mother.

Jase calmly entered the numbers for her, taking the code out of her memory. The Colonies man was startled, but when the code checked out correctly on his screen, he shrugged. "Such trust," he said. "Now the lady's palm—"

Mother looked at Jason coldly. "The old lady's going crazy, so dump her off to another world, you miserable bastard, I hate you, just like your father I hate you, you bastard." She looked at the man. "Do you know who his father is?"

The man shrugged. Of course he knew. He had Jase's records up on the screen.

"He's his father's son, not mine."

"It's the only way to save your life, Mother."

"Who are you, God? You decide who's supposed to live and how?"

Like Radamand, thought Jason, again remembering the deaths of brothers he never had. But I do not use my gift to kill. I use it to save. I am not Radamand. I am not Homer Worthing. Yet he knew, from his mother's thoughts, that she loved Jase so much that she would rather die than lose him, than leave him.

"If you stay," he said coldly, "they will interrogate you."

"I'll tell them everything," she said.

"And that is why you have to go."

The Colonies man smiled. "Everything in the Colonies is in strictest confidence. No prosecutions, all crimes absolved— it's a fresh start, whatever it is you did."

Mother turned on him. "And do you erase the memories, too?"

Ah, yes, Mother. That's the question. How can we forget what we remember having done? How will I forget that to save your life I must destroy it?

"Of course not," said the man. "We dump the memories back into your head as soon as you come out of somec."

"Don't you love me?" Mother asked.

The Colonies man looked baffled.

"She's talking to me," said Jase. "I love you, Mother."

"Then why won't you be there when I wake up?"

Desperate, Jason turned to the one strategy he hadn't tried. The truth. "Because I can't spend my life taking care of you."

"Of course not," Mother said. "After all, I only spent *my* life taking care of *you.*"

The Colonies man was getting impatient. "Your palm, lady."

She slapped her palm down brutally on the reader. "I'll go, you little bastard! But you're going with me! Sign him on, he's coming with me!"

"You don't want me with you, Mother," said Jase softly.

"Enter your number, please," said the man. The Colonies were used to getting unwilling people. He didn't care whether Jason went happily or not.

So Jase entered the man's own personal code. Of course it didn't check out. But Jase knew they printed the incorrect code on the screen, and the Colonies man recognized it.

"How did you—" began the man. Then his eyes narrowed. "Get out," he said. "Get out of here."

Jase was only too glad to obey.

"I hate you!" called his mother after him. "You're worse than your father, I'll hate you forever!"

May that hatred keep you alive, thought Jason. May that hatred keep you sane. You can't hate me any worse than I hate myself. I am Radamand. All that he could do, I could do. Haven't I killed my mother here today? Taken her out of the world. To save her life, yes. But then why didn't I go with her? I am Radamand, remaking the world, breaking and bending other lives to fit myself. I ought to die, I hope I die.

He meant it. He wanted to die. But even as he thought it, he scanned the minds of the people near him in the corridor. None was looking for him. He still had a chance to get away. And despite his feelings of despair, he would go on trying to escape until he succeeded, or until he was caught. So much for willing death.

But how could he get anywhere? The moment he palmed a reader he'd tell where he was. To eat, to travel, to talk to Gracie, anything he might do that was worth doing would alert Mother's Little Boys, and they'd find him. Worse, he was legally an orphan now, since his mother had irrevocably signed on with the Colonies. It made him a ward of the state, and he could legally be searched for and found by anyone, without the lengthy legal process of showing cause. Until he could get himself enlisted with the Fleet, he was vulnerable.

He used a booth and talked to Gracie, just long enough to get a directory and find the location of the nearest recruiting station. It was a good long worm ride to get there. Not as far as Radamand had been, but far enough. Did he dare?

His question was answered almost immediately. Leaving the booth, he again scanned the people near him—and one of them was one of Mother's Little Boys, coming to get him at the booth. He ducked into a crowd and left him behind. For once he was glad he was still small—he disappeared and turned a corner, all the while keeping the man's thoughts in his mind. Lost him, thought the man. Lost him.

But they were looking, and it had taken only a few minutes at the booth before one of Mother's Little Boys had reached him. He couldn't ride a worm. Even if he palmed the reader and immediately got aboard, the worm would hardly have finished acceleration before they got to him. So he had to walk. It was two hundred levels above him and four subs away. There was no hope of reaching there before tomorrow. In that time he would have nothing to eat—only water could be had without palming for it. And where would he sleep?

In one of the twenty-meter parks, under a tree. The lawn was artificial, but the tree was real, and the rough bark felt good on his hand; the needles pricked him but he needed the pain. Needed the pain so he could sleep, with his mind newly crowded with memories of what he never did, and what he had just done. His mother was not sane—he knew that better than anyone, having seen directly how she lost touch with reality, how she lived in the constant hope of Homer Worthing coming home. But how was he any less mad himself, with the vision of his dying brothers before his eyes? Why do I remember it this way? Why can't I see it as a story that happened to someone else? Why does my mother's face blend so easily into these memories? He could not separate what he knew he had done from what he knew he had not done. If he could shrug off Radamand's acts, then would he lose the guilt for what he had done to his mother? He was not willing to do that. Painful as it was, what he had done, he had done, and he would not give up his own past, even at the cost of keeping someone else's. Better the madness of keeping Radamand within him than the worse madness of losing Jason.

So he slept with the prickling needles clasped lightly in one hand, the other hand resting on the bark of the tree. *I am what I have done,* he said to himself as he dozed off. But he awoke saying, *I* was *what I did. I* am *what I will do.*

It was a whole day's walk, up the endless stairs, not daring to palm the public elevators, along the corridors, taking a slide-walk when he could. He reached the Fleet recruiting station just before closing.

"I want to join," said Jase.

The recruiter looked at him coldly. "You're little and you're young."

"Thirteen. I'm old enough."

"Parents' consent?"

"Ward of the state." And without giving his name, he punched in his personal code, calling his data into the air above the recruiter's desk.

The recruiter frowned at the name. *Worthing* was a name not soon to be forgotten. "What, planning to follow in your father's footsteps?" he asked.

Jase said nothing. He could see the man wished him no ill.

"Good scores, strong aptitudes. Your father was a great starpilot, before."

So there were other memories of Homer Worthing. Jase probed, and found something that surprised him. The world that Homer destroyed had refused him permission to draw water from their oceans. They had kept him there until the Fleet could catch him. They were not wholly innocent. The Fleet did not hate Homer as the rest of the universe did. Jase had grown so used to being ashamed of who he was that he did not know what to do with this new information, except to hope there would be a place for him in the Fleet. Perhaps, at last, he had a patrimony.

But the recruiter only shook his head. "Sorry. I just applied you, and you've been rejected."

"Why?" asked Jase.

"Not because of your father. Code 9. Something about your aptitudes. I'm not allowed to tell you more."

He told Jase more whether he meant to or not. Jase was being refused entry into the Fleet because of his scores at school. He was too bright to be admitted to the Fleet without consent from the Office of Education. Which he would never get, since Hartman Torrock would have to approve him.

"Jason Worthing," said a man behind him. "I've been looking for you."

Jason ran. The man behind him was one of Mother's Little Boys, and it was arrest he had in mind.

At first the crowds in the corridors helped him. They were moving quickly, and Jase could dodge among them, moving faster than his pursuer, and always out of sight. Gradually the man chasing him was joined by more, until a half dozen were working their way through the crowd. He could not keep track of them all. It was too hard, to look out of their eyes and try to guess, from what they were seeing, where they were.

They caught him when the crowd was slow, for then he was too small and weak to force his way through. His size was no longer an advantage, the Swipe was no help to him, and he found himself sprawled on the ground with a savagely spiked shoe on his hand. Even so he was not afraid of pain: he ripped his hand away and, despite the agony of flayed skin and torn-open veins, he almost scrambled away into the crowd before they caught him, ankle and wrist, and cuffed and shackled him.

"Tough little bastard," said one of Mother's Little Boys.

"Why are you chasing me?"

"Because you ran. We always figure that anybody who runs should probably be caught." But he was lying. They had orders to take Jason Worthing alive, at all costs. Whose orders? Hartman Torrock's? Radamand Worthing's? Not that the answer made much difference. He should have gone to the Colonies with Mother. He had gambled everything on the chance of turning a foul future into something better; he had lost.

But it was neither Radamand nor Tork who came to take him into custody. It was a short, stout, balding man who ordered them to unshackle him, and to cuff them together. The invisible field kept their wrists within a meter of each other.

"I hope you don't mind," said his captor. "I wouldn't want to lose you again, after going to all this trouble. His hand is bleeding. Anyone have a healer?"

Someone passed a healer over Jase's hand, and the blood coagulated and the flow stopped. In the meantime, the short man introduced himself. "I'm Abner Doon, and I'm the closest thing to a friend you're likely to find in this world. I have every intention of exploiting you unmercifully to carry out my own plans, but at least while you're with me you're safe from Cousin Radamand and Hartman Torrock."

How much did this man know? Jase looked within his mind and saw: everything.

"I was asleep until you took that second test," said Doon. "But when you got half right a question whose answer wasn't known to but a handful of physicists, who weren't too sure themselves—well, the Sleephouse people wakened me. They have their instructions. I wouldn't have missed you for the world."

They went to an official highway, which Doon entered merely by palming the door, the way anyone else might board a worm. A private car was waiting. Jase was impressed, and willingly got inside.

"Who are you?" he asked.

"A question I've been trying to answer since adolescence. I finally decided I was neither God nor Satan. I was so disappointed I didn't try to narrow it down any further."

Jase probed his mind. The man was an assistant minister of colonization. He also believed he ruled the world. And, upon further examination, Jason realized it was true. Even Radamand, for all his machinations, would have been awed at what Abner Doon controlled. Even Mother—not Jase's mother, but Mother, the ruler of Capitol—even she was his pawn. It was not the world he ruled. He could twitch, and half the universe would tremble. And yet he was almost utterly unknown. Jase looked him in the eyes and laughed.

Doon smiled back. "It's flattering that I've had as much power as I have, for as long as I've had it, and yet a good-hearted boy can look into my heart and still laugh."

It was true. There were no murders in Doon's memory. Dwelling in his mind was not the agony that being Radamand had been. Doon did not live to shape the world to his convenience. He was shaping the world, but what he had in mind was not at all convenient.

"I've always wondered what it would be like to have a friend from whom I could keep no secrets," said Doon. "Have you noticed yet your stupid blunder at the Colonies office? You proved you were a Swipe to the counterman. Now I have to put him under somec and wake him up with an old bubble, so he doesn't remember it. It's very unkind of you to clutter up other people's lives that way."

"I'm sorry," said Jase. But he also knew that this was Doon's way of telling him that his mistakes were being covered for. He felt better.

"Oh, by the way, speaking of somec, your mother wrote you a note before she went under."

Jase saw in Doon's mind the memory of his mother handing over a paper, her face stained with tears, yet her lips smiling as Jase had not often seen her smile. He clutched at the paper, read it despite the trembling of his own hands.

"Abner Doon explained everything to me. About Radamand, and the school. I love you and forgive you and I think I won't be crazy anymore."

It was her handwriting. Jase shuddered in relief.

"I thought you'd want to know that."

Jase read the note again, and then they arrived. They went directly from the car into a short hall, and from the hall into a forest.

This was no park. The grass underfoot was real, the squirrels gamboling on the trunks of the trees were not mechanicals, even the smell was perfect, with not a hint of plastic in the air. The door closed behind them. Doon turned off the cuffs. Jason stepped away from him, looked up into a sky for the first time in his life. No ceiling. No roof at all. He was afraid he might fall. How could people stand to live without a roof overhead?

"Dazzling, isn't it?" asked Doon. "Of course, there *is* a ceiling—all of Capitol has a ceiling—but the illusion is well done, isn't it?"

Jase looked away from the sky and back to Doon.

"Why did you save me? What am I to you?"

"I thought Swipes didn't have to ask questions," answered Doon. To Jase's surprise, he was undressing, shedding clothing as he led the way deeper into the woods. They came to the largest open body of water Jase had ever seen in his life, nearly fifty meters across. "Swim?" asked Doon. He was naked now, and he was *not* stout. The bulk had come from protective clothing. Doon poked the armor gently with his foot. "There are those who want me dead."

Of course there were. Doon did not have Radamand's advantage of knowing other men's desires and secrets, to bribe and blackmail perfectly.

"My cousin Radamand will be one of them, as long as you keep me alive."

Doon laughed. "Oh, Radamand. He's due for his next sleep in the next few weeks. He's a loathsome sort of man, and he's not that much use to me anymore. I doubt he'll ever wake up."

Jase was horrified to realize that it was true. Abner Doon could cause the Sleephouse to kill a man. The one unshakeable verity of life in Capitol was this: the Sleephouse could not be corrupted. And yet Abner Doon's influence reached even there.

"Swim?" asked Doon again, walking into the water.

"I don't know how."

"Of course not. I'll teach you."

Jase undressed and followed the man uncertainly into the water. He could see that Doon meant nothing but good toward him. Doon was a man that he could trust. So he followed Doon out until the water was almost to their necks. Doon and he were nearly the same height.

"Water is actually a very safe medium of locomotion," Doon said. Jase only noticed that it was cold. "Now here, my hand is against your back. Lean back against my hand. Now let your legs just come loose from the ground, just relax. I can hold you up."

Suddenly Jase felt very light, and as he relaxed he felt his body bobbing lightly on the surface, only the gentle pressure of Doon's hand under him to remind him of gravity.

Then the world turned upside down, Abner Doon had a back-breaking hold on him, and Jase's face suddenly plunged under the water. He gulped, swallowed; his eyes stung; he desperately needed a breath, and dared not take it. He struggled to come up, but couldn't break the hold. He struggled, he twisted, he tried to strike with his hands and feet, but he did not come to the surface until Doon pulled him up. And in all that time, Doon had meant nothing but good for him. Doon had intended no harm. If this is love, thought Jase, God help me—or is it that Doon is somehow able to lie to me, even in his own mind?

"Don't cough," said Doon. "It splashes water everywhere."

"What was that for?" demanded Jase.

"It was an object lesson. To show you what it feels like to be in something over your head."

"I already knew how it felt."

"Now you know even better." And Doon calmly proceeded with the swimming lesson.

Jase caught on quickly, at least to something as simple as a backfloat. The pseudo-sun was setting, and the sky turned gently pink. Jase lay on his back in the water, stroking the surface just enough to keep moving, just enough to stay afloat. "I've never seen a sunset before."

"Believe me, that isn't how sunsets look on Capitol. The sky of this planet is greasy and dank. Sunset topside is downright purple. Orange is noon. Blue sky is impossible."

"What does this place imitate, then?"

"My home world," said Doon. Jase caught his memories, and they were of the planet Garden. Indeed, this room was only an imitation of a tiny corner of the place. Jason could see Doon's longing for the rolling hills, the thick groves of trees, the open meadows.

"Why did you ever leave it?" asked Jase. "Why did you come *here?*"

Power is the only gift I have, thought Doon. Jason followed his thoughts. How to get power, how to use it, how to destroy it. A human being can only go where his gifts are useful. Capitol is the place where I must be. However much I hate it. However much I long to destroy it. Capitol is my dwelling place, at least for now.

Then, suddenly, Doon's thoughts changed. Jase heard him in the distance, getting out of the water. Jase tried to swim toward shore, but he was awkward and slow, and when he tried to stand the lake was too deep, and he only just recovered himself enough to return to the backstroke. Swimming—staying afloat, in fact—took so much of Jase's concentration, especially now that he was afraid, that he could spare little of his attention to probe in Doon's mind. That was why he taught me. That was why he brought me here. To distract me so I wouldn't know what he had in mind. So I couldn't predict his every move. He fooled me, and now what does he have in mind, what trap has he set for me?

When at last he reached the shore, Doon was disappearing through a door in the garden wall. Jase looked desperately into his thoughts, searching for danger, and found waiting for him Doon's knowledge of the Estorian twick. A small marsupial with teeth like razors. He saw Doon's memory of the little animal leaping at lightning speed onto the udder of a cow before the beast so much as noticed it was there. The twick hung there for a moment by its claws, then disappeared, boring upward and inward into the cow's body, blood gouting from the wound. The cow only then reacted, it had happened so quickly. It shuddered, ran a few steps, then dropped to the ground and died. The twick crawled slowly from the cow's mouth, panting and sluggish and bloated. Jase had read about twicks, too, and knew something of their habits. Knew, too, that twicks had wiped out the first colony on Estoria and even now they were only restrained with ultrasonic fences that kept them confined to reservations.

Why was Doon thinking of Estorian twicks? Because he was releasing one into the park right now. The only prey the twick would want was Jase, and Jase was naked and unarmed beside the lake. Yet still in Doon's mind, Jase could find nothing but good will. That frightened him more than anything else—that Doon meant well for him, and yet had no idea how Jase would survive the attack of the little beast.

Already the twick was perched on a branch not twenty meters off. Jase stood absolutely still, remembering that twicks rely mostly on smell and sound and motion to identify prey. He tried, desperately, to think of a weapon. He pictured himself picking up one of the stones from the lake's shore, and as he tried to bring it down on the twick, the little animal would leap up and eat his hand in midstroke.

The twick moved. So quickly that Jase hardly saw the motion, except that now the twick was in the grass, and only ten meters off.

Jase's hand throbbed where it had been torn under his captor's boot. The smell of blood is on me, he realized. The twick will come for me whether I move or not.

The twick moved again. It was two meters off. Jase tried desperately to see into the animal's mind. It was not hard to get the fuzzy view the beast had of the world, but it was impossible to make sense of the welter of urges. He would not know what the twick meant to do until it happened. Jase could not use the Swipe, and had no other weapon.

Suddenly Jase felt an excruciating pain in his right calf. He reached down to pry the animal off. For a moment the twick clung, still boring into his leg; then it wriggled out and immediately was burrowing into the muscle of Jase's upper arm. The leg gushed blood. Jase screamed and struck at the animal with his left hand. Every blow landed, but it did no good.

I'm going to die, Jase shouted in his mind.

But his survival instinct was still strong, despite the terrible pain and worse fear. Like a reflex he realized that the twick would simply jump from target to target on Jase's body. It was only a matter of time until it hit a vital artery, or until it found the boneless cavity of his abdomen and devoured his bowels.

But with each gram of flesh it ate, the twick would grow more sluggish. If Jase could only manage to stay alive, the twick would gradually lose its frenzied speed. But Jase, too, was growing weaker as the blood flowed out of him through two great wounds. And he had no weapon, even if the twick were slow.

He threw himself to the ground, trying hopelessly to crush the animal under the weight of his body. Of course the twick was uninjured—its skeleton was flexible, and it sprang back to shape as soon as Jase rolled off.

But it had stopped eating for a moment, was not attached to Jase's body, and it would be slower now. Jase scrambled to his feet and began to run.

With a wound in his leg, he was slower, too, and before he got three steps away, the twick struck. But Jase's back was to it now, and the animal only dug into the muscles under the shoulder blade.

Jase threw himself to the ground, backward. This time the twick made a sharp sound and scurried a little further away. Jase tried to run again, skirting the edge of the lake. This time he managed a dozen staggering steps before the twick clutched at his buttocks and began tearing at him again. Jase broke stride, fell to one knee. The lake was only a meter away. I can't swim with all these wounds, thought Jase. Oh well, the coldly intellectual part of his mind answered. Maybe the twick can't, either.

He crawled toward the water, dragging his left leg, for the twick had severed the great muscles of the thigh, and the leg would not respond to him, except with agony. Jase reached the water just as the animal struck bone.

It was impossible for Jase to float. He just crouched under the water, holding his breath forever, trying to ignore the agony pulsing from his buttocks, from his leg, from his arm, from his back. He could feel the twick burrowing along the edge of his pelvic bone. His analytic mind noted the fact that this was taking the animal away from the vulnerable anal areas. Muscles can heal. I can live. Muscles can heal. The repetition kept him underwater despite the pain, despite his lungs bursting for air.

The twick slowed. It emerged from Jase's body at the hip. Immediately Jase grabbed it, fumbled for its neck. The twick was slow, and Jase had it by the throat, crushingly. Now Jase let himself rise from the water enough to take a breath, still holding the twick under. The air came like fire into his lungs, and he almost immediately fell forward into the water again. But he did not let go of the slowly wriggling twick. His hands, if anything, held it tighter. He struggled with his elbows and one good leg to drag himself toward shore again. The water became shallow enough that he could keep his head above the surface without trying to stand. The twick vomited and the water went black-red with Jase's undigested blood and flesh. Then, at last, the twick stopped moving.

Jase found the strength to fling the limp animal out toward the middle of the lake. Then he fell forward, onto the shore, his face slapping into the mud, his bleeding leg and buttocks and hip still under the water. Help, he thought. I'll die, he thought. After a moment he gave up trying to turn his thoughts into words. He only lay there, feeling the blood rush out of him, filling up the lake, touching every shore of the lake, until it was all red, all part of him, and there was nothing left in his body at all, nothing inside him now at all.

4

The Devil Himself

There were tasks as winter came on that books must wait for, even though Lared's bookwork was bringing money to the family. The coming of snow was not taken lightly, and all hands were needed to be sure of food and fuel enough for the season. Especially now, when they knew there was no protection; since the coming of pain, any dark thing was possible. So each day when Lared awoke he did not know whether today would be spent twitching his fingers to move a pen or bending his whole body to some heavy task. There were days when he hoped for one, and days when he hoped for the other; but regardless of what he hoped for, he worked hard at whatever the day required. Even when the story that he wrote was painful; even when the tale was held in memories of dreams that had been near unbearable when they came.

The first snowfall began late on the afternoon of the day Lared wrote the story of Jase and the battle with the twick. The snow had threatened all day; the sky was so dark that Jason had lit a candle at noon to light the page for Lared's work. But now that part of the tale was told, and Lared was already putting away the pen and ink when the sound of the tinker's cart could be heard above the ringing of Father's hammer in the forge. It was the old saying—the coming of the tinker is the coming of the snow. Actually, as everyone knew, Whitey the tinker came several times a year, but always arranged it so he'd reach Flat Harbor before the first hard snow.

Jason looked up from blotting the new ink on the parchment with a linen cloth, for Sala was stuttering up the stairs—both feet hitting each step, she was so short. "The tinker's come," she shouted, "the tinker's come! And there's snow on the ground today!"

It was worth a little rejoicing, that something in the world still worked as it should. Lared closed his pen box. Jason set aside the parchment. So small and fine was Lared's writing, so economical of words, that the first sheepskin was not yet full.

"It was good work for today," said Jason. "We've finished the first part. The worst part, for me, I think."

"I have to make up the tinker's bed," said Lared. "He stays the winter. He's a good bellows mender, and he can make a goatskin bag tight as a bladder."

"So can I," said Jason.

"You have a book to write."

Jason shrugged. "Looks to me like *you're* writing it."

Lared took two tick covers from the shelves in the attic, and together they ran through the innyard without bothering to put on jackets against the cold. The flakes were already falling, the little ones that had come twice before and didn't stick to the ground, but were sticking now, on the grasses and leaves at least. They made their way into the haybarn, which was musty and crowded with the year's straw. Lared went unerringly to the bed straw, which was cleanest, and they began stuffing the ticks.

"The tinker gets two beds, and I get only one?" said Jason.

"The tinker comes every year, and does his work for free, and pays nothing. That makes him kin." *You'll never be kin, because Mother doesn't like you,* Lared said silently. Knowing, of course, that he could be heard.

Jason sighed. "It's going to be a very hard winter."

Lared shrugged. "Some say it is, some say it isn't."

"It is."

"The worms in the trees are furry, and the greybirds flew on by us this year, going farther south. But who knows?"

"Justice and I checked the weather on the way in, and the winter's going to be very hard."

No one knew weather that far in advance, but Lared was long past surprise. "I'll tell Father, then. It's firewood time. I'll have to cut firewood, you know. And we always start at first snow. The trees drop their sap by then."

"You need a rest from writing."

"The more I do, the easier it gets. Words come to mind easier."

Jason looked at him oddly. "But what do you think it all means?"

Lared didn't know how to answer without sounding foolish. He folded over the top of his tick. "Don't overstuff, it goes lumpy."

Jason folded the top of his, too. "If you put shadowfern in it, the fleas go away."

Lared made a face. "And where will we find shadowfern in the snow?"

"I guess it's a little late."

Now Lared had the courage to ask. "Doon is the devil, isn't he?"

"Was. He's dead now. At least, he promised me that he'd die."

"But was he?"

"The devil?" Jason heaved the tick over his shoulder like a collier with his sack. "Satan. The adversary. The enemy of the plan of God. The undoer. The destroyer. Yes. He definitely was." Jason smiled. "But he meant well."

Lared led the way back across the yard to the house and up to the tinker's room. "Why did he put you with the twick? Did he want you dead?"

"No. He wanted me to live."

"Then why?"

"To see what I was worth."

"Not much, if you had lost."

"Not much for a year afterward—it took a long time to heal, and I still get twinges at my hip. Don't ask me to run long distances, for instance. And I sit a little slanted."

"I know." Lared had noticed that the second night, that Jason always leaned a little to the left in a chair. "I know something else, too."

"Hmm?" Jason cast his tick out along the bed first, and together they worked at smoothing it.

"I know how you felt, with Cousin Radamand's memories in you."

"Oh, you do?" Jason was not pleased. "That's why I insisted Justice give the story to you as dreams, instead of waking—"

"They're always too clear for dreams. They feel like memories to me. I wake up some mornings and see these split-log walls and I think—how very rich we are, to have real wood. And then I think, how very poor we are, to have a dirt floor.

I reach out sometimes when I come to the door of Father's forge, to palm the reader."

Jason laughed at that, and Lared laughed, too.

"Most of all, I think, Sala and Mother and Father surprise me, just for being there. It's as if your memories are realer to me than my own. I like to pretend that I can see into their minds, the way I do in your memories. I look at their eyes, and sometimes I even think I know what they're about to do." Lared cast his tick over Jason's. "They never do it, though."

"I wish I had been like you," Jason said.

"I wish I had been like you," Lared answered.

"What Doon did, with the twick—I don't think he meant it this way, but it sorted out my memories. Coming so near to death, having so much pain, it does things to the way you remember the rest of your life. Nothing else seemed quite so real to me anymore. I still was not clean, mind you—I still felt guilty at what I had done to my own mother, at what I remembered having done in Radamand's past. But it didn't matter so much. I counted the days of my life from that moment. Before Doon, and After Doon. He had plans for me. He cleared my record of the blot that Torrock had put on it, he had Radamand's crimes made public—all but the Swipe—and my dear cousin was put on an asteroid somewhere. And then he made me a starpilot. Like my father."

"Justice hasn't given me any memory of that."

"She never will. We're trying not to clutter up your brain with things that don't matter. I became a starpilot the way everyone else does. I was just better at it than most. The hardest thing, though, was to make sure I always won my battles in ways that could be counted as clever thinking—not the Swipe. There I'd sit, knowing exactly what the enemy intended to do, and helpless to save as many lives as I might have, if I had been free. Always I had to wait a moment too long, see the enemy do a little too much, and people died to save my life. That's a problem for you, Lared. If I can save a hundred lives by making it obvious I have the Swipe, which would lead to my death, is that better than to save only fifty lives in order to hide the Swipe, so I can live to save another fifty, and another fifty, and another fifty?"

"That depends on whether I'm one of the fifty that gets

saved either way, or one of the fifty that dies to save you."

Jason frowned. Together they cast the linen sheet over the ticks and tucked it in under them. "The tinker gets linen, and I have to sleep on wool."

"Wool's warmer."

"Linen doesn't itch."

"You didn't like my answer."

"I hated your answer. It doesn't depend on whether you'll live or die. It depends on what's *right*. And what's right and wrong doesn't come down to your personal preference. It never does. If it comes to what you personally prefer, then there's no right or wrong at all."

Lared was ashamed and angry. Angry because he didn't think it was right that Jason should make him feel ashamed. "What's wrong with wanting to live?"

"Any dog can do that. Are you a dog? You're not a human being until you value something more than the life of your body. And the greater the thing you live and die for, the greater you are."

"What did you live for, when the twick was eating you?"

Jason looked angry, but then he smiled. "The life of my body, of course. We're animals first, aren't we? I thought I would live to do something very important."

"Like make a bed for a wandering tinker?"

"That was exactly what I had in mind."

"You speak our language better than I do, now."

"I've spoken a dozen languages. Yours is just an evolved version of one I spoke very early in my life. My native language, in fact. All the patterns are there, and the words are changed in predictable patterns. This planet was settled from Capitol. By Abner Doon."

"When a child is very bad, they say, 'Abner Doon will come in the night and steal all your sleep.'"

"Abner Doon, the monster."

"Wasn't he?"

"He was my friend. He was a true friend of all mankind."

"I thought you said he was the devil."

"That, too. What would you call the man who gave you the Day of Pain?"

Lared remembered, as he did more and more rarely these

days, the sound of Clany's screams, the blood pulsing from the leg of the man they carried upstairs, the death of the old cleric—

"You couldn't forgive him, could you?" asked Jason.

"Never."

Jason nodded. "And why not?"

"We were so happy before. Things were so good before."

"Ah. But before Abner Doon undid the empire, unslept the sleepers, things were not good. Life was empty or miserable for almost every living soul."

"Then why didn't they thank him?"

"Because people always believe things were better—before."

Lared realized then that he had made a mistake. He had thought, from all his dreams, that Doon was Jason's enemy. Now he knew that Jason loved the man. It frightened Lared, that Jason Worthing loved the devil. *What is this work I'm doing? I should stop at once.*

Of course Jason and Justice heard this thought. But they answered not at all. Not even to tell him he was free. Their silence was the only answer that he got. *Maybe I will quit,* he decided. *Maybe I'll tell them to go to some other village and find some other uneducated, ignorant scribe.*

As soon as I find out what happened next, I'll quit.

Lared was the forester for Flat Harbor, and so he had to spend a week in the forest, girdling trees. Jason was coming along. Lared was not glad. Ever since he was nine years old, he had girdled the trees for the winter's lumbering. It meant days on end, wandering the woods that he knew better than any other in the village, seeing the old places made new and naked by winter, discovering where the animals were hidden, and above all spending nights alone in the wattle and daub huts he made himself each afternoon. No sound of anything but his own breathing, and then waking some mornings to see his breath like steam in the air, and other mornings to a thick fog in the woods, and other mornings to trackless snow hiding the ground from him, unmaking all the oldpaths, forcing him to make something new in the world just by walking forth from his night's hut.

But this year he would have Jason with him, because Father insisted.

"We've never had winter before, not like this," said Father. "In past years we've been—protected. This year we're like the animals—the cold can kill us, we can get lost, we can go hungry, a tool can bite us and who will be there to stanch the blood? You go nowhere alone. Jason is needed for nothing else, he can go, and so he *will* go." Father glared at Jason, daring him to argue. Jason only smiled.

It was not a job that needed two men. Lared had been watching the trees all summer, and knew which ones should be harvested this year. Such trees were almost never close enough together that Lared could point out one for Jason to girdle while he did another himself. And if they worked the same tree, Jason was always getting in Lared's way. By noon on the first day Lared made it plain that he did not want Jason there, and so Jason discreetly kept his distance. There was little snow on the ground, and that only in patches. Jason took to gathering mosses from trees and stones, sorting them into pouches in the woollen bag he had sewn for himself while Lared wrote. Not a word passed between them all afternoon. Yet Lared was always aware of Jason. He girdled the trees quickly, deftly, moving faster than he usually did. He knelt before the tree, and his chisel bit into the bark. He tapped it with the mallet and drove it all around the tree, then clawed the bark downward with the iron tool he had drawn for Father. Before Lared they had girdled twice, in two parallel lines around the tree. But that took twice as long as necessary—once there was a single cut, the bark could be clawed off far enough to be sure the tree was dead before harvest in the deep snow. Then, next year, new shoots would come from the stump. It was part of Lared's work each year to trim off the shoots, so they could be dried to shape and then worked into stems and handles and frames on reed and wicker baskets. Nothing was wasted, and Lared was proud of how smoothly he worked, how quickly the job was done.

He worked with such concentration that the sun was already setting when he realized that he had not yet made the hut for the night's sleep. He had never done so many trees on the first day before. He had never had Jason Worthing watching him, either. Now he was well past the remnants of old first-day huts. He didn't want to go back for them. Nor would it be practical to go on to second-day huts—they were too far ahead, and he always scaled the rock cliff of Brindy Stream on the second day, in broad daylight—that wasn't a work for evening. So he would need Jason's help to make a new hut quickly, with no old wattles to start from.

No sooner had he thought this than Jason was beside him, silent and expressionless, waiting for instructions. Lared chose a good house tree, with a long low branch for the central beam, and near enough to a willow that it would not be inconvenient. Jason nodded and began using his own knife to cut the willow withes where they hung from the tree. Lared saw that Jason knew what he was doing, and could reach higher and cut longer sticks than ever Lared could. So after Lared had gathered the deadwood sticks for the wattle frames, he set to work making the daub at the edge of a stream. It was cold work, digging with a hand-spade in the muddy bank, and splashing water onto the soil with his wooden bowl. But he did it quickly, and by the time Jason had the withes woven together into large strong wattles, the mud was ready for daubing.

Jason brought over the wattles one at a time. He quickly learned Lared's way of daubing—taking a handful of large fallen leaves and scooping up the mud with it. They slapped the mudcovered leaves onto the wattle and left them there—the leaves made the wall thicker and warmer and more water-tight than mud alone. Together they carried each finished wattle to the tree and leaned it against the beam. Because Jason had been able to cut such long twigs, the wattles spread out much wider than any hut Lared had ever made before—room for two men inside.

They cut saplings to strengthen the door, and hung on it the sheepskin Lared carried for that purpose. It was fully dark before they had a fire going out in front of the hut. They heated water and simmered the sausage so it would go warm into their bellies for the night's sleep. Lared went and washed the little pot, and when he came back Jason was already asleep on one side of the tent, leaving Lared with half the space to lay out his blanket and sleep. It was a fine hut, and Lared discovered that he didn't mind the sound of Jason's breathing beside him after all. They had not exchanged a word all day. The silence of the forest was complete, except for the noises of owls on the hunt, and a bearkin passing by.

As always on the first night of tree-girdling, Lared drifted off to sleep thinking, Why should I ever go back to Flat Harbor? Why don't I spend forever here?

That night he dreamed. And in his dream he was not Jason Worthing—the first time that he had not been given Jason's own life as a memory.

He was Abner Doon.

He sat before a table, and in the air before him was a world. Or rather, a map of a world, with nations marked out in different colors. He pressed keys, and different colors came onto the globe, and the world turned and showed him other faces, and as Doon studied it he understood that a thing of beauty was being wrought there. It was a game, of course, only a game, but among the players was one of true genius. Herman Nuber, said the computer registration of players. Herman Nuber, who at the moment was under somec, he was the player who had taken the Italy of 1914 and played it into a position of world domination, with an empire of allies, client states, and outright possessions that was larger than anything Earth had seen till that point in history.

Nuber's Italy was a dictatorship, but one that was studiedly benign. In every client state and conquered territory, rebellion was ruthlessly suppressed—but loyalty was lavishly rewarded, taxes were not high, local customs and freedoms were respected, and life for the computer-simulated populace was good. Rebellions profited nothing, and lost all, and so the government was stable, so stable that even inferior players, making stupid blunders while Nuber was on somec, even they could do little damage to Nuber's Italy.

Indeed, that was what had first drawn Abner to the game. He did not pay much attention to International Games, any more than he wasted time watching the endless lifeloops, with their tediously complete reproduction of the lives and loves of dull and oversexed people, in three dimensions and full color. He was busy building his own network of power, turning his office as assistant minister of colonization into the center of the world. But so many people were talking about Nuber's

Italy. Nuber will be waking soon. Nuber will conquer the world this time. The bets were running high, but all the odds were on the actual date of the end of the game, not on whether Nuber could bring it off. Of course he could. Of all the players in the history of International Games, no one had ever started from so weak a position and built it into such a strong one in so short a time. Perfection, it was called. The ultimate empire.

Naturally, Abner had to see.

He studied it carefully for many hours, and all they had said was true. It was the sort of government that could stand forever. A new Roman Empire that made the old one look transient and paltry.

Such a challenge, thought Abner.

And in his dream, Lared understood the thing of beauty Herman Nuber had conceived and brought to be, and he cried out in his sleep against the act that Abner planned. But the dream continued, for it was not in his control.

Abner Doon bought Italy. Bought the right to play that nation. It was expensive, because there had been some illegal speculation in the players' market and the price had inflated, in order to force Nuber to pay bonuses in order to buy it. But Abner had no intention of forcing Nuber to pay anything. Abner never meant to sell Italy. Instead, he would use it as a test of what he planned to do in real life: he would see how well he could bring off the utter destruction of the order of the world.

He played carefully, and in his dream Lared believed he understood all that Abner did. He engaged in pointless wars and made sure they were badly generaled and stupidly fought— but not so stupidly that there were any crushing defeats. Just attrition, a slow wearing away of the army, of the wealth of the empire.

And within the empire he also began a quiet corrosion. Mismanagement and stupid decisions on industrial production; changes in the civil service to promote corruption; unfair, almost whimsical taxation. And the conquered nations were singled out for harassment. Religious persecution; insistence on the use of the Italian language, discrimination against certain groups in jobs, in education; severe restrictions on what could and could not be printed; barriers to travel; confiscation of peasant land and the encouragement of a new aristocracy. In short, he did everything he could to make Nuber's Italy function much the way the Empire did. Only Abner timed and controlled things, watched carefully to be sure that the resentment built gradually, held off rebellions, kept them small and weak, biding his time. *I do not want a few geysers*, Abner told himself. *I want a volcano that will consume the world.*

The only thing Nuber's Italy had that Capitol lacked was Catholicism, a binding force, a common faith that bound at least the ruling classes together, ensured they looked out upon the world with a shared vision. The integrity of the Church, that was the one thing they trusted in the corrupt empire that Abner was giving them.

Like somec. Like the Sleephouse. The common hope and faith of all the ruling class of Capitol and the Thousand Worlds. To sleep, and thus live longer than the poor fools who could not qualify. The integrity, the incorruptibility of the keepers of the Sleephouse was the faith of all. *If through my accomplishment I truly merit somec, I will have it.* It can't be bought, it can't be demanded, it can't be cajoled, it can't be had by fraud. Only by recognized achievement. It was the only thing that preserved the Empire of the Thousand Worlds, despite the rot that holed and softened it everywhere else. The faith in the final judgment of the Sleephouse, which measured men and women and gave them immortality, if they were worthy.

I will bring you down, thought Abner Doon, and Lared shuddered in his sleep.

It was only a matter of time, then, until Nuber's Italy became ripe. In the meantime, Herman Nuber awoke from his three-year sleep—a noble allotment of somec indeed, to sleep three years for each one year waking—a man could live four hundred years that way. But that was the esteem Nuber had won for himself, with such a creation as Italy.

Of course Nuber tried to buy Italy, so he could play. But Abner wouldn't sell. Nuber's agents were persistent, their offers princely, but Abner had no intention of letting Nuber save Italy. Nuber even tried to strong-arm him, sending hired thugs to frighten him. Abner had too much power in Capitol already, though. The thugs already worked for him, and Abner sent them back to Nuber with instructions to do to him what he had hired them to do to Abner. It seemed only just.

Except it was not just. Nuber could see what Abner was doing to his empire. He was no fool. He had spent seven years of his waking life—twenty-eight years of game time—building Italy into a phenomenon that would stand in the annals of International Games forever. And Abner was destroying it. Not clumsily, but deftly, with exquisite timing and perfect thoroughness. It was not enough to provoke rebellion and reorganization. Abner was provoking revolution and conquest that would erase Italy from the map, utterly destroy it so there was no hope that it would ever rise again. When Abner was through, he meant there to be nothing left for Nuber to buy and rebuild.

At last he judged the time was ripe. Abner did a simple thing, but it was enough: he exposed the secret corruption he had brought into the heart of the Church. The outrage, the loathing it caused tore away the last pretense at legitimacy, even decency, that Nuber's Italy possessed. The computer hardly knew how to cope with this, except with instant, overwhelming revolt. All the grievances in every nation were joined now with the anger of the aristocracy—all classes acted at once, and Italy was undone, the empire fragmented, the armies in mutiny.

It took three days, and it was over. There was no Italy left in the game.

Even Abner was stunned at how well it worked. Of course International Games used simplified patterns, but it was as close to reality as any game could be.

I will do it again, thought Abner. And the pattern unfolded in his mind. The seeds of universal revolution were already there, for the Empire was corrupt to the core, with only the hope of somec holding all in check. Abner's work, then, was to postpone revolution until he was ready, until it would all come at once, until revolution would not merely change the government, but undo everything, even cut the threads that bound world to world. Travel between the stars must end along with everything else, or his destroying would be in vain.

But here fate had been kind to Abner's plans—indeed, he suspected, things might have gone the way I wish them to without my intervention. That was the problem with manipulating reality: there was no way to find out what *would* have been. Perhaps I make no difference in the world. But then, perhaps I do. And so Abner began the slow process of corrupting the Sleephouse. Allowing quiet murders and manipulations through somec. Allowing sleep levels to be bought with money or power, allowing bubbles of memory to be tampered with or lost, allowing petty princes of crime or capitalism to think they could use the Sleephouse as they saw fit. When at last it all came out, the way somec had been misused, all the resentment would come at once, all hatreds would explode, with even the somec users themselves revolting against the Sleephouse, so that somec itself would be eliminated, even for the passage between the stars, even for the one legitimate use it had.

I can do it, Abner said, triumphantly.

But he was a man of conscience, in his way. He went to visit Herman Nuber, when it all was done. The man was stricken, to see his life's work undone for no purpose that he could understand.

"What have I ever done to you?" asked Nuber. He was a very old man, it seemed, or at least very tired.

"Nothing," said Abner.

"Did you win much, betting on the fall of Italy?"

"I had no wagers placed." The sums involved would have been petty, compared to what Abner already controlled.

"Why should you wish to hurt me, then, when it profited you nothing?"

"I did not want to hurt you," Abner said.

"What else, man, did you think it would do?"

"I knew it would hurt you, Herman Nuber, but that was a result I neither desired nor undesired."

"What did you want, then?"

"The end of perfection," said Abner.

"Why? What is it about my Italy that made you hate it? What low, small thing in your heart requires you to undo greatness?"

"I don't expect you to understand," said Abner. "But if you had taken this last turn, the game would have ended. The world of your game would have gone into stasis. It would have died. I was not against the beautiful thing you made. I was merely against it lasting forever."

"You love death, then?"

"The opposite. I love only life. But life can only continue in the face of death."

"You are a monster."

And Abner silently agreed. I am the monster of the deep. I am Poseidon, who shakes the earth. I am the worm at the heart of the world.

Lared awoke weeping. Jason touched his shoulder. "Was it as bad a dream as that?" he whispered.

Only gradually did Lared realize he was no longer in the plastic world of Capitol, but under the leaning wattles of a forest hut, with Jason leaning over him in the dim light coming from the edges of the sheepskin door. It was very warm inside the hut, which told Lared at once that it had snowed in the night, making a thick layer on their walls to keep in their bodies' warmth. Indeed, the wattles sagged deeply, and unless they unbuilt them soon they would break and not be usable for next year's huts. The urgency of the work took the dream from Lared's mind, or at least pushed it back enough that he could stop his grieving.

It was late in the morning when Lared brought up the dream with Jason. Lared wanted the man beside him now, in the snow—it was cold hard work, and with Jason using the claw Lared could cut the girdle and go on to the next tree, leaving Jason to follow his tracks in the snow. Only when they reached the cliff were they together long enough to talk.

"We have to climb this?" Jason asked, looking at the snow-covered ledges.

"Or fly," said Lared. "There's a quick way, but it's too dangerous in the snow. We'll take the slanting crevice there."

"I'm getting old," Jason said. "I'm not sure I can climb it."

"You can," said Lared. "Because there's no other choice. You don't know the way back home, and I'm going up."

"It's sweet of you to be so careful with me," Jason said. "If I fall, will you climb back down to help me, or leave me as an offering to the wolves?"

"Climb back down, of course. What do you think I am?" And then his rage burst out. "If you ever send me a dream like that again, I'll kill you."

Jason looked surprised. How could he look surprised, when of course he knew all that Lared felt?

"I thought you'd understand Abner, if you saw that dream," Jason said.

"Understand him? He *is* the devil! He's the one who brought the Day of Pain! He found the world at peace, and beautiful, and he destroyed it!"

"He's dead, Lared. He had nothing to do with the Day of Pain."

"If he *had* been here, he would have done it."

"Yes."

"And he would have come here to gloat, to see how much we suffered at his hands, the way he came to Nuber!"

"Yes."

And then another realization more terrible than the first. "He would have come to see us, the way that you and Justice came."

Jason said nothing.

Lared got up and ran to the cliff and began to climb. Not the safe way, up the crevice, but the dangerous way, the quick way that he used when the rocks were dry and his feet were bare.

"No, Lared," Jason said. "Not that way."

Lared did not answer, just moved even faster, though his fingers had to fight for purchase and his feet kept slipping. Higher up the cliff, it would matter more, but Lared didn't care.

"Lared, I can find the safe way in your mind, you won't harm me by going this way, you'll hurt only yourself."

Lared stopped, clinging to the rock. "That's the only person that a good man would ever willingly hurt!"

So Jason began to climb up after him. And not the safe way, either. Step for step, he followed Lared up the most dangerous part of the cliff.

But Lared would not quit. He couldn't, now—going back down this way would be far more dangerous than going on. So he climbed, more slowly now, more carefully, brushing the snow from each handhold, each foothold if he could, trying to make the way clear to Jason, safe for him as he came up afterward. At last Lared lay at the top of the cliff, reaching down to help Jason up the last difficult clamber. They knelt beside each other on the brink, looking down over the forest below them. In the distance they could see the fields and cook-fire smoke of Flat Harbor. Behind them the forest loomed as deep, as black and white as ever.

"More trees to girdle?" Jason asked.

"No more dreams of Doon," said Lared.

"I can't tell this story without him," Jason said.

"No more of his memories. I hate him. I don't want to remember being him. No more dreams of Doon."

Jason studied him a moment. Looking in my mind, aren't you! Lared shouted silently. Well, see how much I mean it! I would never do what Doon would do—

"Don't you understand, at all, why he did it?"

I don't want to understand it.

"Mankind is more than just these billions of people. Together we're all one soul, and that soul was dead."

"He killed it."

"He resurrected it. He broke it into little parts that had to change, to grow, to become something new. We used to call it the Empire of the Thousand Worlds, even though there were only some three hundred planets with populations. But Doon fulfilled the name for us—it wasn't all destruction. He sent out huge colony ships, spreading mankind farther and farther from Capitol, so that when the end came, when he destroyed Capitol and ended starships for three thousand years, there truly were a thousand worlds, like a thousand spider balls, each one teeming with its billion people, each one finding its own way to be mankind."

And how many people were grateful to him? Were they as glad as Clany's mother, perhaps?

"It has been more than ten thousand years since then, and his name lives on as one of the devil's names. No, they weren't glad of it at all. Is the apple tree glad when you cut it off to graft it into the wild-apple root?"

A man is not a tree.

"As you are to the apple tree, Lared, Abner Doon was to mankind. He pruned, he grafted, he transplanted, he burned over the old dead branches, but the orchard thrives."

Lared stood. "There are more trees to girdle. If we hurry, we can make the third night's hut tonight, and save ourselves some wattling."

"No more dreams of Abner Doon, I promise."

"No more dreams at all. I'm through."

"If you wish," Jason said.

But Lared knew that Jason agreed because he figured Lared

would relent. And Lared knew that he was right. He would not dream of Abner anymore, but of Jason he would dream. He had to know how that child became this man.

So when the trees were girdled and they came home, two days earlier than usual because they had worked so well together, Lared went to his penbox and opened it, and cleaned the pens, and said, "We write tomorrow, so give me dreams tonight."

5

The End of Sleep

The tinker was a cheerful man, and he loved to sing. He knew a thousand songs, he liked to say, a thousand songs, and all but six of them were too filthy to sing in front of ladies.

Truth was he knew dozens, and if Sala's work was done, she'd sit at his feet and sing along with him—she had a memory for words and melodies, and her sweet voice with the tinker's piping tenor were a sound to hear, and upstairs where he wrote for hours each day Lared liked to hear them. Liked it so well that every now and then Jason would say, "The world won't end if you take a breath now and then," and they'd go downstairs and tool the leatherwork that always waited, while the women spun and wove and whispered and Sala and the tinker sang.

"Will you sing?" Sala asked Justice.

Justice shook her head and kept on with her weaving. She was not good with her hands, and Mother only let her do roughspun cloth, the sort of stuff that hardly mattered. The fine wool for shirts and trousers, that was done by cleverer hands; and above all Justice was never let to touch a spinning wheel. The village women kept three of them, besides Mother's own, in the common room of the inn during the winter—when it was the gathering place for Flat Harbor. Each day when they bundled against the cold and came, the women each brought three good faggots for the fire and a pear and an apple, or half a loaf, or a rind of cheese for nooning, and they made a feast of it. The men ate after, at a separate table, a hot meal that somehow seemed less cheery than the laughter from the cold table where the women ate. It was the way of things—women had their society, and the men had theirs. But poor Justice, thought Lared, she belongs to neither.

It *was* sad, for Justice made no effort at all to learn the language, and so while she understood everything—far more than anyone said, in fact—she never spoke a word to anyone, except through Sala or, occasionally, Lared—but usually Sala, for they were always together. Ever since Justice had tasted the pain of the burning man on the raft, from that time on Sala was Justice's comfort, her company, her voice. Of all the women, only little Sala seemed to love her.

So while Sala and the tinker sang, Justice listened intently, and Lared understood that Justice was, after all, capable of love. He could not see into her mind, as Jason could, to see she was drawn as much to the tinker as to Sala.

The tinker was a laughing man, of average height and profound but solid belly, and he alone did not treat Justice as if she were strange. Indeed, he must have made a point of making sure his eyes always included her as he looked from face to face around the room, that his ribald comments were directed as often to her as to any other woman in the place; and Lared also understood if his smile seemed to fall on Justice more often than on any other woman. Justice *was* young, and none of her teeth had rotted, and she had a pleasant body and a face that in certain lights was beautiful, for all its sternness. The winter was long, and this woman seemed unattached, so why not try for her? Lared was old enough to understand *that* game. But the chance of playing heat the sheets with Justice—well, if the tinker did *that* he was more of a miracle-worker than Jason. And I don't care *who* overhears my thoughts, I'll think what I like all the same.

"Think what you like," Jason said, "but Justice might surprise you. She's lost more in her life than *you* have, so she has a right to be stern—and a right to love whomever she likes, whenever she likes. Begrudge her nothing, Lareled."

To Lared's surprise, he *did* care who overheard his thoughts. Angrily he closed his penbox. "Do you *always* listen to my thoughts? When I strain over the hole in the privy, are you there, feeling what I feel? When my father takes me through the most sacred steps of a new man, will you be at his side, along with me?"

Jason raised his eyebrows. "I'm getting older, Lared. If I'm with you in the privy house, it's to recall how easy it is for a young man, compared to the work *I* go through."

"Well, stop it!"

"You don't know what straining *is*."

"*Stop it!*"

From downstairs came Mother's voice. "What's going on up there?"

"She's *your* mother," Jason whispered.

"I'm telling Jason that I hate him!" Lared called.

"Oh good," Jason whispered. "That will make everything so much easier."

But the frank answer turned away Mother's wrath. "At last you've come to your senses!" she called. "Will he go away now?"

"And will she give the jewel back?" Jason whispered.

"No he will not!" Lared called down the stairs. "He's not through studying how country bumpkins live." He closed the bedroom door and returned to the writing table. "Well, if you're ready to work, so am I."

"For your information, I have lived in far more primitive conditions than this. And loved it."

"Stay out of my mind."

"You might as well ask me to go through my days with my eyes closed, for fear I might see someone. Believe me, Lared, I've been inside some of the foulest minds you can imagine—"

"I know! You put the memory in *me*."

"Well, yes, that's right, we did. I'm sorry. It's the only way to tell the story."

"There are other ways to tell stories. You speak the language well enough, even if you can't write it. *You* tell the story. I'll copy down what you say."

"No. I've lied too often in my life. What *you* write will sound truthful. What *I* write is always in the language of lies. For someone like me, that's all language is *for*, is to tell lies. I get the truth in other ways. Other people never get the truth at all."

"Well, I'm not going to dream of Abner Doon again, and we haven't finished his part of the tale, and so you're going to *have* to tell me at least a part."

"Where did we leave off?"

"The Estorian twick."

"That feels like forever ago!"

"We took a long walk in the woods."

"Well, no matter. Obviously I didn't die. It took half a year

for the wounds to heal, and after that Doon arranged for me
to be trained as a starpilot. I lived as a starpilot lives from then
on. Somec kept me asleep and ageless while I traveled in deep
space, and the ship woke me up whenever an enemy ap-
proached. No one ever killed me, and I killed a lot of them,
and so I became very famous and popular, which meant I had
a lot of enemies, and eventually they tried to kill me and so
Doon sent me off as commander of a colony ship."

Lared spun the feathery tip of the quill between his lips.
"You're right. I can tell the story better than you."

"On the contrary. *I* know which things are worth telling at
length, and which things are best skipped over."

"There are some things you *never* explained."

"Like?"

"Like what happened on that second test they gave you. I
remember every bit of how much you worried about it, and
nothing of how it ended."

Jason strained to push the heavy needle through the leather
of Father's new boot. "Whoever tans hides around here does
a miserable job."

"He does an *excellent* job. His boot leather sheds snow and
lets no water in."

"It also sheds needles."

Lared was feeling annoyed and impertinent, a delicious feeling which he intended to indulge freely. "Keep trying and
someday you'll be strong enough."

Jason got in the spirit of the quarrel and handed him the
boot. Lared took the needle and with a circular, twisting motion
drove it quickly and smoothly through the sole. He handed the
boot back to Jason.

"Oh," said Jason.

"The test," Lared reminded him.

"I passed it. But I couldn't have. Because the answer to the
second question had only been worked out by physicists at
another university a few months before. And the answer to the
third question, which I halfway solved—well, *no* one had been
able to answer it at all. That alerted the computer. And the
computer alerted Abner Doon. Woke him up, because there
was a new thing in the world, a person that might be worth
collecting."

Lared was in awe. "As a child you solved a question that the scientists couldn't answer?"

"It's not as impressive as it sounds. Somec was killing physics and mathematics, just like it was killing everything else. They should have solved both problems centuries before. But the finest minds were quickly put on the highest levels of somec—six months awake for six years asleep. The only people awake long enough to accomplish anything were the second-rate minds. Almost every nation does that to themselves, given enough time. They make their great minds so secure, they bog them down so much with being honored and famous, that they never accomplish anything in their lives. I was *not* a genius. I was merely clever and awake."

"So Abner collected you?"

"He watched my movements through the computers and Mother's Little Boys. They could have caught me anytime. He saw that I went to Radamand, he overheard our conversation—the walls *were* ears—and he saw how I shipped my own mother off on a colony ship. Ruthlessness in a child—he found it charming."

"You had no choice."

"No, but you'd be amazed at how often people who have no choice act as if they had one, and lose everything because they could not bear to do what had to be done."

"So then what happened?"

"No. Write what I've told you, and what you dreamed of Abner Doon—tell those stories, bare and clean, and then tonight you'll dream again."

"I hate your dreams!"

"Why? I'm not Doon."

"When I wake up I can't remember who is me and who is you."

Jason pointed to himself. *"I* am me. *You* are you."

"You never answer me."

"That was the only answer. Whatever is contained within your body, whatever acts your hands and feet performed, that's you. And if you remember my acts, then that is you, too."

"I never sent my mother to a world where I'd never see her again."

"No," Jason said. "No, you never did."

"Then why am I so ashamed of myself for doing it?"

"Because you have a soul, Lared. They found it out in early experiments with somec. Volunteers would go under somec, and lose their memories, and then when they were revived, they dumped someone else's memories into their minds. It worked fine with rats. But then, it's hard to think of a rat who would do something that another rat wouldn't mind doing. They woke up remembering a lifetime of performing acts that they could not bear to remember having performed. Why? They had no benchmark to measure against—as far as they knew, it was their own life. But they couldn't bear to remember having made so many *wrong* choices. There was something that remained in a human mind even after somec had taken everything else, the part of you that says, 'This is the sort of thing I do,' and 'This is the sort of thing I do not do.' The part of you that names you. Your soul. Your will. All the old words."

"And it lives after you when you die?"

"I didn't say that. It merely survives when somec takes everything else. If you would let me show you a story from Doon's own life—"

"No."

"Then I'll tell you. He loved a woman once. A bright and clever woman who was ruled by an invalid father and a spiritually crippled mother. All her life, this girl had bent and twisted her life to their bidding, because she loved them. It ruined everything, cut her off from everyone, except Doon, because he had his remarkable ability to understand human nature—even without the Swipe—and he saw her and knew what was locked away behind her parents' door. So he loved her. But she wouldn't leave her family to go with him."

"To marry him?"

"It was nothing like what *you* call marriage. But she wouldn't do it. She couldn't bear to leave her parents without the support she gave them—without her, they would have truly lived in hell. So she stayed. Fifteen years, until they finally died. And in that time she had become miserable, bitter, savage, and she was no longer interested in love, even when Doon came back to her and gave it to her. So he played a trick on her. Back when they were considering, uh, marriage, he had arranged for her to have her memory bubbled for storage, but she backed out before they ever gave her somec. He saved that bubble all those years, and now he put her under somec—he had corrupted the Sleephouse by then—and put the old memories into her head when she awoke. Then he told her what he had done—that she had cared for her parents to the end, but now she could go on with her life without remembering the years that had so embittered her."

"And so they lived happily?"

"She couldn't stand it. She couldn't bear to live without remembering every agonizing moment of her parents' decline. She was the sort of person who had to fulfill every bit of her responsibility, even if it destroyed her—she could not live without the memory of her own destruction."

"Her soul."

"Yes. She made him put her full, true memories back into her. Even though it meant erasing the few good, happy months they had. The pain was more valuable to her than the joy."

"She sounds like the sickening kind of person Abner would love."

"You are so kind-hearted, Lared. You have sympathy for everyone."

"Who would want to keep pain and throw away happiness?"

"A good question," Jason said. "Which you must answer before the end of this book. Now write these stories, and dream tonight."

"What will I dream about?"

"Don't you want it to come as a surprise?"

"No."

"You will dream of how Jason Worthing, the famous warrior and starpilot, ended up in command of a colony ship and lost a battle, for the first time in his life."

"I'd rather write that than the things you've told me to write today."

"Sometimes you have to tell the dull parts of the story so that the good parts will mean something when they come. Go on, write. Your father needs these boots before we go out lumbering next week."

"You're coming with us?"

"I wouldn't miss it for the world."

So Lared wrote, and Jason sewed. In the evening Father

tried on his new boots and pronounced them good. In the night
Lared dreamed.

Starpilots were young for a long time. On each voyage,
which might take years, even at several times the speed of
light, the pilot slept, only waking when the ship alerted him.
It could be another ship, it could be planetfall, it could be some
unexpected hazard or malfunction, but usually a pilot slept from
three days after launch until three days before the voyage's
end. It was rare for planetside duty to take longer than a few
weeks. The result was that starpilots were at unbelievably high
somec levels—an average of three weeks awake every five
years under. Only Mother, the Empress, slept more and woke
less. No politician or actor had more prestige.

And of all starpilots, none was better known or more admired than Jazz Worthing, the hero of Ballaway, the darling
of the trueloops.

Therefore, as Jason well knew, no starpilot was more hated
and envied, because no other starpilot so symbolized the Empire
to those who loathed it.

So it was no surprise to him when he came to port at Capitol
and found himself surrounded by people who hated him. What
surprised him was that most of them planned to kill him. Things
were getting out of hand. What had Doon been doing these
last twelve years?

Only Capitol, of all the worlds, could afford a spaceport
large enough for starships actually to land. It was part of the
majesty of Capitol, the loops they sent out to every planet,
showing the tugs lowering the starships into the gaping bays
in the metal surface of the world. Almost every landing had
some loopers there to watch. Jazz's landing had every looper,
hired or freelance, who could get free of grisly murders or raids
from wall rats. And crowds—

Thousands of people lined the tier on tier of balconies around
the bay. Jazz knew they were there before the door broke open;
without trying, he could feel their adulation. As always before
he cracked the door he paused and asked himself, do I need
this? Have I come to live for this? And, as always, the answer
was: No. I don't think so. I hope not. No.

His agent, Hop Noyock, greeted him as he stepped through

the door. It was one of Hop's perks, to be featured on trueloops throughout the Thousand Worlds. It got him into an amazing number of parties while Jazz was gone. Hop was that rare creature, a starpilot's agent who didn't hate his client. After all, Hop had aged some dozen years since their relationship had begun, and Jazz had aged scarcely six months. Hop was going bald. Sagging a little in the belly. But he was loyal and intelligent and hard-working, a combination few agents ever achieved. Besides, Jazz liked him. He had grown up as a wall rat, and done well enough in the crawlspaces that he had the money and connections to buy papers and get into the corridors before he was eighteen. Doon had found him. Never met him, of course, but he was aware of him, and when Jazz decided he needed an agent to handle his Capitol business, Doon recommended him.

But Hop was taking no pleasure in the cheers of the crowd, not this time. Oh, he strutted and bowed and waved like the wall rat he was, but his heart wasn't in it. Jazz went into Hop's mind and found almost at once what was bothering him.

Hop had been wakened only two days before, when word reached the Sleephouse that his client was arriving. And they brought him a folded, sealed note. A memory slip, which the Sleephouse people kept on hand for the paranoid—people who thought of something after their memories were bubbled and before the drug and couldn't stand the thought of losing the idea. Hop had never used one before, thought they were foolish. But there it was, in his handwriting, a note that said, "Someone trying to kill Jazz. Warn."

Hop couldn't figure it out, and neither could Jason. How could he find it out just before going under? Did someone in the Sleephouse tell him? Absurd—they had no contact with the outside world, the monks and nuns of the god of sleep. What could they tell him? And no one else had access. Hop decided, therefore, that it must be that just before he slept he put together something that he had already known, combined facts so that he realized some plot on Jason's life. For the past two days he had been trying desperately to think of something he noticed on his last waking that might have been a clue. He had come up with nothing, and now Jazz was here, and he knew no more than the note he had written to himself.

Jazz knew something that Hop didn't know. He knew a man who could walk into the Sleephouse and tell something to someone whose bubble was finished, something that had to be written down. The warning came from Doon.

It was two hours before Hop could get away from the loopers long enough to tell Jazz about the note. By then Jason had already found a dozen people in the crowds around him who were in on one or another conspiracy to kill him. One was even armed. It was easy to evade him, and the others had cleverer plans than to pellet him in the presence of three hundred loopers.

"Don't worry," Jason said. "It's probably nothing."

"I hope you're right. But I've never left myself a note before. It must mean something."

"How do *you* know how smart you are between bubbling and the somec? Nobody remembers."

"I'm always very smart."

It was the beginning of a hectic few days. Jazz couldn't go to his rooms at all—there was almost always someone waiting inside to kill him, and Jazz found out about several plots to lay traps for him. Finally, things came to a head at a party held by a former lifeloop star, Arran Handully, who had given up public fornication in favor of a life of ostentatious gentility. She was deep in one of the more dangerous plots to kill Jazz. Sitting against a wall with no one attempting to talk to him, Jazz had a chance to study the question of why all these murder plots were coming at once. He decided to do a little searching in depth. The mind of Arran Handully was convenient.

Jazz had to die—it was one of the foremost imperatives in her mind. But why? Here was where the surprise came: Jazz's death was the beginning of a coup. Not that Jazz had any political power, of course. Just that he symbolized all that Arran hated about Capitol, about the society that had driven the only man she had ever loved to suicide many years before. It was a charming and tragic story, the death of her lover, and Jazz found himself exploring her mind for the sheer pleasure of it, carelessly ignoring the dozen other threats at the party. While he studied her, she came up to him.

"Commander Worthing," she said.

"Call me Jazz," he said, using the charming smile that

played so well on the loops. Of course, there were a few dozen clandestine loopers taking it all in, and Jazz knew enough to please his public, even when the loop was being taken illegally.

"And I'm Arran. You are something of an unexpected guest, Jazz. We didn't know you'd be in Capitol until yesterday. It was kind of you to come."

"The pleasure," said Jazz, "is mine. I have only seen one of your lifeloops, but it was enough to entrance me."

"Oh, which one is that?"

"I forget the name," Jazz said—he never knew it—"but it was one you did with an old actor named—named—ah yes, Hamilton Ferlock."

She felt stricken, but showed nothing. Ham Ferlock was the lover who had killed himself when she refused to break character on a twenty-one-day straight-through loop. It was cruel of Jazz to bring him up—but then, she was planning to kill him.

When? Why not now? A servant came with a single goblet of wine.

"No matter what we might plan," said Arran sweetly, "you are the guest of honor at any party you attend. I give you the cup of the night." She held a silver cup in her hand, and she held it toward his lips, for him to drink. The servant maneuvered closer, so he could take the goblet from the tray and put it to Arran's lips. Jason took the goblet, but refused the cup.

"How can I take such an honor at your hands?" he asked.

"I insist," she said. "No one deserves it more."

"What a remarkable woman you are, Arran. Such courage—to dare to poison me at your own party."

If he had been more watchful, he could have avoided this moment. But now the plots were coming together at once. More than a few of the guests at the party were armed; every exit was watched. The only person here who knew the secret ways out of the room was Arran herself, and they were all keyed to her palm. So he selected the most melodramatic of the would-be assassins, a young clothing designer who had created Arran's costume for the evening. Jazz stepped toward him. He was the murderer of choice, because he meant to be theatrical about it.

"Fritz Kapock," the young man said, to introduce himself.

"How dare you accuse Arran Handully of such a foul crime?"

"Because it's true," said Jazz.

"Apologize, Jazz, and let's get the hell out of here," said Hop quietly.

"Rapiers or pellets?" asked Kapock. Oh, he meant to do it according to the rules, didn't he. Jazz laughed at him and accepted the duel with rapiers.

One thing led to another. Jazz didn't kill the young man, mainly because Mother's Little Boys arrived while the duel was in progress. No one had called—Doon had sent them himself. So Abner is somehow responsible for all this sudden interest in my death, he thought. If only I were sure that Doon knows what he's doing.

Mother's Little Boys created enough havoc that he escaped, with Arran's unwilling help. Jazz had only one objective—to find Doon and point out to him that Jazz's love for him did not extend to a willingness to die for him. Along the way he shed Hop and Arran, figuring they'd be safer away from him, and Hop knew well enough how to take care of himself. And at last he was face to face with Doon, beside the lake in his private garden.

"Very well done, to get away," said Doon. "Some of their plots were quite thorough. You were almost in danger several times."

Jason fingered the cut Kapock had given him on his arm. "What are you doing, Doon?"

"Oh, just isolating and bringing out the best people of Capitol. *You* can get inside their heads and find out who they are. I have to work out little tests like this."

"Next time just ask me."

"I look for things even you wouldn't be able to find."

"It shouldn't be too hard. Your test for the best people is whoever wants me dead."

"What do you expect? You're the foremost symbol of a detestable empire."

"I am what you made me. We're all what you made us."

Doon was genuinely hurt. "Surely you don't think I'm God, do you? I'm just one element in your environment, that's all."

"In theirs, maybe. In mine you're more."

"Because you love me so deeply?" asked Doon, mocking.

"Because the most important events in my life happened to you. The only woman who mattered to me was your little piece of unrequited love. All my best triumphs were your triumphs, all my strongest dreams were yours—"

"Not true."

"Of course it's true! Your memories are more present in my mind than my own!"

"And why is that?" asked Doon.

"Because you cared so much. You have such a strong sense of purpose, even when you don't even know what it is you're trying to accomplish—all your memories *mattered* to the person who went through the experience."

"And *your* own past? Is that nothing? Battles, struggles, fear, conflict—"

"What conflict? What fear? Except for one long moment with a little beast in your garden, Doon, I have never been afraid. A bit tense, to see how the game would go, but the outcome was never in doubt. In battle I could always hear the other fellow's plans as he thought of them, in conversation I always know the other person's hidden thoughts, I've never had to wonder or guess—"

"Your life is such a *bore*. Poor Jason."

"There are times when I wake up thinking that I'm you. I look around the inside of the ship and I think, why am I here? I look in the mirror and I'm surprised to see this face. This face is from the loops. This face is Jazz Worthing, but I remember, very clearly, I am Abner Doon; I am the one who won the confidence of Mother herself and told her when it might be a good time to die—"

As he spoke, Jason looked in Doon's mind to see if indeed the time was up. Abner had wakened the empress herself, had met with her, revealed himself to her many years ago. "I will wreck your empire," he told her. "I thought it only fair to let you know." She took it calmly, perhaps even happily, and gave her consent, on one condition—that he tell her when he was about to do it, so she could be awake to watch. Now Jason looked to see if he meant to tell her soon. To see if Doon was planning to end the empire now.

"Of course not," said Doon. "I have too much to accomplish before that. Give me at least another hundred years."

What did he have to accomplish? He had been sending out colony ships for centuries now. But the ones that he was sending now, they held his hope.

"Mankind is my experiment," said Jason. "Cut the threads that bind the stars together, and each world will spin on its own for a while. Perhaps thousands of years, until someone comes up with a stardrive that needs no sleep, and then we'll see what mankind has become in a thousand different cultures."

"That's *my* speech," said Doon.

"That's all right," Jason said. "You've been playing puppet with us all. My voice, your words."

"Are you angry?"

"Why me? Why am I singled out for the joy of being one of your twelve oddities?"

"I don't know."

"I know you don't know. I know what you know, and I know what you don't know. I even know what you don't know that you don't know. I can find things in your head that you've forgotten ever knowing. You have been planning this for me for the fifty years that I've been gone, and you don't even know what you expect from it!"

"I'm sending you farther than I'm sending anyone else. I'm keeping no record that your ship was ever sent. Officially, all the traitors and conspirators going with you were executed. No one will look for you, not until they find the message that will be released a few thousand years from now. Your little world will have longer to develop than any other."

"What do you expect, evolution in a few thousand years?"

"Not evolution. Breeding."

In Doon's mind, Jason saw himself as Doon saw him. With the eyes pure unflecked blue. Like his father's eyes, and *his* father's eyes.

"The stud for a world of Swipes, is that it?"

"*Sire* is the more delicate word."

"I wasn't raised on a farm."

"You and your family are an anomaly. Your gifts are far more reliable, far more extensive than any known strain of telepathy. Why not see what happens to it in isolation?"

"Then why didn't you isolate me? Why give me a colony full of people who have spent their last few wakings plotting to kill me?"

Doon smiled. "It appealed to my sense of proportion. It would be too easy for you to run a normal colony. It would hardly be enough to keep you awake all day."

"It's kind of you to worry about me being bored."

Doon took Jason by the hair at the back of his neck and drew him down, drew him close, and face to face he said, "Surpass me, Jason. Do more than I have done."

"Is this a contest? Then why not start even? Three hundred and thirty-three colonists against one ship's captain—I don't like the odds."

"With you," said Doon, "no one is even."

"I don't want to go."

"Jason, you have no choice."

Jason saw that it was true. Doon had already given out more than enough proof that Jason was a Swipe. He would be arrested the moment he left Doon's personal protection; if he tried to escape, where could he hide, when everyone on Capitol knew his face?

"The puppet," Jason said, "wishes to be free."

"You *are* free. Stay and die, go and live—you have your choice."

"What choice is that!"

"What do you expect, an infinite selection? To have a choice at all is to be free—even when the choice is between two terrible things. Which is most terrible, Jason? Which do you hate the most? Then choose the other and be glad."

So Jason chose to go; Doon had his way again.

"It's not so bad," Doon said. "Once you're gone, you won't have me manipulating things anymore."

"The only star on the journey through the night," said Jason. "It will comfort me as my colonists sharpen their knives in the darkness." Yet it was no comfort. To be without Doon, that was what frightened Jason most. Doon was the foundation of his life, for good or ill; ever since Doon had found him, Jason had known that nothing could go too wrong in his life—Doon was watching.

Now when he stumbled, who would lift him up? This was freedom after all, Jason realized, because from now on no one would save him from the consequences of his own acts. It wasn't freedom that I yearned for, was it? It was childhood that I wanted, and Doon is barring me from my refuge; he has been my father all these years, and now he's thrusting me away. "I'll never forgive you for this," Jason said.

"That's all right," Doon said. "I never expected to be loved." Then he smiled oddly, and Jason knew he was not as cheerful as he pretended. "But I love *you*," Doon said.

"I'm so much like you that to love me is purest narcissism." Jason was not trying to be kind.

"It's what isn't me in you that I most love," said Doon. "Where I have torn down, you will build up. I have made the chaos for you, and the world is without form, and void. You are the light that will shine on the face of the deep."

"I hate it when you say things you've been practicing up to say."

"Good-bye, Jason. Go meet your colonists—day after tomorrow they go under somec, and then you're on your way."

Lared put down his pen and sprinkled sand on the parchment to dry the ink. "Now I know why I wish you had never come here," he said.

Jason sighed.

"It's like you said. My strongest memories are yours."

"What I said was wrong," Jason answered. "Just because you remember me saying it doesn't mean it was true, or that I still believe now what I believed then."

"Sometimes I even forget and try to look into people's minds, and I can't, even though I remember doing it. It's like someone cut off my hand. Or burst my ears, or cut out my tongue."

"Still," Jason said. He held up the ax handle he was carving. "I cut the wood however I like, but it's the grain that decides the strength and shape of it. You can add and subtract memories from people, but it isn't just your memory that makes you who you are. There's something in the grain of the mind. They found it out from the start, when they tried dumping someone else's bubble into a person's brain. All his experiences, all his past—and the mind that came out of somec was empty, wasn't it? But the new memories wouldn't fit. He remembered only being this other person, he *believed* he was the other person, but he could not bear remembering it. It was not himself."

"You told me. They went mad."

"There was nothing right in their past, how could they stay sane?"

"Will I go mad?"

"No."

"How can you be sure?"

"Because no matter how much of me you remember, me or anybody else, there is at the root of your mind a place where you are safe, a place where you are yourself, where your memories are right, and belong to you."

"But it changes me, to remember being you."

"And me," Jason said. "Do you think I'm the same man, knowing the insides of other people's lives the way I do?"

"No. But are you sane?"

Jason was startled, then laughed aloud. "No," he said. "God help me, but you ask the truest questions! Justice was right to pick you, you've got a mind like ice. No, I'm not sane, I'm utterly mad, but my madness is the sum of all the people I have known, and sometimes I think that I have known all the people in the world—at least all the kinds of people that it's possible to be."

He seemed so delighted, so exuberant, so glad to be himself that Lared couldn't help but smile. "How can all that fit inside your head?"

Jason again held up the half-finished ax handle. "As tight as the handle in the ax. And there's still room to drive in a wedge or two. Always room for more, to set it tighter."

The first heavy snowfall did not come, and did not come. "Bad sign," said the tinker. "It means the sky is saving up." And he climbed on the roof to mend the flashing around the chimney, and took out the flue and rebuilt it so it fit tightly again, no leaking. "Do yourselves a favor with the doors and windows—make sure all the shutters are strong, and the doors fit tight, and caulk the walls."

Father listened to the tinker, went outside and looked at the bright cold sky, and announced that no other work mattered until the house was tight. The whole village then set aside their work and closed their houses. The littlest children slapped more daub on the weak places of the walls, down low; doors were tooled to fit tighter; shutters were remade; and in a time of such work, Jason and Lared found themselves taken again from the work of pen and parchment. They did the ladder work together, fastening in place the shutters of the upstairs windows. Jason climbed the ladder the right way; Lared, who had always climbed like a cat, went up the ladder the wrong way, and quickly, and then perched on the sill of the beams that poked out of the wall of the house. He had no fear of falling.

"Be careful," Jason said. "There's no one to catch you if you fall."

"I don't fall," Lared said.

"Things have changed."

"I'll hold tight."

As they worked, Jason told stories. About the people of his colony. "I called them in, one by one, and while they sweated through interviews that meant nothing, I found out from their memories just what kind of person each was. Some were haters, the sort of people you'd expect to find in any conspiracy to kill. Some were merely afraid, others were dedicated to a cause—but I didn't care that much why they had wanted me dead. I needed to know more the purpose of their lives, what made them choose their choices."

Like Garol Stipock, a brilliant scientist-turned-engineer, who devised the machinery that could diagnose a planet from its ore to its weather in a few orbits. He thought of himself as an atheist, rejecting the strong, fanatic religion his parents had forced on him as a child; in fact, even as he worked hard to reject and break down any authoritarian system he could find, he was still the child who believed that God had definite ideas about what mankind ought to be, and Garol Stipock would give up anything and everything to try to achieve that ideal.

Like Arran Handully, who had devoted her life to entertainment, subsuming her own identity in her lifeloop role, living day after day, minute by minute, in the constant scrutiny of the loops, so that people could circle around a stage and watch her life from every angle. She was the greatest of the lifeloop actresses, and under it all was the desire for others to be happy—when she retired, she never missed the audience, for it was not her own need she had meant to satisfy when she performed.

Like Hux. A dedicated middle-level bureaucrat, on a two-up, one-down somec level. Everything he touched went smoothly, every job was accomplished on time and under budget. Yet despite the great esteem that superiors and underlings alike had for him, he had refused promotion after promotion. He was married to the same wife, had the same block of rooms, ate the same meals, played the same ballsports with the same friends, year after year after year.

"So why did he join a revolution?"

"He didn't know that himself."

"But *you* knew."

"Motives aren't remembered, especially the ones you don't understand yourself—I can't just find a place in his memory where all his unknown purposes are laid out for me to see. To others, to himself he seemed to have only one purpose in life: to keep everything the same, to resist change. But that need was just the outward face of what he wanted most: stability and happiness for everyone he knew. He was no Radamand, remaking the world to his own convenience."

As Lared worked, a face came into his mind, a lantern-jawed face with a hint of weakness around the eyes. Hux, he knew. Justice was showing him the pictures as Jason told the tales. Where are you, Justice? Working somewhere in silence, as always, listening to us talk, with almost never a word to say yourself?

"You're not listening," Jason said.

"You're not talking," Lared answered.

"Put in the pin, my arms are breaking holding this shutter."

Lared put in the pin. The shutter swung smoothly again. Together they set to fastening it down, top and bottom, and barring it from the outside. It was a north-facing window, and the northwest wind had torn shutters away before. Jason talked on as they drove the wooden pins that would hold the shutters closed. "Hux wanted an order of life in which all were reasonably content, and when it was found he didn't want it to change. He was no hypocrite—he willingly inconvenienced himself, sacrificed much in order to keep his corner of Capitol secure and stable. He was also bright enough to see how somec undid and destroyed everything. Separated families as they straggled their separate routes across the years, ended friendships as one went to the Sleephouse while the other stayed up, not having merited sleep—somec kept the empire stable, but only at the cost of unbalancing almost every life it touched."

"So he wanted the empire to go on without somec?"

"One of the few in my colony who didn't long for sleep. And then Linkeree—I remember them together because of what happened later. Link was as opposite to Hux as a man can be, on the outside. He had no friends, no close associates, no family. He was the only person in my colony who had never been on somec in his life, except for the voyage from his home world. He had been confined in a mental institution for years before coming; his parents had been confusing, possessive, cruel, and exploitative—in cases like that it was usually the children who ended up being locked away. So Linkeree even believed himself to be half-crazy, a loner who loved no one and needed no one."

"But you knew better."

"I always know better. It's the curse of my life." Jason frowned. "If you don't hold on with at least one hand while you're balancing on only one foot up here, I'm going to throw you down myself to end the suspense."

"I told you I won't fall. What was the truth about Linkeree?"

"He had an overdeveloped sense of empathy. He could imagine other people's suffering, and felt it himself. His mother had used that against him all his life, torturing him with guilt for all the suffering of her life. The only thing that freed him was seeing what real suffering was." And again an image came into Lared's mind. But not a face this time. It was an infant lying in a clear place in tall, knife-like grass, left to starve or freeze or be devoured by the creatures of the night. With the image came a feeling of desperate compassion—I can do nothing, and yet I must do something or not be myself—and finally the image gave way to another, to a group of uncivilized tribesmen kneeling in a circle in the grass, taking the child's corpse apart in a ritual; I understand, the child must die for the sake of the tribe, the child's death means life. It was a moment of clear understanding for Linkeree, for in the infant he saw himself, torn and broken to keep his mother alive. I am not insane; she is the one who is mad, and I am suffering for her. But does she love me as these tribesmen love the infant they have killed? The answer was no, and so he left, escaped from his world and went to Capitol, a place where everyone looked for someone else to suffer for them. Linkeree was a living sacrifice; he suffered to expiate the guilt of all who touched him.

"Hold tightly when such a vision comes," said Jason. "I think we shouldn't do this when we're perched up here."

"I'm not so fragile as that," said Lared. But the infant stayed in his mind, lying there in the grass with savage insects hanging from its naked body.

"Linkeree was not a loner, after all. He was like Hux, in a way—all he cared about was other people. It made Hux sociable and stable; it made Linkeree shy and skittish; but I knew them both for what they were, and I said to myself, "These I will make my leaders. Because power in their hands would be used for the good of all, and not to please themselves. Or rather, if they pleased themselves they would please others as a matter of course, because they could not be happy in the knowledge of others who were miserable."

"No one is that good," said Lared. "Everyone wants what he wants."

"You are that good," said Jason. "That's what goodness is, Lareled, and if there were no goodness in people, mankind would still be confined to loping across a savannah somewhere on Earth, watching the elephants rule, or some other more compassionate species."

"I don't know," said Lared. "I've never cared much about other people's pain."

"Because they didn't feel any. But you still hear a burned-up child screaming, you still feel a man's blood pumping from a wounded foot. Don't tell me you know nothing of compassion."

"What about you?" asked Lared. "Are *you* good?"

No, came the answer in his mind. It took a moment for Lared to realize that it was Justice who had answered, not Jason. No, Jason is not good.

"She's right," Jason said. "It's the whole meaning of my life, that I inflict suffering on others."

"Did you cause the Day of Pain?" asked Lared.

"It was not my choice," said Jason. "But I believe it was the right choice."

Lared did not say another word that afternoon, thinking how
the man who worked beside him approved of what had changed
in the world since the Day of Pain. And that night he dreamed.

Jazz awakened to see the lid of the coffin sliding back, the
amber light winking at the edge of his vision. His bubble must
have just finished dumping his memories back into his head,
and his body was hot and sweating, as it always was when he
came up out of somec. Push-ups, sit-ups, running in place
made him alert and quick again.

Only then did he notice that it was not the amber light
flashing in his coffin, but the red. Had it been red all along,
or had it just changed? No time to decide the question now; in
a moment he was at the controls, and the ship was telling him
what it knew. An enemy ship had been hiding behind a planet,
almost as if it expected his approach; two projectiles were
already launched.

Even as Jason's fingers sent two of his ship's four torpedoes
into space, his mind searched for and found the enemy captain,
the mind controlling the missiles that dodged and pitched and
weaved their way toward him. The missiles were far more
maneuverable than Jason's massive colony ship, but Jason knew
where the missiles were going, and moment by moment Jason
drew himself farther out of the enemy's way. In the meantime,
his own missiles homed in on the enemy, anticipating her
attempts to dodge. For once Jason didn't care if anyone noticed
that he knew things he could not possibly know, that he was
a Swipe. He would not be going back to Capitol again, and
so at last he could fight with his full ability.

Just before the enemy's ship exploded in a globe of light,
the enemy captain knew that she would die, and in that moment
she took grim satisfaction from the fact that even if she died,
Claren would finish off the enemy.

Claren. She was not alone. Jason and his enemy had been
concentrating on their duel, routing their missiles and their own
ships; only now did he realize that there was another ship, still
behind the planet, which had been using the first ship as its
eyes to route its own attack. Jason's ship was tracking the
enemy missiles, which were already near. Desperately Jason
searched for Claren, the enemy who was so close to success.

He found Claren just in time. Or it would have been just in time, except that Claren was no longer controlling his missiles—when the first ship blew up, he had lost his means of seeing and therefore controlling his missiles' flight. They were homing on Jason automatically, which meant their course was absolutely predictable and easy to dodge, except that Jason had wasted too much time looking for the captain's mind, and while he could avoid one missile, he could not avoid the other. It would strike him. Its high-intensity light would carve through his ship's armor; the skin of the ship would peel back from the wound and allow the missile to enter, to plunge into the core of the stardrive and there, gently, explode. A pathetic little explosion, really, but almost anything would upset the delicate balance of impossible forces, and the ship would explode.

Jason saw his future in a moment, and in that moment decided that he would prefer any alternative to utter destruction. The missile was too close for him to move his whole, massive ship out of the way. But the payload, a slender shaft projecting forward from the massive stardrive, *it* would not go off like a pent-up star if the missile struck and exploded there. Almost instinctively Jason swung himself into the path of the missile. Somewhere back along the kilometer-long tube behind him, the missile would strike, colonists would die, and Jason found himself hoping that the missile would kill only some of the people, and not harm the all-important animals and seeds and supplies and equipment at all.

Impact. The ship shuddered from the distant explosion; alarms went off on the control panels; but the explosion was far enough from the stardrive, shielded enough that the drive was able to cope with the disturbance, balance itself before an unstoppable reaction destroyed everything.

Alive, thought Jason. Then he set about killing Claren. The enemy remained out of sight behind a planet, but Jason used Claren's own eyes to track the missiles when they were in the lee of the world, in a place where Claren knew he would be safe, but the missiles came on as if they had intelligence of their own, as if they could read his mind, for wherever he dodged the missiles were already headed for his new course, and in a few moments he was dead.

I don't like knowing my enemy's name, thought Jason.

The damage was brutal, but not unsurvivable, or so it seemed at first. The 333 colonists were arranged in three parallel corridors at the back of the payload, each of the three corridors completely shielded from the others, to help protect against the whole colony being wiped out in such an event as this. One corridor was a total loss—it had been peeled open to space and the coffins had burst open and erupted with corpses. A second corridor seemed untouched—the bodies all lay peacefully within their coffins. But the controls had been seared as the missile canted into the ship, and none of them would ever be revived.

Still, the third corridor remained, and 111 people would be enough to start the colony; with the supplies and equipment unharmed, they would survive. They would accomplish less work the first year, but they would have all the more supplies to keep them going for a few more years, till things were up to speed. It was sad that so many had died, but the colony had not been undone.

So Jason thought, until he reached the very back of the payload, where the bubbles were stored in a carefully protected environment.

That was where the missile had actually exploded.

Fourteen bubbles had survived intact. Nine from the corridor that had exploded, four from the corridor whose residents would never wake up, and only one bubble from the surviving colonists.

Only one human being left. The others would be incapable of doing anything for themselves, remembering nothing, knowing nothing. How could he deal with 111 adult-sized infants? What good were people without minds?

He walked back through the corridor of survivors and looked down into the coffins at the people who, though not dead, would never again be themselves. His good friend Hop Noyock, the actress Arran Handully; he touched each coffin and remembered what he had seen within each mind, Hux, Linkeree, Wien, Sara, Ryanno, Mase, I know what you will never know again—who you are, what you have done, what you meant to be. Now what are you, if I ever wake you up? You, Kapock, with your fierce, devoted loves, what lovers will you remember now? Their names were broken with your bubble, and your past is dead.

The only bubble that survived belonged to Garol Stipock. Jason studied his face as he lay in his coffin, sleeping. Are you the one that I should waken? The one person committed to undoing authority in any form? What sort of ally would you be? Anyone's bubble but yours, if the choice had been mine. Your childhood is the one I least needed to keep in living memory.

Jason swung the ship through its change of course, but when it was done he did not sleep. Instead he studied, dumped into his head the Empire's collective wisdom on the art of colonization. All the jobs took dozens of able-bodied women and men to make them work. He plunged deeper into the library, to the books rather than the bubbles, unscrolling them in the air over the control desk, trying to find out what he could teach infants to do, how many he could support by the labor of his own hands.

Many times he almost despaired. It could not be done. The high-level technology to farm and manufacture, to create a modern society, required many people with strong specializations. How could he hope to educate a hundred people from infancy to advanced specialties quickly enough that they wouldn't starve while they waited to grow up?

But gradually, inevitably, the answer came. The modern economy would be impossible, but an older society would not. A life with simple tools that could be made by hand; a life of fields that could be plowed by people who had not learned their algebra but could drive an ox. I can plow an acre myself, plant and harvest it, to feed myself and a few others. Just a few at a time, until the first ones have developed enough to help me with the next ones.

The only drawback was that it would take years. The ship would preserve those he had not yet wakened, but each one he brought out would be utterly unproductive for many years, and during that time would still need an adult's portion of food, of clothing, of everything, and would require frequent attention and time-consuming care. The colony would never be able to sustain more than a few of these at a time, for the economy would always be marginal, farming as they would with hand tools and animal strength.

It would take years, but perhaps, if they learned quickly enough, Jason could leave them from time to time, return to the ship and sleep for a year or two, come back just to bring new colonists from the ship, just to check and make sure the colony was running smoothly. After all, these people had been carefully chosen—the best people of Capitol, Doon had said. And if a few of them showed exceptional leadership ability, I could bring them aboard the ship and put them under somec again, and preserve them for a time of great need. I could—

Then Jason realized what he was doing. Planning to create a colony of ignorant peasants, using somec to create an elite class, headed by himself, of people who would withdraw from the world and return to it, years later, without having aged. All that was detestable about somec I am already planning to use again.

But only for a time, Jason told himself. Only until the colony is firmly established, only until we've recovered from the missile that has so undone us all. Then I'll destroy somec, destroy the whole ship, sink it in the bottom of the sea, and somec will disappear from my planet.

It was the only way he could think of to form the colony at all. Even at that, it would require almost unbearable amounts of work from him, especially at the first. But it could be done.

Could be done, and might provide an opportunity no one else had ever had. A chance to create a society out of nothing. To create its social institutions, its habits, its beliefs, its rituals, to design them carefully with no need to compromise with old habits, old beliefs. I can make utopia, if I have wit enough; the power is in my hands, if I can only decide what the perfect society must be.

The idea grew, and he began to write of what he thought his world might be, until at last he realized that he was happy again, and excited for the future, more so than at any time before in his life. The enemy's missile undid all of Doon's designs, and for the first time in his life Jason was truly on his own, without having to account to Doon or anyone else. If he failed now, it would be his own failure; if he succeeded, it would be success for him and for every generation that followed him in his world. And it will be my world, he told himself. By accident I have been made the creator; I am the one who will put the breath of mind into these men and women; let us stay in Eden this time, and never fall.

6

Waking
the Children

The house was sealed; they could all feel the difference, lying in bed in the firelight. The drafts from under the doors were almost gone, so Lared felt no urgency to hide behind the low walls of his truckle bed. The heat sometimes was so great that Sala would cast off her blankets in the night.

And still the snow did not fall. The cold whined out of the north, but the only snows were scattered, a few showers that blew into corners and clung to shingles.

"When it comes, it'll hide your head," said the tinker. "I've got me a weather sense, and I know."

In the night, Lared tossed and turned with the dreams that Justice took from Jason's memory and put into his mind. But it was different now. For some reason, when he awoke, he could not easily remember what he had dreamed.

"I'm trying," he told Jason. "I know it had something to do with plowing. You were doing it all wrong or something. You were trying to drive the oxen the way you lead a well-trained horse. You weren't much of a farmer then. Is that it?"

"Of course I wasn't much of a farmer," Jason said. "It was the first time I had seen dirt in my life."

"What's dirt? Dirt is dirt."

"I see," said Jason. "That's our problem. Before I awakened the cattle and brought them out of the ship and put them in their plastic barn, I had never set my hand on the back of a hot, sweating beast, never felt the play of his muscles under the skin. When I hitched the plow on them, I had to discover the tricks of the straight furrow and controlling the depth of the blade myself—none of the books taught me. The oxplow and the oxen were only sent along in case of a massive power failure. Who was alive in those days who knew how to use them?"

"Even Sala knows more than you did," said Lared. How was he supposed to take this seriously?

"These things stay in my mind as magnificent, hard-won discoveries. They come to you as clumsiness in tasks you do every year without thinking. No wonder you forget."

Lared shrugged, though in fact he felt that he had failed somehow. "I can't help it. It's not as if I don't try to remember. Find another scribe."

"Of course not," said Jason. "Why do you think we chose you? Because you were of this world, you knew what mattered and what didn't matter. I loved the work of the soil because I had never done it before, it was all new at a time in my life when I thought I had already done everything. To you it isn't new, it's drudgery. The little things I do while you write, the ax handles, the boots, the wickerwork, it's all pleasure to me; living here with you, after all these years to be part of a village again, I love it, but what does it matter to you? So don't write about it. Don't write about how I worked as hard and fast as I could to earn an hour to go wandering through the forest, collecting herbs to test in the ship's lab. Don't bother with my first tastes of real food, the way I threw up at the taste of bread after so many years of predigested pap made from algae, fish meal, soybeans, and human manure. What's that to you?"

"Don't be angry," Lared said. "I can't help it that it doesn't matter to me. I'd remember it if I could. But who would want to read about it?"

"For that matter, who'd want to read about any of it? Lared, you dream of civilization, don't you—a life of comfort and safety, with time enough to read whatever you liked, and no one to turn you into a plowman or a blacksmith if you didn't want to do it. Yet what you do—herding the trees for harvest, shuttering the windows, making sausage and strawing the ticks— that is better than any other life I've lived or seen or even heard about."

"Only because your life's never depended on it," Lared said. "Only because you're still just pretending to be one of us."

"Maybe so," Jason said. "Just pretending, but I know my

way around the forest, and I do an ax handle as well as anyone I've seen here."

Lared was afraid when Jason was angry. "I mean then. You were pretending. You must have learned over the years."

"Yes," Jason said. "A little. Not much." He was twisting horsehair into a bowstring, and his fingers were quick and sure. "But I stole the skills from other men, who learned them better than I. I got inside them while they worked, and knew the feel of it without looking. I didn't earn it. I didn't earn anything in my life. I'm just pretending to be one of you."

"Did I hurt you?" Lared whispered.

"And that's another way I'm not like you. *You* have to ask."

"What did I say wrong?"

"You said nothing but the truth."

"If you can hear my heart, Jason, you know I didn't mean to hurt you."

"I know it." Jason tested the cord—it was fine and tight. "So. If we don't allow the farm and forest work into our tale, there wasn't much else. So what do we tell in the book you're writing?"

"The people—the ones who lost their memories—"

"It was the same as the farm work, tedious, filthy work. I just took them from the ship, a few a year, fed them, cleaned them, taught them as quickly as I could."

"That's what I want to know about."

"It's just like raising a baby, only they learned a lot quicker and when they kicked you it could really hurt."

"And that's all?" Lared asked, disappointed.

"It was all the same. It only interests you because you've never had a child," Jason said. "People who've had infants will know. The crying, the demands, the stink, and as they learn to get up and move on their own there's a lot of destruction and sometimes injury and—"

"Our babies have always got by without the injuries. Till lately."

Jason winced. Lared already knew that Jason bore some responsibility for the Day of Pain, and he took some satisfaction from Jason's silent confessions of guilt. "Lared, it was the only happy time of my life. Learning to be a farmer, and teaching the children as they learned. Don't despise it because you were born with what I only learned then. Can't you write that? Can't you write of a single day?"

"Which day?"

"No day in particular. Any day would do. Not the day I first took Kapock and Sara and Batta from the ship—I didn't know what I was getting in for, that autumn; with the harvest in, I thought the year's work was done."

"Winter's when the real work happens," Lared said. "Summer's harvest comes from winter's water."

"I didn't know that," Jason said. "Not that day, anyway. Not the time when I despaired, when they seemed to learn nothing, when I grew sick of their endlessly emptying bladders and bowels. Perhaps when I knew that it would succeed. Perhaps a day when I loved them. Find such a day, Justice, and give it to Lared in his dreams."

That afternoon the snow began to fall. The wind blew harder than ever; they went out only to make sure all the animals were closed in the barns and stables, to make sure everyone in the village knew, and that no children were out in the storm. That took the afternoon, and Lared felt a strange exhilaration in the danger of it, for they had treated him like an adult, letting him go from house to house, trusting him with the lives of some of the families because no one followed after him to be sure he delivered his messages. They have almost decided that I'm a man, thought Lared. I am almost on my own.

By suppertime there was no going out at all, for any reason. The wind was whipping the snow through the innyard, piling it up mountainously against the windward walls of house and barns and forge. Lared looked through the sliding shutter on the door—even with so small an opening, the wind stung his eyes and made it hard to see. What he saw was the storm that the tinker had so long promised. There was never a calm in the wind, only an occasional slackening that would let the snow fall slightly downward, instead of seeming to fly straight across, level with the ground. It was impossible to tell how deep the snow was, after a while; he could see no buildings through the flying snow, had no reference point. Only when the snow drifted up against the door so high that it plugged the shutter hole, only then did he realize that there had never before been such a storm in the village of Flat Harbor. That night Lared went with his father into the cold attic, to see whether the roof

beams could bear the weight. Afterward, he lay awake in bed
a long time, listening to the wind whipping the house, prying
at the shutters; listened to the snow press downward on the
house, making the old timbers groan with the weight. He got
up twice to put another log on the fire, to make sure the rising
heat was stronger than the cold whistling down the chimney,
or else the smoke would back into the room and kill them all.

At last he slept, and dreamed of a day in the life of Jason
Worthing; he dreamed a good day, the day that Jason knew
his colony would work.

Jason awoke to the lowing of the cows that needed milking.
He had been up three times in the night with the new ones,
just brought from the ship. Wien, Hux, and Vary, and they
were trouble—with the first three on their own a little more,
Jason had forgotten how much trouble they could be. Not that
they needed nighttime feedings—their bodies were adult, after
all, and not growing. They awoke because they did not know
yet how to dream. Their minds were vast caverns, and they
easily got lost; they had no store of images to guide them
through the night. So they awoke, and Jason comforted them,
calmed them.

The cows need milking and I must get up. In a moment I
will.

How long till these new ones learn? Jason tried to remember
back through the last months, the long winter, the longer spring
as he tended Kapock, Sara, and Batta, doing his best to keep
them safe, keep them learning, even as he struggled to ready
the land, to plant, to grow a crop. But in the late spring they
began following after him, imitating him, learning the work;
it had not been long. Eight months and they were walking and
talking and helping bear the burden of the work.

Jason knew enough of children, though he'd never had any,
to know that they were progressing far faster than any infant.
It was as if something in their brains that did not depend on
currents of electricity kept a pattern; they learned to walk easily,
in a matter of a few months; bowel and bladder control came
soon, mercifully; their tongues found the tones of speech well
enough. Learning their bodies from the inside was not as hard
this time as it had been when they were very small. But it was
little comfort during the months before they *had* learned, for

no mother had had to contend with a six-foot infant crawling to explore in the night; and with bodies fully developed, Jason had to enforce strict rules about who slept where, and how they must stay dressed, and what may or may not be touched: it was hard enough to deal with them without a pregnancy. Jason meant to build a stable society, and that, he had decided, meant that the customs of marriage had to be firmly embedded in the patterns of their lives.

With Batta, Kapock, and Sara, that was already in the past, and still to come with Wien and Hux and Vary.

Jason sighed and forced himself to get up, to dress in the darkness. Only it wasn't as dark as it should be—light was coming in through the skylight. He had slept more than a moment, and the cows would be angry. Except that he didn't hear them lowing. They should be complaining loudly by now.

It was only when he opened the door and the light fell across the floor that he realized that the others weren't there. The new ones lay in their coffins—the sides kept them from falling out of bed—but the old ones were gone. Jason felt a thrill of fear as he thought of them down at the river. He had taught them to respect the danger of the stream, and the current was weak this far into the summer—he should not be afraid. Should not be, but was.

They were not at the river, but as he walked around the plastic dome they called the House, he saw Kapock out in the vegetable field, hoeing along the rows of beans. He looked farther, and at the forest's edge there was Sara with Dog, letting the sheep out to graze beyond the edge of the fenced fields. He knew then where Batta would be, and walked into the barn.

She had already finished the milking, and was skimming the cream from yesterday's for butter-making. "You're just in time," she said, imitating a phrase that Jason often used, imitating even his intonation. "You're just in time. Let's curdle it." Oh, she was full of herself, but the work was well done, wasn't it? and Jason hadn't been there to help at all. So together they poured the buckets of skimmed milk into the wooden tub and set it in front of the heater to warm. Making curds in front of a solar-powered heater did not seem like such a contradiction to Jason. He knew that he would soon have to begin the use of open fire, but he dreaded it and hoped to put it off at least another year. So it was radiant heat from a unit brought with the ship that kept the milk in the tub at the right temperature, and lactic acid saved from the belly of a slaughtered lamb that did the curdling, and bacteria carefully cultured from the ship's supply that began to grow in the milk to turn it, eventually, to cheese.

"We let you sleep," Batta said. "You were very very tired. The new ones were very bad in the night."

"Yes," Jason said. "Thank you. You've done very well."

"I can do it all," she said. "I know the way." So he only helped her when the job needed more than two hands, and told her nothing; when he was sure she knew what to do he set about the simpler task of butter-making. With the curdling well under way Batta came to him, strutting a little, and smiled as she laid her hands on the handle of the churn. "Butter for summer sweet and cheese for winter meat," she said.

"You're a marvel," Jason told her, and he went back to the House to tend the new ones. He fed and diapered them, carried out the manure to the privy that he and the old ones used, and dropped the urine-soaked diapers into the tub, where the piss leached out for soapmaking later in the fall. Use everything, thought Jason, teach them to use everything, even if it makes your civilized stomach a little sick. *They* have no such fine sensibilities. *They* can learn what matters and what doesn't. How many of the citizens of Capitol had thought nothing of adultery but shuddered at the sight of their own stools? The loops that showed defecation were considered far more pornographic than the ones that depended on interesting variations of sex. Capitol didn't need you, Doon, to make it fall. You only made it so somec would die with it—it was caving in before you came.

Kapock showed himself no mercy in the vegetable garden. Like Batta, he was working to earn Jason's approval, and he gave it gladly. Kapock had killed no table plants, and the weeds were well cleared. "You've put food on the table today," said Jason. That was strong praise, for he had taught them what they had to know to survive: that every day's work had to put food on the table, that every hour of summer sweat was winter survival; and they believed him, though they remembered almost nothing of winter, and never doubted that there would be food enough to eat. Indeed there was—food enough on the ship to feed the four—no, seven—of them for a generation.

But the sooner they were self-supporting, the better.

Jason looked in Kapock's mind, as the tall child hoed eagerly. He had few enough words to think with yet, but he had a strong sense of the order of things. He was the one who had thought of the day's surprise, to let Jason sleep while they did the work, and of course Kapock had chosen for himself the job he hated most, the one of endless repetition while bent over in the hot sun. That was the order of things to him: to do all that Jason taught them to do, without having to be asked anymore. He had taught them that was what it meant to be grown, that you did what must be done even when you didn't want to, even when it hurt, even when no one would know if you didn't do it. That was Kapock's project for the day, to be grown up in Jason's eyes.

But there was more. A sense of the future, too. And Kapock found a way to put it into words. "Will the new ones help tomorrow?" he asked. He had understood: as the new ones were, lying helpless in their coffins, he and Batta and Sara once had been; as he and Batta and Sara now were, the new ones would become.

"Not tomorrow, but in a few more weeks."

To Kapock that still meant an unmanageably long time, as far off as the mythical winter, but it was confirmation that he was right about the way things would go in the world. And so he dared another question. "Will I teach them everything?"

The question really meant, Will I become like you, Jason? And Jason, understanding that, answered, "Not these new ones, but other ones, later ones, little ones, you'll teach them everything."

Ah, thought Kapock wordlessly. I will become you, which is all I want.

They took their noon meal together, without Sara because she was tending the sheep, and they wouldn't come in till late in the afternoon. Jason had never seen Kapock and Batta so happy, falling over their own words as they tried to tell each other all that they did, all the praise that Jason had given them, while Jason quietly moved among the coffins, feeding the new ones some of the cream saved out from the churn. Batta's new butter spoke for itself on the bread from last year's wheat. Last year's wheat, which Jason had planted and harvested himself, testing seven different seeds in this alien soil to find the ones that thrived best. No such loneliness again as when I plowed on the little tractor, and flew in the skiff to place the game animals in the forest, to stock the lakes with fish that my people could eat; I was far more free then to come and go as I liked, and I did not have to work half so hard as now, but I like this better, much better, the sound of their voices in my ears, the pleasure of seeing their joy in learning.

Together they strained the day's curds and wrapped it and put it under a stone to press it into cheese. Thirty other cheeses already growing strong and rank promised plenty to eat in the winter; Jason had been right to bring all but a few of the cows out from the ship, despite the trouble that they had caused him in building fences strong enough to hold them in.

I have done all this, thought Jason. I have come to a meadow by a river and turned it into a farm, with people and animals and food enough to keep all alive. And they are learning, they will someday know enough to survive without me—

It was the promise of future freedom, that they needed him less today than yesterday. It was also the warning of death.

Batta and Jason left Kapock to watch the new ones and went out to the edges of the unfenced fields to split last winter's logs for fence rails. It was hot, exhausting work, but before darkness forced them in from the field they had fenced another hundred strides—before summer was gone they could let the pigs out into the forest to range and root, with a fence to keep them from the crops. Then the forest would feed them, and it would be one less drain on the resources of the little farm; the pigs would harvest the forest for them, and bring it back as bacon for the winter's eating.

Waste nothing. Harvest everything. The geese would glean after harvest, so the spilt grains would become roast meat late in the autumn. The sheep would eat the stubble and turn it into wool and ewe's milk and young lambs for next year's flock. The ashes from the wastewood burning would be used with urine and turned to soap; the guts of the slaughtered pigs and lambs would become strong threads for binding, or casings for sausages. Once it had been the daily life of every man and woman in the world, to turn everything into food or fuel or clothing or shelter; to Jason it was the dawn of creation, and everything he did was new.

Sara and Kapock had the supper ready. It was tasteless but

good enough because Jason hadn't had to watch the cooking. They were serious about this today—twice as much had been accomplished as in any day since Jason took them from the ship. Batta even tried to feed the new ones.. Hux spat it on her, and Wien bit the spoon, and she got angry and yelled at them. Kapock told her to be quiet, what did she expect from new ones? Sara shouted at Kapock to be nice to Batta, she was only trying to help. Jason watched it all and laughed aloud in delight. It was complete. They were a family.

"There," said Lared. "Is it what you wanted?"

"Yes," said Jason.

"I even tried to write it so cheese-making would sound wonderful. Anybody with half a brain can make cheese, you know. And sheep can jump over the kind of fence you were making."

"I know. I learned it before the summer was out, and we raised the fence."

"Human piss makes disgusting soap."

"The books didn't say that. Eventually we started leaching it out of the straw in the barns, the way you do it. We couldn't learn everything at once."

"I know," Lared said. "I'm just saying—you were as much a child as they were. A bunch of big children. Like you were five years old, and they were three, and so that made you like God to them."

"Just like God."

Kapock came to him one night late in autumn, in the darkness when the others were asleep across the room. "Jason," he said, "did everything come out of the starship?"

He used the word *starship* but did not know that it meant a thing that could move among the stars. It was just the word for the tall, massive building an hour's walk from the House.

"Everything that you didn't help me build," Jason said. He had been too careless in his use of the word *everything*, for Kapock at once believed that somehow the land and the river and the forest and the sky had come from the starship, too. Jason tried to explain it, but the words were gibberish to Kapock. What did *voyage* and *colony* and *planet* and *city* and even *people* mean to him? Just an incantation that only Jason understood. It remained his belief that everything had come from the starship, and that Jason had brought the starship to this place. Later I'll teach him, Jason thought, later he'll understand more, and I'll teach him that I'm not God.

"And the new ones, did you make them?"

"No," Jason said. "I only brought them with me. They were just like me, before we came. They slept all the way here. There are more of them in there, sleeping."

"Won't they wake up and be afraid, without you there?"

"No—they're asleep longer than that. The way the river is asleep under the ice. The way the fields are asleep under the snow. They won't wake up until I waken them."

Of course not. Nothing wakes till Jason wakes it. Winter comes when Jason wills it. And the people who sleep like the river under ice, they come as Jason calls them. I also do as Jason teaches, for I was also Ice.

The wind let up late in the afternoon. "Just a lull," said the tinker. "Don't go far, and don't go alone."

"Not far," said Father, "and Lared will come with me."

They went out the south-facing kitchen window, bundled to the eyes so that they climbed like clumsy infants. On the south side the snow wasn't quite so deep, though walls of drifted snow flanked the house left and right. The snow was still falling, straight down this time.

"Where are we going?" Lared asked.

"To the forge."

It was almost painful, the sound of their footsteps in the silence. For a while, between inn and forge, neither building was visible. Only the unfamiliar landscape of the drifts. Only his father, plowing awkwardly through the waist-deep snow ahead of him. Then the forge became a dark streak in the snow ahead, only the edge of the roof of it visible. Lared had never been outside in such weather before, but Father unerringly found the shallowest snow, avoiding the deep drifts that were higher than their heads.

A trick of the wind had put a drift in front of the south-facing door of the forge. They forced through it to the wide window in the top of the left-hand door; it opened inward, and the snow gave way, and they lowered themselves inside.

"Help me stoke the fire." It was still alive, from the day before. But what work was so urgent that they had to risk their lives in such a storm?

The answer came when Lared tried to close the window.

"The fire!" said Father. "And leave the window. The others need to see the light."

The others. Lared understood at once. They would make him be a man tonight. It was a great honor, to do it in such a storm as this, provided that the others came. And they did come, two by two, until eighteen men were crowded, sweating, into the hot smithy. They left a clear aisle from the open window to the fire of the forge.

"We stand," said Father, "between fire and ice."

"Ice and fire," said the others.

"Will you face the fire, or will you face the ice?"

What did it mean, to face one or the other? How could he pass a test if he didn't know what the question meant?

So he hesitated.

The men murmured.

Lared tried to imagine what they meant to do. Fire was Clany, dying in agony; ice was the snow outside, and no track to guide him home. Give me ice over fire any time. But then he thought again: if I have to face two dangers, which would I rather have before me, and which behind? I will face what I fear most—perhaps that is the test.

"Fire," he said.

Many hands took him and faced him toward the fire. The bellows coughed. The cinders flew upward. The many hands took the clothing from him, until the fire seared his skin in front, and the wind from the door froze him behind.

"In the beginning," recited Father, "was the age of sleep, when all men and women longed for night and hated all the days of waking. There was among them one with power, who hated sleep, and all his ways were destruction. His name was Doon, and no one knew him until the Day of Waking, when there came a shout from the world of steel: Look at the man who has stolen sleep! Then the name of Doon was known everywhere, for the sleepers belonged to him, and there was none left who was not forced awake."

What would this have meant to me, wondered Lared, if I hadn't had Doon's face in my memory? All a mystery, all a myth if I hadn't known, but I *know* the truth behind it, I have spoken with Doon face to face, and I can tell you the way his eyes look when he knows you are afraid. I have also been Doon, and evil as he was, somec was worse.

"Then," said Father, "the worlds were lost in the light. They could not find the stars in the sky anymore. For five thousand years they were lost, until men learned to travel against the light, to travel so quickly they could do it without the sleep that Doon had stolen. Then they found each other again, found all the worlds but one, the world known by the holy name."

"Ice and fire," murmured the other men.

"Only here, between the fire and ice, may the name be spoken." Father reached out and put his thumbs on Lared's eyes. "Worthing," he said. Then he whispered, "Say it."

"Worthing," Lared said.

"It was the farthest world, the deepest world, and it was the place where God had gone to sleep when men awoke. The name of God is Jason."

"Jason," said the men.

"And the world was full of the sons of God. They saw the pain throughout the worlds, the pain of waking, the pain of fire and light, and they said, 'We will have compassion on the woken, and ease their pain. We are not Jason, so we cannot give them sleep, but we are the children of Jason, so we can keep them from the fire. We are Ice, and we will stand at your back, and hold the light at bay '"

They know the end of the story, Lared realized. They know what became of Jason's world when he was done.

"Now," said Father, "they have given ice to us. But we remember pain! Here between the ice and fire, we remember—"

He stopped. The men murmured. "Remember," someone said. "Pain," someone whispered.

"It has *changed*," Father said. He wasn't reciting anymore. "It isn't the Day of Waking anymore, and it isn't the Day of Ice. It's the Day of Pain, and I won't let it go the old way."

The men were silent.

"We saw it coming down the river, what happens when you

do the ice and fire now! And I said that day, we will not do it here!"

Lared remembered the man burning alive on the raft. From upriver, where there is still ice in the mountains. "What is supposed to happen now?" asked Lared.

Father looked sick. "We throw you in the fire. In the old days, we were stopped. Our arms would not do it, though we threw with all our might. We did it so we would remember the pain. And to test Worthing."

The men were still wordless.

"We saw what happened to Clany! We know that Worthing is asleep again! The Ice has no power anymore!"

"Then," said Clany's father, "give him ice."

"He chose the fire," said another man.

"Neither one," said Father. "We did it before because we knew there'd be no pain. Now we know pain and death."

"Give him ice," said Clany's father. "We did not make you speaker so that you could save your son."

"If we keep this alive then all our sons will die!"

Clany's father was on the edge of weeping—or was it the edge of rage? "We must call them back to us! We must wake them up!"

"We do not kill our children, even to waken a sleeping god!"

Lared understood it now. Naked, the boy-who-was-to-be-a-man was cast into the fire or out the window into the snow. He could see in the faces of the other men that they weren't sure what they wanted. There were many generations in this ritual. All the uncertainty since the Day of Pain was in their faces. And Lared knew his own value in their eyes. A bookish boy and so not trusted; not strong for his age and so not valued; the son of the most prosperous man in the village, and so not liked. They do not long for my death, but if someone is to die and wake the children of Jason they are willing for it to be me. And Father is shaming himself to save my life. If they consent to let me live, it will be because my Father begged, and he will never have his pride again in the village.

The fire is too much for me, thought Lared. But I can face the snow.

"Are the children of Jason in the fire or in the ice?" he asked.

He was not supposed to speak, but then nothing was supposed to happen as it had.

"They are Ice," said Hakkel the butcher.

"Then I will go into the ice," said Lared.

"No," said Father.

As if in answer, the wind howled outside. The lull in the storm was over.

"Tell me what to do, once I'm outside," said Lared.

No one was sure. The children of Jason had always stopped them before the end. "The words we say," said Father, "are, 'Till you sleep in ice.'"

"In the fire," said Clany's father, "we say, 'Till you wake in flame.'"

"Then I will go until I sleep."

Father put his hand on Lared's shoulder. "No. I won't allow it." But his eyes said, I see your courage.

"I will go," Lared said, "until I sleep."

No, said a voice in his mind. I will not save you.

I'm not asking you to, Lared answered silently, knowing he was heard.

Do not choose to die, said Justice.

"I will go until I die!" Lared shouted.

Their hands reached out to him like dozens of little animals, set to devour him. The hands lifted him, rushed him toward the window, and cast him out into the wind and snow.

The snow stung him, and as he struggled to right himself it got in his nose and mouth. He came up gasping and trembling, his legs weak under him from the shock of the cold. What am I doing? Oh, yes. Going until I sleep. There was enough light from the window to cast his shadow a short way into the snow— he stepped forward into his shadow. The wind caught him and he fell again, but he got up again and staggered forward.

"Enough!" cried his father, but it was not enough.

Until I sleep. Sleep was ice to them, in their story. There would be ice along the edges of the river. Not that far. I can run it in three minutes in summer. I must bring them ice from the river, I must take the cold and bring it back to them, the way Jason took the twick into his body and brought it out, and lived. From this night, if I live, Jason's memories won't steal me from myself.

No one will save you, said a voice in his mind. But he

wasn't sure if it was Justice or his own fear speaking.

It wasn't far, but the wind was cruel, and it whipped along the river worse than anywhere in the village. Lared dug numbly in the snow until he uncovered stones that until yesterday had been half-buried in mud. Today it was already freezing, and he cut his clumsy fingers before he could persuade a sharp stone to rise into his hands. Then he knelt at the water's edge, where snow spilled out onto the new ice, and the ice reached arms out into the river. A few blows with the stone and the ice at the edge broke up; the water splashed and felt warm on his arms. He fumbled in the water to get hold of a large fragment of the ice, and then half-crawled back up the slope of the bank.

He had the ice from the river, it was enough that he could go back and no one could say he failed, but the wind blew the snow into his face now, and as he staggered forward the world was nothing but dots of white coming toward him. He could not see the village, saw nothing but the snow around him, forgot where the river even was. A moment ago he could hardly hold the ice for shivering; now his body had forgotten it was cold.

Then, out of the endless points of snow, there came two shadows. Father, and Jason. It was Jason who led the way, but it was Father who put a blanket around him.

"I got to the river," Lared said, "and I got this ice."

"It doesn't even melt in his hands," Father said.

Together they lifted Lared and carried him through the snow. They shouted, and someone answered; someone also answered, faintly, farther on. It was a chain of men through the snow. Lared did not see the end of the chain. He slept in his father's arms.

He awoke trembling violently in a tub. Mother was pouring hot water on him. He screamed from the pain.

Seeing he was awake, she gave him the sort of sympathy he was used to. "Fool!" she shouted. "Naked in the snow! All men are fools!" She returned to the fire to heat more water.

She's right, said the voice in his mind.

"But so were you," whispered Jason.

The other men were there, their faces shifting in the firelight. The room was hot and it hurt to breathe, and Lared didn't want them to watch him that way. He ducked his head, turned to

the side, turned back again, shaking his head back and forth
slowly.

"Leave him," Jason said. "He got the ice for you, he came
home asleep, he did all you said for him to do."

The men pulled on their heavy coats and capes, began to
glove themselves.

"They say your name is Jason," said Hakkel the butcher.

"My name is Jason Worthing," Jason said. "Did you think
Lared's father lied to you?"

"Are you," whispered Clany's father, "God?"

"I'm not," said Jason. "I'm just a man, getting old, wishing
he had a family, and wondering why you are all such fools as
to have gone from yours on a night like this."

They left through the kitchen window, guiding each other
home through the darkness.

7

Winter Tales

The snow had been deeper in previous years, but there had never been so bad a beginning to the winter. Everyone in the house kept saying it, over and over: "And this is only the first real storm." For three days the wind kept up, though after that first night the snow was only a few inches at a time, and they could get around enough in daylight to make sure the animals were fed and watered.

Lared did not get around, however. He lay in Father's own bed during the day, while the life of the house went on around him. The women of the village gathered on the third day, to resume the work of weaving. Though Lared was in the room with them, they did not much converse with him. He was feverish and didn't feel like speaking, and the others had such awe of him that they had little to say to him. After all, they had taken the storm without loss, and many suspected that it was because Lared had offered himself to the storm that it had been no worse than it was.

During the work, the tinker sang his songs and told his tales. He was good for several hours' entertainment, but then there came a lull in the conversation, just the sound of the shuttlecock flitting back and forth in the loom. Then Sala got up from her needlework and walked into the middle of the room. She turned around twice, looking at no one, and then turned to face Lared, though he was not sure if she looked at him or not.

"I have a story of a snowstorm like this one. And a tinker."

"I like that," said the tinker, laughing. But no one else laughed. Sala's face was too serious. The tale she meant to tell came from someone else. Lared knew it was Justice. So did the others—they kept sneaking looks at Justice, who was doing coarse weaving with horsehair strands. She paid no attention to them.

"The tinker's name was John, and he came to a certain

village every winter, to stay at a certain inn. The village was in the middle of a deep forest called the Forest of Waters. The name of the village was Worthing, because the name of the inn was Worthing. John Tinker stayed at the inn because it was his brother's. He lived in a room in a tall tower in the inn, with windows on every side. His brother was Martin Keeper, and he had a son named Amos. Amos loved his Uncle John, and looked forward to winter, because the birds came to John Tinker. It was as if they knew him, and all the winter they were in and out of his windows; during the storms they huddled together on the sills."

Lared looked at the women in the room. They showed little reaction to the name, but there was a set to their lips and a steely look in their eyes that made Lared wonder if they, too, held that name as sacred.

"The birds came to him because he knew them. When they flew he saw through their eyes and felt the air rush by their feathers. When the birds were ill or broken, he could find the hurt place in them and make it well again. He could do this with people, too."

A healer. The name of Worthing. They knew then that Sala's story was somehow a story of the Day of Pain.

But Lared heard it a different way. This tale was from the story of Jason's world, but it came after everything that he had written in his book so far. Justice had given a tale to Sala that Lared had never heard before. Were they forsaking him?

"When he came to the village, they brought their sick to him, their lame, and he made them well again. But to do it he had to swell inside them for a time, and become them, and when he left he took the memories with him, until the memories of a thousand pains and fears dwelt in him. Always the memory of pain and fear, never the memory of healing. So that more and more he was afraid to heal others, and more and more he wanted to stay with the birds. All they remembered was flight and food, mates and nestlings.

"And the more he withdrew from the people of the village, the more they feared and were afraid of him because of his power, until at last they didn't think of him as a man at all, even though he had been born among them, and he did not think of himself as one of them, either, though he remembered almost all their agonies.

"Then came a winter like this one, and the snow was so deep in one terrible storm that it cracked the roof beams of some houses, and killed and crippled people in their sleep, and froze others so the sickness crept up their dead legs and arms. The people cried out to John Tinker, Heal us, make us whole. He tried, but there were too many of them all at once. He couldn't work fast enough, and even though he saved some, more died.

"Why didn't you save my son! shouted one. Why didn't you save my daughter, my wife, my husband, father, mother, sister, brother—and they began to punish him. They punished him by killing birds and heaping them up at the door of the inn.

"When he saw the broken birds he was angry. He had taken all the years of their pain, and now they killed the birds because he would not do enough of a miracle to please them. He was so angry that he said, You all can die, I'm through with you. He bundled himself in his warmest clothes and left.

"When he was gone, the storm came again, and pressed on every house, and tore at every shutter until the only house left unbroken by the wind and snow was Worthing Inn. To the inn the survivors came, then sent out parties to search for others who might be trapped in broken houses. But the storm went on, and some of the searching parties disappeared, and the snow was so deep that only the second-story windows could be used as doors, and many of the low houses were covered and they couldn't find them.

"The fourth day after John Tinker left was the bottom of despair. Not a soul left alive that had not lost kin to the storm, saving only Martin Keeper, who had but the one son, Amos, who was alive. Amos wanted to tell the people, Fools, if you had only been grateful for what Uncle John could do he would not have left, and he would be here to heal the ones with frozen legs and the ones with broken backs. But his father caught the thought before Amos could speak, and bade him be silent. Our house stands, said Martin Keeper, and my son lives, and our eyes are as blue as John Tinker's eyes. Do we want their rage to fall on us?"

No one looked at Justice's blue, blue eyes, but everyone saw them.

"So they held their peace, and on the fourth night John Tinker came back, frozen from wandering in the storm, weary and silent. He came in and said nothing to them. And they said nothing to him. They just beat him until he fell, and then kicked him until he died, because they had no use for a god who couldn't save them from everything. Little Amos watched John Tinker die, and as he grew up and found strange powers within himself, like the power to heal and the power to hear and see through other people's ears and eyes and the power to remember things that had never happened in his life, Amos kept these powers to himself, and did not use them to help others, even when he knew he could. But he also did not use his powers to get revenge for John Tinker's death. He had seen the villagers' memory of John Tinker's death, and he did not know which was worse, their fear before they killed him, or their shame when he was dead. He did not want to remember either of those feelings as his own, and so he went away to another city, and never saw Worthing again. The end."

Sala broke from her trance. "Did you like my story?" she asked.

"Yes," said everyone, because she was a child, and people lie to children to make them feel better.

Except the tinker. "I don't like stories where tinkers die," he said. "That was a joke," he said. Still no one laughed.

That night, when everyone was asleep, Lared lay awake, bundled in blankets in his bed near the fire. He had rested so much these last few days that he could not sleep. He got up and climbed weakly up the stairs, and found Jason and Justice sitting awake in Jason's room, with a candle for light. He had thought to have to wake them. Why were they still up?

"Did you know I was coming?" Lared asked.

Jason shook his head.

"Why did you tell the tale to Sala?" asked Lared. "It's from after. It's from a time when Jason's descendants were getting much stronger than he was. It must have been hundreds of years."

"Three thousand years," said Jason.

"Which of you remembers it?" asked Lared. "Were you still there, Jason?"

"I was under somec, in my ship, at the bottom of the ocean."

"So it was you," Lared said to Justice. "You were there."

"She wasn't born for thousands of years after John Tinker died," said Jason. "But there's an unbroken chain. Every child at some point dares to penetrate his parents' memories. So generation after generation, some of the memories survive— the ones that each generation has found important enough to keep. It's not a purposeful choice—they just forget what doesn't matter to them. I found the memory of John Tinker in Justice's mind. I've even looked back to try to find a memory of me." Jason laughed. "I suppose it's because my children only knew me for a little while, and what they found in my memory made no sense to them, I guess. I'm not there. I search for the oldest memories, and I'm forgotten. Just a name."

It was not Jason's reverie that Lared had come for. "Why did you give it to Sala, and not to me?"

Justice looked away.

"We were just quarreling about that when you came in," said Jason. "It seems that Sala *asked* her—why the Day of Pain had to happen."

"And that was the answer? The story of John Tinker?"

"No," said Jason. "It's the sort of answer you give to children. It doesn't explain the Day of Pain, it's part of another story. It belongs in another place in your book. The Day of Pain did not come because there was too much suffering for my children to handle all at once. My children did not run out of power to heal mankind's ills."

Lared was determined to make Justice herself speak to him. "Then why did you stop?"

Justice still looked away.

"It is to tell that story," said Jason, "that we're writing our book."

Lared thought of how his book had been given to him, and remembered the tale that Sala told, and shuddered. "Did you give her that story as a dream? Did she see John Tinker die?"

That finally provoked Justice to speech. Into his mind she said, *I gave it to her in words. What do you think I am?*

"I think you are someone who sees pain and can heal it but walks away."

Lared did not have to be able to see behind the eyes to know that his words stung her.

"What," said Jason, "and if she walked in from the snow would you kick her to death? Wait until you understand before you judge. Now go to bed. You had your brush with death the other night, you've matched my survival in Doon's garden, that's what you wanted. No one helped you till you had accomplished what you set out to do. If I had found you and stopped you, or if Justice had warmed you on your way, so that you were never in any danger, what would it have meant, your hour naked in the snow?"

Lared did not say the answer, because it would have felt like surrender. Or apology. Did not say it, but of course they heard it anyway, and he went back down the stairs to sleep.

When he got there, he found his mother awake waiting for him. She did not say a word, just covered him up and went back to bed. I am watched, he thought. Even my mother watches. That was a better answer than the one that Jason and Justice had given him. With that answer, he could sleep.

And when he slept, he could dream.

It was morning, and Kapock got up early to raise the fire. There was a new smell in the air. The others joked that with sheep around him all the time Kapock couldn't smell anything, but it wasn't true. He could smell everything, but everything smelled just a little bit like sheep.

The new smell was snow, a mere thumb-thick blanket on the ground. It was early. Kapock wondered if that was a sign of a hard or easy winter. What weather would Jason send this year? he wondered. This was the first winter that Jason was not with them, the first winter that Kapock was the Mayor. I wish you would not go, Kapock had said. And if you go, I wish you would make Sara the Mayor. But Jason said, "Sara is best at naming and telling tales, and you are best at knowing what is right and wrong."

It was true that Sara was good at naming. She made Jason tell her again and again about the Star Tower where the Ice People slept—she was the one who named it Star Tower. From the stories she decided that the place where they all lived on the north side of the Star River was Heaven City, and the huge river an hour's walk to the north was Heaven River, because it was as wide as the sky. And when she and Kapock took all the sheep across the Star River and lived there with them, Sara said in surprise one day, "We don't live in Heaven City anymore. We have a new place." And she promptly named it Sheepside.

Sara was good at naming, but Kapock wasn't very good at right and wrong. Jason could not be wrong, but Kapock was never sure what right and wrong *were*. Sometimes what he thought was right turned out to be right. Today everyone would know that he was right when he told them to make the thatch early, before it was even cold. Now every house was dry and warm inside, except the newest house, the one they were building for Wien and Vary. The early snow would make them all say, You were right.

But sometimes he was wrong. He was wrong when he tried to get Batta and Hux to marry. It seemed like the right thing. They were the last two of the first six Ice People—Kapock had married Sara and Vary had chosen Wien. Hux thought it was a good idea. But Batta got angry and said, "Jason never told you to marry, did he?" and Kapock admitted she was right and he was wrong. Jason was never wrong, and so they were all disappointed that he was not as wise as Jason. This snowfall would help them trust him again.

Kapock remembered four winters in the world. The first was a very dim memory of light too dazzling to see—he remembered being afraid because the snow was much too large, and he fled back into the house. The second winter was better, because that was the winter when he and Sara and Batta lived only from the food they had worked to grow themselves, and it was the winter when Jason taught Hux and Wien and Vary to walk and talk.

The third winter was the winter when Kapock and Sara first lived in their own house across the Star River from Heaven City. Theirs was the first marriage and theirs was the first new house, and come summer theirs was the first child born. Sara named him Ciel.

But the fourth winter would be this winter, with Sara nursing Ciel and wanting Kapock not to talk so much, and Kapock was afraid. For now there was a problem in Heaven City that he did not know the right and wrong of.

It was the law that when there was a large work to do, all the people worked together. That was how they built new houses in two days, and how they harvested and harrowed, how they threshed and thatched, how they cut the winter's wood and cleared new fields. The tools belonged to all of them together, and so did the hours of the day.

So he did not know what to do when Linkeree asked him for an ax and a day. "What for?" asked Kapock. But Linkeree would not tell him. Kapock never knew how to talk to Linkeree, because Linkeree did not say much, even though he knew how. Linkeree was perhaps the cleverest of the Ice People from the second spring—he was the one who made the fish trap in the Star River, and no one taught him how, unless Jason did it secretly. It was Linkeree who first put berries in new wool so that five shirts were made blue. Linkeree was so strange that he never wore a blue shirt himself. Still, it did not take Jason to tell Kapock that Linkeree was different from the others, and in some ways better, and it made Kapock not want to argue with him, but to trust him to do right.

"Take the ax today," said Kapock, "but tonight you must chop your day's share of firewood."

Linkeree agreed to that and went.

But all day Hux was angry. "We all work together," he said, over and over. "When Jason was here no one went off to do secret work." It was true. But it was also true that no one had ever before spoken against a decision of Kapock's, after it was made. And all day Hux kept saying, "It's wrong for Linkeree to change everything this way."

Kapock could not argue with him. He, too, felt uneasy with the change.

That was five days ago, and each day in the morning Linkeree asked for the ax, and each night he came back and did a good day's work while the others sang and ate and played games in First House, where the New Ones, who were just learning to crawl, would laugh and clap even though they couldn't yet speak. It was as if Linkeree were no longer one of them, as if he lived alone. And each day Hux would complain all day. Then at night when Linkeree came back, Hux would be sullen and watch Linkeree, but never said a word of complaint, and Linkeree didn't seem to notice how angry Hux was.

But yesterday Hux followed Linkeree into the forest, and last night he told Kapock what he had seen. Linkeree had built a house.

Linkeree had built a house, all by himself, in a clearing in the woods a half hour's walk from Heaven City. It was all wrong. Houses were built by everyone together, and they were built for a woman and a man who meant to marry. The man and woman always went in the door and closed it, and then opened every window and through each one shouted together, "We are married!" Kapock and Sara had been the first, and they had done this for the sheer joy of it; now everybody did the same, and you weren't married until you did it. But where was Linkeree's wife? What right did he have to have a house? The next marriage, as everyone knew, would be Hux and Ryanno. Why should Linkeree have a house? All he would have there would be himself. He would be alone, and far from the others. Why would he want that?

Kapock didn't understand anything. He was not as wise as Jason. He should not be Mayor. Sara and Batta were both wiser than he. They had both made up their minds quickly. Batta said, "Linkeree may do what he likes. He likes to be alone and think his own thoughts. No one is hurt by it." Sara said, "Jason said that we are one people. Linkeree is saying he does not want to be part of us, and if he is not part of us then we are all less than we were." They were both very wise. It would be so much easier for Kapock if they had only agreed with each other.

This morning Linkeree would ask for the ax again. And this time Kapock had to do *something*.

Sara came outside, bundled to protect her and little Ciel against the cold.

"Are you going to do something about Linkeree today?" she asked.

So she had been thinking of it all morning, too. "Yes," said Kapock.

"What are you going to do?"

"I don't know."

Sara looked at him in puzzlement. "I wonder why Jason made you Mayor," she said.

"I don't know," Kapock answered. "Let's go to breakfast."

At breakfast Linkeree came to him, already holding the ax. He did not ask. He just stood and waited.

Kapock looked up from his gruel. "Linkeree, why don't we

all take axes, and help you finish the house you're making?"

Linkeree's eyes went small. "It's finished."

"Then why do you need the ax?"

Linkeree looked around and saw that everyone was watching. He fingered the ax. "I'm cutting the trees to clear a field."

"We'll all do that next spring. We'll cut into the forest north of First Field, up the hill."

"I know," said Linkeree. "I'll help you with that. May I take the ax?"

"No!" shouted Hux.

Linkeree looked coldly at Hux. "I thought that Kapock was the Mayor."

"It isn't right," said Hux. "You go off every day to do work that no one needs you to do, and during the day no one sees you, and during the evening no one talks to you. It isn't right."

"I do my share of work," said Linkeree. "What I do when work is done is mine."

"No," said Hux. "We're all one people, Jason said so."

Linkeree stood silent, then handed Kapock the ax.

Kapock handed it back. "Why don't you take us to see the house you built?" he asked.

At that, Linkeree grew calmer. "Yes, I'd like to show you."

So they cleared up breakfast and left Reck and Sivel with the New Ones as they followed Linkeree eastward into the forest. Kapock walked in front, with Linkeree.

"How did you know I built a house?"

"Hux followed you."

"Hux thinks I am an ox, always to stay in my pen except when I'm needed to pull."

Kapock shook his head. "Hux likes things to stay the same."

"Is it so bad for me to be alone?"

"I don't want you to be sad. I'm sad when I'm alone."

"I'm not," said Linkeree.

The house was strange-looking. It was smaller from end to end than the other houses they had built, but it was taller, and there were windows up high, under the roof. And strangest of all was the roof itself. It wasn't thatch. It was chips of wood overlapping, and the only thatch was at the very top.

Linkeree saw Kapock looking at the roof. "I only had a little thatch, and so I had to do something to finish it. I think this will hold out the rain, and if it does, I won't have to make a new roof every year."

He showed them how he had put split logs across the tops of the walls and made a second floor to the house, above the first one, so that the inside of the house was not smaller after all. It was a good home, and Kapock said so. "From now on," Kapock said, "we will put this second floor in all our new houses, because it makes more room indoors." Everyone agreed that this was wise.

Then Hux said, "I'm glad you made this fine house, Linkeree, because Ryanno and I are going to be married."

Linkeree was angry, but he answered softly. "I'm glad you and Ryanno are going to be married, Hux, and I will help you build a house."

Hux said, "There is a house, and Ryanno and I are next to need a house, so it is ours."

And Linkeree said, "I made this house myself. I cut the wood, I split and notched the logs, I cut the blocks for the roof and tied them all in place myself. No one helped me, and no one will live in this house but me."

And Hux said, "You used the ax that belongs to all of us. You used the days that belong to all of us. You ate the food that belongs to all of us. Your house is on ground that belongs to all of us. Your life belongs to all of us, and all of us belong to you."

"I don't want you. And you don't have me."

"You ate the bread that I helped grow last year!" shouted Hux. "Give me back my bread!"

Then Linkeree doubled up his fist, and with arms strong from lifting and pulling logs, he hit Hux in the belly, and hurt him. Hux wept. Such a thing had never happened before, and it did not take much wisdom for Kapock to see that this was wrong.

"What will you do now, Linkeree?" asked Kapock. "If you want to keep the ax all to yourself, and I say no, will you hit me? If you want to marry a woman, and she says no, will you hit her, too, until she says yes?"

Linkeree held his fist in his other hand, and stared at it.

Kapock tried to think. What would Jason do? But he could not be Jason—Jason would see into their minds and know what they thought. Kapock couldn't do that. He could only judge what people said and did. "Words should be answered with words," said Kapock. "A person is not a fish, to be beaten on a rock. A person is not a goat, to be whacked when it doesn't move. Words should be answered with words, and hits should be answered with hits." People agreed. It seemed fair.

Hux seemed willing to supply the vengeful blow himself, but Kapock wouldn't let him. "If you hit him it would be the same quarrel going on. We must choose someone else to hit him, so that the blow comes from all of us, and not just from one."

But no one wanted to do it.

At last Sara handed little Ciel to Batta. "I will do it," she said, "because it must be done." She strode to Linkeree and hit him hard in the belly with her fist. She was as strong as any man, from lifting sheep and making fences with Kapock, and Linkeree got the worst of it.

"Now for the house," said Kapock. "Hux is right that it isn't fair for a man with no wife to have a house before he and Ryanno have a house. But Linkeree is right that it isn't fair for someone else to have a house that Linkeree built alone. Jason would know what to do, but he isn't here, and so I say that no one will live in this house until a house is built for Ryanno and Hux. We will build that house as soon as we can, but until then this house will stand empty." Everyone agreed that it was the right answer—even Linkeree and Hux.

But the snow melted that day, and that night it rained, and the ground was deep and wet. They couldn't build a house on such soft ground. And after four weeks of rain, the cold set in suddenly, and the snow fell thick, and they had to build a new barn quickly because there was danger that the animals would have no shelter if the barn roof broke. So instead of a house for Ryanno and Hux, they built a barn, with daub and wattle walls, and then the winter was too deep to build at all. "I'm sorry," Kapock said. "We couldn't help the weather, and the barn had to be built, and now it's too cold and deep to build a house—the snow won't be clear till spring."

Then Hux and Linkeree both grew angry. Hux said, "Why should Ryanno and I wait, when a house is built and ready for us!" Linkeree said, "Why should I have to stay here all winter, when the house I built for myself stands empty! I built my house, and I'm tired of waiting."

Kapock told them to be quiet, and said that it wasn't right for there to be an empty house. "But I don't know which of you should have the house. When Jason was here, people only got their own house when they married. He never gave a hosue to someone who wasn't going to be a family."

"No one ever built a house alone then, either," said Linkeree.

"That's true. So this is what I decide. The house belongs to Linkeree because he built it alone. *But.* It isn't right for one man alone to have a house, when Ryanno and Hux want to be married and have no house to be together in. So all this winter, until we can build them their own house in the spring, Ryanno and Hux will live in Linkeree's house, and Linkeree will live with us."

Everyone said that it was fair and right, except Linkeree, and he said nothing.

Ryanno and Hux went to Linkeree's house and shouted from the windows, even the little windows high up, but no one was quite as happy as usual because they knew it wasn't their true house.

That night, Linkeree set his house on fire, and then shouted to wake up Hux and Ryanno so they could run outside. "No one will live in the house I built but me!" shouted Linkeree, and then he ran off into the snow. Hux and Ryanno walked barefoot in the snow to get back to First House, and Batta, who had learned the rules of healing, cut off two of Ryanno's toes and one of Hux's fingers, to save their lives.

As for Linkeree, he had stolen an ax and some food, and he was gone in the snow.

How could a man live alone in the snow, with no house and no friend? They were all sure that Linkeree would die. Hux raged that he should die, because of the finger he lost and the toes that Ryanno lost. But Batta said, "A toe is not a life," and in the morning she, too, was gone, with a pan and a dozen potatoes and two blankets made of blue wool.

Kapock was afraid now. Jason would come back and he would say, "How are the people that I left in your care?" And Kapock would answer, "All are well except Hux and Ryanno, who lost their toes and finger, and Linkeree and Batta, who ran off and died together in the snow." He couldn't bear to let things be that way. The toes and finger he couldn't help now. But Batta and Linkeree he could.

He left Sara as the Mayor, though she told him not to go, and he went off with a saw in his hand and a coil of woolen twine around his shoulder and a bag of bread and a cheese slung on his back. "If you die too, how will that help us?" Sara asked, holding Ciel up so Kapock would remember his child.

"I would rather die than have to tell Jason that I let Linkeree and Batta die."

So Kapock searched in the forest for three days before he found them, living in a cold wattle-and-daub shelter leaning against a hill. "We're married," they said, but they were cold and hungry. He gave them some of his cheese and bread, and then together they chose a place on firm ground, but in the shelter of a hill, and they cut switches from a tree and swept away the snow from a section of ground, and all afternoon Kapock and Linkeree and Batta felled and split logs. With the saw Linkeree cut shingles, and in three days the house was built. It was windowless and small, but it was the best they could do in the cold, and it was warm and dry enough inside.

"This house belongs to me as much as you," Kapock said when it was done.

"That's true," said Batta.

"I will give you my share of this house, if you will build Hux the same house you burned. The very house, and you must build it alone. Before you do one thing to make this house larger, you must build a fine house for Hux."

"I can only do that in the spring," said Linkeree. "The work's too fine to hurry it, or do it on soft ground in the snow."

"In the spring is soon enough."

Then Kapock went home, and all that winter he and Sara and Ciel lived in First House, with the New Ones, while Hux and Ryanno lived in Kapock and Sara's own house across the river. Every day Kapock and Sara would cross the river and care for the sheep, but whenever Hux and Ryanno wanted to give back their house, Kapock said no—while Linkeree and Batta had a house of their own, Ryanno and Hux would also have a house. Sara saw the wisdom of what Kapock was trying to do, and so she did not complain. And there was peace.

Jason had not said when he would return. For a long time Kapock hoped for him every day. But spring came, and fields were plowed and planted, and then summer, and trees were felled and houses built. It was near autumn when Jason came again. It was early morning, and Kapock and the dogs and Dor, one of last year's New Ones, were taking the sheep to a meadow in the hills southwest of Heaven City. Dor, who knew the way, was leading. Kapock brought up the rear, crook in hand, watching for stragglers. The sheep were drinking at a brook when he heard footsteps behind him. He turned, and there was Jason.

"Jason," Kapock whispered.

Jason smiled and touched him on the shoulder. "I've seen all that happened, all that was important enough for anyone to remember. And you've done well, Kapock. The quarrel between Linkeree and Hux could have destroyed Heaven City."

"I was afraid that everything I did was wrong."

"Everything you did was right, or as right as anyone could hope for."

"But I didn't know. I wasn't sure."

"No one ever is. You did what felt right to you. It's all we ever do. The way I did when I named you Mayor. It worked pretty well for both of us, didn't it?"

Kapock did not know what to say. "Yesterday my Ciel spoke. He called me by name. It's like you said, Jason—the little ones we make aren't as strong as your Ice People, but they learn, and they grow, just like the young lambs becoming rams and ewes. He said my name."

Jason smiled. "Bring all the people to the west end of First Field, under the arm of Star Tower, fourteen days from today. I'll come then, and bring New Ones."

"Everyone will be glad." And then, "Will you stay?" Stay, so I can be Kapock the shepherd again, instead of Kapock the Mayor.

"I will not," Jason said. "I'll never stay again. A few days, a few weeks if there's a need, but never longer than that. But I'll come every year on the same day, for a few more years at least, to bring New Ones."

"Do I have to be Mayor forever?" asked Kapock.

"No, Kapock. There'll come a time, not too many years from now, when I'll take you with me into the Star Tower, and leave someone else as Mayor. Someone else who doesn't want the job. I'll take you, and then someday, later, I'll bring you back, not a day older than you were before, and you'll see how the world has changed while you slept."

"I'll be Ice again?"

"You'll be Ice again," said Jason.

"And Sara? And Ciel?"

"If they earn it," said Jason.

"Sara will. And Ciel, I'll do my best with Ciel—"

"Enough. Your sheep are waiting. And Dor will wonder who I am. I don't think that he remembers me."

"Fourteen days," said Kapock. "They'll be there, all of them. There are nine houses now, and four children born, and five women growing big. Sara again, she's one of them—"

"I know all that," Jason said. "Good-bye."

He walked away, and left Kapock with the sheep and the dogs and Dor.

Dor's eyes were bright. "That was Jason, wasn't it?" he said. "He talked to you."

Kapock nodded. "Let's get the sheep to the hills, Dor." And he told him tales of Jason all the way.

Lared wrote the story as he sat in bed, with the parchment on a board on his lap. Everyone in the house saw him writing, and the women asked him to read it aloud. It was not really about Jason, and Lared saw no harm in it, and so he read the tale.

Before the end they all took sides, some saying that it was Hux in the right, and some saying that it was Linkeree.

When it was done, Sala asked, "Why did Kapock have to lose his house? He and Sara didn't do anything wrong at all."

Mother answered, "When you love people, you do whatever it takes to make them happy."

If that is true, thought Lared, why doesn't Justice protect us, the way she and the other children of Jason used to?

When Father came in from tending the animals, they told him the story, too, and then asked him the question Sala had asked. "He paid the price," Father said. "Someone has to pay the price." Then he turned to Lared. "As soon as the weather clears, we're taking the sledges out to bring home the trees you marked. We can't do it without you."

"No," said Mother. "He isn't well yet."

"I'll be ready," Lared said.

8

Getting Home

They set out at first light, twenty-two men with eleven teams of horses pulling sledges. Lared led the way, and this year, for the first time since he had begun to mark the trees, he was counted in the total of men. He had marked forty-four trees, four for each team. And Father rode beside him on the foremost team.

One by one they came to the trees that Lared had marked. Two men with axes and saws stopped at the fourth tree. They would cut it, then haul it back to the third tree, cut that and go back to the second, then to the first, and then home, each team—with the surest foresters and the strongest horses saved for last, for they had the farthest to go to bring their timber home. Lared and Father would be last this time. They both had earned it.

Only six of them were still together at nightfall, when they had to make camp. They had brought wattles and poles on the sledges, enough to make a stable for the horses and a large hut for the men. It took only half an hour to set it up—they built the same structure every year, and they practiced doing it in the common field at Midsummer.

"Pretty proud of yourself," said Jason. "Oh, did I startle you?"

Lared looked up. "You wouldn't know what it feels like. No one ever startled you in your life."

"Every now and then."

"What am I supposed to be proud of myself about?"

"Riding at the head of the company. And the way you pointed out the weakening at the top of the mast tree, so they agreed that you had to cut it this year, and not wait for it to be the best mast ever to float down the river—you were magnificent."

"Don't mock me."

"I wasn't. You earned it. Like my first solo in a cruiser. Rites of passage. I've lived a long time, that's all, and yet I still watch the young ones pass through into responsibility, before they realize that irresponsibility was better, and I can't help but love them for it. There's no better moment in your life."

"It was," Lared said, "until you pointed it out."

"Shall I show you how you looked?"

"What do you mean?"

In a moment he saw it before his eyes, supplanting his own vision: himself as Jason had seen him earlier in the day, talking oh-so-gravely with the older men. Only now he saw the half-veiled smiles. All very good-natured—they liked him—but still patronizing. He was still a boy pretending to be a man. And when the vision faded, he was ashamed. He walked away from Jason in the thickening darkness.

"I thought you'd had enough of wandering off in the snow," Jason called.

"You and Justice! You with your visions! Have you seen yourselves!"

"Always," said Jason, walking toward him.

"What do you gain from it? Making me ashamed?"

"Now look at it again."

"No."

But protest was meaningless. Again came a vision, but this time it was his own memory, with the way he felt at the time. Riding at the head of the company, talking business with his father, explaining his decisions about each tree to the listening men. Only now there were his present bitterness and shame like tinted glass, coloring everything darker. He felt again the happiness he had felt all day. Only now he thought himself a fool, and was angry.

"Stop it!" he shouted.

"Lared!" His father's voice rang out from the distant camp. "Is something wrong?"

"No, Father!" Lared called back to him.

"Come on back, then. It's getting dark, if you can't see it!"

Lared could not answer, for again Justice put a vision in his eyes. The same memories of the same day, but this time not through Jason's eyes, nor through his own, but rather himself the way his father saw him. Constantly through the day as

Lared spoke, Father saw that he was foolish, but also remembered him younger, remembered him as a child; remembered, too, himself on such a day. Remembered the boy who clung numbly to a chip of river ice, for the sake of honor or faith or manhood. The love and admiration were so intense that when the vision at last faded Lared's eyes were filled with tears. He had never been a father, but he remembered fatherhood, and he ached for a little child that was gone forever, that he had never held, that had been himself.

"What are you doing to me?" he whispered.

A branch cracked overhead, and snow dribbled down near them.

"This is the last time," Jason answered.

The same scenes, in his own memory again. Only this time he saw himself more clearly than before. He no longer believed the happiness, of course, but neither did he believe the scorn. He saw himself as if from the distance of years. He saw that he was young, but did not hold it against himself. He saw also that he was happy, but he did not wish that he still felt that way. He remembered too well the pain of discovering how foolish he had been. He saw himself more as Father had seen him, as a boy on a path of years, echoing childhood with every move, promising manhood also. And that combination of foolish happiness, shame, and love—meant something. Until then, the memories had meant nothing. But these visions of today had taken on a powerful resonance; his whole life trembled with it. And yet Lared could not think why this day should be so important, after all.

Jason leaned close to him, held him by the shoulders, almost in an embrace. "Were you happy before?"

"Before what?"

"Before we showed you how it really was?"

"Yes. I was happy." And the remembered happiness was somehow stronger than the happiness itself had been.

"And then what?"

"Angry. Ashamed." Was it the pain, then, that made the joy so strong? Was that Jason's lesson? Truth or not, Lared was not grateful. He did not like being carved into whatever shape suited Jason's purpose at the time, jammed in place and wedged like the handle of an ax.

"Now, Lared. What is it that you feel now?" asked Jason.

I've been wounded, and you're using the bloody place to teach me, and if that's what gods are supposed to do, then I wish there were no gods at all. "I don't want you near me." He ran from Jason toward the light of the cookfire.

As he ran, Justice spoke to him comfortingly in his mind. *Joy, Lared. What you feel is joy. The happiness, the pain, the love. All at once. Remember it.*

Get out of my mind! Lared screamed inside himself.

But he lay awake remembering it.

"Lared," said Father, lying beside him. "We were all proud of you today."

Lared did not want to be lied to, and he knew the truth. "The others laughed at me."

Father did not answer at once. "With affection, yes. They like you." A longer silence. "I didn't laugh at you."

"I chose the right trees."

"Yes, Lared."

"Then why did they laugh?"

"Because you were so proud of the first horse. They all rode the first horse once."

"They laughed because I was strutting like a cock in the chickenyard."

"Yes," said Father. "What are you, God? Must everyone always take you seriously?"

It sounded harsh, but Father's hand on his arm told him that it was meant kindly. "Like I said, Lareled. I was proud of you today."

Lared felt Jason's blue eyes burning inside his mind. *I am alone with my father, Jason. Can't I be alone with him?* He felt Justice haunting him, ready to put a veil across his sight and make him see whatever dream she chose. *Because you give them to me, Justice, have I forgotten how to dream?*

What are you, Jason? God, that's what you are. Going into and out of your starship, never aging as your people lived and died. A select few you took with you, and they, too, passed the time and stayed young. Kapock was taken up before his son was grown; Sara, too, left little ones behind. You gave them great prestige, and cut them off from all that they loved. They worshiped you, Jason Worthing, and what did they gain from it? Anyone can tell a lie to children, and win their love. It worked with me.

Ah, whispered Justice in his mind. So you don't like the way that they believed in Jason. You prefer doubt. You prefer those who know what Jason really is.

Lared remembered the one bubble that had been preserved. Garol Stipock. The one man who could remember Capitol, who knew that Jazz Worthing was mortal. A man who had once sought to prove it. You gave him his memory?

What do you do with another man's past? Jason rocked the case of Stipock's bubble in his hands. All of Stipock's past in his hands, and Stipock's living body hot with somec in the corridor, the last of the original colonists, waiting to be wakened.

Before the missile plowed this ship, I was full of plans, how I would deal with three hundred people who wanted to murder me. I had ideas, I remember. Keep them off balance, quarreling with each other, reliant on me for any kind of stability at all. I didn't need to do it after all. Now, instead of keeping them disturbed, I keep the peace. I find the best of them, the wisest, they serve a few years as Mayor and then I bring them here, I save them for when they're needed next. I never asked them to think of me as God, but the honor it gives to those I take into the ship makes Heaven City a safe and stable people. Sixty years so far, safe.

And stagnant.

He tossed the bubble gently into the air, caught it. Stipock wasn't one of the haters. He hadn't wished for my blood, he only wanted what Doon wanted: the breaking of the game. Stipock was one who did not believe. He had believed too much religion as a child. I could not have created a society to gall him more than this one, with their naive faith, their willing compliance with authority. Why do you obey the Mayor? he would ask. Because Jason isn't here, they would answer. Well, why do you obey Jason? he would ask. Because he was the first. Because he made us. Because everything obeys Jason.

Will you tell them, Stipock? Will you teach them all the ways of Capitol? Teach them about stars and planets, bending light and gravity? No, you're not such a fool as to think you can build utter ignorance into true science. You'll see the oxen and the wooden plows, the brasswork and the tin, the faith in

Jason and the peaceful trust in Jason's Mayors, and it won't be physics that you teach them.

It will be revolution.

I would be a fool to wake you up with your memories. Just one more New One, one more infant, the last of all, and you would trust me as faithfully as you trusted in your parents' god, until your disillusionment. But *I* would never disillusion you. I'm what you longed for all your life—someone you could believe in. I know the thoughts of your heart, I never age, I come and go as I like, I produce people from my tower and whatever question you have, I can answer it, and you'll never know my answer isn't truth. I'm the god that will not fail.

But if you have your memory, we will be enemies, and you are the one I fear most of all. Without malice, without a lust for power, not a rival for my people's faith, but an enemy of faith itself. You will undo the stories that they've chosen to believe, change the meaning of everything that happens. They're waiting for you, as they wait in every generation of the world: the young, the resentful almost-men and almost-women who want to move into their parents' places. They were the built-in catalysts in every culture I have found in the ship's computer. No society can stay the same, because the young ones have to *change* things, to show there's a reason for them to be alive. They're waiting for you to come and tell them not to believe.

Jason pressed the clear case between his palms. I will erase you, and you will be mine. No one will know it, life in Heaven City will be better because of it.

But he did not crush the case. He found himself walking back to Stipock's coffin, holding his memory, holding Stipock's childhood in his hands.

He tried to understand why he was going to do it. Some sense of fairness, some idea that you don't steal the past of a man? It was all right for it to happen accidently, it was fine to take advantage of the thieveries of fate, but to do it deliberately would be murder, was that it?

But he had killed before, he had been inside a man's mind at the moment when Jason's missiles took him into the bright tunnel of death. He would do it in a moment, if he thought his people would be better for it. No moral scruples would stop him, if his children needed it.

His children. It was for them that he would put the bubble

in its place, let it dump Stipock's life back into him. Jason did not even know what good would come of it. Perhaps it was a taste of evil that they needed. Someone to do for his stable society just what Doon had done for Capitol. Trouble was, he never had found out how Doon's revolution had turned out.

Who is Mayor? Noyock. Poor Hop—what am I doing to you? Putting a rebellion in your city. Indeed, a rebellion in Noyock's own house. It was a troubling situation as it was. Noyock was here for his second stint as Mayor; he had slept forty years. He was still in his late thirties, physically, and his son Aven was older, in his fifties, going gray. Aven had guessed by now that Jason would not take him into the tower. How could he? Aven was a stubborn, vengeful man, the sort that would never do as Mayor. Now Aven was taking it out on Hoom, his youngest son, ruling him as cruelly as he would have ruled the city, given the chance, proving over and over again how right Jason was not to take him up. Hoom was another matter. He was Noyock again, he had ability, if his adolescence didn't ruin him.

Last year, when he had first realized how bad the situation was, Jason had toyed with the idea of taking Hoom from Aven's house. But the good of all was more important than the good of one—if he once violated the family, now in the third generation, the echoes would be heard throughout history. Hoom would pay for the safety of Heaven City. It was cruel, but necessary.

So why am I bringing Stipock out, if the good of the whole is more important than any individual? Jason hesitated again before starting to waken his sleeping enemy. How dare I do this, when I don't even know why I'm doing it?

Yet he knew that he must do it, and could only trust his own blind impulse. Any other mind he could probe and understand. With his own, he was as helpless as everyone else. For some reason, not in spite of but because of his love for the people of his city, he must let Stipock loose to do what he inevitably would do.

He depressed the levers, then leaned back against the other wall to wait for Garol Stipock to wake up. Now that he had committed himself to giving Stipock his memories, he had to figure out a way to explain to him why the colony was as it was, and why it had taken Jason sixty years to wake him.

• • •

It was almost sunrise when they brought the boat to shore.
Stipock was almost naked and dripping wet and a little cold,
and the others laughed at him as he shivered, but it was ex-
hilarated laughter, and they loved him for what they had done
this morning. Stipock had made a hobby of sailing on the great
indoor lake of Sector ff3L, and it felt good to swim again, even
if the river was a little silty. But it was not swimming and
boating *again* that pleased him. The joy of it was its firstness:
never before had a boat rested on the waters of this world;
never before had these children seen a human being swim.

"You will *teach* us!" Dilna demanded. "If I'm going out on
this boat again I want to know how to swim!"

"If I can find time between road-building and shingle-cutting
and answering your ridiculous *questions* all the time—" Stipock
said.

Wix laughed at him. "If we didn't ask questions you'd talk
anyway. You're a talker, Stipock."

"But Hoom here is the only real listener."

Hoom smiled but said nothing. Just sat by the boat, holding
the wood that he himself had worked and shaped to do what
Stipock had said that it must do. There were few carpenters to
match Hoom's handwork. He was slow, but when he was
finished the boat was tight as a barrel, and scarcely needed the
coat of gum they gave it. Stipock had thought of starting with
a canoe, but it was too easy to spill from one, and the young
ones couldn't swim. If he hadn't had Hoom as a carpenter, he
couldn't have done it.

"Well," said Dilna, "when do we hold a public demonstra-
tion?"

"Today," said Wix. "Right now. Let's call the whole of
Heaven City to see us ride on the water like a woodchip."

Dilna poked at the boat with her toe. "It *is* a woodchip."
She grinned at Hoom to show him that she meant no harm by
it. He smiled back. Stipock enjoyed seeing how much he was
in love with her. It was one of the best things about being with
young people—everything was for the first time, everything
was new, they were still young enough to believe in the future.
No one had ever plucked them up from their life, thrown them

into a colony ship, and sent them out to the edge of the universe in the power of a starship pilot who liked the idea of being God.

"I think we should wait to show everybody," Stipock said. "I'm supposed to meet with Noyock this morning. Let me talk to him about it. Besides, it isn't enough just to go out on the water with it. We have to *go* somewhere. The other side, I think. *Your* father should go with us, Hoom."

Why did Hoom look alarmed? "I don't think so," he said.

"Imagine meadowlands that went on forever. Room for millions of cattle to graze."

"Millions," said Dilna. "That's what I like best about you, Stipock. You always think small." Then, as usual, Dilna brought them all back to reality. "We have to get home now. It's morning, and people will wonder where we are."

Stipock left first, with Wix, because he could tell Hoom wanted to hang back and be alone with Dilna for a while. Wix took his leave as they crested Noyock's hill, and went on down into the city. Stipock walked up the dirt road to the house where Mayor Noyock lived.

It was hard for Stipock to take the Mayor seriously. He had seen him too often before, on Capitol, Jazz Worthing's oily, ubiquitous agent, getting into every loop, as if by appearing often he could become more than ten percent of a man. Everything was different here, of course. Hop Noyock had never been sycophant or a parasite, as far as *he* remembered, anyway. Stipock had seen the wound in the ship, the damaged coffins, the ruined bubbles. He knew that it meant a fresh start for everyone, to come into the world empty-minded again.

But not quite open-minded, after all. Because Jason was present in every part of the colony, Jason's mind was imprinted all over so-called Heaven City. Jazz Worthing, the starship pilot, had finally got what he longed for: absolute worship by backward, debased peasants. He had made no effort at all to teach them what the human mind was capable of. What the universe itself was like. Just a mumbo-jumbo of religion, like an ancient emperor trying to convince his people that he was a god. Only Jason had done much better than most. He had the miracles to prove it. Only Stipock knew that his apparent agelessness was nothing but somec, that his wisdom was nothing but a decent education in Capitol's school system, that the miracles he wrought were all machinery hidden in the Star Tower—no, the colony ship; they've got me saying it, too.

Stipock knew what was in store for him. Jason had put his memory in place and let him come into the colony unfettered. Stipock could think of only one reason for such an act: the egomaniacal Jazz Worthing still needed an audience, still needed the people of Capitol to worship him. Stipock was the only person available to watch and then applaud. You'll get damn little cheering out of me, he told himself with anticipation. I've spent my life undoing pompous, dogmatic, self-serving tyrants like you, and I'll do it again. I'll do it the way I've done it every time before: with the truth. It's the one thing that the Jazz Worthings of the universe can't bear for long.

Stipock was not naive. He knew what he was up against. Sixty years of Jason's lies and miracles, his power and authority had made this a rigid, powerful theocracy, with the Mayor like Jason's archangel standing guard at the tree of life. Jason still has the power of the rulers of Capitol: he still controls somec, and if he wishes he can leave me behind as he and his chosen servants skip like stones across the face of time. But while Jason slept, Stipock could do his own work of undoing. I will unweave your little fabric, Jazz, I will ravel it out before you wake again. Three years you've given me, or so you said, before you'll come again. See what I can do in that amount of time.

Jason had inadvertently given him a powerful tool. Because Stipock was the last of the New Ones, because he had let Stipock come from the ship walking and talking, with a store of knowledge and a vocabulary as elevated above the rest of the colony as Jason's own, some of Jason's aura of divinity had fallen upon Stipock. The most pathetically ardent of Jason's worshippers hardly dared argue openly with Stipock, his prestige was so high. It made him free.

Till now. No doubt Noyock had called for him today to try to silence him. Well, Noyock, you can try. But already I have wakened enough people that your authority is shaken, and any punishment you try to measure out will only martyr me in the eyes of those who have realized the backwardness of Heaven City. I've taken the young people out on the water and shown them how to swim. They won't be trapped here between rivers anymore.

Still, Stipock was honest enough to admit to himself as he knocked at the door of Noyock's house that he was afraid. Noyock was not just a creature of Jason's shared prestige. It wasn't just the office of Mayor that made him powerful. Noyock had been Mayor before, for seven years, and on his own he had done much to change and improve the life of Heaven City. He was the one who had started the little villages miles away; he was the one who had divided up the land so each family farmed their own, and the common work was limited to road-making, lumbering, and harvest. The result had been much greater prosperity, a spurt of growth, and now, in his second term as Mayor, Noyock was still energetic, a good leader, with the trust and confidence of everyone whose trust was worth having. Including Stipock. Stipock's contempt for him as Jazz's agent did not make him blind to the fact that Noyock was a benevolent despot. Unfortunately, benevolent despots were the worst kind: it was so much harder to convince people they ought to get rid of them.

The door opened. It was Aven, Noyock's son. He greeted Stipock coldly. "Come in."

"Thank you, Aven. How are things going?"

"Your hair is wet," Aven said.

"It was in water," Stipock answered.

Aven studied him for a measured moment. "You've built your boat, haven't you?"

"I'm not a carpenter," Stipock said. It was a stupid thing to say, he realized, for it instantly incriminated Aven's son. There was no better carpenter in Heaven City than Hoom. And from the anger in Aven's face, Stipock realized Hoom had lied when he said his father didn't mind all that much. The man looked capable of killing in his rage.

"Because my father built this house many years ago," said Aven, "before Jason took him into the Star Tower, I allow him to use two rooms upstairs to conduct his business as Mayor. That means I must permit any sort of scum to come into my house—but only long enough to walk up the stairs and into the Mayor's office."

"Things are going well for me, too," Stipock answered. He

waved cheerfully at Aven as he went up the stairs. Hoom was right—his father was as pleasant company as a boar in the woods.

Noyock's office door was open, and Stipock could see him, bent over a table, writing on a piece of sheepskin. Stipock thought of a paper mill, using rag and pulp, and decided there wasn't need yet for so much paper; nor were there people enough to spare from other work for such a task. Still, it might be worth teaching people how to do it. Parchment was so primitive, and only one fair-sized sheet of it from each animal killed.

"Oh, Stipock," said Noyock. "You should have said something."

"It's all right. I was thinking."

Noyock ushered him into the room. Stipock glanced at what Noyock had been writing. "The history," Noyock said. "Every month I take a few days to write what happened that was important."

"What *you* thought was important."

"Well, of course. How can I write what *you* thought was important? I'm not you. Jason settled that years ago—anyone who wants to can write a history. A few of them have. It's always interesting to compare them. It's like we lived in different worlds. But the Mayor usually knows more of what's going on. After all, what's important is usually a problem, and the problems always end up coming to the Mayor. It's been that way since the time of Kapock."

"There are some things you don't know about."

"Fewer than you think," said Noyock. "For instance, I know that you've been telling the children that Jason shouldn't choose the Mayor, that everyone ought to vote on it."

"Yes, I've said that."

"I've been giving that a lot of thought. And it occurs to me that if we did that, we'd usually choose someone that we liked. The trouble is, the Mayor has to make a lot of decisions that no one likes. Then no one will want him to be Mayor anymore, and so either we'd keep changing Mayors or we'd choose Mayors who govern very badly but never offend anybody. Now, before you start arguing with me, Stipock, let me tell you that those are just my thoughts of the moment, and I wonder if you'd be kind enough to think about them at least as long as I thought about your ideas before trying to answer them."

Noyock smiled, and Stipock couldn't help smiling back. "You're a clever bastard, you know."

Noyock raised an eyebrow. "Bastard? I wish you and Jason would write down all these words that none of the rest of us knows, so we can learn them."

"It's just as well. A lot of them aren't worth knowing."

Noyock leaned back in his chair. "Stipock, I've been very interested in what you've done in the six months since you've been here. You work hard at every task that's been put to you. No one calls you lazy, and no one calls you a fool. But I keep hearing complaints about you. Mostly from the older people. They're concerned because of the things that you've been teaching their children."

"I won't stop," Stipock said.

"Oh, I don't want you to stop," said Noyock.

"You don't?" asked Stipock, surprised.

"No, I just want to make it official. So they'll stop complaining about it. I want you to be a teacher all the time. I want it to be your work, the way the sheep are Ravvy's and the cattle are Aven's. I've calculated that we'll give you a plot of land and require your students to farm it for you. They'll pay in sweat for what you put into their heads."

Stipock was genuinely surprised—and puzzled. "You *want* me to teach them? Do you have any notion of what I say?"

"Oh, yes. You tell them how the world is a spinning globe, and the sun is a star. You tell them how sickness is the work of tiny animals, how the brain is the seat of the mind, and your story that Jason is only one of many who drive Star Towers through the sky has filled the children's minds with interesting speculations about what other worlds might be like, with all the miracles you talk about. It has little practical value, of course, but I'm not afraid of what will happen with the children thinking things that none of us have ever thought before. I think it's more to be encouraged than discouraged. But that isn't why I want you to be our teacher."

"Why, then?"

"You know things that will solve problems for us. You've talked of a water-powered mill to grind the grain—I want to build it, and I want you to teach some of the children the principles behind it so we can make more. You've talked of boats, so water-tight that we could cross the Great River and sail out to the ocean."

"You know about the ocean?"

"Of course."

"The children don't."

"Those of us who have been in the Star Tower—Jason shows us the maps of the world, where the grasslands are, the forests, the metals hidden in the earth, the great rivers and the seas. He's shown us the computer and the pictures it draws in the air, he's shown us the coffins where the Ice People sleep. He showed me *you*, in fact, and warned me he might waken you this time."

"But you've told no one about it."

"There's been no need."

"But—they don't even know the shape and size of the world they live on."

"If they ask, I tell them. No one asks."

"Why should they ask? No one knows that you know."

"Well, *you* haven't kept your knowledge a secret, and that's all that matters now. Build your boats, Stipock, and take the children who adore you across the river. I'll help you—I can keep the frightened parents at bay. Start a new village there, with a river that only those who've learned to drive your boats can cross, and give these children a chance to become men and women without their parents breathing down their necks."

It was not at all what Stipock had expected. He had looked for a reprimand; he had come steeled for a quarrel. "Don't you realize how that will dilute your power, Noyock?"

Noyock nodded gravely. "I know very well. But Heaven City is growing larger all the time. Jason told me to separate my work and give bits of it to the best men and women for the job. I've put Worinn in charge of the building of roads, and he's doing well. Young Dilna is a master of tools, since everyone knows she does fine metalwork better than anybody else. Poritil is harvestmaster and keeper of the grain—"

"And doing well. I didn't realize how new they were. I thought Jason set the system up."

"He suggested it. I only carried it out. But you—he didn't tell me what to do with you."

"But you said he warned you."

"That the children would follow you, and I was not to interfere, except—"

"Except?"

"That the peace and law of Heaven City must be maintained."

"And what does that mean?"

"That means that when you take the children across the river, Stipock, you will not teach them to disobey the law. I know more about the life of the Ice People than you think. Jason told us how they thought nothing of marriage, and coupled where they pleased, and killed their children—"

"I can see he gave you a neutral picture of it—"

"We need our sons and daughters, Stipock. I was here when there were only fifteen of us, besides Jason. I was here when the first babies grew, before they were ever men and women. Now there are nearly a thousand. Now there are people who can spend all their working time at the forge or at the loom, so that those who are best at a job don't have to drop their work to weed the fields or shear the sheep. We're free now, to follow our desires. We do not need two or three or four separate cities, each one doing for itself what we could all do more easily together. We are too few for that. And Jason warned me of another thing."

"What was that?" Stipock expected it to be something about him.

"War. Do you know the word?"

Stipock smiled tightly. "It was Jason's main line of work."

"The closest we've come to it was the burning of Linkeree's house, back in the first year of Kapock. Jason told me stories of what it could be like. I believe him."

"So do I."

"The seeds are there, Stipock. The seeds of war are in this house. My grandson Hoom hates his father, and my son Aven has done his best to earn that hate. Look among the young ones, Stipock. Find the best of them. Not a hot-headed fool, like Billin. Perhaps Coren, though she tends to play favorites. Perhaps Wix—calm, not quick to anger. Or Hoom himself, though I fear he's learned too much of bitterness, and not enough of love. Before you take the children across the river, come to me and we'll name a Little Mayor for the other side."

"No."

Noyock smiled. "You have another suggestion?"

"On the other side, if the new town is to be settled by the people who believe in me—and they aren't children, Noyock, not anymore—then we'll choose our leader *our* way."

"Interesting. Shall we compromise? Let's choose a Little Mayor for the first year, and after that year we can let the people choose a leader by their own voice."

"I knew you before, Noyock, knew who you were, at least."

"I don't want to hear about it. I have trouble enough being who I am now, without being troubled with thoughts of who I once was in another life."

"No, I didn't mean to dwell on it. I just wanted to tell you— I never would have believed that you were the same man. Whatever else might be wrong with the way that Jason has things going here, it's made a good man out of Hop Noyock."

"But *you*, Stipock, you *are* the same man you were before."

Stipock grinned. "And no better, is that it? Well, I'm good enough for this—when the man in power is as flexible as you, it's hard to hate you. But I can promise you that if you let me do what you yourself have just proposed, in ten years the office of Mayor will be elected, and the laws will be made by the people of this place, and not by the dictates of a one-man judge and king and legislator."

Noyock laughed and shook his head. "Not only do you use words I've never heard of before, but you even pretend to be able to see the future. Don't overreach yourself, Stipock. Even Jason cannot see the future."

But Stipock knew that change would come, and knew that he was giving shape to that change already. Noyock was giving it to him as a gift. A town of his own, with a river between his people and the Mayor; authority to teach as he saw fit, and begin to modernize this backward place; and a promise of democracy to come. I'll hold him to that, thought Stipock. And when Jason comes back, he'll see what a little dose of truth and freedom can do, even to the medieval society he created.

He took his leave of Noyock and opened the door to leave. Downstairs he could hear shouting.

"Will you do what I forbid?"

And the sound of a blow.

"Will you do what I forbid?"

Silence. And another blow. A crash of chairs falling. "I ask you, boy! Will you do what I forbid?"

From behind him Stipock heard Noyock emerge from his office and close the door. "I think your son is beating your grandson, Noyock."

"And I think you know the cause of it," said Noyock.

Stipock turned and answered abruptly. "Hoom told me that he had consent!"

"Are you so wise, Stipock, and yet you can't tell from his face when a boy is lying? No, don't go downstairs. Not yet. It's between father and son."

From downstairs: "Will you do what I forbid? Answer, Hoom!"

Esten, Aven's wife, began to plead with her husband to stop hitting the boy.

"He's beating the boy. Is that part of what parents are allowed to do?"

"If the child is small, we take it away to save its life. But Hoom is old enough that he can't be beaten without his own consent. Listen—he's telling his mother to leave them alone. He doesn't want protection, Stipock."

"Answer me!"

From downstairs Hoom cried out in pain. "Yes, Father, I *will* do what you forbid! I will sail on the river, I will go where I like, you were a fool to forbid it—"

"What do you call me! What do you—"

"No! Don't touch me again, Father! You've beaten me for the last time!"

"Oh, do you think you're a match for me?"

Noyock brushed passed Stipock and headed down the stairs. *"Now* we step in," he murmured as he passed. Stipock followed him.

They got there just as Aven picked up a broken chair leg and began advancing on his son, who stood defiantly in a corner.

"Enough," said Noyock.

Aven stopped. "It's none of your affair, Father."

It seemed somehow pathetic that this fifty-year-old man called Noyock, who was fifteen years younger in appearance, *Father.*

"It became my affair when you laid a hand on the boy,"

Noyock said, "and it became an affair for all of Heaven City when you took a weapon in your hand. Is Hoom a badger that you need to kill to protect your herd of rabbits?"

Aven lowered the chair leg. "He threatened me."

"When you are striking him and he merely offers to strike you back, Aven, I think the threat is hardly out of line."

"What right do you have, as my father or as Mayor, to interfere with what goes on within my own home?"

"An interesting point," said Noyock, "to which I offer this solution. Hoom, I have just asked Stipock to build boats, larger ones than the one that lies hidden at the river's edge."

Noyock is a deep one, Stipock realized. He gave me no hint that he knew that we had already built a boat.

"You are the only carpenter to see that the boats are built well and safely. I am making it a project for the whole city, so the boats will belong to us all—but I place you in charge of the building."

Hoom's eyes widened. "For my man's share?"

"For your master's share," answered Noyock.

"Master's share!" cried Aven. "You might as well say he's not my son!" It would have been bad enough to give Hoom a man's share, enough entitlement to food and clothing that he could live on his own. But a master's share was enough for him to build a house, and it freed him from a young man's constant liability to be called to road work or timbering. Indeed, Noyock had called it a city project, which meant Hoom would have the power to call others to work some part of the seven weeks of seven hours that each man and woman owed the city. Noyock had elevated Hoom above his father. It was Hoom's freedom from his father's house and his father's rule.

It was also Aven's humiliation before his son. And Noyock knew that he was doing it. "When you took that chair leg in your hand, Aven, you declared that he was not your son. I only finish properly what you so badly began. Stipock, these things take effect immediately—would you help Hoom take his clothing from his father's house, and let him live with you until he finds a wife or builds a house?"

"I will," said Stipock. "Gladly."

Aven silently walked out of the room, brushing Esten out of the way. The woman came in and took her father-in-law by the hand. "Noyock, for my son I'm glad," she said. "But for my husband—"

"Your husband likes to wield authority he doesn't have," said Noyock. "I raised nine daughters and one son. I have concluded that I'm a better father of girls than of boys." He turned to Hoom. "What are you waiting for?"

Stipock followed Hoom up the stairs. It didn't take long to get everything that Hoom owned. Three shirts, two pairs of trousers, winter boots and a winter coat, gloves, a fur hat—it all wrapped easily inside the coat and made a bundle under Stipock's arm. Hoom took the only other things he prized: the saw and the adz that Dilna had made for him, the work that Noyock had seen before he made her master of the tools. Stipock marveled at how little Hoom possessed, how little any of them owned. How pitiful—a carpenter forced to use tools of bronze, when there was iron to be had in the world, if only Jason cared to bring his colony out of the dark ages.

That is the best gift I can give these people, Stipock thought. I can take them south to the desert land, where the trees have taproots two hundred meters long, I can take them there and let them mine the iron that lies locked in cliffs just waiting to be taken, the only iron in the world in easy reach, and I will give them tools and machines and bring them out of darkness into light.

Hoom stopped at the door of his room and looked back into it.

"A house of your own soon enough," Stipock said.

"It was this house I wanted to belong in," Hoom whispered. "He hates me now, and I'll never have a chance again to make it right."

"Give him time to see you as a man on your own, Hoom, and he'll come around, you'll see."

Hoom shook his head. "Not me. He won't forgive me." He turned his face toward Stipock and smiled. "I look too much like Grandfather, don't you see? I never had a chance here."

Hoom turned and walked away. Stipock followed him down the stairs and out of the house, saying to himself, Remember that Hoom sees more than anyone thinks he sees.

• • •

On the morning of Midsummer Day, Hoom and Dilna left their house, and with every other man and woman and child of Stipock's city, they climbed aboard a boat and let the southwest wind carry them against the current to the landing place at Linkeree Bay. There were nine boats now, and Hoom had built them all; and because of his boats there were cattle grazing on the broken meadows to the north, and a new tin mine with a richer vein than any they had had before, and above all, Stipock's city, where Wix was Little Mayor because the citizens had voted for him themselves. All because Hoom could make a boat that was tight enough to hold water out. He looked at the others, in his own boat, in the other boats strung out along the river, and he said to them silently, I gave this to you with my own hands. These boats, this river, the wind in the sails, they are who I am in Heaven City.

And Stipock gave them all to me, when he taught me how a boat could be.

And Dilna gave it all to me, when she made the tools that fit my hand.

And Grandfather gave it all to me, when he set me free of Father.

So in their way, they also made these boats. But between them and the water, I am. These boats are myself, and someday they will take me to the sea.

"You're quiet," Dilna said.

"I'm always quiet."

Little Cammar was nursing. "The wind over the water makes him hungry," Dilna said. "The wind makes me want to shout. But you—the water makes you still."

Hoom smiled. "Plenty of chances to shout today, when we vote."

Dilna tossed her head. "Do you think that it will pass?"

"Grandfather says it will. If all of us from Stipock's city come and vote for it, then it will pass. We'll have a council to make our laws, and I have no doubt, Dilna, that you'll end up a member of it, shouting at people to your heart's content."

Wix shouted from the tiller. "Stop talking and get ready for shore!"

Dilna started to pry Cammar's mouth away from her breast. Hoom stopped her. "You don't have to do every job, every time. There are enough of us to pull the boat ashore without interrupting Cammar's breakfast." Then he jumped over the side, rope in hand, and splashed ahead, pulling the boat into the channel it had dug for itself on previous landings. The others quickly joined him, and soon the boat was firmly aground. On *their* side of the river, they had built floating platforms tied to shore, and they moored the boats in the water, without having to get their feet wet. But the people on the Heaven City shore wouldn't build such docks, or even allow them to be built. "If you want to live across the water," they said, "you shouldn't mind getting wet." Just one more of the reasons why Grandfather's compromise had been so hard to reach—there had been so much vindictiveness over the two years that Stipock's city had existed. Petty things, like when a group of older people had demanded that Noyock not count roadwork and land-clearing on the Stipock side of the river against the seven weeks of seven hours. Father had been part of that. And the long quarrel over whether Dilna should be allowed to carry tools across the water—that had been Father's idea from the start, and he began it right after Dilna married Hoom. He couldn't bear the thought that Hoom would have children of his own, that Hoom was really free of him at last.

But you can't hurt me now, Father. I have Dilna for my wife, and Wix and Stipock for my friends, I have my child, my house, my tools, and above all, my boats. That was the one thing they hadn't argued with—when Hoom decided to locate his boatyard on Stipock's side of the river. "I hate the sight of the things," Father had said. "Build them under water, if you ask me."

They walked together up the road. Of course no carts were sent to greet them, and no horses. Hoom could almost hear his father saying, "They have horses and carts of their own on the other side of the river, why should they use ours?" But it was all right. They were all friends, or almost all, and the exceptions were tolerable. Billin, for instance, with his sharp tongue and his love of quarreling—but Hoom knew how to avoid him, most of the time. Today, for instance, Billin was off with the dozen or so friends who thought that he was wise. They walked behind the rest, no doubt plotting something absurd, like how to climb up into the Star Tower and bring Jason down, or some such thing.

At the crest of Noyock's hill they could look down the way

they came and see their boats on the shore, then look the other way and see the Star Tower, rising still higher than they were, even here on the top of the hill, a vast, massive thing of stark white, so pure that in winter it almost disappeared, and now, in summer, it dazzled in the sunlight.

And at the foot of the Star Tower, there was Firstfield, where two-and-a-half years ago Jason had brought them Stipock. Stipock, who feared no one, not even Jason. Stipock, who had opened up the world to them. Stipock, who was even greater than Grandfather.

For an hour in Firstfield they talked again, as Noyock again explained to them all the agreement he had worked out over these last months, despite the quarrels, despite the ones who insisted that the only solution if the "children" would not come home was to divide the world at the river, and have no more to do with each other. The compromise was simple and elegant, like Dilna's tools, which were beautiful because they worked. All of Heaven City was divided into sections: Heaven City, Stipock's city, Linkeree's bay, Wien's forge, Hux's mills, Kapock's meadow, and Noyock's hill. Each separate group had some authority to decide their own way, and each would choose someone to sit in Council, where with the Mayor they would decide the laws, and try offenders, and decide disputes between the towns. "We are too many now," said Noyock at the end, "too many for one man like me to know everyone and decide everything. But even with these changes, *because* of these changes, we are still one people, and when Jason returns after harvest, he will find that we found a way to settle our differences without hatred, and without division."

It was a hopeful speech. It promised much, and it was plain that Noyock believed in it. Hoom believed it, too.

Then the vote was taken, and Billin and his friends voted with Aven and the others who hated Stipock's city, and the compromise failed.

The meeting broke up in chaos. For an hour afterward, the people of Stipock's city quarreled and argued. It was finally clear that Billin would settle for nothing less than complete separation, and when he took to calling Wix a dog because he always barked when Noyock told him to, Wix declared the meeting over and started up the hill. Hoom and Dilna at once followed him, with Cammar in Hoom's arms. So it was that they were the first to crest Noyock's hill, the first to see the ships on fire.

They cried out and called the others to help, but it was too late. Many of them worked, trying to get water up onto the boats, but it was too late, and the fire burned too hot for them to get very close, and Hoom never bothered at all. He just sat on the shore, Cammar in his lap, watched the flames dancing above the water, and thought, You have burned me up, you have killed me on the water, Father and whoever helped you bring the flame. You have undone all that I have ever done, and I am dead.

Hours later, exhausted, their boats mere skeletons of blackened wood along the shore, they all watched the sun go down and talked dispiritedly of what they ought to do.

"We can build new ships," Dilna said. "I'm still the master of tools, and Hoom still knows how it's done. You know that Noyock will allow us. Our enemies can't stop us!"

"It takes three months to build a ship."

"The cows will go unmilked," someone answered.

"The gardens will go to seed."

"The cattle on the meadows will go wild."

"Where will we live for the months of building?"

"With our parents?"

And then, amid the weary, hopeless anger, came Billin's voice. "Where in Jason's law is our protection? We trusted Noyock, but he didn't have the power to save us, did he? If we're to be protected then we must protect ourselves!"

Wix tried to silence him. "It was you that did this, voting against us."

"Do you think that made a difference? They planned this before the meeting ever began. Fice and Aven, Orecet and Kree—they knew that this would be their one chance, the one time that every one of us would come, that all our boats would be here, and no one back in Stipock's city to sail across and bring us home. They burned our only road home. And I say we ought to answer them in kind!"

For once, Hoom agreed with Billin. What else was there to do? Nothing would undo the harm that this had done them. It was Father again, just when I thought that I was free.

The talk got wilder and angrier as the night came on. They built fires on the beach, and their friends from Heaven City came to them and offered food and beds for the night. One by one the families went away, leaving behind only the angriest, only those who still cared to hear Billin talk of hate and vengeance.

"Come with me," Dilna said. "Roun and Ul have offered us a place to sleep, and Cammar and I need the rest."

"Then go," said Hoom.

She waited for a while longer, hoping he would come. But he stayed, and finally she left, and at last there were only a dozen of them gathered at the fires on the beach, and the moon was setting in the west, so the darkest of the night was soon to come.

It was then that Hoom finally raised his voice to be heard.

"All you do is talk," he said to Billin. "All you do is talk how they'll pay. I say we answer them as simply as we can. They used fire to steal our homes from us. What right do they have to sleep content in their own homes, after what they did to us?"

"Burn Heaven City?" Billin asked, incredulous. Even he had not thought of something as insane as that.

"Not Heaven City, fool," Hoom said. "Were they all consenting to the fire? Justice is all I want. It was my father who did this. You know it's true: my father who hated me so much that he would burn my boats."

So they pried off boards from the half-burnt boats, water-soaked on one end, easily alight on the other, and carried them a roundabout way up the hill, so they'd not be seen from the city. Hoom led the way, because the dogs knew him.

But someone was awake and waiting for them as they passed behind the stables, where the horses stamped at the smell of fire.

"Don't do this," Noyock said.

Hoom said nothing.

Noyock looked past him to the others. "Don't do this. Give me time to find those who burned your boats. They'll be punished. We'll turn all the resources of Heaven City to build new boats for you. It won't take months, but weeks, and in a few days Stipock assures me we can have a small boat so a few of you can cross and tend the animals."

It was Wix who answered him—at heart he still hoped for compromise, probably. "What sort of punishment will *you* give the ones who did this?"

"If we can be sure who did it, then the punishment is in the law—they lose their property, and all they own is given to you."

Billin spat. "And of course all you have to do is ask who did it, and they'll step right forward, won't they?"

Noyock shook his head. "If they won't admit it, Billin, then Jason will be here in four more months. You will have long since gone back to your homes, and he will settle it. I promise you, he'll have no tolerance for what they did. But if you do this tonight, he'll have no more tolerance for you. What kind of justice is this? What if you burn the house of an innocent man?"

"He's right," someone murmured. "We don't know for *sure*."

But Hoom said, "If we burn *this* house, Noyock, I think it won't be an innocent man who suffers."

"It'll be an innocent woman, then, your mother. And me. I live there."

Billin laughed. "That's all he's thinking of. His own roof."

"No, Billin. I'm thinking of you. Tonight all Heaven City is outraged; their sympathy is with you. But if you come and burn a house in the night, you'll lose every friend you have, because they'll all be afraid that sometime in the night *their* house will burn, too."

Hoom took his grandfather by the shirt, and pushed him back against the stable wall. "Don't talk anymore," he said.

"It's the Mayor," someone whispered, aghast that Hoom would touch him.

"He knows who it is," Billin said. "Hoom doesn't have the courage." And Billin stepped up, pushed Hoom aside, and struck Noyock a blow in the jaw, jamming his head back into the wall. Noyock slumped and fell to the ground.

"What are you doing?" Wix demanded.

Billin whirled on him. "What is Noyock to us?"

"Stipock told us that if we strike a man, then his friends will only strike us back. No one said anything about coming to blows, like children playing in the grass."

Hoom didn't hear anymore of the argument. He took a sheaf of long straw from inside the stable door. The horses looked in fear at the torch in his hand. "Not for you," he murmured, and strode from the stable to the house. The others fell silent when they saw him go, and some of them, at least, soon followed him. Hoom went in through the kitchen door, set the straw and some of the cookfire wood near the curtains in the big room with the table. The room where Aven had struck him for the last time. He did not hesitate—when the kindling was ready, he put the torch to it. The flames erupted at once, and the curtains soon caught. It was hot enough that Hoom had to step back right away, and step back again a moment later. The fire quickly caught on the timbers of the house, and the smoke rushed along the ceiling toward the opening of the stairs.

Wix stood behind him. "Come on, Hoom. We've got fires well set outside, too—it's time to give the alarm to them."

"No," said Hoom.

"We didn't bargain to kill anybody," Wix said.

Father killed *me*, Hoom answered silently.

"Your wife and son are alive," Wix said. "Don't let it be said that someone besides you gave the alarm to save your mother's life. Don't let it be said that you wanted your father dead."

Hoom shuddered. What was I doing? What am I? He ran to the foot of the stairs and shouted, "Fire! Fire, wake up! Come out!"

Wix joined in the shouting, and when no one came from the rooms upstairs, they ran up. Smoke must be seeping through the tops of the bedroom doors. He ran to his father's room and opened the door. His mother was staggering from the bed, coughing, brushing smoke away with her hands, trying to see. Hoom took her, led her out, rushed her down the stairs. The other end of the house downstairs was all aflame. "Who else is in the house?" Hoom demanded.

Mother shook her head. "Just Aven and Biss."

"Father wasn't in bed," he said.

"I made him—I made him sleep somewhere else," she said. "He burned your boats," she said. Then all at once she realized. "You set this fire! You burned my house!"

But by then he had her out the door. He rushed back in. Wix had Biss and was carrying her down the stairs. "Where's Father!" Hoom shouted.

"I didn't see him!" Wix shouted back. Hoom pushed by him and ran back up. Flames were already lapping around the edges of the stairwell, and the door of his parents' bedroom was bright with flame. The fire was spreading faster than Hoom had expected. He could see the flames coming in from the windows now, spreading across the ceilings of each room in turn. Father wasn't in his own room, wasn't in Biss's—of course not, you fool, Wix would have seen him!—wasn't in Noyock's room.

"Come down, Hoom! He isn't there!" Wix shouted from downstairs.

Hoom ran to the head of the stairs. The stairway itself was on fire, at the edges.

"Come down before it's too late!" Wix was standing at the front door. The porch was also on fire now.

"Is he down there?"

"If he were in the house he'd be awake by now!" shouted Wix.

So they hadn't found him. He must be here. Hoom opened the door of Noyock's office. The flames leaped out at him when he opened the door, singeing his hair, catching his pants on fire. But he didn't stop to beat out the flames. Only one room left—his own. He forced his way down the little hallway, kicked in his door. This room hadn't caught fire as badly as the others, but it was thick with smoke. His father lay coughing on the floor.

"Help me," he said.

Hoom took him by the hand and tried to drag him to the door, but Aven was too large and heavy for him. So he took him under the arms and tried to lift him. "Get up!" he shouted. "I can't carry you! Get up and walk!"

Aven finally understood, and staggered to his feet, clung to his son as he led him from the room. Hoom rushed him as fast as he could toward the stairs, but as they passed the open door of Noyock's office, Aven pulled away from him. "The history!" he shouted. "Father will kill me, Father will kill me!" He staggered toward the door. The pages of the history were already curling with flame. Hoom tried to hold him back, shouted that it was too late, but Aven only knocked him down and stumbled into the room. Hoom got up again in time to see the flames reach out to greet Aven as he clutched at the parchments and screamed and screamed. "I'm sorry," he cried. He turned to face Hoom through the doorway, his clothing all afire, and screamed again, "I'm sorry!"

Then he fell backward onto the burning floor, just as someone grabbed Hoom by the ankle and pulled him to the stairs. Desperate hands took him and carried him outside. But all Hoom could think of was the sight of his father in the fire, clutching the burning parchment, screaming "I'm sorry" as the flames uncovered his heart.

Lared awoke sobbing, his father holding him close, whispering, "It's all right, Lared. Nothing's wrong, Lared, it's all right."

Lared gasped at the sight of his father's face, then clung to him. "Oh, I dreamed!"

"Of course you did."

"I saw a father—a father dying, and I was afraid—"

"Just a dream, Lared."

Lared breathed deeply, tried to calm himself. He looked around and saw that the other men were also awake, looking at him curiously. "Just a dream," he explained to them.

But it was not just a dream. It was a true story, and a terrible one, and when the other men finally looked away, Lared gripped Father's hand and held it to his lips and whispered, "Father, I love you, I would never harm you."

"I know it," Father said.

"But I mean it," Lared said again.

"I know you do. Now go back to sleep. It was a terrible dream, but it's over now, and you didn't hurt me, whatever happened in the dream."

Then Father turned away, curled back under his blanket to sleep again.

But to Lared it was no dream. What Justice put into his mind came with too much clarity to be dismissed as mere madness of the night. Lared knew now how it felt to watch his father die, knowing that he caused it. And then, with her unsurpassed ability to intrude in his thoughts when Lared wanted her the least, Justice asked him, Did you know you loved your father before now?

Lared answered only, I hope I die before you make me dream again.

At sunrise Lared felt spent from the night's experience. He felt shy now before the other men—they had seen him vain as a cock yesterday, and tearful as a babe last night. This morning he was quiet, speaking little, embarrassed now to be in the lead with the others watching him.

Above all, to Jason he said nothing. Rather he stayed with his father, spoke to him when he needed to, and kept the pure blue eyes out of his sight.

At noon, Lared and Father mounted their horses to leave the last team behind. Jason would not be put off then. "Lared," he said.

Lared looked at the harness of his horse.

"Lared, I remember it, too. Before you dreamed your dreams, I have dreamed them all."

"Only because you wanted to," Lared said. "I never asked to see."

"I was given eyes. If you had them, would you leave them closed?"

"He has eyes," Father said, puzzled.

"Let's go now, Father," Lared said. They rode in silence past each of the last four trees in turn, until they reached the hut that Jason and Lared had built the last night, not all that long before. There was the final tree, girdled and ready for cutting.

And suddenly Lared was afraid. He did not know why. He simply felt—unprotected. Exposed. He stayed close to his father, following him when it had no purpose, even when his father went back to the sledge for another ax, because the one he used was too light for him, and kept twisting when it hit the tree.

Finally, Lared had to speak, just to calm his fear. "What if there weren't any iron in the world? Or so far away we couldn't get it?"

"I'm a blacksmith, Lared," Father said. "Those words are like telling a woman she's barren."

"What if?"

"Before iron, people were savages. Who would live in such a place?"

"Worthing," Lared said.

Father stiffened, rested on his ax for a moment.

"I mean the world, the planet. The iron only came shallow enough to find it in one place in the world. A desert."

"So you go to the desert and dig it out. Cut wood."

Lared swung his ax and made a chip fly. Father swung in turn and made the tree shudder.

The tree fell, and together they hacked away limbs, and rolled and levered it onto the sledge. It was not a mast tree; it was not so heavy that the horses had to be used just to pull it into place. By nightfall they had the second tree as well, and then they lay down to sleep in the hut.

Lared did not sleep, however. He lay awake, staring into darkness, waiting for the dream that he knew would come. Whenever he began to doze, he pictured Aven in his mind, Aven burning like shavings in the forge. He did not know whether it was his own memory of the dream, or Justice putting it in his mind afresh. He dared not sleep for fear of worse dreams, though he did not know how he might stop Justice even if he could stay awake forever. It was not a rational decision to stay awake—it was pure dread, dread of the woman waiting in the night to take his mind from him and make him be someone else and do another man's acts. *I would die for my father, I would never harm him.*

Sleep never came, and neither did the dream. For once they had done precisely what he asked. They told him nothing, they showed him nothing. But waiting for it cost him rest, and at first light his father, thinking him asleep, poked him to wake him up. Now, with his father awake, now suddenly Lared felt himself able to sleep; and once he could dare to do it, his desperate body demanded it. Sleep. He staggered through the morning rituals, the hitching of the team; he almost fell from his horse when he dozed. "Wake up, lad," Father said, annoyed. "What's wrong with you?"

Chopping at the third tree invigorated him somewhat, but he was still not alert. Twice Father had to stop him. "You're cutting too high here. Bring it down, we don't want the branches to get caught up in other trees and never fall."

Sorry, Father. I thought I was cutting where you said. Sorry. I'm sorry.

And when the tree was ready to fall, it tipped the wrong way and tangled up, as Father had warned.

"Sorry," Lared said.

Father stood looking upward in disgust. "I don't see what's holding it up as it is," he said. "There's hardly a branch touching, if you look closely enough. Go bring the team, unhitch the team and bring them here, we'll have to pull it down."

Lared was still unharnessing the horses when he heard the crash of the tree falling.

"Lared!" cried his father. Lared had never heard such pain in his father's voice.

His left leg lay fully under a great branch of the tree; his left arm was pierced by a smaller one, that drove in at the great muscles of the upper arm and passed clear through, snapping the bone so the arm bent upward like another elbow at the break.

"My arm! My arm!" Father cried.

Lared stood stupidly, unable to understand that something was expected of him. Father's blood seeped out on the snow.

"Lever it off me!" Father cried. "It's not such a big tree, son! Lever it off me!"

Lever. Lared got the lever quickly from the sledge, got it into place, and heaved. The tree rolled up and away from Father, and with his good arm he struggled to slide away, but the balance of the tree was still wrong, and it rolled back down again. This time it caught only his foot, and didn't fall so far, so that there was little new pain. "Lared, stop the bleeding," Father said.

Lared tried pressing on the break in the arm, but the blood came too quickly. The bone was in tiny fragments there; the arm was so soft all the way through that there was nothing to press against. Lared knelt there in a daze, trying to think what else to do.

"Cut if off, you fool!" Father screamed. "Cut it off and tie off the stump and burn away the end of it!"

"Your arm—" Lared said. To cut off a blacksmith's arm, either arm, was to take the forge from him.

"My life, you fool! An arm for my life, I'll pay it!"

So Lared stripped the sleeves off his father's arm, then took an ax and this time struck accurately, taking off his father's arm just above the break. Father did not scream, only gasped. Lared used the torn-off shirtsleeve to tie the end so at last the bleeding stopped.

"Too late," Father whispered, his face white with pain and cold. "I've got no blood left."

Don't die, Father.

Father's eyes rolled back in his head and his body went limp.

"No!" Lared shouted angrily. He ran to the lever and this time forced the tree upward hard enough that it achieved a balance and stayed off his father's body. He dragged his father away, closer to the sledge. The leg was broken, but nothing had pierced the skin there. It was the stump of arm that made Lared so furious. There was nothing that had prepared him to see his father's body so mutilated. Those were the arms that went in and out of the fire—

Burn the stump of the arm. But there was no point in that if Father was dead. I should see if he's dead or not.

He was breathing, and there was a weak pulse in his throat.

But the wound was not bleeding now. It was more important to get him home than to do anything else. Muddled as his thinking was, Lared still knew that. It took him fifteen minutes to lever yesterday's trees off the sledge, and another quarter hour to get his father on, his body bundled and covered with every blanket, then tied in place. Lared mounted the right-hand horse, the lead horse, and the sledge lurched forward.

Once they were underway, Lared realized he wasn't sure which way to go. Ordinarily he would follow the smoothest path home, which meant retracing their route. But they had gone far out of their way, leading the others to their trees. By far the shortest journey would be to go direct. The only trouble was that Lared didn't know the way for sure. On foot he could get home with no trouble. But he couldn't be sure of finding a path that was smooth and wide enough for the sledge.

He could not decide. His mind refused to clear. At last all he could think of was that home was closer if he left the path. As long as he stayed alert, as long as he kept in mind the way the forest was in summer, he could find a safe, quick route. He might yet save his father's life.

But he could not stay awake. Now, with the steady rhythm

of the horse's walk, the hiss of the sledge over the snow, the endless whiteness of the winter forest, he could not concentrate on anything, kept waking to find his face pressed against the horse's neck. Desperately he clung to the horse and urged it on, faster and faster, crying out against himself. Why didn't you sleep last night! You've killed your father! And Aven's face loomed against the whiteness of the day, Aven stood in every bright place, clinging to the burning parchment, his clothes awash with flame.

Help me, he cried silently. "Help me!" he screamed aloud.

Of course Jason was watching. Of course Justice heard. But what they sent him was not a miracle, but another dream. He watched the snow ahead of him, he guided the horses among the trees, but it became sand, and his mouth grew dry and thirsty, and he was Stipock at the end of his dream of steel.

It was time for the rains to come, and the water in the cistern was getting low. Three jars had been broken in the last month, and now the memory of so much water spilling over the sand haunted Stipock.

Haunted him all the more because at last they had reached the iron. Carving into the cliff face with bronze and stone tools, they had penetrated some twenty meters into the rock. He thought it would be closer. Perhaps he had chosen the wrong spot. But the waiting had taken its toll. If they had found iron at once, it would have been too easy, it would have meant little. So it was just as well that the first year of their colony they spent most of their time turning the streams into ditches to make the sand produce food, and hacking at the ironwood trees a few miles away to bring down logs for their wooden houses. Heaven City had been generous with their tools, and Jason had brought more than a year's supply of ship's food when he flew them down to the southern desert. All had looked promising.

Except that even then the dust had choked them whenever they ran; even then there was always a thin film of dust on the top of the water, settling into deeper and deeper mud at the bottom, so that they learned not to stir the water in the cistern or the drinking pots. And the second year, when Hoom and Wix and Billin took their turns leading the diggers into the rock, then the dust was always in the air, until they became accustomed to filth, to white streaks in blackened faces, to the coughs at night as the diggers took their gritty breaths.

And now drought. The rains were due. The winds had come on schedule, whipping sand and dust along the plain in gusts. Here the wind was visible, and Stipock shielded his eyes, squinted and watched each wall of wind as it came, dark as a wave of the sea. The rains were due, and they had struck iron; for rain, they would have been grateful. But the iron was nothing. The iron was useless stone.

"We can't eat it," Billin said, standing on the pile.

The others listened wordlessly. A dust devil whipped by, skirting the heap of ore.

"We can't drink it."

Stipock grew impatient. Usually at these meetings he held his tongue, let the younger people reach their own conclusions, and only stepped in with advice if they became deadlocked. But he knew where Billin was leading, and it would be the end of them, the end of the hope of bringing steel to Jason Worthing's world. "Billin," he said, "we can't drink words, either. If you're going to list the useless things in the desert, you might include those."

They laughed, some of them. Even Billin smiled. "You're right, Stipock. So I won't make a speech. Don't all thank me at once."

They laughed again. We aren't finished yet, thought Stipock, if you can still laugh.

"You know that I went south for ten weeks. But since I came back, I've told no one what I saw. No one but Stipock. He asked me not to say anything because it would distract you from the work. But now I think, since we do things by vote here, that you ought to decide for yourselves what you do and do not want to hear."

They wanted to hear about his journey south. Stipock bowed his head and listened to the tale again. How Billin went up the stream into the hills, where the ironwood grew broader and taller, where some animals lived; and then up through a pass in craggy mountains, and when he reached the other side, the world changed. There was not an exposed rock without moss, thick grass sprang up underfoot, the soil was moist, and as he walked down the far slope, the forest became unimaginably thick. Fruits that he had never seen before grew from the trees. He tried some of them, and they were good—he dared not try too many, for fear one would be poisonous and so he could never return to tell the rest.

"And it was that way all the way down the river to the sea. All the way to the sea I went, where the sand is only in a ring around a bay, and water comes in pure streams down to the beach, and fruits and roots are so plentiful that you could eat forever and never have to farm at all. I'm not making that up. We've had enough disappointment. I wouldn't promise more than is there. It rained four of the five days, downpours so heavy the sea splashed with the raindrops, but it was over in an hour and the sun was bright again. You know it's true! I left with five days of food, and came back ten weeks later. I was tired and hungry, but not ten weeks worth of hungry. There's food there! And Stipock knows it. Stipock knew all along that those lands were there. I say we should go there. I say we should live there, where there's plenty to be had. It doesn't mean giving up on the iron. We can send an expedition back here every year, well-stocked with food and tools. But our families won't have to eat this dusty bread all year, they won't have to live with hunger every hour of every day. We can wash in the sea and be clean, drink from clear streams—"

"Enough, Billin," Stipock said. "They get the idea."

"Tell them that it's true, Stipock. They don't believe me."

"It's true," Stipock said. "It's also true that for half the year terrible storms come and ravage the shore, raising huge waves, with winds that kill. That's a danger. But there's a worse danger. And that is the danger that in a place where you don't have to work hard and think keenly to stay alive, you'll forget how to work and forget how to think."

"Who can think with his tongue thick as a stone in his mouth?"

"What Billin says sounds like perfection. But I ask you to stay. The rains are late, but they'll come soon. We aren't starving yet. There's still water."

They said little, but when the meeting was over, they agreed to stay.

As always, that night Stipock and Wix ate with Hoom and Dilna because otherwise they would have had to eat alone. "Why haven't either of you married?" Hoom asked from time to time. "I highly recommend it."

But Wix and Stipock never answered. Stipock never answered because he didn't know why—he had never married on Capitol, either. Perhaps he was so much of an anarchist that he didn't want the government of a wife and children. Stipock knew much better why Wix didn't marry. It was because he already loved a woman, but the woman was Hoom's wife.

It was an open secret in the iron colony: when Hoom took his shift at the rock, leading his diggers deeper into the cliff, Wix called upon Dilna where she worked with the tools, or Dilna visited him in his house. People were busy at their work; no one was watching; perhaps they thought they were undiscovered. Stipock confronted Wix one day and said, "Why are you doing this? Everyone knows."

"Does Hoom know?"

"If he does, he doesn't show it. He loves you, Wix, you've been his friend since you used to sneak out of his father's house together. Why are you doing this?"

Wix wept with shame and vowed to stop, but he didn't mean it, and he barely hesitated. As for Dilna, Stipock did not even ask her. When she was with Hoom it was plain she loved him— he was a good father, a loving husband. Yet she did not bar her door to Wix. With Bessa and Dallat asleep, and Cammar outside playing or working in the sand, she took Wix into her bed like a thirsty man takes water. Once, when Stipock came to the house and found them together, she looked at him with eyes that begged him to forgive. That surprised him—he had seen so much adultery on Capitol that he did not see it as a sin anymore. Yet he could hear his father give the sermon: The coin of sin is pleasure, but the payment is death. Watch out for death, Dilna. Of course, you'll die if you live a chaste life, too. The beauty of chastity is that when death comes, you'll regard it as a blessed relief.

"They won't stay long now," Wix said, "if it doesn't rain soon."

"I know it," Stipock said.

Hoom broke the bread, and it crumbled like the sand outside

the door. He smiled grimly and passed the dish. "Take a handful of bread. Also swallow an ironwood seed—there's soil enough in our bellies for it to grow."

Dilna poured the crumbs on her tongue. "Delicious, Hoom. You're definitely the best cook in the family."

"That bad, is it?" Hoom took a mouthful of water and swished it in his mouth, tasting it as if it had been palatable. When he finally swallowed, he looked disappointed that it was gone. "Stipock, I want to go, too. The children—we've got to do something before we run out of water, or it'll be too late, they'll not have the strength to go anywhere. It already dries them out, the sun and wind dry them, and they walk around here as if they were thinking of dying. We can't stay."

Dilna looked angry. "We came here for a purpose, Hoom—"

"I'm sorry," Hoom said. "Once these dreams of machines that could move themselves, and of tools that could cut through bronze were all I wanted with my life. When Jason sent us away from Heaven City to dig this iron, I was glad. But now that it comes to a choice between the future of the world and the future of my children, the choice goes the other way. For me there's no world without Cammar and Bessa and Dallat. They're asleep in there right now, and for me all that matters is that they wake up tomorrow, and every tomorrow after that. You and Wix, you have no families, you can decide for yourselves. And Dilna, she has courage that I can't find. But I am a father and that's all that matters to me now, with only four inches of water left in the cistern."

Stipock thought of Aven's house burning like a vast torch on the top of Noyock's hill, remembered Hoom screaming and screaming all night, so that they could hear him from Heaven City to Linkeree Bay. They all thought it was the pain of burning, and it was true that he had heavy burns. But it was his father that he called for, hated Aven that he pleaded with. And now his fatherhood meant more to him, apparently, than motherhood to Dilna.

"I know what you're thinking," Dilna said. "You're thinking I don't love my children."

"It never crossed my mind," said Stipock.

"But I do love them. I just don't want to see them growing

up to be useless and lazy and stupid. I am what I do. I'm a toolmaker. But what if they live in a place where they need no tools? Where they don't need clothing or shelter or—what would they be then? I won't go south. Stipock is right."

Wix nodded. "I'll wait for the rains, too, as long as I can. And then I'll go. But not south. The way I see it, it's time to go home."

They took that in silence for a while. Stipock watched them eat, watched them savor their water, watched them remember Heaven City and the boats on the water.

"We could make a boat from the ironwood trees," Dilna said, "and go out to sea, and let the water carry us home."

Stipock shook his head. "There's a falls five hundred meters high well down the river, when the river flows at all. And even if we made it out to sea, we can't drink the sea water. It has salt in it."

"I don't mind a little salt."

"It has so much salt that it makes you thirstier and thirstier, and the more you drink the more you want until you die."

Hoom shrugged. "That means we walk."

"It's a long way," Stipock said.

"Then let's hope it rains," said Hoom.

It didn't rain. The winds shifted to the west, but didn't move northwest; there was no water from the sea, but now the sand and dust became much worse than ever before. The dust seeped into every crack. It was millimeters deep on their beds and bodies when they woke in the morning. Children choked on it and cried out. After two days of it, one of Serret and Rebo's young twins died.

They buried him in the sand during one of the brief lulls in the wind.

The next morning the dessicated body was in the open, the skin flayed away. The wind, in one of those cruel tricks of nature, carried the baby up against the front door of his family's house. Serret had to shove to get the front door open in the morning; his screaming once he saw what had jammed it closed brought everyone out of their houses. They took the body from him, tried to burn it, but the wind kept putting the fire out, and finally they carried it out into the desert, to the lee of their settlement, and let it lie there for the wind to carry it away.

That night they did the same with two more children, and then carried Wevin's body to the same place after her baby tried to come four months early.

Billin went from house to house in the morning, his face muffled against the wind, and said, "I'm going today. I know the way. In three hours we'll be among the ironwood trees. By nightfall we'll be in a place with water. I'll wait there for three days, and then whoever is with me, I'll take them through the pass. Next year we'll come back to dig for iron. But this year we'll leave while our children are alive."

An hour later they huddled together in the lee of Billin and Tria's house, carrying their precious skin-covered jars of water, carrying or leading children. Stipock did not argue with them or try to make them stay. Nor did he listen to them when they whispered, "Come with us. We don't want to follow Billin, we want to follow you. You can keep us together, come with us."

But he knew that in a land where life was easy, no one could keep them together except with magic or religion, and he wasn't much with either—he wasn't cynic enough for the trickery of the first, or believer enough for the latter. "Go," he said. "I wish you well." They moved off into the desert at midmorning, the wind whipping across their path, erasing their footprints almost before they were made, the sand whipping out from under their feet with every step. "Live," Stipock said.

For three more days, Stipock, Wix, Hoom, Dilna, and the children survived by living in the mine, sealing it off as best they could by tearing apart an empty house and rebuilding the walls at the mine entrance. At the back of the mine, in the darkness, they could breathe more easily. On the third day, they awoke to the sound of rain.

They ran to the entrance, tore away the wall, and caught their first glimpse of hell. It was as if the whole sea had fallen on them. The ground was all mud, and the houses themselves were sliding along the gentle slope as the mud flowed slowly toward the river. Yesterday the river had been dry. Now it was a torrent, well over its banks.

"Rain," said Wix. "Should we stay?"

It was a bitter joke. Wix and Hoom plunged out into the rain, which soaked them by the second step, and they went from house to house, gathering up what they could salvage before the houses were swept into the river. As it was, they barely made two trips each before the river lapped out to carry the huts away. Then they watched from the mine entrance, glad that it sloped upward so they were in no risk of drowning. They drank and drank, filling and refilling the same jars. Well back from the mine entrance they poured water over the children, washed them and let them play naked on the blankets. They had never been so clean, it seemed, and the sound of their laughter made the rain joyful.

Until the storm ended. The sun came out within minutes, and before nightfall the ground was baked and cracked. A few sticks remained of one house; all the rest were gone. The river continued to flow well into the night, but by morning it was back down to a mere trickle, a few stagnant ponds.

The heap of iron ore was gone. It had been too close to the river.

There was no need for discussion. They had little food and only the water in their jars and waterbags. It was madness to go anywhere but south, so they went east, following Stipock's memory of the maps that Jason had showed him. Cammar walked, and Hoom and Wix each carried a child. Dilna and Stipock carried their pitiful belongings. A few blankets, an ax, a few knives, crumbly bread, clothing. "We need clothing and blankets," Stipock warned them, "because it's going to be cold a few times on the way home."

Now, on the journey through the desert, it was harder for Wix and Dilna to pretend they did not love each other. Sometimes, in their weariness, they would lean on each other as they walked. Stipock watched Hoom at such moments, but he only held Bessa or Dallat and walked on, perhaps singing or telling a story to the child. Hoom is not blind, Stipock decided. He sees but chooses not to see.

Before night the dust began to rise again, and Stipock led them south into the shelter of the ironwood forest. The next day they moved eastward among the trees, and the next day did the same, until they came to a broad riverbed heading northeast. It flowed, not strongly, but with water they could drink. So they followed its course for five days through desert and occasional grassland to the sea.

One of the days along the river, Stipock crested a hill and stood beside Hoom and saw what he was watching: Wix and Dilna embracing. It was just for a moment; they must have thought they were far enough ahead not to be seen; or perhaps they didn't care anymore. It was not passionate but weary, their embrace, like a husband and wife long married and returning to each other for familiar comfort. It occurred to Stipock that this might well be more galling to Hoom than if they had looked furtive and eager.

Hoom stepped down from the rise, and the lovers were suddenly out of sight behind a low ridge of dirt. "I thought," said Hoom with a self-deprecating laugh, "I thought that of the two of us, she felt *that* way toward *me*."

Stipock set his hand on Hoom's shoulder. Little Bessa breathed hotly on his hand. "They both love you," he said. It was inane to think that such words would comfort Hoom.

To Stipock's surprise, however, Hoom smiled as though he needed no comfort at all. "I've known since we lived in Stipock's city. It began not long after we were married. Before Cammar was conceived."

"I thought—that it began here."

"I think it was something they couldn't help. It was here that they stopped trying to hide it. How could they?" Hoom held Bessa tightly to him. "I don't much care whose seed it was that grew. I'm the one who hoed, and I will harvest. These children are mine."

"You're a kinder man than I am."

Hoom shook his head. "When Jason was with us, before he brought us here, and I was trying to take the blame for my father's death, he said to me, 'You are forgiven as you forgive Wix and Dilna.' I do, you know. It's not a lie. I had already forgiven them before Jason said that. And because I knew that I had no blame or hate for them, I believed Jason when he said there was no blame or hate to hold against me, either. Will you tell them that? If I should die sometime before the journey's through, will you tell them that I forgive them, that it's all right?"

"You won't die, Hoom, you're the strongest of us—"

"But *if*."

"I'll tell them."

"Tell them that it's true. That I meant it. Tell them to ask Jason if they doubt it."

"Yes."

Then they crested the low ridge, and Wix and Dilna were there resting, playing with Cammar, trying to pretend that they were only friends weary from the journey.

From the mouth of the river eastward until they finally reached the isthmus leading north, it was the worst desert they had yet crossed. Stipock warned them, and they filled their water jars and waterbags and drank from the river for two days until they could hardly bear to drink. "Keep this up and we can all piss and float home," Wix said, and they laughed.

It was the last time they laughed for a while. The desert was wider than Stipock had thought. The smooth and sandy beach gave way to cliffs and crags. There was as much vertical as horizontal travel, and each day Stipock insisted that they drink less and less. They ran out of water anyway, except for the little bit they saved for the children. "It's not that far," Stipock told them. "There are streams on the isthmus, and it isn't far." Indeed, from the tops of hills they could look across the sea and catch a glimpse of land going northward, a coastline leading toward the land of pure water.

It was too far, though. They buried Bessa under a pile of rocks before dawn one day, and walked on more slowly, even though their burden was lighter by her scant weight. That night they reached an oasis of sorts, and drank the foul-tasting water, and filled their waterbags and jars again. They thought they had made it. An hour later all were vomiting, and Dallat died of it. They buried him by the poisoned pool, and weakly walked on, emptying their jars and bags along the way through the sand. They did not weep. They hadn't the water in them to make tears.

The next day they reached a clear spring in the side of a hill, and the water was good, and they drank and didn't get sick. They stayed at the spring for several days, building back their strength. But now their food was getting low, and with full jars and bags they set out again.

Two days later they reached the top of a rocky rise, and stopped at the edge of a cliff that plunged down nearly a kilometer. To the west they saw the sea, and to the east another sea, the water winking blue in the sunlight of early morning. At the bottom of the cliff the land funneled into a narrow isthmus between the seas. The isthmus was green with grass.

"Do you see the green down there, Cammar?" asked Hoom. The boy nodded gravely. "That's grass, and it means we'll find water, and perhaps something more to eat."

Cammar looked annoyed. "If we were going where there was food, why didn't you bring Bessa and Dallat? I know they were hungry."

No one knew how to answer, until Hoom finally said, "I'm sorry, Cammar."

Cammar was a forgiving child. "That's all right, Papa. Can I have a drink?"

They found a way down the cliff before noon; it was not sheer, but broken with many possible paths. They slept on the grass that night, and in the morning, for the first time in years, they awoke to a world that was wet with dew. Only then, with Cammar throwing wet grass at them, only then did they cry for the ones who died.

Lared shook himself, looked around. The horses were stopped facing a thicket. Behind him Father was moaning softly. It was afternoon. Lared could not remember any of the journey until now. Where was he? He looked behind him at the trail left by the sledge. It wound well enough among the trees. Had he guided the horses? Or had he slept? All he could remember was the desert, and Hoom and Wix and Dilna, and the children dying, and how at last it looked like life. But Father was moaning on the sledge behind him. Lared dismounted and walked stiffly back to see him.

"My arm," Father whispered, when he saw Lared. "What happened to my arm?"

"A branch broke clear through it, Father. You told me to cut it off."

"Ah, God," cried Father, "I'd rather die."

Lared had to know where they were. He walked back into an open area, found the rise of the mountains to the south. He was still headed in the right direction. But he couldn't picture this place in the summer. It looked all new to him. And if it was new, it meant he must have drifted far to the south, so far

that he was in forest that he didn't wander in. Or perhaps he
had passed Flat Harbor entirely.

Then, suddenly, he felt something shift in his mind and he
recognized where he was. The clearing he was standing on was
a pond, that's why it was so unfamiliar. He was on thick snow
over the ice of the pond. There was the low mound of the
beaver house. Somehow, in his sleep, in his dreams, he had
followed the right course. Only the thicket stopped the horses,
and it was a simple matter to turn them and follow the course
of the frozen stream for a while, leading the horses to bring
some life back into his own legs.

"Lared," Father called out. "Lared, I'm dying."

Lared did not answer. There was no answer to that. It was
probably true, but it didn't stop him from pushing on. The
trees opened into meadow, and he mounted again. And again
the snow and the sound and the movement dazed him, and
Justice brought him onward with a dream.

Stipock was tired. They had been climbing every day for a
week into the highest mountains in the world. Nowhere near
the peaks, of course, but still fighting for every step.

They crested another grassy hill, with higher, craggier
mountains on either side; but this time, instead of another,
higher hill beyond, there were only lower hills, and clearly
visible beyond them was an endless sea of deep green.

They had reached the top before him. Cammar was running
around in erratic circles while the others contemplated the scene
ahead.

"I feel like I'm falling," Dilna said. "It's been so long since
anything ahead of us was down. Are we almost there?"

"More than halfway, now, and the worst behind us. No
more desert. We should reach a large river soon, and we follow
that for a long, long way. We might build a raft, and float
down until it meets with a river nearly as large from the south.
Then we go north, straight north, and cross low and gentle
mountains, and soon we'll strike the Star River and follow it
on home."

"No," Wix said. "Tell me that we only have to go down
this slope and Heaven City will be there. The world should not
be any larger than this."

"How do you keep the world in your head like that, Stipock?"

"I studied the map in the Star Tower. Searching for iron. I once thought of leading an overland expedition. I didn't expect Jason would be willing to fly us there."

"Will they be glad to see us?" Dilna asked. "We didn't leave under happy circumstances."

Stipock smiled. "Do you really care how glad *they* are? We've had our stab at trying to build a perfect place. The climate was bad and the goal was all wrong. It isn't iron that makes a civilization." He thought of Hoom, loving his children and tolerating the intolerable between his wife and his friend. That is civilization, to bear pain for the sake of joy. Hoom grew up before I did, Stipock realized. He found out that if you try to eliminate the pain from your life, you destroy all hope of pleasure, too. They come from the same place. Kill one, you've killed all. Someone should have mentioned that to me when I was younger. I would have acted differently when Jason put me in his world. I was the devil when I might have been an angel if I tried.

"People," Dilna said.

"What?"

"Civilization. People, not a metal, not a parchment, not even an idea."

Wix eased himself to a sitting position on the grass, then lay back. "Stipock, admit it! All your talk of Jason being just a man was sham. You and Jason are both gods. You made the world together, and now you're here just to see what use we're making of it. And to impress us with miracles."

"Mine haven't been too impressive so far."

"Well, it takes a while to get in practice. Like chopping wood. The first few strokes are never right. That's when people lose legs and feet, the first few strokes, when they aren't accustomed to it."

"A clumsy god. Well, I confess it. That's what I am." He was about to say, And so are you, but a piercing scream interrupted them, and they jumped to their feet. "Cammar!" Hoom shouted, and they quickly saw that he wasn't on the crown of the hill. They ran in different directions; Stipock went to the northwest brow of the hill, and saw with hope that there were depressions marking small footprints in the grass; then saw, with horror, that the running steps had carried the child, unsuspecting, to the brink of a cliff. There was a mark of scraping at the very brink, torn grass where Cammar had clutched. If we had been watching, if we had been near, we might have saved him before he fell.

"Here!" Stipock called.

As the others ran up, Cammar's voice came from below the edge of the cliff. "Stipock! Where's Papa? I'm hurt!"

Hoom ran along the edge of the cliff, out to an angle where he could see. "Cammar! Can you see me?"

"Papa!" Cammar cried.

"He's just over the brink, on a ledge. Almost in reach!" Hoom shouted, and he ran back to them. "I can reach him. Stipock and Wix, hold onto my legs. Dilna, stay near the edge to help me with him when we get him near the top. Don't lean out, though. The edge isn't too secure."

His confidence, his air of authority calmed them all. It will turn out all right, thought Stipock. It only vaguely occurred to him that this was Hoom's blind spot, that he might not be willing to believe that saving his son was impossible. Still, the child was alive. There were piles of stone in the desert for the other two; Dilna was pregnant again, but the unborn child could not compare with Cammar, the oldest and the last now alive. They had to try, even at risk of their own lives.

Hoom lay on his back, not on his belly—it was an admission that Cammar was so far down that he could not be reached by a man bending at the waist, only by a man bending at the knees. Stipock gripped his leg and together he and Wix lowered him backward over the cliff.

"Almost there!" Hoom shouted. "Just a little farther."

"We can't," Stipock said, because they were already so close to the edge themselves that he had to double his legs up under him to keep them from dangling over the edge. Stipock only had Hoom by the ankle now, and his grip was none too sure. But somehow they lowered him another few centimeters.

"Almost! A little farther!"

Stipock was going to protest, but saw that Wix was grimly moving closer to the edge. Of all people, Wix cannot fail to help Hoom save his son, Stipock knew that, and so he began to carefully adjust his grip to allow him to lower Hoom a little more.

Then, suddenly, Hoom screamed, "No, Cammar! Don't jump for me! Stay there, don't jump for me!" And then a high-pitched child's scream, just as Hoom kicked powerfully, lunged downward, pulling his leg out of Stipock's grasp.

By some miracle Wix held on, crying out in the pain of the exertion. Dilna held onto Wix to keep him from falling over, too. Stipock could not get near enough to help Wix hold onto Hoom; he could only help Dilna in her effort to keep him from following Hoom over the edge.

"We could use a miracle now," whispered Wix.

"Cammar!" cried Hoom, his voice echoing among the mountains. "Cammar! Cammar!"

"He doesn't even know that he's in danger," Dilna said, panting and whimpering from grief and terror and despair. Stipock knew the feeling. They were safe. They had come this far, they were surely safe now. Something was very, very wrong with the world.

Then Wix screamed and his fingers gave way and Hoom slipped over the edge. They heard him strike ground; they heard him strike again. Not far away. Not all the way down. But definitely out of reach.

Dilna screamed and struck at Wix. Stipock got above them, pulled them both until they came up with him, up away from the lip of the abyss. Only when he was sure they would not accidently follow Hoom, only then did he shout, "Hoom! Hoom!"

"He's dead, he's dead!" Dilna cried.

"I tried to hold him, I really tried!" Wix sobbed.

"I know you did," Stipock answered. "You both did. Neither of you could have done more. You did the best you could." Then he called again for Hoom.

This time Hoom answered, sounding exhausted and afraid. "Stipock!"

"How far down are you?" Stipock called.

Hoom laughed hysterically. "Far. Don't come down. You can't get here. Can't get down or up."

"Hoom," Dilna said. But her voice was not a shout, it was a prayer.

"Don't try to come after me!" Hoom shouted again.

"Can't you climb up at all? Or down?"

"I think my back is broken. I can't feel my legs. Cammar is dead. He jumped for my hands. I touched his fingers, but I couldn't hold him." Hoom wept. "They're all gone, Stipock! Do you think I'm even now?"

Stipock understood what he meant: trading his children's lives for his own guilt at the death of his father. "This isn't justice, Hoom. It doesn't come out even."

"It must be justice!" Hoom cried. "It sure isn't mercy!" A pause. "I can't hold on for very long, I think. Just my arms holding me."

"Hoom, don't let go! Don't fall."

"I thought of that already, Dilna, but it's going to happen anyway—"

"No!" Dilna shouted. "Don't fall!"

"I tried to hold onto you!" Wix shouted.

"I know. It was Stipock who let go, the old turd. Stipock, do your miracle now."

"What miracle?" Stipock asked.

"Make us clean."

Stipock took a deep breath, and then he spoke, loudly, so Hoom could hear him, too. "Hoom told me that if he ever— if something happened to him—"

"Yes, go on!" Hoom shouted.

"That he has known since before Cammar was conceived. And he loved you both anyway. And loved the children. And he—forgave. I believe him. He has no anger in him."

Dilna was weeping. "Is it true?"

"Yes," said Hoom.

Wix turned over and lay face down in the grass and cried like a child.

"I'm going to let go now," said Hoom.

"No," said Dilna.

So he didn't let go. But there was nothing to say, nothing to do. They just waited at the top of the hill, listening as Wix cried, listening to the birds calling each other in the canyons.

"I have to let go now," Hoom said. "I'm very tired."

"I love you!" Dilna cried.

"And I!" shouted Wix. "I should have died, not you!"

"Now you think of it," Hoom said. Then he let go. They heard him slide a little, and then heard nothing at all.

"Hoom!" Dilna cried. "Hoom! Hoom!"

But he didn't answer. He never answered.

So after they spent themselves in tears, they got up and took their burdens, they climbed carefully down the safe slopes, and made their way out of the mountains into the great forest. They found the river, built a raft, and the three of them floated for weeks, it seemed; they lost count of days.

They wintered north of the river, and Dilna's child was born. She thought of naming him Hoom, but Stipock forbade it. She had no right to saddle the child with her guilt, he said. Hoom had forgiven them, they owed no debt to him, the child should not be forced to remind them. So she named him Water. And in the spring they crossed the mountains and entered Heaven City, where they were greeted with rejoicing.

"Lared," said Jason.

Lared awoke. He was on horseback. Villagers were all around him. "Lared, you brought your father home."

Lared turned to look at his father on the sledge behind him. Justice was bending over him. Sala stood beside her, nodding. "He's alive and probably won't die," she said, her voice calm and almost adult-sounding. "Cutting off his arm saved his life."

"He told me to," Lared said.

"Then he told you well." The words were strange, coming from his younger sister. Strange to her, too, for suddenly it was as if the water had poured from a goatskin bag. She began to cry. "Father! Father!" And she knelt on the sledge and held her father and kissed his face. He awoke then, opened his eyes and said, "He took my arm, damn the boy, he took my arm."

"Never mind," Jason whispered to Lared. "He's not himself."

"I know," said Lared. He slid from the horse, stood shakily on the ground. "The day went on forever. Take us home."

It was less than a kilometer back to the village. Jason had cut loose his team, abandoning the sledge, and rode down the whole path, alerting all the timbering crews. They, too, unharnessed the horses and rode on quickly, gathered along the six men who had already brought their logs home, and only just got to where Lared had brought his father.

"Did Justice guide me?" Lared asked. "I dreamed the whole way here. Stipock and Hoom and—"

"She sent you the dream, but she didn't guide you. How could she? She doesn't know the way."

"Then how did I get here?"

"Perhaps there's more in you than you thought."

Jason helped him through the door of the inn, where Mother hugged him tightly, savagely, and then demanded, "Is he alive?"

"Yes," Lared said. "They're bringing him now."

Then Jason helped him to his truckle bed, which waited ready by the fire. He lay there trembling while four men carried in the mutilated body of the blacksmith. He was unconscious. Jason set to work at once, boiling herbs and dressing the stump. While Father was still unconscious, Jason set the leg and splinted it.

All the time, Justice sat in a chair, watching. Lared watched her from time to time, to see if she winced at his father's pain. She showed no sign of noticing. No sign that she knew that she could heal him with a thought, could even restore his arm. Lared wanted to shout at her: If you can heal it, and don't, then you consent to it!

She did not speak into his mind. Instead, Sala came to him and touched him on the forehead. "Don't torment me, Lareled," she said. "Think of Hoom and Cammar and be glad you're home."

He kissed his sister's hand and held it for a while. "Sala, please say your own words to me."

Almost at once Sala began to cry. "I was so afraid, Lared. But you brought Father home. I knew you would."

She kissed his cheek. But then it suddenly occurred to her. "But Lared, you forgot to bring his arm. How will he beat the iron, without a hand to hold it?"

Then Lared wept softly, for Father, yes, and for himself, and tears for Hoom and Cammar, for Bessa and Dallat, for Wix and Dilna and for Aven, for the innocent and guilty, for all the pain. I never knew I loved Father till he lay there at the brink of death. Perhaps I never *did* love him, until he was nearly gone. It seemed a very powerful thought, until it occurred to him that Justice probably put it into his mind. At that he went to sleep. He could not escape them, and the price of trying was too high. He had somehow gotten home, and he had kept his father alive somehow, and that was enough for now, he feared nothing now, not even dreams; no, not even sleep.

9

Worthing Farm

Father lay on his bed, sleeping like death for several days. But whenever anyone asked how he was, Sala answered, "He'll be fine."

Fine, thought Lared, good as new, but with his left arm missing and a memory of his son, staggering like a drunken man, chopping at the tree like a child; I took his arm, and not because I swung the ax to cut it off—there'd be no blame in that, God knows—but because I made the tree fall wrong, I made it hang in the branches of the other trees.

He tried not to blame it on Jason and Justice. Forcing me to have dreams of fathers dying, so that I lay awake in terror of it, and so caused my father to as much as die. Was this in their design from the start? Did they show him Aven's death so that he would maim his own father? What then does Hoom's death mean? What fall is in store for me? But when he thought like that, he would become ashamed, because it was the dream of Stipock's journey home to Heaven City that had kept him moving when on his own he could never have brought Father home.

The others in the village wanted to make much of him. Lared, the treeherd who saved his father's life and brought one-armed Elmo home on an unknown path. The tinker kept threatening to make up a song about the deed, and the other men, who had been so amused at him before, now treated him with unfeigned respect. With awe, in fact, falling silent when he entered the room, asking his opinion as if he had some unusual wisdom. Lared took all these changes courteously—why should he rebuff their love?—but each kindness, each honor galled him, for he knew that rather than praise he should have blame.

He hid from them in the book. There was much to write, of Stipock, Hoom, Wix, and Dilna, he told himself. So he closed himself in Jason's room all day, writing and writing.

He came down for meals, and to do the work that must be done with Father lying deathlike on his bed, but even that became unnecessary, for Lared began to find that whatever job he thought that he must do, Jason was already doing when he got to it. Lared had nothing to say to Jason, just walked away. Obviously Jason was hearing the need to do the job from Lared's own mind, and then rushing to do it so that Lared would get back to the book. Lared even wondered sometimes if they hadn't plotted out the entire thing so that he would spend more time writing. Very well, he thought, I *will* write, as quickly as I can I'll write, and finish the book and send you and it away as far from me as possible.

One day, when the snow was falling thick outside and the house was full of the smell of sausage frying, Lared bent over the table and wrote at last of the death of Cammar and Hoom. He wept as he wrote it, not because of the dying, but because of the forgiveness Hoom gave to Wix and Dilna as he died. Jason found him there; Lared resented his coming in—Jason, at least, couldn't plead the excuse that he didn't realize Lared didn't want him there.

"I know you don't want me here," Jason said. "But I *am* here, all the same. You've written all you know so far."

"I want no more dreams from you."

"Then I have delightful news. You've finished all the tales I have that are worth seeing yourself. I will tell you how I ended my time with my people, and then—"

"And then I give you the parchment and you go away."

"And then Justice will give you the memories that my own descendants preserved through all the generations. Like the tale of the tinker."

"I want no more dreams and tales."

"Don't be so angry, Lared. You should be glad of the dreams you've had. You might take a lesson from Hoom, for instance, and instead of punishing yourself and me and Justice for your father's injury, become as generous as Hoom and forgive us all."

"What do you know and understand of Hoom?" said Lared.

"You forget that I'm the one who sent my mother off to a colony against her will. Very much the way you cut off your father's arm. You have in you the memory of every pain I've suffered in my life. You loved Hoom the more for knowing him—why not me?"

"You are not Hoom."

"Yes I am. I'm Hoom and everyone else whose heart I've had in me. I've been so many people, Lared, I've felt so much of their pain—"

"Then why do you cause more? Why don't you leave me alone?"

Jason struck the wall behind him with the butt of his fist. "Why don't you realize that I feel even what you're feeling now, you fool! I know you and I love you and if I could spare you one bit of this, if I could ease your burden and still accomplish what must be done—"

"Nothing *must* be done! You only *want* to do it."

"Yes, that's right. I want to do it the way you want to breathe. Lared, for thousands of years my children watched all the worlds of men, protected you all from pain and suffering. In all that time, Lared, in all those years there *never* was a Hoom! Do you understand me? A Hoom or Wix or Dilna is impossible in a universe where actions have no consequences! Why do you love Hoom, if not because of what he did in the face of suffering? Without the suffering, what was he? A clever carpenter. Without his father's beatings all his life, without the face of his father haloed in the flames, without his wife's adultery and the deaths of Bessa, Dallat, and Cammar—yes, without the touch of Cammar's fingers as he leaped and fell, what would there be in Hoom to make you love him? What would there be of greatness in him? What would his life have meant?"

Jason's passion shocked Lared. He was usually so calm, it made his rage the more fearsome. But Lared would not be put off, even so. "If you could ask Hoom, I think he would gladly have foregone the greatness if he could have lived his life in peace."

"Of course he would. Everybody would prefer that everything go smoothly for them. The worst bastards in the world are those who devote their entire lives to making sure things go smoothly for themselves. Individual preference has nothing to do with what I'm saying."

"That's plain—you've never been one to go out of your

way to do good for other people, except when you need them to do something to further your grand design."

"Lared," Jason said, "people aren't individuals, even though we all think we are. Even before I came, what did you know of yourself, except what your family told you? Their tales of your childhood became your vision of yourself; you imitated your father and mother both, learned what it means to be a human being from them. Every pattern of your life has been bent and shaped by what other people do and what other people say."

"So what am I then, a machine that echoes everyone around me?"

"No, Lared. Like Hoom, you have in you something that makes a choice—something that decides, This is me, this is not me. Hoom could have become a murderer, couldn't he? Or he could have treated his children as his father treated him, couldn't he? It's the part of you that chooses that's your soul, Lared. That's why we couldn't dump one person's bubble into another's mind—there are some choices you cannot live with. So you aren't just an echo. But you are one thread of a cloth, a vast weaving; your life forces other people to make choices, too. The men who honor you for saving your father—don't you realize that it gives meaning to *their* lives, too? Some might be jealous of you, you know—but they are not. They love you for your goodness, and that also makes them good. But if there were no danger, if there were no fear, then what would it matter that we live together, that our lives touch? If our actions have no consequences, we are just machines, contented machines, well-oiled and running smoothly with no need to think, nothing to value, because there are no problems to solve and nothing we can lose. You love Hoom because of what he did in the face of pain. And because you love him, you have become him, in part; and others, knowing you, will also become him, in part. It's how we stay alive in the world; in the people who become us when we're gone." Jason shook his head. "I tell you all this, but you don't understand."

"I understand, all right," Lared said. "I just don't believe you."

"If you understood it, Lared, you'd believe it, because it's true."

Then Justice spoke in Lared's mind: Jason tells you only half the truth, and that is why you don't believe.

Jason must have heard her, too, because his face went dark with anger, and he slumped down and sat on the floor and whispered, "So I'm not human; so be it."

"Of course you're human," Lared said.

"No, I'm not. Justice knows me better than any living soul. It's what she told the Judges: I am not human."

"You have flesh and blood like any man."

"But no compassion."

"That much is true."

"I *feel* what other people feel, but I have no pity for them. I saw a universe without pain and I said, This is foul, undo it, and then I chose to remain in it because I prefer to live here, surrounded by fear and suffering. I would rather live in a world where there can be agony like Hoom's—so that there can be a man like Hoom. I would rather live in a world where a man does a mad thing like walking naked through the snow just for the sake of honor, or where a blacksmith chooses and says, Take my arm to save my life, or where a woman sees her husband come home one-armed and almost dead and goes that day to tell her lover, I will never come to you again, for now if my husband learned of this, he would believe I hated him because he wasn't whole."

Lared held the quill tremblingly in his hand. "I hate you."

"Your mother is a woman, and nothing more. She had no face until the Day of Pain."

"We were happier without faces, then."

"Yes, and the dead are the happiest of all. They feel no pain, they have no fear, and the best sort of human being is the one most like a river, flowing wherever it's carried by the slope of the land."

"You're glad for other people's pain, that's what you are. That's why you came here—to relish it."

"Think of me what you like," Jason said, "but now tell me this: which of all the dreams I've given you would you most like to forget? Which of them would you like to have taken completely out of your mind, as if it had never happened? Which of these people do you wish you had never known?"

"You," said Lared.

Jason looked as if he had been hit. "Besides me. Who would you like Justice to remove from your memory, the way you scuff out a drawing in the dirt?"

"You've done enough to my memory. Leave me alone."

"You fool. What do you think all your protection *was* but changes in your memory? You tell me to leave you alone, but you hate me because we have done exactly that. Which do you want, boy—to be safe or to be free?"

"I just want to be alone."

"As soon as I can, Lared, I'll let you be as alone as your heart desires. But we have a book to finish. So listen and I'll tell you all the rest of the story that's mine to tell. No dreams— your precious memory will be undisturbed. Are you ready?"

Lared set down the pen. "Make it quick."

"Do you want to know what happened to Stipock and the others?"

Lared shrugged. "You'll tell me what you want." He knew he was infuriating Jason all the more; it was what he wanted.

"Wix and Dilna married, of course. I took them both into the Star Tower, and they each served several terms as Mayor. I made Stipock write a few books on machinery and fuels and general knowledge—something that future generations could build on. He married the Mayor then, Arran, and fathered eleven children. Then I took him into the ship. Later, he was Mayor twice.

At the end of three hundred years there were some two million people in Heaven City. Though it wasn't a city like Capitol; only twenty thousand people lived in the city proper. They were spread well onto the northern plain, and south into the forests and mining country clear to the headwaters of the Star River, and already there were some who had gone to live at the mouth of Heaven River. They were all one culture and one language and one people, and I decided that they had foundation enough. They had learned all that I could teach them, and so I brought out all the people I had saved in the Star Tower, and chose a few dozen from among those who had never gone under somec, and I sent out colonies year by year, five thousand people at a time. Stipock sailed in ships to the land where his mining effort had failed before; Kapock and Sara went overland with two thousand sheep to crop the grasslands east of Stipock's desert; Wien the bronzesmith went to the mountains of the northeast, and Wix and Dilna led their people eastward. Noyock sailed westward to the islands, where his cattle were fenced only by the sea. Linkeree and Hux each founded cities at opposite ends of the Forest of Waters, on the river that Stipock, Wix, and Dilna rafted on their journey home. Those are all the ones you know—there were many others. And the one colony I didn't wish to send—Billin's people in the islands of the south. As I heard it, they became uncivilized rather sooner than the rest. But the peace I established wasn't permanent, not anywhere. There was commerce and there was war, exploration and concealment; lies were told and truth was left forgotten. Still, every people in every land remembered the golden age of Jason, the time of peace. People have a way of longing for lost golden ages. *You* know about that."

"It isn't you I miss," said Lared.

"When the last of the colonists left Heaven City, I raised the starship from its resting place in First Field. It wasn't fit for flight among the stars, but that hardly mattered. I put it into orbit and then I went to sleep. For fifty years."

"Perched like God in the sky," said Lared, "peering through the clouds to see how the world got on."

Jason went on as if Lared hadn't spoken. "It was only when I awoke that I began my real work. After all, I hadn't tried to make a utopia—all I had done, really, was teach the people how to work and prosper and live with the consequences of their acts. I had some other business to attend to. I was feeling and looking nearly forty then, and I had had no children. And Worthing's World, Lared, was going to be a place where my gifts would grow and develop and perhaps become something more than I had made them.

"So I took a landing craft and some equipment, and I chose a place beside the West River in the densest part of the Forest of Waters, a place where no highways would go, at least not until the world filled up, which I doubted would be soon. I set off a circle ten kilometers across, and marked it with an inhibitor."

"I don't know the word."

"I know you don't. It sets up an invisible barrier that's very uncomfortable for an intelligent being to cross. Birds fly through

it. Dogs and horses are a bit annoyed. We had no dolphin
problem, for obvious reasons. I embedded the inhibitor in a
stone, and lasered an inscription on the stone:

WORTHING FARM

> From the stars
> Blue-eyed one
> From this place
> Jason's son.

"I can see you were determined to stop this nonsense of
people worshipping you," Lared said.

"I didn't start it—you know that, Lared. But I could use
it, couldn't I? Already every colony had legends of Jason, who
took the Star Tower into heaven, but someday would return.
I only had to change that a little. I went to Stipock—the nation
of Stipock, since Garol had already died. His grandson, Iron,
was the Mayor of the place. I didn't tell them who I was, just
asked for a place to live. But they weren't blind—it's hard to
hide my eyes. Stories sprang up at once, and people came to
see me, but I never admitted being Jason. I only lived there
six months, but in that time I told some stories. Enough to tell
the world to look for the coming someday of my son, and to
give them some reason not to hate and murder my children if
they found them. You must remember that I had lived half my
life—more than half, then—in fear of being called a Swipe
and killed.

"At the end of the six months I married Iron's daughter,
Rain, and took her north with me, to Worthing Farm. Oh, did
I mention? I never told my people the name Worthing. I only
gave the name to Worthing Farm, and only told it to an inner
circle in Stipock. They were my watchers, to protect the world
in case one of my children should be a Radamand—it was,
after all, in the blood.

"I took poor Rain with me to Worthing Farm, and we had
seven children, and it was the happiest time of my life. But
I'm not like Hoom, Lared. I loved my children, but I loved
them less than I loved other things. I was like my father, I
suppose, or perhaps like Doon—I had work to do and things

to learn that I valued more than love. You're right. It's as you said—I have no heart." Jason smiled cruelly. "At the end of ten years—and to me, remember, Lared, this was a year ago— I put the gate of the inhibitor in her hand and taught her how to use it, and then I left. I had to know what would come of things. How the world would end. So I said good-bye to Rain and told her that it was vital that she only leave Worthing Farm when it was time to choose a husband or a wife for one of our children. No child with these blue eyes would ever be allowed to leave. And any child who did not have these eyes was to be sent away at adulthood with whatever inheritance the farm could spare."

"What a happy family it must have been," Lared said, "with the children prisoners."

"It was cruel and miserable. I never thought they would keep it up. I was just trying to give them time, perhaps three or four generations, to establish themselves in some numbers before they went out and put themselves at the mercy of the world. Someone would rebel, I was sure, and steal the gate, open the inhibitor and leave it open. How was I to know how patient they would be? Perhaps it lasted so long because I told Rain that each keeper of the gate, before she died, must name a daughter or daughter-in-law to own the gate after her, and control the ins and outs. When I founded my little family, remember, my particular gift was passed from father to son, linked to sex. I had no way of knowing that would change— and it didn't, for a long, long time. So the gate passed from one woman to the next, women who did not have this gift, whose only power in their families was the gate itself. They handed down the gate for a thousand years. For a thousand years only the children stayed who could look behind the eyes. What I didn't count on was that many of those who were cast out simply went beyond the inhibitor's range and started farms, and it was their daughters who became the wives of Worthing. After a while the inbreeding became quite intense. It changed the power as it doubled and redoubled. It made them brilliant and intense, weak and sickly, frightened of the world and conscious, always, of the invisible wall and the stone in the middle of the farm. I should have foreseen it, but I didn't. I gave them powers beyond anything men had conceived of except in their dreams of God; but I also made them less than human in their hearts. The miracle is not that they grew powerful. The miracle is that when they finally left Worthing Farm, any of them had any humanity at all."

"And where were you, while your beautiful family grew up?"

"I went back up to the starship, and got everything ready, and then took the ship down to the bottom of the sea. I would only waken when the world had technology enough to notice I was there and bring me to the surface. Or when the rest of mankind discovered my little world, and woke me. Either way, I thought that would be a good time to wake up. I never doubted that I'd waken. I didn't know it would be fifteen thousand years, of course, but I would have done it anyway. I had to know how things would end."

Lared waited. Apparently Jason was finished. "Is that it, then? I'll write it in an hour, you can take the book, and then you can leave here and never disturb us again."

"I'm sorry to disappoint you, Lared, but it isn't the end. It's only the end of the part of the story I can tell. Justice will give you dreams for all the rest."

"No!" Lared shouted, and he got up from the table, knocking it over, spilling the ink across the floor. "Never again!"

Jason caught him by the arm, spun him back into the middle of the room. "You owe us, you ungrateful, self-pitying little bastard! Justice dreamed you home. You owe us your father's life."

"Why doesn't she change me, then, and make me *want* to endure these dreams?"

"We thought of that," Jason said, "but we're forbidden to do that, in the first place, and in the second place it would change who you are, and anyway, you've told us not to play with your mind. There aren't many more dreams, Lared, because we're nearly finished. Besides, the dreams aren't so clear now. They're not memories of direct experience, as Stipock's were, from him to me to Justice to you. These memories were passed on through generations of my family, just the bits and fragments that each new generation found to be vital enough to remember. What you'll dream tonight is the oldest memory that survived. A thousand years after I left them, and this is how they finally ended their imprisonment."

"Don't give it to me in the night. Tell me now," said Lared.

"This one must be seen in memory. If I tell you, you won't believe or understand it."

There was a knock at the door. It was Sala. "Father's awake," she said. "He isn't very happy."

Lared knew that he must go downstairs, but dreaded facing his father. Father knows what harm I did him. He could see all too clearly in his memory the way Father's arm looked, impaled and crushed on the end of a broken branch. He could remember all too well the feel of the ax as it cut through flesh and split the bone. I did it, Lared said silently. I did it, as he went down the stairs. I did it to you, as he stood beside his father's bed.

"You," Father whispered. "They say you brought me home."

Lared nodded.

"You should have left me, and finished what you began."

His father's cold hatred was more than he could bear. He ran upstairs and threw himself on Jason's bed and wept for grief and guilt. He wept until he fell sleep, and Jason didn't waken him when he saw him there, but slept on the floor himself so Lared could have his dreams.

Elijah held the plow as the oxen pulled, making straight furrows across the field. He did not look to the left or the right, just followed as steadily as if he and the oxen were all one animal. It was almost true, for Elijah's mind was not on his plowing. He was seeing through his mother's eyes, his old mother's mind, watching as she committed the unspeakable act.

"There are flecks of black in Matthew's eyes," she said. Her eyes, of course, were brown, since she was a child of over-the-wall. "He isn't one who has to stay. He has to leave."

Wants to leave, that's all, wants to go away because he hates this place and hates *me* because I am stronger than he is, he wants to get away from *me* to over-the-wall, but it is forbidden. His eyes have flecks of black in them, but Matthew has the power of Worthing nevertheless, and so must stay; he has *one* power, whatever else he lacks: he has the power to shut me out. He has the power to keep me from peering in his mind. In all of Worthing, in all of time that anyone remembers, never has there been a one who had the power to close himself to our Worthing eyes. What does he hide? How dare he keep secrets? He must stay, he must stay—we want no one in the world whose children might have power to close us out. He must stay.

As Mother took the gate from its place above the fire, Elijah called silently to all the children. Come. Mother means to use the gate. Come.

And so they came, all the blue-eyed men of Worthing, all their wives, all their children. Wordlessly, because they had so little need of speech. They gathered at the low stone wall that marked the edge of Worthing. They were waiting when Mother came to let Matthew go.

"No," said Elijah.

"The decision is mine," said Mother. "Matthew isn't one of you. He can't see the way you see. He doesn't know the things you know. Why should I make him live here with you, like a blind man in a world of sight, when out there in over-the-wall he's like everyone else?"

"He has a power, and his eyes are blue."

"His eyes are bastard, and the only power he has is privacy. I wish to God I had it too."

Elijah saw himself through Mother's eyes, felt the fear she felt of him, but still he knew she would not bend. It made him angry, and the grass grew dry and brittle beneath his feet. "Do not betray the law of Worthing, Mother."

"The law of Worthing? The law of Worthing is that I am keeper of the gate, and the decision is mine. Which one of you will dare to take the gate from me?"

No one, of course. None of them would dare to touch the gate. Defiantly she squeezed it and held it open. They felt it as a sudden inward silence, the absence of a noise they had always heard before but never noticed till it ended. The gate was open, and they were afraid.

Matthew started forward, carrying his inheritance—an ax, a knife, a pouch that held a cheese and a loaf of bread, a water-bag, a cup.

And Elijah stood in front of him, to block the way.

"Let him go," said Mother, "or I'll leave the gate open every moment of every day, and your children will climb the wall and wander off, and Worthing Farm will become the same as over-the-wall! Let him go or I will do that!"

Elijah thought then to take the gate from her and give it to another woman who would keep the law, but when the others saw that thought in his mind they forbade him, and said that they would kill him if he did.

You are all unworthy, Elijah said in silence. You are all cursed. You all will be destroyed because you consented to her breaking of the law. Then in silent rage Elijah stepped aside and let his brother go. Then he walked back to the field. Behind him, the grass where his feet had stepped went dry, and withered, a small trail of death. Elijah was angry, and there was death in him. He saw his mother notice this, and it pleased him. He saw that his cousins and his uncles also were afraid. There has been none like me in Worthing until now. Worthing has given me such power now, at the time when the law was broken by a woman who did not understand the danger of her most-beloved son. Worthing made me at the time of trouble, and I will not let Matthew leave here without punishment. The law will not be broken without revenge.

He did not decide what his revenge would be. He merely let his anger grow. Soon Mother began to shrivel like the grass, her skin drying and flaking off her, her tongue thick in her mouth. She drank and drank, but nothing could quench her thirst. Four days after Matthew left, she handed the gate to Arr, Elijah's wife, who did not want it; handed the gate to Arr and died.

Arr looked at her husband in fear and said, "I don't want this."

"It is yours. Obey the law."

"I can't bring Matthew back."

"I don't expect you to."

And in her mind Arr said, She was your mother.

And into her mind Elijah put his answer: Mother broke the law, and Worthing is angry at her. Matthew also broke the law, and you will see what Worthing does.

But nothing seemed to happen as the days went by. Matthew did not go far—he walked among the people of over-the-wall, the cousins and sisters and aunts with all their families, and the ones whose eyes were not the blue of Worthing, and he persuaded many of them to come away. Elijah could not know

what Matthew planned, only what he told the others. He spoke
of building a town, where he would keep the inn, a place ten
miles to the west, where the north road crossed the river and
travelers often passed. We will learn something of the world
of men and women, he said. And of all blasphemies, this was
the worst: As he laid the foundation of his inn he named it
Worthing.

There is only one Worthing in the world, and that is Worthing Farm.

It took two months before they realized how terrible Elijah's
vengeance was going to be. For in those weeks no rain fell,
and the sun beat down mercilessly every day. A stretch of
pleasant weather became a dry spell, and a dry spell became
a drought. No cloud came over the sky, and the heavy mustiness
of the air was gone, the air was dry as desert. The people's
lips chapped and split; the dry air hurt like a knife to breathe
it; the river fell, and hidden sand bars became islands, and then
peninsulas, and finally the river did not flow at all. The trees
of the Forest of Waters went grayish green, the leaves hung
limply from the branches, and in the fields of Worthing Farm,
despite the wells they dug and the water that they hauled from
the slackening river, the seedling crops went brown, went black,
and died.

It was much the work of hate, of Elijah's anger; even he
had not realized he could do so much.

And as the days went on, the people and animals began to
weaken. They came to Elijah then, and pleaded with him. You
have punished us all enough, they said. Our children, they
said. Let it rain. But Elijah could not do it. He had never
decided that the rain should stop; he had only filled himself
with anger, and he could not cease to hate just because he was
asked to; not even because he wanted to.

He wasn't even sure that he had done it. He heard travelers
telling Matthew in his fine new inn that droughts like this came
every now and then, but usually in Stipock across the sea. It
was natural enough, and it would end soon with a great storm
that near tore roofs from houses and drowned the world—it
happened every century or so, to renew the world.

Others said it was just chance. Storms passed to the south;
there was no drought in Linkeree, far to the west, or eastward

in Hux. Even the West River flowed strong and bold from Top
of the World down past Hux, only to dry up when it reached
the area of the drought. "I'd say you're in the center of it here,"
the travelers would say. "But it's just chance."

The children began to sicken, and because the water was
saved for the children, the animals began to die. The squirrels
dropped from the trees and lay dead in the field. The rats died
under the houses, and the dogs tore at them to drink their blood
and live another hour. The horses were found stiffening in the
stall, and the oxen staggered once or twice, and dropped.

If it is me, I wish to stop. If I have caused it, let it end.
But no matter how often he said it, or even shouted it aloud,
the drought only deepened, the heat grew worse, and now in
distant corners of the forest men and women patrolled to kill
anyone who lit a fire; even cookfires were forbidden, because
the slightest spark could burn the Forest of Waters from end
to end. And wagons rolled over the Heaven Mountains or
upriver from the sea or down from the Top of the World, filled
with water jars and water barrels, to buy a farm for a barrel,
a house for a jar, a child for a cup, and a woman's virtue for
a swallow of it. But water was life, and so worth the price.

The cousins and uncles came to Arr and said, Use the gate
and let us go. We must go where the water is being sold. Even
if we must sell Worthing Farm, we'll do it to save our lives.

But Elijah raged at them. What were their lives, compared
to Worthing Farm?

And in return they threatened him with death, until one of
them said that whatever Elijah had done to the world, he must
be left alive to undo it.

What are you waiting for? they finally said. Kill us now or
let us go—or does it please you to watch us die?

As for Elijah's wife, Arr, and their sons John and Adam,
they had no more to drink than anyone else. But it was as if
they sucked moisture from the air, or perhaps sank tap roots
deep into the earth, for their breath did not rattle in their throats
and their lips and noses did not bleed and they did not scream
for water in the night before they died, like the others. Even
those who lived over-the-wall did not suffer so badly, for they
could sell their souls for water, and survive. Nothing, however,
passed the wall of Worthing Farm.

One day Elijah heard Arr planning to use the gate and let the water sellers in. But Elijah knew the hearts of all the cousins and the uncles, and he knew that if the wall were opened they would all leave, all do as Matthew had done, and Worthing Farm would die.

It's dead anyway, they answered him. Look at the desolation. You have killed it.

But he did not open the gate, and he could not wish away the drought.

So on a day of maddening grief, those who survived began to carry all the corpses and lay them on the ground in front of Elijah's door. The babies and the children, the mothers and the wives, the old men and the young men: their parched corpses were a monument in the yard before Elijah's house. He heard them planning it and forbade them. He screamed at them but still they went on. And finally his rage at them was murder, and they died, adding their own fresh bodies to the pile they had made, and there were none left alive within the walls but Elijah's own family.

In an agony of hatred Elijah cursed them for having provoked him. I never wanted you to die! If you had stood beside me and kept my brother here—

And as he railed at the dead, they began to smolder, they began to burn; flames erupted from their abdomens, their limbs were crisp as tinder, and the smoke leapt up into the sky. When the flames were at their brightest, Arr ran from the house and flung the gate into the fire, where it exploded almost at once, the fire was so hot. And then she threw herself among the bodies of her friends and neighbors, whom her husband had made her kill: she blamed him for it with the last passion in her heart, because he had not let her use the gate to set them free.

It was only then, in utter anguish, that Elijah wept. Only then that he himself gave water to the world. And as he cried, while his sons watched the awful fire, there came a cloud in the west, so small at first that a man's hand held out from his body could cover it. But Matthew Worthing saw it from the tower of his inn, the tower that he had built to rise above the treetops so he could see Worthing Farm. Matthew saw the cloud and shouted to the people of his new village, Look, water!

And their hope for rain came into Elijah's mind like an earthquake, and he gasped with the power of it, and he, too, longed for water with all their longing, and his own besides; and with all the force of his anger and his guilt and his grief at what he had done, all that together in him called for the rain. The cloud grew, and the wind came up, and the brittle branches of the trees began to shatter in the wind; thunder pealed out and lightning raced across the blackened sky, and the rain began to fall like seas upon the forest. The rivers filled almost at once, the ground was torn and stripped, the trees caught fire from lightning but the rain soon put the fires out.

Then through the eyes of the villagers, Elijah saw the one fire he was glad of. The tower of Matthew's inn began to burn, with him in it; but Matthew raised his hand and the fire went out, vanished as if it had never been. I was right, thought Elijah. I was right, he lied to us, he had more power than to shut us out, I was right, I was right.

When the storm died away Worthing Farm was desolate; even the corpses had been swept into the torrent of the river. The gate was gone, which meant the wall was also gone; Elijah had nowhere else to go now, but to take his sons, leave Worthing Farm, and go west ten miles to his brother's inn, and beg forgiveness from him for the great harm he had done the world. But I was right, he said to himself, even as his brother galled him with his kindness and cruelly named him half owner of Worthing Inn. I was right, and Mother should have kept you in.

But he never said it aloud. Said, in fact, almost nothing for the rest of his life. He even held his tongue when Matthew took Elijah's sons into the street and said to them, "See that sign? That says Worthing Inn. That's all that's left of Worthing now, you and your father, me and my wife and our children yet to come. We're all that's left of Worthing now, thank God. It was a prison, but at last we're free."

Lared woke in darkness, to find Jason kneeling beside his bed. "Justice told me the dream was over," he said. "Your father calls to you."

Lared got up and went down the stairs. Mother was bending over Father, holding a cup to his lips. Lared wanted water, too, but didn't ask. Father's eyes had caught him.

"Lared," Father said. "I had a dream."

"So did I," said Lared.

"In my dream, I saw that you blamed yourself for this." He raised his stump. "I dreamed that you thought I hated you. By Worthing I swear it isn't so. There is no fault to this, I hold you blameless, you are still my son, you saved my life, forgive me if I said a thing to make you take the blame upon yourself."

"Thank you," Lared said. He went to his father and embraced him, and his father kissed him.

"Now sleep," said Father. "I'm sorry that I had them wake you, but I couldn't bear it if you went another hour with such feelings in your heart. By Jason, you're the finest son a man could have."

"Thank you," Lared said. Then he started for his truckle bed, but Jason led him up the stairs instead. "Tonight you've earned a better bed than that miserable straw bed by the fire."

"Have I?"

"You had the memory of Elijah Worthing in you, Lared. It's not a pleasant dream to have."

"Was it true? There was a drought like that in Stipock's colony, and it ended with that sort of storm, and no one made it happen."

"Does it matter? Elijah believed that he caused the drought and caused the storm. The rest of his life was shaped as if it were true—"

"But *was* it true?"

Jason pushed him gently down onto the bed and covered him with blankets. "Lared, I don't know. It's the memory of memory. Did all the people of Worthing die that way? Certainly there were no others in the world with my blue eyes, except those they could trace to Matthew and Elijah, but perhaps all the rest were hunted down and killed. As to the storm, there's no one now who can control the weather. But Justice can do other things, things with fire and water, earth and air. Who's to say that once there might not have been one man of all my children who could cause a drought like hell itself, and a storm like the end of the world. Certainly there's never been such hate as his. Never in all the memories I've seen has there been such hate."

"Compared to him," Lared whispered, "my hate for you is love."

"And so it is," said Jason. "Go to sleep."

10

In the Image of God

Father was out of bed now, but no one was rejoicing about it.
He was foul to be with, stamping around the house with his
crutch under his one arm, leaning like a tree in a hard wind,
snapped at everyone when he spoke at all. Lared understood
why he was so short-tempered, but that didn't make it any
easier. Gradually Lared found himself more interested in being
upstairs in Jason's room, working on the book, while others
found their own strategies for avoiding him. The women stopped
coming to the inn for their work; the tinker started visiting from
house to house; soon only Mother and Sala and Justice were
left in the empty downstairs of the inn. And even Mother
avoided him, forcing him to be alone more and more, and his
rage and shame grew, for he blamed it on his mutilation that
no one came near him if they could help it.

Except Sala. She haunted him. If Mother made her sweep,
Sala would soon be sweeping near Father's bed, where he lay
brooding; if she played with her mannikins, they danced the
May at Father's feet, where he rested by the fire. At such times
Father would watch her, and it would keep him quiet for a
time. But then he would try to do something—put a log on
the fire, grind the pease for the week's porridge—and she
would be there also, taking the other end of the log as he
struggled with it, brushing back the hard pease that he spilled;
and then he would grow savage, railing at her for a clumsy
fool and ordering her away. She went, and in a moment returned, quietly, and stayed always within reach of him. "If you
don't want trouble," Mother whispered to her once, "stay away
from him."

"He lost his arm, Mama," Sala answered, sounding as if
she thought he had mislaid it somewhere.

One evening as the tinker returned to the inn for supper,
and Lared came down from upstairs, Sala said to Father, loudly,

"Papa, I dreamed of where your arm is!"

There was no talking then, as they waited for Father's rage. But he surprised them: he only looked calmly at her and said, "Where is it?"

"The trees have it," she said. "So you must do as trees do, and when they lose the end of the branch, they grow it back."

Father whispered, "Sarela, I'm not a tree."

"Don't you know? My friend can tree you and wood you." And she looked at Justice.

Justice looked down at the table in front of her as if she hadn't understood a word. For a long moment they all stood there, looking at Justice. Then Sala began to weep. "Why is it forbidden?" she cried. "It's my Papa!"

"Enough," said Mama. "Sit to eat and stop your crying, Sala."

Father sat gravely at the head of the table, laying down the crutch beside him. "Eat," he said. And he began lifting the spoon to his mouth, again and again, to finish the meal as quickly as he could.

Jason had not been at table, but of course it was no accident that he came in now. He walked to Father carrying tongs from the forge and a bar of iron. "Somehow," he said, "this is supposed to become a scythe."

Mother took in her breath sharply, and the tinker looked at his plate. Father, however, merely studied the bar of iron. "It's too short for a scythe."

"Then I need you to find me a bar that *will* do."

Father smiled wryly. "Among all your talents, Jason, are you also a smith?" Father touched Jason's upper arm, which was strong as a man's arm should be, but slim as a child's compared to Father's.

Jason touched his own arm and laughed. "Well, we have a chance to see if a man gets an arm like yours from hammering, or hammers well because he has the arm."

"You're not a smith," said Father.

"Then perhaps I can, with both hands, serve as the left hand of a smith."

It was a bargain, and Father was good at bargaining. "What's to gain for you?"

"Little to gain, except good company and something to do

that's worth doing. Lared is writing things now that I never knew. He doesn't need me."

Father smiled. "I know what you're doing, Jason. But let's see if it will work." He turned to Sala. "Perhaps I can have two arms where I used to have one."

He got up from the table and put on his layers of coats and scarves; Jason helped him, and did not get shouted at once, because he knew just when Father wanted help and when he didn't, and just how much to do.

Lared watched them leave, thinking: I should have been the one to stand beside him at the forge. But I must write Jason's book, and so he takes my place beside my father. Yet he could not convince himself to be angry, or jealous, or to grieve. He had never longed to be a smith. He was almost relieved that someone else would stand with Father before the fire.

In a half hour they all heard the welcome sound of the hammer ringing in the forge, and Father cursing at the top of his lungs. That night Father stormed through the house, raging about muddleheaded fools who can't handle anything right and a scythe that will never be good for harvesting anything but hay. Father was interested in something again, and life would be bearable for the family.

And in the night Lared dreamed an ancient memory of a boy who lay in bed discovering the hearts of men.

John snored softly beside him, his breath sour from the night's cheese, but Adam was content to let him sleep. As long as John had lain awake, Adam couldn't go exploring. Now he could send his mind away to wander with no fear of John distracting him.

Adam had found this power only a few weeks before. He had been stalking a squirrel, to kill it with a thrown rock, and as he crept slowly forward he kept saying silently to the animal, Hold still, hold still. Squirrels had always held still for him longer than for any of the others—he thought it was because he was so stealthy. But this time the squirrel did not so much as twitch, and when Adam threw the stone and it missed, the squirrel did not scurry up the tree. It still sat, still waited until Adam came right up to it and picked it up and beat it against the tree. It never moved at all.

He played with the boys at the swimming hole. They had always ducked each other in the water, played at drowned man; Adam could do it better now, and when Raggy swam under the water, he made him think that up was down until the air was a knife in his lungs. Then he let him up. Raggy came out of the water crying, terrified, and would not go in again whatever the boys said. But once Adam had done it to enough of the boys, they grew afraid and said there was a monster in the water, and they wouldn't swim anymore.

That was all right. Adam had grown into other amusements. Now he lay awake at night, and went exploring in the minds of the villagers of Worthing Town. Enoch Cooper first, because Adam was doing a thing to him each night when he went at his wife. Last night he had made him go limp as a leaf just before the end. Tonight he stayed with him for an hour, never letting him finish, until his wife, who was long since satisfied, begged him to quit and go to sleep. Oh, Enoch Cooper did swear and call on Jason, and he couldn't sleep for the tightness of his groin.

Then Adam found Goody Miller, who kept cats. Last night he made her favorite hiss and scratch at her, so she cried herself to sleep. Tonight he made her hold the cat's head under the millstone. In the old days it would have been the crushing of the cat that Adam relished, but there was far more pleasure in being inside Goody Miller's mind as she screamed and grieved over the cat. "What have I done to you! What have I done?"

And Raggy—he was always fun to do things to, because for so long he had bossed them all in whatever game they played. He got Raggy to stand out of his bed, take off his nightgown, go to Mary Hooker's place beside the river and stand at her door, playing with himself, until her father opened it and drove him off with kicks and curses. Oh, this was a grand night.

In the back of his mind, each person that he did things to became a little dry corpse, and he added it to a growing pile of corpses at the door. Is that good, Papa? Is that enough?

He made Ann Baker think that there were little spiders on her breasts, and she scratched and tore at them until they were bloody and her husband had to bind her hands behind her.

Is that enough?

Sammy Barber went to his shop and filed his razors flat.
Is that enough?

Veddy Upstreet nursed her baby in the night, and suddenly
the child refused to breathe, no matter what she did.

Stop.

Wouldn't breathe no matter—

"Stop."

Adam opened his eyes, and there stood Father in the doorway. John stirred beside Adam in the bed. "Stop what, Papa?"
asked Adam.

"What you have came to you from Jason. Not for this."

"I don't know what you're talking about." In the Upstreet
house, the baby breathed again, and Veddy wept in relief.

"You are no son of mine."

"I'm just playing, Papa."

"With other people's pain? If you do this again I'll kill you.
I ought to kill you now." Elijah held a knotted hemp in his
hand, and he dragged Adam from the bed, pulled his nightgown
up over his head and arms, and began to beat him.

From the bed, little John cried, "Papa, stop! Papa, no!"

"You're too soft-hearted, John," Father said, grunting from
the force of the blows he gave. Adam writhed in his grasp, so
the rope struck him on the back and belly, hip and head, until
Adam did what he had never dared to do, and made his father
hold *still*.

And Elijah held still.

Adam pulled free of his father's grasp and gazed in wonder
at him. "I am stronger than you," he said. Then he laughed,
despite the pain of the blows his father gave him. He took the
hemp from his father's hand and raised his father's nightgown
over his head. He tapped his father with the hemp.

"No," whispered John.

"Hold your tongue or I'll do you, too."

"No," said John aloud.

In answer Adam struck his father across the belly with the
rope. Elijah did not so much as flinch. "See, John? It doesn't
hurt."

"Why doesn't Papa move?"

"He likes it." He kicked his father in the groin with all his
strength. Again not a sound; but the blow overbalanced him,

and Elijah toppled over backward, lay helpless and unmoving on the floor, looking for all the world like one of the corpses on the pile. What are you doing, Papa, lying on the pile? Do you want to burn with Mama? Are you dry? Adam kicked and beat and stamped and John screamed, "Uncle Matthew! Uncle Matthew!" And suddenly Adam felt himself flying across the room, slamming into the leathers hanging on the wall.

Uncle Matthew stood at the top of the cellar stairs. "Get your clothing," Matthew said.

Adam tried to make him hold still, just like Elijah, but he couldn't seem to find Uncle Matthew's mind. Suddenly he felt himself burn up inside, so that he clawed at his belly to let the fire out. Then he felt his eyes melting, dripping down onto his cheeks, and in terror he screamed and tried to push them back in place. Then his legs began to crumble like a sugar man, and he lurched closer and closer to the floor; he bent over and watched the pieces of his face fall off and lie shriveling on the floor, ears and nose and lips and teeth and tongue, his eyes last like jelly, only now he looked up from those eyes at his empty face, just blank and featureless skin with a gaping hole for his mouth, and he saw the mouth suddenly fill from inside, and out came his heart, and then his liver, and then his stomach and bowel as his body emptied itself, until he was light and empty as a flourbag in spring—

And then he lay on the floor, weeping and pleading for mercy, for forgiveness, for his body back the way it was.

"Adam," John said softly from the bed, "what's wrong with you?"

Adam touched his face and everything was there, as it should be; he opened his eyes, and he could see. "I'm sorry," he whispered. "I'll never do it again."

Elijah was crying where he sat now, leaning against the wall. "Ah, Matthew," he wept, "what have I made here? What monster have I made?"

Matthew shook his head. "What harms have you done to Adam that you haven't also done to John?"

Then Elijah realized something, and smiled despite his pain. "I *was* right. You are one of us, just as I said."

"Please don't do it again," Adam whispered.

"You and your father," Matthew said. "Neither of you knows

what your power is for. Do you think Jason made us to live forever on a farm, Elijah? Or to play cruel pranks on people who can't protect themselves? I am watching you now, both of you, I'll have you do no more harm. You have both done enough harm in your lives. Now it's time that you began to heal."

Adam lived at Matthew's inn for two more years. Then, on a day when he could bear it no more, he fled empty-handed, stole a boat and went downriver to Linkeree. On the way he searched backward, looked in Worthing Inn until he found his uncle's son, little Matt, a baby just learning his first words. He made the baby speak aloud: "Good-bye, Uncle Matthew." And then he killed it.

He waited for the answering blow from Matthew's mind, but it never came. I am beyond his reach, Adam realized. I am safe at last. I can do what I like.

He made his way to Heaven City, the capital of the world. Adam was safe on every road, for who could even think of harming him? And he was never hungry, for so many people yearned to give him food. In Heaven City he waited and watched. This much he had learned from Uncle Matthew: his power would not be used for games. He had read the stone in the middle of Worthing Farm, as all the blue-eyed children read it: From the stars blue-eyed one, from this land Jason's son. I am the first to leave the Forest of Waters. I am Jason's son. I will not be content with a plot of ground, or even an inn, but the world should be enough for me.

And bit by bit, the world came to him.

Came to him in the shape of a girl, not so little anymore, the granddaughter of Elena of Noyock. She haunted the palace, always just out of sight, holding still in a corner, under a stair, by a curtain. It was not that she was unsupervised. Some of the servants were probably detailed to keep an eye on her. But it didn't matter much. No one cared that much about her, for she had a younger brother, and Noyock's rulers were succeeded by the eldest male. Elena of Noyock was merely guardian, in favor of her grandson, Ivvis. What was Uwen, the granddaughter, the invisible? When Adam first came to live at Elena's palace, he noticed her, determined that she was nothing, and ignored her.

So a year passed, in which Adam had made himself indispensible to Elena of Noyock. He had risen quickly, but not suspiciously so—no higher or faster than native genius might make a young man rise. Elena sent him to conduct delicate negotiations for her—he always seemed to extract the very most that could be won from any situation. Elena had him choose her servants and her guards, for the ones he chose were loyal and served well; he was never deceived. And when he told her what her enemies were planning, his information always turned out to be correct. Elena prospered. Noyock even prospered. Above all, Adam prospered. Everyone watched him as he made his way through the chambers and porches of Heaven City. Watched him with envy, or hatred, or admiration, or fear.

Except for Uwen. Uwen watched him with love. Whenever Adam noticed her, he noticed that. Saw in her memory that she came sometimes to his room at night, as he lay alone on his mat in the darkness. In the night she studied him, when he was alone and when he was not alone, studied him and wondered how this man from nowhere had managed to be powerful, to be noticed, to be somebody, when she, the daughter of a lord, granddaughter of Elena of Noyock, had never been noticed at all. What do you do? she wondered. How do you know what you know? How do you say what you say?

But by the time Adam noticed that Uwen was asking these questions, she had the answer. Adam was the enchanted man. Adam was the man of wood from the forest. She knew all the old tales. Adam was the Son of God. When he climbed the stairs to the third floor to go to bed one night, she was leaning on the banister at the top. Not hiding anymore. It was time, she had decided, to be seen.

"What did you do, Adam Waters?" asked Uwen. "For a living, I mean. Before you came here." She perched on the banister above the steep drop down the stairwell.

"I looked for little girls who wanted to die, and I pushed them down stairwells," said Adam.

"I'm fourteen years old," said Uwen, "and I know your secret."

Adam raised an eyebrow. "I have no secrets."

"You have one very big secret," said Uwen. "And your secret is that you know all the other people's secrets."

Adam smiled. "Do I?"

"You listen all the time, don't you? That's how *I* find out secrets. I listen. I've seen the way you pay such close attention to everyone who comes to our house. Mother says you are very wise, but I think you just listen."

"We wouldn't want people to think I'm wise, would we."

Uwen entwined herself into the rails like a weed grown up through a picket fence. "But when you listen," said Uwen, "you even hear what people didn't say."

Adam felt a thrill of fear. In all his maneuvering to rise through the ranks of diplomats and bureaucrats in Heaven City, no one had guessed his secret until now. How many people had he whispered to, who had recoiled in fear and said, "Who told you? How did you know?" But none had said, You even hear what people didn't say. Already Adam imagined Uwen's death. It would annoy her grandmother, but not seriously. The child was not particularly useful until she could be married to political advantage. It was not as if the child were loved. Adam felt no debt to Elena of Noyock. He had benefited her as much as she had him, and that made them even; he did not owe her his life itself. And it *was* his life at stake. For if people once guessed that instead of controlling a network of informers, as they all supposed, Adam Waters had only his own mind supplying him his secrets, then everyone he had blackmailed would be out to kill him, and Adam would be dead within a day. My life or yours, Uwen. "How could I hear them?" asked Adam.

"You lie on your back in bed," said Uwen, "and you listen. Sometimes you smile, and sometimes you frown, and then you wake up and write letters, or go make visits, or tell Grandmother, 'The governor of Gravesend wants this much and no more,' or 'The bank of Wien has let all its gold slip away to build the highway, and they're buying at a premium now.' It gives you power. You're going to rule the world someday."

"Don't you know that if you tell people such things, someone might actually believe you, and then my life would be in danger?" I could make the banister break right now, but the fall might not kill her.

"I don't tell secrets. I'll never tell yours, if you do one thing."

I could make her erupt into flames from the inside out—it

would be thorough, but perhaps too flamboyant. "You were a cute little girl, Uwen, but you're becoming something of a bitch as you get older."

"I'm becoming an unusually interesting young woman," said Uwen. "And if you're planning on killing me, I've already written everything down. All my proof."

"You don't have any proof. There's nothing to prove."

"As Grandmother always says, innuendo is everything in politics. It's much easier to be believed when you're telling people that a powerful young man is really a monster."

The banister creaked and began to crack.

"I love you," said Uwen. "Marry me, get rid of my brother, and Noyock will be yours."

"I don't want Noyock," said Adam. The banister began tilting backward.

"You wouldn't dare," said Uwen. "I'm second in line to the throne of Noyock. I can help you."

"I can't think now," said Adam.

"I know things."

"Everything you know, I know," said Adam.

"I would be the one person," she said, "that you could tell the truth to. Don't you ever wish that you could tell the truth to somebody? You've been in Heaven City for five years now, and you're just about to play for everything, and when it's done what will you have to do with yourself?"

The banister righted itself. "You'd better get off," Adam said. "It isn't safe."

She unwound her legs from the rails and clambered off, then walked to Adam where he stood leaning on the wall; she walked to him and pressed herself against him and said, "So you'll marry me?"

"Never," said Adam, putting his hands behind her, holding her close to him.

"You want to marry power, don't you?" she said, lifting her skirt and guiding his hand to rest on her naked hip.

"You aren't the heir. Your brother Ivvis is."

She lifted his tunic, too, and began to fumble with his codpiece. "I don't *have* to have a brother."

"Even if you had no brother, Noyock isn't strong enough for what I want to do. You will never be powerful enough."

He checked the servants and made sure none of them had the slightest desire to come up to the third floor of Duchess Elena's Heaven City palace.

She looked angry. "Then why did you let me live?"

He lifted her up, his hands behind her thighs, and carried her into her room. "Because I like you."

Adam was very careful with her. He could feel everything she felt, knew what she enjoyed, what she did not enjoy, when she was unready, when she was eager, when she needed passion, when she needed gentleness. He was her only memory of lovers; the other women he had taken were too cluttered with faces in their minds, names to cry out in the moment of delight. Uwen had only him. She would never need anyone else. "You love me," she whispered.

"Whatever you need to believe," said Adam, "is fine with me."

Adam was in no hurry. There was little suspense in the final outcome. Heaven City was not like Worthing Farm. Here there was no one to undo him, no one whose power matched his or surpassed it. When he was challenged to a duel here he knew that he could win; and did, until the challenges stopped. When someone thwarted him he could easily move them aside. He could flatter almost anyone, and when he tired of that, he could frighten or seduce or, ultimately, strike down whoever stood in his way.

Except Zoferil of Stipock. Zoferil was a woman of honor and deep faith, who alone of all the rulers of the world had never lied and never would. When she could not speak the truth she said nothing, and when she did speak the truth her words were knives that cut to the heart of all hearers. They feared her, even those whose armies were larger, because they knew that the people of Stipock truly loved Zoferil as she loved them, and would die for her, and she for them; they could not get her to conspire with them in any dishonorable thing, and so she remained aloof from all their plans, a constant threat because if she brought her army into any war it would easily swing the balance. Without her as an ally there was always the risk that she would be an enemy. People of every nation said, Jason must love the land of Stipock, because he gave them Zoferil.

"I will have Zoferil's power and I will have her love," said Adam. "She is mine."

"She's an old lady and you'll never love her," said Uwen.

"But with Stipock and Noyock both mine," said Adam, "the rest of the world will slip into place quietly."

"Noyock isn't yours," said Uwen. "It's Grandmother's."

Adam didn't need to argue. Didn't need to say, *she* is mine, and you are mine, and your little brother Ivvis is also mine. Everyone was his; Uwen simply knew it, that's all, and it gave her a sense of freedom, to at least be aware of her possession.

Elena of Noyock grew old, and her grandson Ivvis was still a child; with the weight of death upon her, she felt a need to name a regent—Adam was her choice, of course. She died soon after when her ship was lost at sea. Adam was a scrupulous regent, protecting the child-magister from all harm, teaching him studiously to be a man of virtue. At the court of the Heaven King they watched how the young man grew, a model of what a ruler ought to be; and in a world where regents more often had to be removed by bloodshed than by law, Adam surprised them all by turning power over to young Ivvis two years before the law required, because the boy was ready to be magister in his own right. The world admired how gracefully Adam stepped back at once into his role as one adviser among many. No one thought it anything but a fortunate coincidence that this happened just as Zoferil's eldest daughter and, sadly, only surviving child came of age. No one but Uwen.

"If you can kill off Gatha's brothers, why couldn't you kill off mine?" demanded Uwen. "And why didn't you just keep the power, when you had it?"

"Doesn't it occur to you that sometimes I like to win things by merit, and not by secret compulsion?"

"You'll never compel *me*."

"I never had to."

"She's not as beautiful as I am. What does Gatha have, that you want to marry her and not me?"

"For one thing," said Adam, "she's a virgin."

Uwen kicked at him, and Adam laughed at her as he went to call on Zoferil.

"All my sons have died during these last few years," said Zoferil to Adam. "I would have hoped that, if they lived, they would each have become a man like you. Adam, it is time for my daughter to have a husband, and the desire of her heart is like the desire of mine: that you be my son, and help her rule Stipock after I am gone."

"I would say yes at once," said Adam, "but I cannot deceive you. I am not what I seem."

"You seem to be the best and wisest and most honorable of men," said Zoferil.

"No," said Adam. "I have deceived the world and disguised myself all these years."

"Who are you then, if you are not Adam Waters?"

"My true name is Worthing. I think you know the name."

"Jason's son," whispered Zoferil.

"I thought before you gave me your daughter, you ought to know."

"You," she whispered. "For a thousand years the secret rite of the men and women of Stipock has called upon the sacred, holy name of Worthing, Jason's son. When I saw your eyes like a perfect sky, I wondered. When I saw your virtue like the purest of all men, I hoped. Now, Adam Worthing, now I know you, and I beg you to take my daughter and my kingdom both, if only you think us worthy."

She crowned him with the crown of iron, and put the iron hammer in his hand, and he vowed that never a sword would come from the forges of Stipock, as all the philocrats of Stipock had sworn before him. All the world looked to him in love or jealousy, and the people of Stipock honored him as if he had been born among them.

Adam had some mercy. He waited until Zoferil was dead to unmask himself.

Then, with a pathetic plot of Wien and Kapock as his excuse, Adam sent the armies of Stipock and the fleets of Noyock to bring blood and terror to every kingdom of the world. Adam's enemies could not stand against him. Their armies could not find him until he stood behind them; their own guards turned against them and assassinated them; and within three years, for the first time since Jason had taken the original Star Tower into heaven, all the world was ruled from Heaven City, and Adam named himself Jason's Son, the true Heaven King.

Even then there were still some who loved him. But through

the years of his misrule they learned what he truly was. How could he pursue power now, when there was no more power to be had in all the world? He plumbed the secrets of death and pain by torturing and killing while tasting the experience in his victim's minds. He broke great men and women, and impoverished great families. He took his pleasure with the virtuous daughters of noble houses and then sold them for whores. He took as much in taxes as he could, and more, so that famines came to lands whose harvests had been good; when the desperate people begged for food at any price, he bought them as slaves to build his monuments. It was as if he set himself the task of proving that he was so powerful that even when everyone in the world hated him, he could still rule them, could still keep his power. His wife, Gatha, wept to see what he had become; his mistress, Uwen, urged him on, for she loved the pleasures of power even more than Adam did. In Heaven City she built the Star Tower the same size and same shape as the one described as Jason's own, and sheathed it in silver, and the bodies of five thousand dead were buried under it. And any who spoke or acted against either of them was ingeniously undone for all the world to see, for all the world to hear the screams. I am God Himself, Adam said at last, and there was no one who dared to say that he was not.

But Adam lived in fear. For he had sent an army to a certain village in the Forest of Waters, and they had killed all the inhabitants and brought their heads to him, and he had looked from head to head, the eyes sewn open, and not one of the eyes was pure as the sky, and not one of the faces belonged to Father Elijah or Uncle Matthew or Brother John; not one of the faces seemed even to be kin. Somewhere in the world there was someone, he knew it, someone who could see into his mind. And yet, like Matthew, they could hide their minds from him. He dreamed at night of the way that Matthew had poured his face upon the ground, and woke up screaming, and then searched the minds of those around him, trying to find out who might have seen a blue-eyed man, who might have heard of someone who had power to rival his own.

Poor me, thought Adam. There is no pleasure for me in the world, so long as I have not found and killed my kin.

• • •

"Jason's son," said Lared scornfully. "That is what came of all your plans?"

"You've got to admit that as a breeding experiment it worked out beautifully. More power than I dreamed could come of what *I* had. I can't control other people's thoughts or actions. All I can do is see through their minds and memories. And don't believe that he's as singularly monstrous as the dream says. This came to you through too many people who loathed him. He was the devil, the Abner Doon of Worthing's world. I suspect he lived in a cruel time, and differed from other rulers only in that he was far more successful in exercising his power. The tortures—I suspect he didn't invent them, though he didn't refuse to use them, either. He was a very bad man, but by the standards of his time I think he wasn't monstrous. But then, I may be wrong. Write him as you dreamed him, and your tale will not be lies."

"What about the others—his father and an uncle and brother?"

"Oh, his father died desperately soon after he left. His brother—you know the tale. His brother became a tinker and a healer and a lover of birds. As for Matthew—his baby, Little Matthew, did not die. In the thirty years of Adam's rise to power, little Matthew grew, and had a son named Amos, and inherited the inn when his father died. After the death of John Tinker, which happened the year of Adam's wedding to Zoferil's daughter, Matthew and Amos went away to live in Hux, near the place where the West River flows out of Top of the World. They became merchants."

Amos looked out the window of his tower onto the streets and rooftops of Hux. He always lived in a tower and worked in a tower, and left seed for the birds at the sills of every window. They came to him all winter, all summer, and he never failed them. Sometimes, with the birds fluttering about his tower, he could pretend that he was worthy of his uncle John Tinker, who lay in a grave at Worthing.

"You remember Uncle John," said Amos.

"Not myself," said his youngest daughter, Faith. It was her way, to try to make differences in words.

"You remember my memories of him."

"He should never have let them have power over him. He should have changed them."

Ah, Faith, sighed Amos. Of all my children, will you be the first that cannot bear the burden that we have taken on? "Oh? And what would he have made them, then?"

"He would have made them stop. Hurting him. He didn't have to let them hurt him."

"They've paid with their lives," said Amos. "Their heads were all cut off and taken away to Stipock City, for Jason's Son to view them."

"And he," said Faith, "he is another one we ought to stop. Why should we allow a man like that to—"

Amos touched her lips with his finger. "John Tinker was the best of us. Infinite patience. None of the rest of us has it. But we must try."

"Why?"

"Because Jason's Son is also one of us."

He watched her face. Since childhood there had not been much that could surprise her, but this was the most painful and dangerous of secrets, and so the children were not shown until they came of age. But are you of age, Faith? Or will we have to put you into the stone for safekeeping, for the sake of the world? To ourselves we must be crueler than cruel, so that to the world we can be kind.

"Jason's Son! How can he be one of us? Whose child is he? You have seven sons and seven daughters, and grandfather has his three and eight, besides you. I know all my brothers and sisters, all my nieces and nephews, and—"

"And hold your tongue. Don't you know that all your brothers and sisters are watching their little ones, to be certain that they do not overhear us? We can't take too much time for this. I have much to explain, and there is little time."

"Why so little time?"

"Because Adam and his children are asleep," said Amos, "but soon they will waken, and you must be decided before they do."

"What do you want me to decide?"

"Hold your tongue, Faith, and hear me, and you will know."

Faith held her tongue, even as she probed for answers in her father's head.

"Foolish child, don't you know that I can close my mind to you? Don't you know that this is what makes us different from Adam and his children? He has no guard in his mind against us, but we can shut him out. Power for power we match him, but we can also keep him out. It makes us stronger than he is."

"Then why don't we throw the devil out!" cried Faith. "He has no right to rule the world!"

"No, he has no right. But who has a better? Who will take his place?"

"Why does the world need to be ruled at all?"

"Because without rule there is no freedom. If people do not walk their appointed path, and obey a law, and unite themselves to say a single word, at least from time to time, then there is no order in the world. And where there is no order there is no power to predict the future, for nothing can be depended on; and where the future cannot be known or guessed at, who can plan? Who can choose? There is no freedom, because there is no rule. Must I teach you the lessons that I taught you from your infancy?"

"No, Father, you don't need to teach me anything."

"If you've learned it already, why are you such a fool? Why did you strike down Vel when she quarreled with you in the street?"

Faith immediately looked defiant. "I hardly touched her."

"You made her remember, for just a moment, the grief she felt at her mother's death. You took the worst hour of her life and gave it back to her, just because she said something you didn't like. You did to her the worst thing in the world, and only for your petty vengeance. Tell me, Faith, what is the difference between Jason's Son and you, that you think you should rule in his place?"

"A hundred thousand dead, that's the difference."

"He killed more because he had more power. Take his power, and won't you be the same? There is more at stake here than you think, Faith. When Father and I first came here, we understood for the first time how much power we really had, as Adam must have realized when he went to Heaven City more than a generation ago. We could make people lend us money and then forget that we owed it to them; we could make our debtors pay us first; we could buy properties whose owners didn't even want to sell. We could be very, very rich."

"You *are* rich."

"But no one is poorer because of it," said Amos. "We stole from no one. We only made new land where there was none before, and found gold where it was hidden in the earth, and above all made the city safe and prosperous, so that all who lived here did well. There are no poor in Hux, Faith. You've never known it any other way, but I tell you that is our achievement. It is our achievement every day."

Faith looked narrowly at him. "What do you gain?"

"John Tinker doesn't reproach me with his death," said Amos. "John Tinker's birds still come to me."

"That's not a reason."

"Yes it is. He lived his life and did no harm."

"And look what it got him."

"Death. But we've learned from him."

"Yes—don't let them near you."

"No. Don't let them know. Uncle John could have healed them to his heart's content, and never would have tasted their resentment if they hadn't known he was the healer. So the people of Hux look at the countinghouse of Matthew and Amos and see nothing but a prosperous business with what seems like half a hundred blue-eyed children constantly about. They don't know that their children live through childhood because of us, their cows give milk and do not sicken and die because of us, their marriages remain unbroken and their contracts all are kept, because somewhere in this house, always, there are two or three or five or half a dozen of us listening, watching, making sure this city is safe from pain—"

Faith shook her head and smiled. "I know what you are. You think that *you're* Jason's children."

Amos shook his head. All the other children had nodded, had understood. They had done nothing to deserve their gift; it was a stewardship; the city had been given into their care, and they must keep it safe. "In all the history of this world," said Amos, "there has never been a happier place than this, the city of Hux, under our care. Mothers no longer fear childbirth, because they know that they will live. Parents are willing to love their children, because they know the children will survive to be adults."

"And yet you still let Jason's Son rule the world."

"Yes," said Amos. "Your very desire to destroy him, Faith, tells me that you are more kin of his than kin of mine. Child, today is the day I ask you, Will you protect the secret and keep the covenant? Will you use your gifts only for healing, never for vengeance, punishment, or harm?"

"What about justice?" demanded Faith.

"Justice is the perfect balance," said Amos, "but only the perfectly balanced heart can be just. Is that you?"

"I know good from evil."

"Will you take the covenant?"

She did not need to answer. He knew her answer from the fact that she closed her mind to him. When she said, "Yes," it only made it worse.

"Do you think that you can lie to *me?*"

She tossed her head defiantly. "Jason's Son is a wound in the world, and I'll heal it. If that's keeping the covenant, then I'll keep it."

"And plunge the world into war again."

Faith got up. "The world is in pain, and one little city is all that you can think about. What good is Hux's happiness, while the world is ground down?"

"It takes time. The children growing up now—then there'll be enough to reach out farther, accomplish more—"

"I won't be part of this," said Faith. "I'm a match for Jason's Son, and I will take his place."

"Will you?" asked Amos. "I hope that you will not. But for the world's sake, Faith, we must put you in the stone."

She did not know what he meant.

But she knew when they took her out into the wilderness, up into the foothills of the mountains, to a place where the living rock cropped out and lay smooth and flat as the sheets on a virgin's bed. "What are you doing to me?" she demanded, for, being violent-hearted, she feared violence.

We have to know, said Amos silently, who you are.

"All these years, and you don't know me?"

We can know your memories, and we can know our memories, but how can we know your future? How can we know how much evil can dwell comfortably in you? The seeds of destruction are there—will they take root, and will you crumble away the rock at the heart of the world?

"What will you do to me?"

Why, we'll make you someone that you are not, and learn from that who you are. We'll float you over the stone, where you're cut off from all life; make you part of the stone, so you're cut off from your own flesh; and then see how much of Adam Worthing you can be.

"Will I die?" Faith asked her father.

I've gone into the stone myself, and came out whole. I did it—we did it because only in stone can we set our memories aside and let someone else's whole mind enter into ours; I floated the stone, and brought each of Adam Worthing's children, one by one, into my mind, to judge them.

"And did they fail?"

Failure would have been not to know them fully. I did not fail. We know them now from the inside out.

"Were they good people?"

As much as I am good, they are good, because their whole memory could fit into my mind and did not drive me mad. So now you will float the stone, and put yourself out of yourself into the living rock, and take another mind into your own.

"Whose?"

That's your choice, Faith. You may take mine. Or you may take Adam Worthing's. Whichever will be most like you. Whichever you think least likely to destroy you.

"How can I know? I don't know either of you. Not really."

That's why we float the stone. It's more than remembering someone else's memories. It's becoming someone else, and measuring his life against your own soul. If the person is too different from you, then you will die.

"How do you know? Who floated the stone and died before?"

Elijah. He was the first. When Adam ran away, when Adam murdered and ran away, Elijah floated the stone and searched for him. And found him. Young Adam was so monstrous that it killed the old man.

"But Father—didn't you say that you had floated the stone for Adam, too?"

No. Only for his children.

"And for me? Would you float the stone for me?"

Faith, I would do it for you if I thought that I would live.

"Do you think that you're so different from me, then? That I'm as monstrously evil as Jason's Son?"

I think that his memories can dwell in your heart better than mine can. I think that if you had a perfect memory of every act and every choice and every feeling I have had in my life, child, that it would drive you mad and you would never find your own self in the stone, and you would die.

"Then I'll take Adam into me. But I'm not a fool, Father. I know what this means. If I can *be* Adam Worthing, then I am not worthy, by your standard. And if I can't endure him, then I'll be justified, but unfortunately I'll also go mad and die."

That's why the choice is left to you.

She took the memory of floating the stone from her father's mind: he opened the memory to her, so she could see. Then, wearing nothing between her and the naked stone, she lay down on it and did exactly what she remembered that her father did.

It was Father who worked on the stone, Father who knew how to make it flow, cold as water, smooth as water, so that she sank backward into the liquid stone and floated on the cold face of the world.

And as she lay there, letting herself seep into the stone, letting her memories flow away, the others guided her to Adam Worthing. They were gentle with Adam, so that he would not know what was being done. They could not be kind to her.

So Faith became Adam Worthing, from his childhood up, from the first terror in his cellar room at Worthing Inn, through each vicious act, each seizure of power, each undoing of other men and women, each slaughter on the battlefield, each massacre of innocents for the sheer joy of doing it.

And when it was done, and she had borne the weight of his terrible past as if it were her own, and it had not driven her mad, she wept with shame, and let herself flow back into herself, and wished that she had died upon the stone.

The others looked at her coldly and turned away. Only her father did not turn from her, and he was weeping. "I couldn't do it," he said aloud.

In his unguarded mind she saw his failure: when it was clear that she could bear to be Adam Worthing, it was his duty to let the liquid stone solidify, and hold her there; to kill her, and keep her memories imprisoned in the rock, rather than to let her live and become another Adam in the world.

"It isn't true," she said. "It isn't just. I can bear him, but I could bear you, too. I'm not like him, not wholly. I'm like you, too. Father, you won't regret it that you let me live."

But he did regret it. They all regretted it, until Faith could hardly bear the shame that she was still alive. I am not like him, she said to herself, over and over. They're wrong about what the stone means.

They were not wrong, though. She knew it, deeper than all her silent protests, she knew that the judgment was just. It took her months of living as a pariah in her father's house, but at last she understood that, yes, all the malice of Adam's life fit easily into her heart, with room left, still. Room for more.

But where is it written, where was it said that I can't change?

The others were never glad to talk to her. They shared with her no tales of their work in healing all the wounds of Hux. But they also could not stop her from watching, from letting her mind wander through the city and see how each wound, each grief, each fear was healed. This is how it's done, she saw; all my instincts were to break, but this is how the broken heart is made whole again.

And when she was confident of herself, she went to Adam Worthing.

She went to Adam Worthing, not in the mind, but in the flesh. She had kept her mind closed to the others; they did not know where she had gone. It hardly mattered—they would not miss her if she died, and as for any danger from Adam, she would not let him know where the others were, or that they even existed. But even if he did know, even if her act endangered everyone, she would do it. For she had taken Adam Worthing into herself, and knew where he was broken, and hoped to heal him, if it was in him to endure the healing.

Still, in case they feared her enough to stop her, she left Hux furtively. Down the West River to Linkeree, then by sea to Stipock City. She made her way easily from wharf to city, from city to castle, from castle to the palace on the red rock cliff overlooking the sea. She knew the words to say to get past every guard and every servant. Until she stood in the anteroom of the court of Jason's Son. She sat calmly and waited as the people came and went for audiences with the Son of God.

"You're too late," said the tired-faced woman beside her.

"For what?" asked Faith.

"To stop him," she said. "You should have come years ago."

The woman was worn, and the elegant clothing could not hide the emaciation. She was dying.

"And he could heal you, if he would."

"Healing isn't what he does." She lifted her chin defiantly. "But I had what I had of him, and it was better than the world gives."

"Uwen," said Faith, naming her.

"He knows you're coming," said Uwen.

"Does he?"

"He's known for all these years. Always waiting. I saw it in him. I was good at watching. Always looking southward from Heaven City, or northward from here, toward the village he destroyed in the Forest of Waters. You come from there, don't you? You can tell me. I won't whisper a word." She smiled. "He knows your heart already. He does that, you know. He knows your heart."

So there was no surprise in her coming. It hardly mattered. She knew Adam better than Adam knew himself. She was not afraid of him. "I'll go in now," she said to Uwen.

"Have you come to kill him?" asked Uwen.

"No."

"Will he love me, when you're through?"

"You're dying, aren't you?"

Uwen shrugged.

Faith reached for her, found the sickness, and made her whole.

Uwen said nothing, just sat and stared at her hands. Faith got up and walked into the hall. The guards did not so much as think of stopping her. She saw to that.

She knelt before the white-haired Son of Jason on his throne. "I've been waiting for you," Adam said.

"I didn't send word ahead. I think we've never met," said Faith.

"She comes with eyes as blue as mine, as blue as my children's eyes, and when I look behind those eyes I see nothing. There was a man once who hid from me. I'd kill him if I could. I'll kill you, too, if I can."

Behind her she heard the footsteps of the soldiers, the whisper of metal rising through the sheath.

She stilled the soldiers with their own memories of the fear of death.

"I know you," she said to Jason's Son. She froze him with the memory of Uncle Matthew standing at the door, the image he had feared most, all his life—the man who could undo him, treat his power like the strength of a squirrel, all quickness but no force in it. And while he sat transfixed, she went into his memories and changed them.

Some things would be possible, and some would not. She could not change his ravening appetite for power, or the fear of failing that gnawed at him—that was deeper than memory, that was part of the shape of himself. But she could make him remember controlling those appetites and fears, refusing to be ruled by them. In his memory now he never killed, though he was tempted to; never seduced, never bullied, never tortured, though the opportunities had come. And when the blood was too thick and deep for her to scrub it out of Adam's memory, she gave him reasons why these acts were not sheer exercise of power. Reasons why each was necessary, why each was good, in the long run, for the people.

And when she was done with him, he was no longer an irresistible tyrant jaded by so many crimes that he hardly noticed them and destroyed by mere habit. Now he was a ruler who feared nothing but his own desires, and avoided his lust for cruelty with the same fear that once he had devoted to the memory, now lost, of Uncle Matthew.

No, not lost. For his memories, the most vivid of them, lived in Faith's own mind. The stone had given her back herself, but nothing could take from her Adam's past.

They were surrounded by people, courtiers and bureaucrats who had come to marvel at the sight of the blue-eyed tyrant and the girl who stood before him, matching him gaze for gaze, hour after hour, in utter silence, while they hardly breathed. What power did she have over Jason's Son? What death would this result in? Who would suffer?

But then it was over, and Adam smiled at her and said, "Go in peace, cousin," and she turned and walked away and they did not see her again, and Adam forbade them to look for her.

It was a clumsy job she did—for years afterward there were curious lapses in Adam's memory, and sometimes he rebelled against the life of self-restraint that he believed that he had led. But on the whole, he was healed, and all of Worthing's world knew it, bit by bit. The monster in the Son of Jason had been tamed; the world could bear his rule.

Amos was waiting for her when she returned to Hux. He met her at the city gate, and walked with her out into the orchards that organized the hill into neat columns and rows. "Well done," he said.

"I was afraid," she said, "that you would stop me."

He shook his head. "We all hoped for you, child. Only you of all of us could understand him well enough to heal him. If you had failed, we would have had no hope short of killing him, and that would taint us forever."

"So I was part of your plan from the start?"

"Of course," said Amos. "There are no accidents in the world anymore."

Faith thought about that for a while, trying to discover why she was sad that the accidents, the agonies were over. It is part of the Adam in me, she finally decided, and put it behind her, and worked with the others to spread the healing influence of Worthing farther and farther out into the world. I will heal the world, and there will be no more accidents anymore.

"The story's almost dull from there on, Lared. Stories of good people doing good works are never very thrilling. For the first many hundreds of years Adam's descendants used their powers to learn the true needs and desires of their subjects and make sure they had good government and were treated kindly; in the meantime, unknown to Adam's family, the descendants of Matthew and Amos watched an ever-growing portion of the world, sparing them pain, removing from their minds the memory of grief, healing the sick, calming the angry, making the lame walk and the blind see. Then, in the Great Awakening, they made themselves known to Adam's kind, and the groups joined their work together, and intermarried. By the time they woke me and brought me up from the bottom of the sea, every living soul on Worthing was descended from me. They conquered the world by marriage.

"When the starships came at last from the other worlds, they saw it as the challenge their power had been created for. They began to watch all the worlds of men. The ships came back to worlds like yours, and told of what they had found on Worthing's world, the lost colony, and how it meant the end of pain. That's when the ritual of fire and ice began here, Lared. And since that day *nothing*, nothing in all the universe of men, has changed."

Lared sat at the writing desk, tears dropping onto the page. "Until now," he said. "Your children could have made all mankind their slaves, but they chose to be kind instead—why did they undo it all? Why did they stop? Why are you glad of it?"

"Lared," Jason said. "You don't understand. They *did* make all mankind their slaves. They just kept them happier than any master did before."

"We were not slaves. And my father had two arms."

"Write the story that you know so far, Lared. We have to finish soon—winter's almost over, and they'll need you in the forest and the fields again. Finish the book, and then I'll leave you as you wanted me to."

"How much more is there, after this?"

"One more dream," said Jason. "The tale of a man named Mercy and his sister, Justice. And how between them they undid the pattern of the universe. Maybe when it's over, you'll not hate me anymore."

11

Acts of Mercy

The wind was out of the southeast, warm and dry. The ice on the river broke up in the night; great rafts of ice floated downstream all day. The snow was still white with flecks of ash from the forgefire, but underneath it Lared heard the running of water. He tossed a bale of hay into every stall, forked it loose, and checked the village sheep for lambing. The time was getting near for more than one of the ewes. And hard as the winter had been, there was still hay enough from last summer to last two more months. A good year for crops and animals. Not so good for men.

The tools stood ready for the summer's work; soon it would be time to spade and ditch the hedges and take the faughter to the peasepatch and the harrow to the fields. Today is warm enough, Lared decided, and he let the geese out into the yard. It was a measure of how much had changed since fall that he didn't even think to ask Father if it was time.

Mother was pregnant. Mother was going to have a little baby and Father was certain it was his. Well, it might be, Lared thought. I wonder who her lover is? It occurred to him to wonder if it might be the tinker—Mother liked him well enough. But no, he had no opportunity. Indeed, when did anyone have time? With the women always visiting and Father never far away, how could it be at home? And Mother ran no errands, except when she worked in company of other women at some clothwork or to carry grain to the mill—

The miller? Surely Mother could not prefer him to Father. No, impossible.

"That's not a very worthy line of thought," said Jason.

Lared turned to him. He stood in the doorway of the barn, silhouetted in the sunlight. "I'm going out to mark the hedges," Lared said. "Do you know the work, or does Father need you in the forge?"

"I need you at the book," Jason said. "That's spring work you're thinking of, and the book's not done."

"The spring work needs doing in the spring. That's why we call it spring work. It's spring, and so I'm doing it. Whatever the value of whatever you paid to Father and Mother, it isn't worth a winter with no crop. Starving to death is possible these days, you know."

"I'll come with you to the hedges."

They each took sawhooks with them, and walked the rows. The snow was wet and slippery underfoot, and the south-facing slopes of the hedgebanks were plain mud, the snow already gone from them. Lared stopped at a plant that was broken from the weight of the winter's snow, so it lay over half into the hedgeroad. "You hardly need to mark one like this, but you do it anyway," Lared said. "When they come along to do your rows, sometimes they're tired and they don't much like the landmaster by then, and anything without its twist of straw gets left, even though they know they'll have to do it over." He plaited a straw on the outmost branch and they went on, cutting off branches that were broken from the stem, marking plants that needed to be rooted or moved back into line.

"Mother's pregnant," Lared said. "I know you know it, but I thought you might be able to tell a bit about the father."

"Same as yours."

"Is that the truth?"

"Yes," Jason said. "Justice says so. She knows how to tell. In the old days, she would have stopped it being born if it were a bastard. It was one of the ways they kept life simpler."

"How can she have a child at all? She already has two."

"All the women who aren't virgins or too old are pregnant, Lared. Most of their children will survive, but not all. You'll have to make this land produce much more, or more will die. No one is watching you now."

"The way it used to be," Lared said. "I'm an expert now on how things used to be. I think I've lived more in your history than I've lived in my own life."

"I know you have. Has it changed you?"

"No." Lared stopped walking and looked around him. "No, except the hedges have no mystery anymore. I know there's nothing on the other side. When I was a child I used to wonder, but not now."

"You're growing up."

"I'm getting old. I've lived too many lifetimes this winter. This village is so small compared to Heaven City."

"That's its greatest virtue."

"Think that Star Haven would have need of a country-born scribe?"

"You write as well as any man."

"If I can find a man to help Father at the forge, or perhaps another blacksmith to take his place there, and let him run the inn—then I'm going. Maybe not Star Haven. There are other places."

"You'll do well. Though I think you'll miss Flat Harbor more than you think you will."

"What about you? When you leave? Will you miss this place?"

"More than you know," said Jason. "I've come to love it here."

"Yes, you would. A nice place to find pain."

Jason said nothing.

"I'm sorry. It's coming on spring and Father hasn't got his arm and even with you helping at the forge it isn't the same. The farming is on my back now, and I don't want it. It's your fault, you know. If there were any justice you'd stay and bear the burden of it yourself."

"Oh, no, not at all," said Jason. "Sons have always taken over when their fathers faltered, and daughters have always done the same for mothers. This is the natural way now. This is justice. What you had before was pure mercy. You never did a thing to deserve it, so don't complain now that it's taken away."

Lared turned away from him and went on up the hedge. They worked in silence till the job was done.

When they got home, Father was in the big copper tub, taking a bath. Lared saw at once that he was angry to see them. He couldn't understand why—Lared had seen Father bathing naked since he was as little as he could remember, Mother pouring the hot water into the tub and Father crying out, "What, do you want to boil my balls off?" Then Lared saw how Father tried to hide his stump behind his body. He must have waited for his bath till Lared was gone hedging, and because of Jason's help Lared had come back too soon. "Sorry," Lared said. But he didn't leave the room. If he had to hide forever from his father's bath, he'd soon be afraid to come indoors, and Father would bathe but once a year at most. Instead Lared walked to the kitchen and took a crust of old bread from the bin and dipped it into the porridge simmering before the fire.

Mother slapped playfully at his hand. "Will you rob the dinnerpot, and the porridge not yet half cooked?"

"It's already delicious," Lared said, his mouth full. Father had stolen porridge that way a thousand times before. Lared knew that Mother wouldn't mind.

But Father minded. "Keep your hands out of the food, Lared," he said gruffly.

"All right, Father," Lared said. No point in arguing. He'd do it again, and Father would get used to that, too.

Father arose from the tub, water dripping. Almost at once Sala, who had been playing silently nearby, ran to him and looked up at the naked stump. "Where are the fingers?" Sala asked.

Father, embarrassed, covered the stump with his hand. It was sadly funny, that he made no effort to hide his loins, but only tried to hide what wasn't even there.

"Hush, Sala," Mother said sharply.

"There should be fingers," Sala said. "It's spring."

"There'll be no new growth on this stump," Father said. And now, the shock of it over, he took his hand away and began to towel himself with a thick wool cloth. Mother came over to towel his back, and on the way she gave Sala a push. "Run along, Sala. Go away."

Sala cried out as if in terrible pain or grief.

"What is it? I didn't push you so hard, girl."

"Why didn't you do it?" Sala screamed. "Where is it?"

Only when Justice appeared at the foot of the stairs did they realize what Sala meant. Sala ran to her. "You can do it! I know you can do it! So where is it? You said you loved me! You said you loved me!"

Justice only stood there, looking at Father, who held the towel in front of him. Then, defiantly, he thrust the towel into Mother's hands and stepped out of the tub toward Justice. "What have you promised the child?" he asked. "In our house we keep our promises to children."

But Justice didn't answer. As usual, Sala did. "She can put an arm back where you lost it," Sala said. "She told me in my mind. I've dreamed of it, I saw it open like a flower, all five fingers back again."

Jason stepped between them.

"Stay out of this, Jason. That woman's been living like a ghost in my house all winter, I want to know what she promised my daughter."

"Put on some trousers," Jason said.

Father looked at Jason coldly for a long moment, then reached for his longshirt and put it on.

"Justice didn't promise anything to Sala. But Sala still saw— what Justice would like to do, if she weren't bound."

"Put a hand back on my stump? Only God could do that. And God is gone."

"That's right," Jason said.

"How does Sala know what the woman thinks? Or does she talk when they're alone?"

"When one of Justice's people loves someone, she can't hide her thoughts from them. She never meant to deceive your daughter, or to disappoint her. What Sala saw is forbidden."

"Forbidden. Bound. But if she weren't bound and forbidden, does she have the power to heal my arm?"

"We came here," Jason said, "to write a book, with Lared's help. He'll finish it tomorrow, and then we'll go." He walked to Justice and pushed her gently back up the stairs. Sala stayed at the bottom step, crying. Father pulled his trousers on, and Lared sat before the fire, watching the flames trying to escape up the chimney, always dying before they quite made it out.

Mercy was the firstborn, and a boy; Justice was his sister. Their mother had known them well in the womb—their names fit them. Mercy could not bear it for another to suffer anything; Justice was sterner, and insisted on fairness and equity regardless of the cost.

Justice's name was not just decorative; it was the path that pulled her through the wilderness of childhood. For almost as soon as she could walk and burble sounds her gift came to her and she began to reach into the memories of those around her, or the memories were forced on her against her will. Father,

Mother, and the thousand other lives that dwelt within their minds, all the other *I*s, all the events of their lives that mattered enough to be held in memory, and somehow in all this Justice had to remember who she was, which memories were hers. She herself was so small, her life so slight, that for a long while she was lost. What brought her out into a sane world, knowing who she was, was a need to set things to rights, to make things balance, to have all right things rewarded, all wrong things done away.

She also emerged from childhood with a yearning to be more like Mercy, her compassionate brother. In ways they were alike—they both lived in dread of undeserved suffering. But Mercy's desire was to bear the misery himself, to simply take it from the sufferer. Justice, on the other hand, sought to find the cause of it, to strike it at the root. She had to know the why of everything. It was a trial to her teachers. Mercy was able to become a Watcher at a very early age, because he had a keen sense of other people's pain, and soon mastered the technique of healing it. Justice, on the other hand, kept getting distracted from the main task. Her teacher wondered to her once, What if it should turn out that you are not a Watcher? There are other works to do, which must be done.

I will Watch, said Justice silently, because Mercy Watches.

So she left behind the games of childhood still unready for Watching, and spent her youth perched in the trees of the School, bending herself to the task that came so easily to Mercy, that was such agony for her. She dwelt in his mind as often as he would let her, to try to discover what it was that made him so quick to sense a hunger and satisfy it, so good at finding pain and healing it. But it was no particular skill that she could find. At last she realized that it was this: Mercy loved at once anyone he knew, and cared more for their joy than for his own. Justice, on the other hand, loved almost no one, but instead measured each person against the standard of what that person believed was right and wrong. Few people were good by such a measure, and Justice's love was not easily given. So when she tried to Watch, she had to learn it as an unnatural skill, and she was twenty years old before she finally left the School-trees and was taken into Pools.

By that time all her childhood friends had been Watching for years, and Mercy was already a master, entrusted with the

Watching of a world for a third of every day. Still, Justice did not condemn herself for being so slow. She was just, even with herself; she knew she was succeeding at a task she was not suited for, and so the price she had to pay was higher.

She passed her trial hour on a day, and on the next day went to Pools for the first time to Watch alone. She came to Gardens, shed her gown to dress herself in wind, and found a Pool with room for her. Gently she lowered herself to her knees in the shallow water, then lay forward until her face was flat on the smooth pebbles. Toes, belly, breasts and face were in the cold water; heels, buttocks, back, and ears were in the breeze that scattered tree-cotton across the surface of the water. She did not breathe, but that was almost second nature now; how many hours as a child had she hung upside down from a tree-branch, learning to close off her body and free her mind to wander among the stars.

Because she was so new, she was allowed to Watch only a village on a primitive world that still shunned electricity, had not yet turned to steam. It was a little place beside a river, with one inn, whose keeper was also the blacksmith—that's how small the village was.

She came to the village in the last hour of night, so there were no waking eyes for her to see through. Instead she coasted the currents of life itself, the dim wash from the serene and stupid trees, the frantic energy of the nightbirds, the beasts of dawn looking for water or salt. She thought, in such an hour as this, that Watching would be joyful.

Just as hunger awoke the first child of the village, she felt a hand on her shoulder. It was Mercy, she knew at once. She did not lift her face from the pool, for Watchers never do. Gently his fingers pressed up and down her back, to say, This is life, you are alive now. She did not need to make any answer to tell him that she heard. But he was not through. Of course he could not speak into her mind—her mind was closed to any thoughts but those of the village that she Watched—so he spoke to her in words, aloud. She hardly knew his voice, or perhaps it was the water that made it strange to her. "They say that Justice is bright and beautiful, and she brings equity behind her eyes. They say my sister is dark and terrible, for she can live with truth."

The words chilled her like his breath on her wet cheek. She

dared not leave the village long enough to look into his mind, even if it were open to her. But there was something final in his words, and it made her afraid. He was bidding her good-bye, and she could not understand it.

Or is it a test? On the first full day alone, do they try all new Watchers by giving them dreadful words from the one they love the best? If it is a test, I will not fail it. She kept her face into the water, kept her mind among the villagers, and Mercy went away.

Justice began to have eyes to see with, sleepy, rubbed eyes as cows and ewes were milked and porridges were stirred over hearthfires. Everything was wood and wicker, pottery and leather—it was an old place, a once-lost place, where the machines did not help the Watchers in their work. Here the horses pissed hot in their stalls, dust seeped unfiltered into houses, children let caterpillars crawl up their arms, and one Watcher had to care for each town, since so many things could harm them.

A child began to choke on a sausage. The parents looked up, uncertain what to do. Justice spasmed the child's diaphragm, ejecting the sausage onto the table. The child laughed, and thought of doing it again, but Justice let his mother scold him, and the child stopped. Justice had no time to waste with games at the breakfast table.

The cobbler sheared off his thumb along with the leather he was cutting. He was not used to pain, and screamed, but Justice took the pain from him, made him pick up the half-thumb from the bench and put it back in place. It was a simple thing to grow vein to vein, nerve to nerve, and then reach into his mind and take away the memory. She also made his wife forget she heard the sound of terror in his cry. What you do not remember, did not happen.

There was anger, which she calmed. There was fear, which she comforted. There was pain and injury, and she healed all. Disease could not take root, for she quickened the body's power to purify itself. Even hunger could not last, for everyone wanted to work hard in the morning, as Justice spread vigor through the village with the dawn, and soon the fields were dotted with workers, and bench and barrel, forge and oven had each its worker in place.

In the afternoon an old man's heart stopped beating. Justice quickly did the death check. It would take more than three minutes' work to heal him; he had no children under twenty; his wife was healthy of mind and heart; and so he would be allowed to die. Instead of healing him, Justice brought his son to his house, the thirty-year-old innkeeper with blacksmith's arms. She kept the young man's mind a blank; he did not recognize the old man, merely picked him up and carried him out to the burying place, where friends were waiting with a hole half-dug. Within the hour the old man was laid into the ground. The men who dug the hole would remember the burying, but they remembered it as long past, a year ago, and they had long since gotten over the grief of the old man's death.

On his way back home, Justice put into the mind of the dead man's son all the joyful moments of his childhood, a generous eulogy; but he believed that he had only walked to his father's year-old grave today, to remember him on the anniversary of his passing.

The dead man's widow blankly packed up all she owned and moved into her son's inn, where she was given a bed in the wall downstairs not far from the fire, with her grandson near her in a truckle bed, and her granddaughter across the room. As far as they all remembered, she had moved in a year before, when Grandfather died. She was long since past grieving, or even feeling strange to live with her daughter-in-law. Everyone was comfortable with each other by now, and life went smoothly on, with Grandfather a beloved memory and no grief to darken their days.

She tended wombs, to be sure the right ones were filled and the rest stayed empty; she came to the aid of the girl who decided it was time not to be a virgin any longer, and made it a pleasure to her, despite the boy's over-eagerness. And at last night came to the village, and the Sleep Watchers touched her gently and told her she was through. Good work, they said silently, and Justice lifted her face from the pool hot with pride, cold from the breeze on her wet face and body. It was noon on Worthing, and the skin of her back and buttocks and thighs was hot and brown. She let the breeze dry her, saying nothing to the other Watchers who had shared Pool with her.

She walked into Garden, and then allowed herself to breathe, letting the air come like snow into her throat. She untied her hair and let it fall over her shoulders. Five more days of Watching, and if she did well they would let her cut her hair. She would be a woman then, her test completed.

She found her clothing and put it on. Only then did her friend Grave come to her, and tell her the news.

They've found God, he said silently. In his starship at the bottom of the sea. He's asleep, but we can wake him if we want to. One thing is certain, though. He's just a man.

Justice laughed. Of course he's just a man—we knew that, didn't we? We *are* his children.

No, Grave told her. Just a *man*.

And she understood now, that Jason Worthing, the father of their race, did not have their power after all.

Oh, he could see behind the eyes, but he couldn't *put* anything there, he couldn't *change* anything.

Poor man, thought Justice. To have eyes, but then no hands to touch with, no lips to speak with. To be dumb and motionless in the mind, and yet see—what torture it must have been. Better to leave him sleeping. What will he make of us, his children, if he's such a cripple among us?

There are those, said Grave silently, who want to waken him anyway. To have him judge us.

Do we need judging?

If he is strong enough to bear the disappointment of not being as powerful as we are, then they say we ought to waken him and see what he can teach us—what other man is living who knew the universe *before* we began to Watch? He can compare, and tell us if our work is good.

Of course it is. And if he is too weak to bear inferiority, then we have only to change his memory and send him somewhere else.

Grave shook his head. Why wake him, if we only mean to take away his memory? What good, then, were all his centuries of sleep?

When a man is grieved or sick or weak, we heal him.

He has memories that are otherwise lost to the world.

Then learn his memories and heal him.

Justice, he is our father.

Then it comes to special cases, and that is unjust. Bring

him up because he is alive, and heal him if he is in pain.
There's no reason to determine first if it would cause him harm
or not. Especially since we could not find *that* out unless we
float the stone—

And she realized then what Grave had hoped to hide from
her, at least for a while longer, that they had already decided
to float the stone while she was Watching, and that her own
brother Mercy was to do it.

Justice waited for no other thought from Grave; she ran at
once to the Hall of Rock. All she could think of as she ran
was that Mercy had come to bid her good-bye, had known
even then what he meant to do, and had not told her. It was
not because she was in Pools; he had waited till she was there
before coming to her, so she would not try to stop him. But
she must stop him, for to look into the mind of the dead meant
death or madness. Of course Mercy would say, Let me be the
one. Here I am, let me—he would gladly give his mind and
his life to dwell within the mind of God.

When Justice got there it already was too late. Only she,
of all who were not at that moment Watching, only she had
not been told of this. Everyone else was gathered, here or at
the other Halls of Rock, and they already waited inside Mercy's
mind. He lay on his back on a flat rock, his arms spread out
to hold him as the stone softened under him, letting his body
sink gently. The breeze began to ripple the surface of the stone,
as Mercy arched his back and let his head sink downward into
the stone, down until his whole head was immersed.

She had no choice, then, but to join the others, as if she
were a willing participant in this act—not merely that she could
not bear to be the only one who was not with him in his
sacrifice.

As she looked beneath the stone, she felt within her a familiar mind. It was her mother, and she said, Welcome, Justice.

How could you let him! cried Justice in her anguish.

How could we not, when he wanted so much to do it, and
it needed to be done?

It isn't fair for him to give all, when I give nothing.

Ah, said Mother silently, so it comes to fairness after all.
You want to match your brother pain for pain.

Yes.

You can't. Even if you wanted to, you could not float the stone. It takes more compassion than you were born with—there are few of us who could. But you can help us, all the same. You know Mercy better than anyone. When the mind of God is in him, you better than anyone can tell us how much of himself is Mercy, and how much is Jason Worthing. And with your perfect sense of measure, you can tell us when the ordeal is done, and from you we can learn what we should do.

I do not consent to this.

But if you do not help us, you may be letting Mercy give himself in vain.

So Justice was not merely an observer, but the leader of all the world as they Watched in Mercy's mind.

Mercy dwelt now at the bottom of the sea, inside a cold and silent chamber where a mind had lived. Now the memories were in an unfathomable bubble, and Mercy had to go into the brain where they once had lived and dwell there, strike out all his own memories and all that he had learned from everyone else, and see what his mind did in the space where Jason once had been. If all went well, he would become Jason, and from him they could learn what Jason would do when he awoke, how he would respond; but it was always less than perfect, this technique, because no one had ever been able to drive out all his own memories, and leave the dead man's mind alone. Always there was something of the floater left, to distort the result. Justice's work was to measure the distortion, and to compensate.

But there was no distortion. They had not counted on how little Mercy loved himself. There was no memory, however deep, that he had to cling to to survive. There was no part of him that had to live on, no matter how much he willed to die. So as Justice searched for Mercy in the cold liquid granite, she found nothing. Only a stranger in Mercy's place. Only Jason Worthing, a poor crippled man who could see but could not speak.

It was already a long, long time, and still she had not found her brother. Where is he, demanded Mother. You must find him, for he can't go on much longer.

At last Justice cried out in despair, He isn't there, he's gone. And in awe at Mercy's perfect gift, all of Worthing withdrew from Mercy's mind at once, having learned from Jason all they needed to know. Justice opened her eyes in time to see the stone go solid again, with Mercy's head still inside, his back arched, his hands clutching the surface. For a moment it seemed that he moved, that he was alive, still trapped and trying to get out. But it was only an illusion, caused by the pose he died in. His flesh was not flesh now, but also stone, and he was gone.

Justice searched inside herself for the balance, the perfect balance that should be there, but it was gone.

Lared stood over Justice's bed where she pretended to be asleep.

"You were giving me dreams," he said. "You are not sleeping."

Slowly she shook her head, and he saw, by the light of the candle that he held, tears seeping from the corners of her eyes.

Before he could speak to her again, there was a hand on his shoulder. He turned, and it was Jason. "She Watched our village, Jason."

"Only the once," he said. "After her brother floated the stone, she never Watched again."

"But I remember the day. I saw myself in her memory, I saw her go inside me and it was as if I understood myself whole for the first time. Nothing that you showed me before, nothing was—"

"Everything else came from lesser minds than hers. What she sees, she understands."

"All these months she's been with us, and I never knew her, never guessed. *She* is God, not you."

"She was the least of the gods, if you want to call them that. But then, at the end she was the greatest. She came to know me, you see. She insisted that she be the one to tend me when they raised me from the sea. I remember waking, with my ship going crazy with warnings—something was moving the ship, and it wasn't anything the poor ship's computer had met before. When we rested on the surface of the sea, I opened the door, and there was Justice, standing on the water in front of me, looking back at me with eyes as blue as mine, and I thought, My daughter. It was only a few days to me, then, since I left Rain and the children in the Forest of Waters. And this was what they had become. She hated me, of course."

"Why? What had you done?"

"It was unfair. She knew that. But it made her the fairest judge of what I might have to teach them. If anyone had reason to disbelieve and doubt me, it was Justice. She showed me everything; they even let me watch them Watch, so that I saw through their eyes what they were doing in the world. It was beautiful, and kind, a world full of people devoting themselves to nothing but the service of mankind. I cursed them and told them that I wish I had been castrated at the age of ten before I spawned any such thing as them. I was quite upset, as I remember. And, as you can imagine, so were they. They couldn't believe that I loathed so much what they were doing. They could not understand, even though they could see into my mind, why I was angry. So I showed them. I said, Justice, let me take from you all memory of your brother's death. And she said—"

"No!" cried Justice from her bed. The word was not in Lared's language, but he needed no translation to understand it.

"Hypocrites, I said to them," said Jason. "You dare to rob mankind of all its pain, yet treasure your own agonies. Who Watches you?"

"Who Watches you?" cried Jason.

No one, they answered. If we ever forgot our own pain, how could we care enough to protect *them* from *theirs?*

"Did you ever think that however much they railed against the universe or fate or God or whatever else, that they might not thank you for stealing from them all that makes them human?"

And they saw in Jason's mind the things he treasured most, the memories that were strongest, and they were all the times of fear and hunger, pain and grief. And they looked into their own hearts, and saw what memories had endured through all the ages of time, and they were memories of struggle and accomplishment, sacrifices like Mercy's when he floated the stone and gave the perfect offering of himself, agonies like Elijah Worthing when he watched his wife cast herself upon the flames, even cruel Adam Worthing with his terror that his uncle would find him and punish him again—these had lasted, while the simple contentment had not. They saw that this was what had made them good, even in their own eyes; and because they had left the rest of man no evils to overcome, they had robbed them of the hope of greatness, of the possibility of joy.

Full agreement did not come at once. It came only gradually, over the weeks and months. But finally, because they could see themselves through Jason's eyes, they decided that mankind was dead as long as they Watched, that men and women would only become human again with the possibility of pain.

"But how can we live," they asked, "knowing of all the suffering that will come, knowing we can stop it, and yet withholding ourselves? That is more suffering than *we* can bear; we have loved them all too long and well."

And so they decided not to live. They decided to finish what Mercy had begun, the perfect offering. Only two people in the world refused.

"You people are crazy," Jason said. "I wanted you to stop controlling everything, I didn't ask you to kill yourselves."

Some kinds of life are not worth living, they answered mildly. You're too uncompassionate to understand.

And as for Justice, she refused to stay because she wasn't worthy to die in Mercy's cause. It would be giving her more value than she was worth.

But you'll have to live among the people in their suffering, they said. It will destroy you, surely, to see their grief and yet not save them.

Perhaps, said Justice. But that is the price that Justice pays; that will balance me with Mercy, in the end.

So Jason and Justice took a starship to the only world beyond Worthing that Justice had ever known, as behind them the world of Worthing tipped inward toward its sun and spiraled down to die in fire.

Justice heard the deaths of a hundred million souls and bore it; felt the horror of the Day of Pain in Flat Harbor, and bore it; felt Lared's hatred as he learned of her power and yet did nothing, and bore it.

But now, lying on her bed, it was Sala's grief that struck too deep, Sala's suffering that she could not bear. She gave that moment to Lared as he watched, let him see her from the inside even at the moment of her pain.

"You see," said Jason, "she is not like me. She isn't un-compassionate, after all. There's more of Mercy in her than she thought."

12

The Day of Justice

Lared and Jason stood at Justice's bedside, and for the first time Lared did not fear her and did not hate her; for the first time he understood what lay behind her choice, and though he thought that it was wrong, he realized it was not Justice's fault.

"How could they decide wisely," Lared whispered, "when they only had your mind to judge by?"

Jason shrugged. "I didn't lie to them. I only showed them the way things seemed to me. Remember, Lared—they didn't just take my word for it. It was only when they saw that they were taking away from others what they would not willingly give up themselves, that what mankind was missing then was the only thing that was worth remembering about the time before—"

"That's fine," Lared said, "if you stand above mankind in a tower, looking down. But here, Jason, when you have the power to heal, and do not heal, I call that evil."

"But *I* don't have that power," Jason said.

At that moment someone screamed downstairs. Screamed in pain, again and again. It's Clany, thought Lared. But Clany's dead.

"Sala!" he shouted, and flew down the stairs, Jason after him.

Father was daring the flames to pull Sala from the hearthfire. There was no part of her that was not afire. Lared did not hesitate, but plunged his hands into the flames and together he and Father pulled her out. The pain of his own burnt flesh was excruciating, but Lared hardly noticed, for Sala writhed in his arms, screaming over and over, "Justice! Justice! Now! Now!"

"She was in the fire already when I woke!" Father said frantically.

Mother kept reaching for her daughter, but shied away each

261

time before she touched the charred flesh, lest she somehow
add to Sala's pain.

Lared thought for a moment that her eyes were closed, but
then realized that they were not. "She has no eyes!" he cried.
And then he looked at the foot of the stairs and saw Justice
standing there, her face a mask of anguish.

"Now! Now! Now!" cried Sala.

"How is she alive?" cried Father.

"God in heaven, not three hours!" cried Mother. "Not like
Clany, let her die now!"

And then Father and Mother were pushed aside, and Justice
seized Sala, tore her from Lared's arms, and gave a wail so
terrible that Lared could not stop himself from crying out at
the pain of hearing it.

And then silence.

Not even Sala crying.

She is dead, thought Lared.

But then, as he watched, Sala blinked her eyes, and they
were bright again, not the empty sockets Lared had seen a
moment ago. As he watched, he saw the burnt skin flake from
her body, leaving a pale, smooth, perfect layer of unburnt,
untouched, unscarred flesh.

Sala smiled and laughed, threw her arms around Justice and
clung to her. Lared looked down at his own arms, and they
were healed, then reached out to Father and touched the bud
of fingers blossoming on the stump where once his arm had
grown. In only a few minutes the arm was whole, as strong
as ever.

Justice sat on the floor, Sala in her arms, weeping bitterly.

"At last," Jason murmured.

Justice looked up at him.

"You're human after all," Jason said.

You *are* good, Lared said to her silently. I was wrong. You
are so good that you could not stop yourself, with the test that
Sala set for you. There is more mercy in you than you thought.

Justice nodded.

"You didn't fail," Jason said aloud to her. "You passed."
And he leaned down and kissed her forehead. "You wouldn't
be my daughter if you had made any other choice."

· · ·

For the small village of Flat Harbor, the Day of Pain was over. It would not be as it was before. Justice played no tricks on memory, and death itself she would not hinder, but the pain was at an end in Flat Harbor, and would be as long as she lived.

It was a spring day, and the snow was gone. The men and women were out among the hedges and the fields, replanting bushes that the snow had moved, harrowing the stubbled fields, getting ready for the plow.

The last of the logs were bound together in a raft, to be floated down the river to Star Haven, where they would fetch a good price, especially the great mast tree in the middle of the raft. Jason and the tinker stepped aboard. The raft shifted slightly, but did not rock for long. It was sturdy, and the tent they had pitched already in the middle would make a pleasant house for the two-week river journey. The tinker had his pots and pans, his tin and all his tools carefully arranged with floats in case the raft broke up—he could not afford to lose all that. Jason carried only one thing with him, a small iron-bound chest. He opened it only once, to be sure all seven closely-written sheets of parchment were neatly rolled and stacked lightly within.

"Ready?" asked the tinker.

"Not quite yet," said Jason.

They waited for a moment, and then Lared came running onto the bank, carrying a hastily-packed bag over his shoulder and shouting, "Wait! Wait for me!" When he saw that they were still against the shore he stopped and grinned foolishly. "Got room for one more?"

"If you promise not to eat much," said Jason.

"I decided not to stay here. Father's arm is whole, and they don't need me much, they never did, and I thought you might need someone along who can read and write—"

"Just get aboard, Lared."

Lared stepped carefully aboard, and set down his bag beside the iron chest. "Will they use a printing press and make a real book of this?"

"If they don't, they won't get paid," said Jason, and he and the tinker poled the raft away from shore.

"It's a good thing to know they'll all be safe," Lared said, looking back at the villagers in the fields and hedges.

"I hope you don't think that you'll be safe with *me*," said Jason. "I may be getting along in my years, but I intend to live. I intend to sleep as little as possible, for one thing. And I hope you remember how many things there are that I cannot do."

Lared smiled and opened his bag to reveal four cheeses and a smoked shoulder. "It's going to be a terrible life, I know," he said. He cut off a strip of meat and gave it to Jason. "Still, I'll take my chances."

BEST-SELLING
Science Fiction
and
Fantasy

☐ 47807-7	**THE LEFT HAND OF DARKNESS**, Ursula K. Le Guin $2.50	
☐ 16012-3	**DORSAI!**, Gordon R. Dickson $2.75	
☐ 80581-7	**THIEVES' WORLD**, Robert Lynn Asprin, editor $2.95	
☐ 11577-2	**CONAN #1**, Robert E. Howard, L. Spragúe de Camp, Lin Carter $2.50	
☐ 49141-3	**LORD DARCY INVESTIGATES**, Randall Garrett $2.50	
☐ 21889-X	**EXPANDED UNIVERSE**, Robert A. Heinlein $3.95	
☐ 87328-6	**THE WARLOCK UNLOCKED**, Christopher Stasheff $2.95	
☐ 26194-0	**FUZZY PAPERS**, H. Beam Piper $2.95	
☐ 05463-3	**BERSERKER**, Fred Saberhagen $2.50	
☐ 10254-9	**CHANGELING**, Roger Zelazny $2.75	
☐ 51552-5	**THE MAGIC GOES AWAY**, Larry Niven $2.75	

Available at your local bookstore or return this form to:

ACE SCIENCE FICTION
Book Mailing Service
P.O. Box 690, Rockville Centre, NY 11571

Please send me the titles checked above. I enclose _____
Include $1.00 for postage and handling if one book is ordered; 50¢ per book for
two or more. California, Illinois, New York and Tennessee residents please add
sales tax.

NAME _____

ADDRESS _____

CITY _____ STATE/ZIP _____

(allow six weeks for delivery)

SF 9

AWARD-WINNING
Science Fiction!

The following titles are winners of the prestigious Nebula or Hugo Award for excellence in Science Fiction. A must for lovers of good science fiction everywhere!